For Kelly.

I hope you enjoy the adventure.

With Love
Nikki

# A Momentary Darkness

Nikki Martin

Thorncraft Publishing
Clarksville, Tennessee

ISBN-13: 978-0-9979687-1-2
ISBN-10: 0-9979687-1-0

Cover Design by etcetera...
Cover photo by Tobi Martin-Flemming.

Library of Congress Control Number: 2017959704

Thorncraft Publishing
Clarksville, TN
http://www.thorncraftpublishing.com
thorncraftpublishing@gmail.com

10 9 8 7 6 5 4 3 2 1

For Tobi, who believed in me always.

For Paul, whose love marks the beginning of a life in which I learned to follow my heart.

For Heidi, who helped me find my way.

# CONTENTS

# ACKNOWLEDGEMENTS

As a writer, you learn that stories, no matter how fantastical, are built around your life. They are extensions of your hopes and dreams, fears and beliefs, loves and losses, and ultimately the kinds of people you have around you. And so, I am going to do my best to thank the people who in one way or another helped me find my way to publishing this book.

Giving a life out in the world to *A Momentary Darkness* has spanned more than fifteen years, but really it began long before that, as far back as I can remember, with my love of reading and losing myself in stories. That deep love was a gift from my amazing mother, Valerie, and my Nana, Helen, who both always had a book on the go and passed on to me the delight that could be found losing yourself in the pages of a book.

To my dad, who I hope in his heart knew this day would come before he left us, and his wife, Paula, you both always saw in me infinite possibilities for success and happiness. I can't thank you enough for being a soft place for me to land over and over again, until I found my footing.

No matter how many times I began to believe this oldest and deepest dream of mine might not come true, my sister never stopped believing this day would arrive. Tobi, for your unfailing certainty and for a friendship as old as we are, thank you. To my brother, Travis, and the rest of my beautiful family for believing in me and cheering on all of my successes, small and large, I am forever grateful.

None of this would be possible without the time and space to dream, write, and find the kind of joy in my life that inspires me to create. Paul, you are an amazing partner and friend. Thank you for believing in me, for being so damn happy for all my success and happiness, and for supporting this dream as it found its way into the waking world.

When we are lost in the fabric of our own stories, we don't always see the big picture. But over and over again, I have found myself surrounded with the kind of strong and amazing people who believed in me and held space in some way for me to believe in myself.

Connie, and all of the RIO Tribe, I hope you know how grateful I am for the love, support, and space to find my voice. HWs: Heidi, Regan, Jen, Angela, Stephanie, Joy, Emma, Kira, Lucy, Haley, Nina, Andrea, Karen, your friendship and belief in me changed the course of my life, and I will never stop loving you and what we built together. Liv, Elly, and Sandra, I am so grateful for the kind of women, friends, who can only be filled with joy and excitement for each other's happiness and successes. I am so glad the threads of our lives were woven back together again. Jennifer, over and over again, you've found ways to support, help, and cheer me on, and I hope you know your friendship and all it has entailed over the years has been the most wonderful gift. Jody, Leslie, Liseanne, Erika, you sometimes light up my darkness and sometimes sit with me in it; both have given me the space to do the difficult work of finding myself every time I got lost. Amanda, yours was the first call I answered to put my writing out into the world and believe it would lead me where I was meant to go. That first step was a big one, and I'm so grateful it was with you and for every step we've taken together since. Grace, Nelson, Kelly, and the whole lululemon family in Halifax, you've given me the chance to be brave and get out of my comfort zone over and over again, and that is powerful magic; don't stop spreading it.

To all the storytellers out there who gave me a safe place to dream and sometimes escape over the years, who offered up worlds and stories and adventures that satiated my aching and lonely heart, or that healed those parts of me that longed for a more fulfilling and adventurous life, or simply leant me love affairs and happiness when I did not have any of my own, I hope this story is my way of giving back just a little of what you gave me.

Lastly, but certainly not least, Shana, publisher, friend, inspiration, fellow dreamer, believer, and leap-taker, we found each other because of a short story, and yet you saw so much more. Because of that, the deepest longing of my heart, to share my words and characters with the world, has been answered. Because you are a fellow a writer, I am going to trust you know some of what I cannot find the words for because it's just so big and wonderful and heart bursting-ly amazing that I am speechless. Thank you for seeing me and for making this first of our many adventures together possible.

To all you dreamers out there: Don't stop dreaming. Some of them do come true.

With love and gratitude,
Nikki

# A Momentary Darkness
Book One of *Awake While Dreaming*

# Prologue
## The Prophecy

Read the Scriptures:

Before time began in this place of virtue, the Founders arrived, led through the ocean of space by a widowed being who served the higher powers in this universe. They came from a tiny planet in the Milky Way known as Earth. The planet had fallen under a deep shadow that had been crossing the universe since the beginning of time. And from the darkest regions of space came a lone traveler given counsel from the Heavens to salvage the beauty that remained among the swarming humans teetering on the brink of their destruction. It would take many generations before they would choose to leap into their self-proclaimed abyss, but the traveler came to them then and chose their freedom. Five beings perfect in all and every way brought with them across the vast darkness a sixth to the empty shores of Alpha Iridium, one of five planets the beings created with their minds along with the giant star it circles, Polaris Mu. And there they dwelt alone, their guide and savior lost to them. Only a name will echo through the ages, the Ocean Widow, they called him Froste.

The Founders arrived to these virgin shores and lived alone outside of regular time and space. They lived in peace and solitude for many years without interruption. They were unaware that time had not begun for them and the moment they had left Earth had yet to pass. They could have lived this way for eons, but eventually longing and loneliness filled their days and so they journeyed south to one of Alpha Iridium's most southern continents, Berdune. They arrived with purpose. Their human nature had finally found them.

They slept beneath the stars that night and together dreamed a wonderful dream that around them a beautiful world would be born. People swarmed into existence and with them came civilization and intelligence.

Thousands of years passed in that single night for the six Founders. As they dreamed, the universe stood still around them like it always had, but they were tempting time and fate. Both had their scent and were now swiftly approaching.

During this sleepless dream, Berdune began to evolve into a civilization bound by love, hope, and freedom as well as deeply felt respect and awe for the Founders who had brought them into being. It was a beautiful place to live and the joy surrounding it was immeasurable. In the dream the Founders lived among the people and were at one time more loved than life itself. Life was pleasant but it wasn't really life at all. What the Founders came to realize as the dusk of their dreaming approached was that though they had written the story until then it was not theirs to live or tell anymore. And so they woke on a golden morning, unaware things had changed for them. Unaware, they had become much like the human ancestors they had left behind on Earth. Unaware that time had caught them and on its tail was the Darkness they thought they'd escaped forever.

The Founders left the shores of Berdune for the home they'd known before. They have since never returned to the peaceful shores of Berdune. It is said they live their days in secret, and some wonder if they were ever really here; if the dream they lived wasn't merely a dream.

Reads the Prophecy:
Set in stone are accounts of an ancient being who is no being at all. It is the same being that chased the Founders from Earth and to these shores so many years ago. It is without mind, thought, or physical existence. Without conscience, without need as we may understand it, without chaos most of all, haunting all of time and space, and hunting in a way that cannot be satiated, it gives itself no name and is known only as the Darkness by those who choose to give it one.

This Darkness knows no home and no science could ever beg to understand it. It is beyond any life form and more capable and powerful than any single god, for it does not find itself slave to any one people or planet.

These Prophets have foreseen that this Darkness will one day choose to creep calmly over the countless worlds of the universe and challenge all species to survive it. All times, all spaces, all dimensions, though unable to have accepted the coming of the dark, will fall victim to it. Only the worthy will survive.

To fight it, the Heavens will send tumbling to Berdune a chosen one to begin the test and therefore end it. The

Heavens will send the chosen one who is born from the stars. The Heavens will send the chosen one who is a dreamer. Fallen from heaven, the chosen one can heal the sick, can but once forfeit one soul for another, and will lead the people of Berdune to the light of overcoming the evil born from power, ignorance, and hatred.

If they are unable to see past the darkness of these things, unable to come together to fight for their survival as a whole, then the Darkness will prevail and all will be lost.

The future ends when the Darkness comes. No time exists beyond then. To survive the Darkness, we must give ourselves over to it. Choose to awaken from the Darkness and there is born the Light.

# Part One
Sleeping

# ONE

Randall Caine sat on the floor of his home office, set adrift on a sea of papers, charts, and calculations. Buoyed by the realization that at any moment the violent storm of his genius might wash him up upon the shores of discovery. When it did, he would be crowned the greatest pioneer mankind has ever seen. He just knew it. He could be an explorer for the history books; one unlike any who'd come before him.

It had begun as a whisper, a dark and sinister insistence deep in the back of his mind. The voice came in waves, both violent and sultry sweet. It was an ocean vast and threatening, with depths that unsettled him like nothing had before. What it said exactly he did not know, but it urged him forward towards a truth that he may not have discovered without it. It called to him day and night, and the longer it spoke, the more he listened and the surer he became of his destiny.

His vision swam in and out of focus, an affliction fueled by tired eyes that hadn't seen sleep in almost four days. Still, there wasn't a page around him that he couldn't recall from memory if he closed his eyes, and so he wasted no effort in trying to refocus; instead he let his mind drift blurrily along with the possibility of blindly bumping into the truth he knew was his alone to realize. *No, the answer wouldn't strike him suddenly,* as he'd once thought, *but instead would wash over him gently.* It would be a storm of a different kind, and yet still, it would pull him under and threaten to wash him away from familiar shores and the man he was now.

Before Randall could wrap his mind around the epiphany hovering just beyond his reach, he heard a shrill cry from down the hall. His five-year old daughter had woken and it was his turn to answer the call.

As he stood, swaying, body aching from being seated too long, a multitude of iridescent spots jumped in and out of existence in front of his eyes. Reaching his hands up to the bare ceiling as if they were in search of a prize just out of reach, he ignored the spots and they soon tired of trying to grab his attention and faded out of sight. After a moment, he let his arms drift down to his sides without their imaginary trophy and sighing deeply, shoulders sagging with the weight of what seemed like two worlds, he made his way to the door and then stepped into the shadows the hallway offered just beyond the threshold. As that darkness wrapped itself around him, a strange and eerie feeling took hold of Randall Caine so that he stopped, startled, then closed his eyes and listened. For what, he did not know. He felt the embrace of the dark like a blanket being wrapped around him, but cold and unsettling. Oppressive. Suffocating even. And then, he felt an immense pressure, like the Darkness was trying to get in. Then, came a whispering in his ears, then deeper than that, in his mind and in his heart, and he had to strain to try and hear so that he could understand what was being asked of him.

Deep down inside he could feel, with absolute certainty, that if he could just understand what it wanted, then he could understand what he was meant to give. The truth was both an exhilarating discovery and a terrifying fact that he wasn't quite sure he was ready to face.

Down the hall, his daughter cried out again. Again the spell was broken. *Had it ever really been cast*, he wondered, as he started, shook his head, and smiled sheepishly at how foolishly he'd allowed himself to be carried away. *Must be the exhaustion*, he thought to himself as he continued down the dark hallway, a little lighter than just a moment before.

Randall Caine loved his daughter more than anything else in the world, but he'd still managed to let his research consume all of his time and energy, making him neglect daily the person dearest to his heart. When he dared to confront his shame over this reality, he told himself that his research was not only for mankind but for his daughter as well. He wanted to make sure she had a future. He wanted to give her the world. If all went as he thought it would, it would soon be in his power to do just that.

Entering his daughter's room, he clicked the light on and revealed a haven swathed in gentle pinks and soft purples. This was a place where light lived and thrived. He stared into the frightened, tear-streaked face staring back up at him and as always the angel he called daughter brought a smile to his dry and chapped lips.

"Daddy," she managed before she began to cry again and for a moment, just a moment, he forgot about his research, about the eerie moment in the dark hallway, and about the discovery that awaited him down the hall. He hurried over to the bed and sat down beside her before scooping her up into his arms and cradling her lovingly.

"What is it darling? Did you have a bad dream? Did you have a nightmare?"

"Uh-huh," she replied, fear squeezing her throat tight and causing her voice to come out in tiny squeaks.

Concern furrowed his brow as he ran his hand gently along her cheek, wiping away the remnants of her tears as he did so.

"Well, it was just a dream. I'm here now, baby, and it was just a dream."

"You were there, Daddy, but you were a bad man. Mommy wasn't there. Just me and you. *You* were a bad man."

The child moaned. It was a helpless and heart-wrenching sound and Randall found himself holding her tighter, as if the threat from her dream had followed her into the waking world and he could somehow be her shield against it.

"It was just a dream, baby. Daddy loves you and would never do anything to hurt you." As his words coaxed her to relax in his arms, he began to loosen his grip on her. After a moment, she pulled her head away from his chest so she could look up into his eyes, searching for reassurance and love. She may have been too young to recognize all that lay in those eyes staring down at her, crinkled at the corners in a smile, but that didn't change what was there: Randall Caine was a man who could change the future and he knew it, and so did all the other forces in the Universe, working and watching and waiting while the Earth turned.

Strangely, it was what he had seen in his daughter's eyes that sparked the first true flames of realization somewhere deep inside him. Whatever it was had passed in a shimmer, so quickly he didn't really even see it at all on a conscious level, but it had affected him just the same. Something had rushed out of his daughter and into him, and he'd glimpsed the future, both hers and his own.

The truth had walked into this room. He could feel it. Somehow it was all tied together; what he'd seen in her eyes, what he'd felt in the hall, and what he needed to do. Again, he could feel the Darkness begin to creep and crawl along his skin as it searched for a way in, and all the hairs on his arms and neck stood up on end. Again, he could hear a whispering but this time as he strained he began to understand. He shivered. The pieces began to fall into place and in that moment something began to change inside of the brilliant but rather ordinary Randall Caine.

"The pretty people were there, too," his daughter said in a much lighter tone. "I liked them. They were very colourful." She ventured a smile and he returned it warmly.

"Come on, darling, back under the covers, back to bed sleepy head." He kissed her forehead after tucking her under the sheets and she beamed up at him; her horrid dream suddenly long forgotten. "I've got lots of work to do still before I can sleep," he added, careful not to sound reproachful.

"Too much work, Daddy."

"One day, it will all be worth it, sweetheart. One day, you'll see."

Her tired eyes hung heavy. Her face, only moments ago bright with fear and anticipation now betrayed a longing for the sleep that was about to take her. Randall stood after placing another kiss on her forehead and clicked the light off on his way out. When he reached the darkness of the hallway, she was already dreaming of things to come and things that might never be; neither one important to him just then. He marched down the hall towards his office, hurrying, ready to dive back into the world of possibility he'd left scattered around his office floor. The terrified child who just moments before had taken all of his attention was now just a memory, the kind no one bothers retrieving.

He had it. He had the answer.

The Darkness had finally spoken, clear and loud.

TWO

Randall Caine woke with a start. He'd been dreaming again. Dreaming of the day when the answer to his life had become clear to him. Dreaming of a day almost twenty-eight years ago when he'd run to his five-year old daughter's aide while subconsciously realizing he would never be the father she needed him to be.

He stood and walked to the window of his large room so he could stare down at the world that was his home now. It was not Earth he looked upon, though he'd looked upon it in his youth.

Randall Caine was now a handsome man in his late fifties who didn't look a day over thirty. Power had agreed with him and so had time in more ways than one.

On Earth, he'd been a talented but unappreciated scientist. On Alpha Iridium, the planet he now called home, he was a greedy, selfish, power hungry ruler who delighted in the torment and torture he could inflict upon the people that he ruled.

He'd been led to Alpha Iridium both through his research back on Earth and by forces he still struggled to understand even as he knelt down before them and obeyed. It had taken many years of his life and countless hours of research before Caine was able to make the journey to Alpha Iridium alone. Originally, he'd planned to use his research to save humanity from destruction. But after many years of being ridiculed for his ideas and innovation, and being looked down upon by the rest of the scientific community, Caine decided his revenge would be to starve humanity of their salvation. Over the years, as he searched and struggled and failed, the Darkness ever whispering to him about power and destiny, he came to believe he'd found Alpha Iridium for another reason. He believed he was fated to rule the tiny world.

The people of Alpha Iridium believed Caine had come to lead them into a better and brighter world. They believed he'd come to fulfill the Prophecy, their savior, and were ready and willing to follow him into the future. The Founders were those who first came to live on the tiny world, created the Alpha

Iridians, and dreamed them into existence to cure their loneliness. It was a choice made without any understanding for the forces at work in the universe or for the consequences of defying them. The people of Alpha Iridium are indeed the victims of creation, as are the Founders. But, then, aren't we all?

After Caine, the Founders started to become myth instead of memory—Creators, Gods even, but never to be seen again. They belonged to an old world, a lost way of life, and most everyone on an Alpha Iridium had accepted it was a way that would never return. You could pray to them for help, for hope, for mercy, but only Caine was here to deliver or deny any of it.

He became an all-knowing and deeply feared ruler whose words were law. He was known for having an intuition that was otherworldly, as if he was privy to the inner workings of the universe that made it both impossible to outsmart him and advisable not to try. He was vicious and uncaring, ruthless and unforgiving, cruel and capable, worshipped by most and feared by almost everyone.

He'd created an army in his first years on Alpha Iridium and it grew daily. They're known as the J'Kahl and they surround Caine day and night. They are his protectors and the weapons he uses to inflict pain and carry out judgment on the people who question his rule or his motives.

Most people thought Caine's actions were those of an angry and vengeful God, and they believed what he told them—that the way they'd lived their lives in chaos before his arrival was the reason he was punishing them now. Once they'd served their sentence of fear and oppression, the people of Berdune believed that Caine would deliver paradise. They believed he'd grant them their wildest dreams and improve upon the torment they now called life. Just as the Prophecy promised, they had faith that he would save them all. They had to, as he had taken everything else from them but that.

It had been almost fourteen years since Caine had arrived and things had only become steadily worse. The streets were always filled with the J'Kahl and citizens were executed regularly for betrayal and opposition, guilty or not.

Many were captured to work in Caine's mines and factories, never to be seen again by their family or friends. Most suffered. Many died in their beds or in the streets. Only the most horrific ghettos of Earth are able to match the destitution and suffering found in the ghettos of Berdune.

People slept in the streets. Some never woke. Children played among the corpses as if they were commonplace; on that planet, they were. Being born was a curse, for you had to live a lifetime, no matter how short, in terror and dismay, with little hope of change. Caine had his kingdom but those who dwelt in it were mere shadows of the living.

Still the people were not willing to lose faith in Caine; he was all they had, the only thing left to place their hope in. If only they could have remembered that they should have been placing it in themselves. Instead, they feared opposing him because they believed he would either abandon them or destroy them, and so they trusted him and did as he asked or ordered. They served him fearfully and loyally and questioned nothing.

There were those who opposed him. Not everyone believed in the Scriptures or the Prophecy, and they were preparing to try and convince others of that. What would come to be tested was something Caine had not bothered to contemplate since a long ago night back on Earth. Was the human spirit strong enough to conquer the darkness that was its opposite and essential other half?

As he stood on his balcony watching the golden sun break over the horizon, Caine thought solely about his plans. He would become the most powerful and feared ruler in the history of time. Once a shy and insecure individual, he had a lot of making up to do. He thought often of the people he'd left behind on Earth. He thought of their journey as a species towards destruction and how once he'd been a part of that trek.

Once upon a time, he'd worked to save them. Now, he couldn't wait until they blew themselves to hell.

Caine looked down on the city of Braedon Ridge just as he liked to do every morning. The first light of day was washing through the empty streets. The tired houses sagged and drooped like time-ravaged gravestones too old to even remember the days when they stood proud and tall; too worn to boast openly the names they once presented to the world as keepers of history.

Caine loved being far above them all; it made him feel more powerful, as if the whole world was down on its knees before him just as he felt it should be. He drank in his power for another moment and then turned and walked back into his huge office. It was a suffocating space. Dark walls pressed in so that the impression given to anyone standing inside it, always in Caine's presence, was one of being pressured to curl up and submit. One wall was covered in shelves stacked with books, all of them haphazardly tossed there, as if they'd been leeched of their knowledge and now had no use. In the center of the space sat a large desk littered with papers. The only place that still spoke of ideas and plans. The rest of the large room was a place of death, a place that demanded Caine refute both the person he once was and the person he'd once dreamed of becoming. He needed a place like this because it demanded he be the person fate had bargained with him to become. In the dimness of those confines, he was able to forget hope and joy and was able to let slip out of sight the strength of the human spirit. Sitting down at his desk, he could let the power control him and let destiny and darkness lead the way. He had work to do still. But even he, in all his power and wisdom, could not imagine or dream up what it was that he was meant for. What instrument might be made of him as the true Darkness crept ever closer to the shores of Alpha Iridium?

THREE

Like a midnight moon, she stood still and silent—her light a sentry in the dark, waiting for the dawn.

A thick fog billowed through the night, predatory and determined as the darkness shrank and stumbled around it.

She should have been cold, but she was not. She could have been scared, but she chose not to be. Instead, she was ready.

Kayla was alone in the night. She was alone in life. Standing only feet from where the ocean met the sand, she felt for the first time as if her loneliness was melting away. As if the warmth summoned inside of her, by letting everything go, was enough to ruin and wreck all her past pain and sorrow. As if the sea, retreating down the sand to rejoin the ocean, was somehow taking her sadness with it. Drawing it out and away. She felt as if some unknown force was lurking in the night, pulling her *home*. Tearing her away from her sorrow and carrying her piece by piece to the place she was meant to be.

It was not the first time she felt the strange combination of emotions moving within her, the fear and the sorrow, the exhilaration and deep longing all at once. Since childhood, an incomprehensible void swam within her. When she was young, and still, she could stand under a star-clad night sky and feel the vastness of what lay beyond that blanket reaching down into her until her entire being ached with longing for a truth that was waiting just out of reach. It was a longing to understand, to know, to be certain there was more than what she could simply see, feel, and touch. She could sometimes feel the vastness of existence itself, beyond the waking world, and knew that both it and life contained within them mysteries bold, terrifying, and terrible. Even if she didn't know how she understood, she knew it just the same.

Kayla craved adventure. Craved a deeper understanding for the mystery and the magic. Craved a life more demanding and exciting and fulfilling than the one she lived, yet she had no idea how to claim that life. And so the void remained. She found ways to make it okay. She daydreamed, often imagining wondrous worlds that must have existed beyond Earth and the adventures she would embark on when there. And, of course, she lost herself in books, the great escape of lonely teens yearning for lives seemingly out of a reach.

Kayla was almost nineteen years old and at times that made her ashamed of her slipping grip on the realities of the world. She thought by now she'd be past this deep and aching sense of not really being connected to it all, but in fact she'd been drifting further and further away. She often wondered whether it was her lack of ties to the world that kept opening up all that space, or if the space had first opened up making it hard for her to bridge the gulf; to find and build those ties that closed the gap and drew her closer to the world. She had no boyfriend, no siblings, and no real friends. She'd always been a solitary person and she was starting to wonder if that was what kept her from loving life in its entirety. Her longing to belong was always overpowered by her need to remain indifferent and keep herself just a little apart from the rest of the world and the people around her.

At times, she was a contradiction. She loved knowing that she needed no one, but ached to let go and let someone hold her for even just a moment. She was modest and shy, yet if you put her in a room full of people she could easily become the center of attention and the life of the party. She was smart, yet had no desire to do anything with her intelligence and had almost no ambition for a career that would feed or challenge her mind. She found school boring and would rather do well on a test by winging it than do great by studying. She was confident when on her own, but could easily become insecure when around others, yet in the end she cared little for what they thought. At least that's what she told herself.

Kayla was often too aware of how different she was than most other people. She needed no one, as her solitude was her longtime companion. She relished it. When she was around others, she sometimes faltered, envying their love and friendships. As she watched them laugh, talk, and joke, comfortable, companionable, and connected, she would wish deep within herself that she could be more like them. She longed to let someone into her world, her life, her heart. But somewhere within her, deep down where no one might glimpse the truth, was a debilitating fear of letting someone see her, really see her. Her strengths and weaknesses, hopes and fears, were secrets she saved for herself. She'd spent so long locking up her faults and flaws that letting anyone near them was impossible now. She spent her time inside worlds she dreamed up or read about. Only there could she find freedom.

Kayla daydreamed of many things. Often she dreamed she was normal. Not because she wanted to be, but because she thought it might be easier and the only way she could ever know happiness. In truth, Kayla, who'd always suspected she knew nothing about herself, had finally learned one real thing that she could trust, the only certainty that dwelt within her, that the prospect of being normal was a terrifying and terrible thing, easier or not, and she could think of nothing worse than being ordinary. And so, a battle of conflicting selves raged within her. If she was so frightened of being normal, then how could she envy such an affliction as well?

Sometimes, even physically, she longed to look like the ideal just so that she could blend into the world of the normal person. She was tiny. Barely 5'1, barely a hundred pounds, barely beautiful. Yet, at the same time, she had a huge presence, and sometimes appeared so strange and exotic that her beauty, though fleeting, was real and overwhelming to those who glimpsed it. She had shy brown eyes that turned a shade of dark red in the sunlight and her hair was the same color. It was curly and long and she almost always wore it the way it looked when she jumped out of the shower. Her skin was golden and smooth, and if she'd ever had a pimple or a blemish, she couldn't remember when. In the way that one accepts what they are, Kayla loved herself completely. Yet, she could wholeheartedly dislike herself as well. She could see and feel her potential but also felt it wasting away and suffered both huge spells of indifference and vast stretches of sadness over this unfortunate reality. Most times, the only way she understood herself was when she realized that she was somehow incomplete, empty, not really a whole person.

In truth, there flows emptiness through us all. We differ only in how great the current runs and whether or not we let it sweep us away violently as we struggle against it or calmly let it carry us downstream. Kayla has been fighting the current of her emptiness for far too long, like many, and her exhaustion begs her to stop struggling and let herself drown in the deep.

She is alone.

She no longer feels like she belongs. She barely belongs to herself.

And yet in her panic, in her hopelessness, in those moments of gasping for air wide-eyed, she glimpses something, unidentified but bright and shining, and waiting for her alone to reach up out of the cold dark and grab hold.

It waits for her like she waits for it.

We are all waiting for something.


FOUR

Like a midnight moon, she stood still and silent—her light a sentry in the dark, waiting for the dawn.

Kale loved the early morning hours, when before the sun had risen she could steal the ocean for herself. Her favorite place on all of Berdune was Sunshine Bay. From the north, three rivers swiftly flow and spill their waters into an ocean bay. To the south is the ocean, where a small, sandy island parts the salt water into two other branches. If you stood far above, the bay looked like a sun with five golden watery rays flowing outward.

Sunshine Bay was how Kale began every day.

When she was a child her father had brought her every morning to watch the sun rise. They would always play the same game, over and over again. They would think up one absurd thought and they would have to take it seriously. Kale's father always said that it made your own problems seem small and silly if you could make something absurd seem important. The simplicity of this wisdom had always awed Kale, even as a child. Her father, a simple man, had often found ways to leave her awed. He had a way about him, an easy sort of being, that could both charm and calm anyone in his presence. His wisdom had always inspired confidence and trust in those whom he met. Alongside his carefree humility and grace, he was a man relied upon by many, including his only daughter who'd almost always looked upon him with stars in her eyes.

Thinking about him now wasn't the first time it began to dawn on Kale that maybe he wasn't as simple as he'd let on. How could a simple man have managed to live such a complicated life, and have it ended in such a complicated way? As always, she pushed and shoved at the truth until it was far enough out of reach that she couldn't feel it pulling at her to try and understand. She came back to the task at hand.

Kale still followed the routine every day.

One absurd thought taken seriously.

On this particular morning, for the first time in a long time, she had trouble thinking up something absurd. The problem was that she had too many real problems on her mind. The source of them all was Caine.

"Alright, Dad," she whispered to the wind, "I guess, just for today, I'll have to use one we've already done before. Let's see...something fun." She said without much conviction, and then paused, listening to the rolling thunder of the waking waves. She waited for inspiration to strike. "I know. What if everywhere we went we felt the rocking of the sea like we were afloat on the waves?"

She thought back to the day her father had first suggested that to her. It had been a long time since that day, and though it reminded her of how much she missed him, it still made her smile. They'd walked home stumbling as if being swayed by the ocean's rhythm, and when they arrived home, Kale's mother had come running out of the house thinking something was wrong. They'd all laughed hysterically together.

It was then, while wandering through that pleasant memory, so long ago, that the sun peeked over the Harjon Mountains to the east, and Kale realized she should go. She let the memory tumble away. *It's so hard to hold onto anything beautiful in Caine's Berdune*, she thought sadly to herself and sighed.

"I'll see you tomorrow morning, Dad," she whispered, turning away from the beauty of Sunshine Bay to begin her walk back toward town. She could hear the waves crashing behind her, that mating of sea and rock far below, and already missed the ocean and all it remembered for her. As she hurried away, something deep down inside of her tried to rise. It was the part of her that knew that if something like the ocean, the moon, or the stars can remember all of time with ease, then is any of what's past really gone or out of reach? Like a wave, the knowing rose and then fell. The moment was past. Kale barely noticed it had come, and gone.

She walked northward towards the town of Braedon Ridge, which was the next stop in her morning routine. She headed north, following the boisterous rapids of the Craden River, drinking in the hurried tumbling of the rapids as they sped away from her, south towards Sunshine Bay and the sea. She took a moment to envy their journey towards the shore but never paused in her own journey away from it.

From the northeast came the Harjon River, which fell into the bay from far above. Between the Harjon and the sea towered an imposing mountain range that seemed to touch the heavens and carry them down to earth with their majesty. From the northwest, the Braedon River lumbered through a dense and angry forest before it met the sea. The house that Kale called home stood on a bluff on its eastern bank, hidden within the mangled woods.

Kale thought about her home, and warmth immediately began to spread through her. It was not a conventional home. She didn't live there with her parents because they'd been dead for years. She didn't live with her siblings or any other relatives because she had none. As far as she knew, she didn't have a single relative on all of Berdune, let alone the whole universe. But, she did have a family. She lived in the secluded house with the people she thought of as her best friends. Three other people like her in one essential way; they were all robbed of their families by Caine.

When Kale's parents had been killed in an accident, she thought her world would end. Yet, somehow, that's when her life had really begun. She swore that day, at the age of fifteen, that she would avenge the death of her parents and one day destroy Caine. She'd never really understood the mistrust she had harbored towards the great and powerful Caine, even from a very young age. She'd always been certain, even when he first arrived, and she was only a child, that his charming exterior was simply a mask that the monster beneath it wore. It always made her parents extremely nervous, and they'd implored her time and time again to keep her feelings toward him a secret, but she had never quite been able to hide how she felt about him. In recent years, he proved all of her suspicions and though she always waited for him to do so, even Kale, in all of her certainty and sight, couldn't have foreseen how evil he would become or the kinds of horrors he would inflict on the people of Berdune.

There were other reasons she turned against him. Those reasons she kept secret and safe until she needed to use them. They were the same reasons she was certain she could find a way to beat him.

Now, at the end of the year 13 AC (After Caine), Kale was almost nineteen and almost done biding her time. Her parents had believed deeply in Caine, but she felt no guilt in betraying their faith because Caine had betrayed theirs.

As she saw the city of Braedon Ridge up ahead, anger swelled up from deep within her. She could still recall what the city had looked like years ago. It was a glittering jewel of happiness and hope in Berdune's lush countryside. She still marveled at how far they'd fallen in the years since Caine arrived. And, still, they tumbled. Every day, she saw a little more despair and darkness, creeping through what was once bright and beautiful, consuming everything in its path. Every day, she faced it and fought it. One day, not far ahead, she will come up against the truth of it in a way she could never have imagined.

Her morning routine wasn't simply out of compassion and love for the people, though those things mattered a great deal to Kale. For her, there was also the reminder of what Caine had brought to Berdune. She saw it in every sad and sorry house she passed, long ago abandoned; the families wrecked or left in ruins. In every hopeless gaze that met hers, in every broken and aching heart that reached out with a belief the pain could be eased, in the terrified scurrying through the streets of people not wanting to be noticed or seen by the J'Kahl for fear of the consequences for the crime of simply being, Kale saw it all. What Caine had brought to Berdune and its people was a promise of darkness like no other, and coming up against the relentless wave of it, over and over and over again, fueled Kale's determination to bring an end to it, no matter what it cost her.

Kale showed up in Braedon Ridge every morning shortly after the sun was up. She would first stop at the Mission and help hand out food and provisions to those who couldn't afford them on their own. She would then walk through the streets visiting old friends of the family, sometimes stopping to join a game of hide-and-seek or soccer with the neighborhood children. Everywhere she looked, she saw pain and suffering, as the weight of Caine's rule pressed down upon them all. One day, she promised herself that she would find a way to inflict it all back on Caine.

On all of Alpha Iridium, only the continent of Berdune was known to be populated. Small tribes were rumored to live on the other northern continents and those who believed that the Founders really did exist said that they must live there as well, but no one really knew for certain. Many towns and villages populated Berdune and the number of people who knew each other across the continent was large. Kale knew more people than she could count. She knew many because of her parents. They were well known across Berdune; especially when near the end of their lives, they'd become part of Caine's inner circle.

Kale was only fifteen at that time, and she never understood why two regular people had been asked to stand at Caine's side. They were loyal and enthusiastic toward Caine's cause but had never really earned the right to outrank those who stood by him faithfully for many years. Kale wondered whether she really knew everything about her parents but quickly, as always, shook this thought away. Of course, she didn't know everything about her parents. Her closest, dearest friends knew close to nothing of the truth about her. That was life. We are the keepers of our own secrets. Some of them we keep even from ourselves.

"Good morning, Mrs. Blanchard. How's my little Emily today?" Kale called out.

A woman wrapped in rags looked up from what she was doing and immediately smiled. Her entire demeanor brightened at the sight of Kale.

"Kale," she replied with pleasant surprise. Warmth and love emanated from the woman as she watched Kale pass. "Em is a little under the weather," she said. "She'll be glad to see you though. She's been asking for you, and Jaren. I think she's got a crush on him." The woman laughed. Kale kept walking but never once gave the impression she had somewhere more important to be.

"Tell Em I'll stop by on my way home." She called back to Mrs. Blanchard. "I've got a little surprise for her."

As Kale got farther into town and the areas that marked the most poverty, she saw less and less of Caine's soldiers, the J'Kahl, and people moved more freely through the streets. She made her way toward the Mission and now couldn't take more than a few steps without being greeted. Some people approached her with gifts, or home baked goods they'd made and wanted her to share with her friends. Some joined her on her walk, either going to help out at the Mission or on their way there for breakfast. Every shining, smiling face and those glimpses of hope and love made Kale's conviction stronger that she would one day destroy Caine. Every sad, sagging house that hid heartache and desolation made her fight to keep the tears of outrage from spilling from her eyes. Still, she saw what she didn't want to see. It was the very same thing she needed to see in order to live the life of sacrifice she knew she must if she was going to defeat him. Braedon Ridge, like all of the once beautiful and sparkling fairytale towns of Berdune, had become stained, ravaged, and ruined by Caine and all of the destruction that he created.

Braedon Ridge was a town, like most on Berdune, without purpose. What few jobs there were, people fought over in order to get coupons for food and clothes. Once able to sustain themselves through farming and trade, the almost fourteen years of Caine's presence had robbed the people of their self-sufficiency. Long ago, they traded their goods with other towns across the continent. Now, the train that ran across their lands carried people to the slavery of Caine's mines and factories and carried back goods of which Caine alone controlled the use and distribution. He shipped some food to the Mission, but it was often so damaged and rotten that he would never have eaten it himself or even fed it to his soldiers.

Yet, still, the people held onto their certainty that he would someday come to champion their salvation. They felt indebted for Caine's aide, as if they suffered against his will and there was nothing he could do to change their lives for the better. Kale knew Caine was a man made of lies and deception, and all she could hope was that he'd starved his people long enough to make them ready to taste change; even if they had to fight and die for it. When she considered this, the sacrifice they'd all have to make, some willingly, some not, to taste their freedom, Kale was always surprised by her acceptance of it. It didn't surprise her, however, that she was willing to die in her pursuit of Caine's destruction, as long as she took him with her to whatever came next. Late at night, lying in bed alone and letting thoughts wander through her mind of what was chasing all of them down, it did disturb her a little that she could so easily ask others to march to their own death if it meant destroying Caine. She wasn't a fool. She knew there would be casualties. If it meant his end, she'd gladly be one of them. This was war. All would play a part before it was done, willing or not.

Destroying Caine consumed her every hope and desire, and not even the ruin and wreckage that might lie in its wake could deter her. Whenever she began to falter in her convictions, all she needed to do was visit Braedon Ridge. There, the J'Kahl roamed the streets, thugs dressed as protectors, hassling the harmless or arresting another innocent person. She would visit the Mission and the people who depended on its charity. She'd see another abandoned home only to find out Caine had found more workers for his mines and destroyed yet another innocent family. It was here that the fires of her hatred were fueled. Here, and somewhere long ago and out of reach.

At the Mission, in the mornings, Kale passed out warm meals and chatted lovingly with friends and acquaintances. The mood was never bleak at the Mission no matter how bad life was outside of it. Looking around at the gaunt, sick, and sallow faces of the people as they ate and talked with their neighbors, Kale wondered if the strength she knew they had would ever get a chance to see the light. She wondered if the strength of the spirit could outweigh the physical weakness that more than thirteen years of deprivation, starvation, and terror had inflicted.

"Kale, when you gonna say 'yes' to marrying me? I've been asking you every day for a year and not a glimmer of hope. I know it's hard to tell but I'm getting on in years and I'd like to settle down," a kind black man said and blushed at Kale, eyes dancing with laughter.

"I've told you, Mr. Carlson, I'm not ready to settle down yet," Kale replied, as if taking his question seriously.

"It's that boy, ain't it? It's 'cause of that boy. I see the way he looks at you. If you gonna marry him, I tell you right now, I better be the best man." Howling with laughter, Mr. Carlson turned and started looking for a place to sit down and eat his sparse meal. Kale had already forgotten his comment about a boy, and the way that boy looked at her. Kale didn't have time for thoughts like that.

Another man stood smiling in front of Kale. Thinning grey hair framed a kind, old face with bright and knowing eyes.

"Mr. Wilson, you're early this morning. Still up from partying last night, I imagine."

It was obvious by the swiftness of his response that this conversation, like the one Kale had with Mr. Carlson, was a morning routine.

"You know it, Kale," he said. "I know I don't look it but I don't feel a day over fifty."

In response, Kale gave him a playful smile and waited for him to move on but he stood, rooted to the spot.

"Kale, I've been worried about you. I hear things. If you're anything like your parents, you're getting crazy ideas in your head. These are dangerous times. Promise me, you'll be careful Kale? We need you here."

Kale's smile changed, softened.

"I promise I won't do anything that doesn't need to be done."

After squeezing her hand in his, Mr. Wilson walked away, tray in hand, shaking his head, muttering, "Just like her father." Not many people left in Braedon Ridge knew how true that statement really was.

FIVE

After spending an hour and a half at the Mission, Kale stopped in to visit Emily and give her the bracelet she'd made for her out of shells she'd found on the beach. Emily was a sickly young girl, often found in bed, coughing and wheezing but never without a smile on her face and the bright hope that youth and inexperience afforded, emanating from her sunken eyes. Her enthusiasm for life and adventure, despite being forced to waste most of her youth in bed, had instantly drawn Kale to the girl and they'd become friends quickly and easily. Kale would never admit, even to herself, that she also envied this girl, healthy or not, the possibility of the life she could live without Caine. If they stopped him soon, and she was certain that somehow they would, then Emily could have the life that Kale had not.

"Can you take me to the beach one day, Kale? Mom won't let me go alone but I'm sure she'd let me go with you." Emily smiled a devious childlike smile and Kale couldn't help but return it.

"Well, Em, I'll tell you what, if you ever want to go somewhere you can't go when you're awake, just go while you're sleeping. That's what I do." Kale gave Emily a serious look as if to assure the girl she wasn't joking. "I can meet you there. Would you like that?"

Emily squealed. "Oh, Kale, that would be wonderful. Can we go there tonight?"

"How about we meet at eleven on our dream beach and we'll stay all night just to watch the sun come up?"

"Will Medea be there? I haven't seen her in days." Emily's eyes overflowed with her anxiousness to learn all she could about the adventure Kale was painting in her imagination.

"She might...if you're lucky," Kale replied.

"What about Corin?" Emily asked, then she added sheepishly, "and Jaren? Could we have a party on the shore?"

Kale laughed. "How about I meet you tonight and we'll figure the whole thing out?"

Kale left Emily smiling ear to ear and counting the hours until it was time for bed so she could dream a night of peace and laughter with her friend.

After the Blanchard's, Kale stopped in with some acquaintances. The visit was short and had one purpose alone.

"We're getting ready to move. We'll keep you informed. If anybody wants out, this is the time. If you're still in, we'll figure everything out at the next meeting."

Her last stop on the way home was by the house of an older couple who were both unable to leave their home. Everyone in Braedon Ridge lent a hand in taking care of them; they'd been widely known and loved before the coming of Caine. Kale always stopped in the mornings and often took the time to have tea with them before hurrying on. Mr. Weston had worked with her father and their friendship, despite the gap in age, meant he could talk about him undeterred for hours. It was the gift he gave Kale over and over again for all she and her friends did for him and his wife. When she knocked on the door, it opened right away. Mrs. Weston, looking older and frailer than usual, moved aside to let Kale step in through the doorway, casting a furtive glance out into the streets of the city beyond, before stepping back inside herself.

"Oscar's not up this morning. He's got a terrible cough, worse than yesterday. I'm not feeling too well either dear. Up all night listening to Oscar hacking away. Can't sleep without him at my side though."

Kale hugged Mrs. Weston then stepped back so she was standing in the doorway.

"Well, I promised Mr. Weston that I would pick up that package for Jaren. He's been wanting to surprise him with that jacket and I know he would want me to take it."

"I've already got it ready," Mrs. Weston said, passing Kale the parcel. "Will you be by tomorrow?"

"Of course I will." She handed Mrs. Weston a small package. "For Mr. Weston. Medication for his cough."

Mrs. Weston opened the small paper bag and pulled out a glass jar with three tiny blue pills trembling together inside. Her eyes widened in surprise and she had to fight to keep the tears from spilling from her eyes.

"How did you get this, Kale?"

"Don't thank me. Thank Corin."

Mrs. Weston threw her arms around Kale's neck.

"You give him a big hug from me, okay? I don't know what we'd do without you and those friends of yours, Kale. Take care of each other."

Kale left the Weston's in the very same manner she did every morning, with rage coursing through every cell in her body and a renewed determination to fulfill the promise she'd made to herself only a few short years before.

On the walk back home, Kale contemplated the sadness, terror, and despair that Caine had brought with him to Berdune. Instead of letting her anger overwhelm her, she allowed it to feed her obsession with destroying him. Though few people openly opposed him, primarily out of fear, Kale was certain that the people of Braedon Ridge and the surrounding areas would be ready to rise up against him if given the chance. She planned to give it to them. She just had to figure out how.

Walking southwest, she came to the ridge that ran from the Craden River across the forest westward to the Braedon River. This was her favorite path home and she wasn't really sure why. Something about it brought her comfort. A secret familiarity deep within her welled up every time she passed by that spot. She couldn't know it was a kind of remembering, a pulling at her by a day long ago and long forgotten, tying her to another life by the thinnest of threads but with the fullness of truth.

Once she got to the Braedon River, she would have to turn north and climb a steep slope to get to the house on the ridge above. That was the hard way to get to the house but she loved the physical exertion. She loved it because it drained her of the energies of the morning. When she got home, she needed to be composed, calm, and ready to plan. She was unwilling to let her friends see her weakness. The fury that boiled just below the surface or the hatred that fought to consume her, they knew these things were in her but not how deep they ran or how long they'd lived there.

Kale loved her new family dearly. They were all she had in a world waiting to fall apart, but she hid a lot from them. She told herself it was because she didn't want them to see her in any moment of weakness. That even though she was the youngest of all of them, she thought that she had to be the strongest, and that they needed her to be. The truth was a far darker thing, as it often could be. She felt safest and surest with that barrier of secrecy between them, that expanse that meant she hadn't given herself entirely to anyone. 'Not until Caine's gone,' was what she told herself over and over again.

"Hello, Kale," a stranger's voice startled her out of her contemplation and she almost stumbled and fell.

Kale caught herself and turned to see who'd spoken out of the shadows that the towering, mangled trees cast in all directions. She was surprised to see it was a woman no taller than she was. Her skin was lighter than Kale's but looked as if she'd spent many years in the golden sun so that it glowed as iridescent amber. Her hair was black as night and though her eyes were a friendly brown, there was within them the depths to hide the entire midnight sky. The sunlight that had wormed its way through the canopy far above glinted off them mysteriously. Kale immediately felt uncomfortable. This was the first time she'd ever met anyone in these woods and the stranger made her anxious.

"Don't fret, Kale. I'm a friend."

Kale felt the day constrict around her. It pressed in on her in a way that felt both familiar and unwanted. Panic began to poke and prod at her but she shoved it away.

"I'm sorry. I don't know who you are," Kale said. "Are you from Braedon?"

The woman smiled and Kale suddenly had the urge to run. This woman, she slowly began to realize, had the answers to a thousand questions, questions she wasn't ready to ask because the answers would change everything. Kale knew her hatred for Caine afforded her a kind of ignorance this woman could swiftly sweep aside and she wasn't ready to let go of it.

*Who was this woman,* Kale wondered, *and why do I feel so drawn to knowing what she knows and yet so afraid?*

The strange woman startled Kale out of her ruminations. Her eyes seemed to express, in their worry and in their acceptance, that she'd heard every thought turning through Kale's turbulent mind.

"Kale, it doesn't matter where I'm from or who I am. What matters...is who you choose to be." The voice, calm and confident, was pleading as well.

Kale shook her head, confused.

A bird cried out behind her and she turned, drawn away by the sound. A moment later when she turned around again, the woman was gone.

Kale stood completely still, scanning the woods, but in the eerie silence that lingered, it seemed as if the woman had vanished into thin air. Kale started home again. She walked quickly, the absurd discomfort the woman had brought still trailing behind her.

Kale felt...reminded.

There was, deep within her, a stirring which had always been, but that was now a little more persistent and demanded to be noticed. Like always, she shoved at it angrily and shoveled it away out of sight, but this time it had become a little harder to do so. The answer was sneaking and skulking about inside her and though she fought to keep it buried, it struggled with every ounce of her being because she wasn't ready to know what she already knew; and the encounter with the strange woman had begun to unearth it.

When, at last, she started the steep climb to the house she called home, she'd begun to put the woman out of her mind, though uneasiness still hung about her like a mist. Years of being able to keep some things hidden, even from herself, couldn't quite help her set the puzzle aside entirely.

The truth, now glimpsed, was asking to be seen.

SIX

When Kale walked into the kitchen of her home, Medea, her best friend, was standing over the stove looking comically perplexed. As Medea poked at what might have been eggs only ten minutes before, Kale realized with fondness that this was a pretty common look for Medea while she was cooking. She couldn't help but pause, smiling, appreciative that some things were certain and unchanging. Above their heads, a thin layer of black smoke hovered like a bad omen, writhing and twisting, snakelike, as a breeze spilled in the doorway and coaxed it to life. When Medea heard Kale walk into the room, she turned and a look of relief washed over her face.

"Thank god you're here, Kale. Are these eggs supposed to be hard on the outside?" She poked at them again with a sigh of exasperation. "Like really hard?"

Kale walked over to the stove and couldn't stop herself from laughing as she pushed her best friend out of the way.

"How 'bout you pour me some coffee and I'll see if I can salvage any of this?"

Medea tried to look hurt but she couldn't help smiling.

"Oh, and do you mind grabbing the food out of my pack and putting it away for me?" Kale added as she turned her attention to the blackened mess Medea had hoped would be breakfast.

Shaking her head, Medea picked up the bag and started to put the food away while Kale threw the tortured eggs into the garbage and cracked new ones. The eggs were a luxury, of course, gifts from people they'd helped or from friends. The coffee, too, was a rarity in Braedon Ridge, but they always managed to have enough to get through the exhausting task of starting a new day in Caine's world.

"They really love you, Kale. They really do," Medea said, as she rummaged through the gifts and food the people of Braedon Ridge had given Kale that morning.

"It's for all of us, Medea, don't be so dramatic," Kale said with a laugh.

Medea and Kale had been friends since childhood. Neither had siblings, making way for a friendship that had brought them as close as sisters in many ways. Neither had parents, accidents having claimed the lives of both Kale's and Medea's. Both girls felt personally assaulted by the loss and held Caine responsible. To them, he was no longer a god or a savior but a demon, a plague, and one that needed to be stopped.

Though Medea was more than three years older at twenty-one, it was often as if Kale was the older sibling. In fact, amongst their friends Kale was most like the parental figure, if not the leader. Kale was five when Caine came to Alpha Iridium, to Berdune. By the time she was eleven, she'd become aware of the problems that came along with creating a god out of a man. When most people were willing to bow down to Caine, Kale had always been ready and willing to openly oppose him, much to the horror of her parents and friends.

She'd even been strong enough at the age of fifteen to take care of Medea when both their parents had been killed. Later, just two years ago, Jaren and Corin had joined their family, and though Jaren was now twenty-two and Corin was twenty, they both looked up to Kale as well. She was fearless and unrelenting. Certain of their cause and uncompromising in her conviction, they would prevail. She was strong, passionate, and loving, even if she could be distant and sometimes seemed out of reach. No one really knew why but Kale was what held their family together and if it weren't for her, the rebel movement would never have started or endured all it had.

Despite how she was seen in the eyes of her friends, Kale could be a solitary and lonely person. She could walk through the streets on her own for hours and be completely content. Sometimes, she'd spend hours sitting by the ocean, listening to the waves, a song sung of eternities, and not once would she think of the world outside the one she was staring at. Though surrounded by the people she loved, at times she was so lonely that she ached. A rare and simple loneliness grew from somewhere deep within her like she was missing pieces of herself. It made her feel as if she was somehow only half a person, a fraction of a whole. She never told her friends how she felt. They needed her to be strong.

"I smell something burning. Was Medea trying to cook breakfast again?" Jaren asked, as he walked into the kitchen through the back door. As always, he had an air of accomplishment about him. His movements were swift, sure, and efficient, as if he had no time to waste. Yet, there was elegance to the way he moved that made you want to watch him for a little while. Everywhere he went, Jaren inspired gazes to follow, and being entirely unaware of it only added to his charm. He rarely wavered in his outward appearance of competence and confidence. This was the mask he wore, his shield and shelter. They each had one.

"At least I try, Jaren," Medea defended, but her words were without reproach or insult. This sibling-like bickering was too common to be anything less than comfortable and comforting. It was another staple in a world with too few. "Don't worry. Kale's cooking now. Why don't you have some eggs?" Medea offered.

"Thanks, little sis, but I ate hours ago. I will have some of that coffee." Jaren walked past Kale and paused to kiss her on the forehead.

Before Medea could object, he took the coffee she'd been pouring for Kale and sat down at the table taking cautious sips from the steaming cup without adding any cream or sugar. Both things were hard to come by on Berdune and not important enough for taking risks. It helped to know that Caine took his coffee with cream and sugar. Somehow that made the bitter, black coffee more agreeable, delightful even in its defiance of the great and powerful Caine.

"I'll give you one thing though, Medea, you make a great cup of coffee," Jaren said, raising his mug in a mock toast.

She smiled at him sarcastically, while pouring another cup for Kale who was just finishing the second batch of eggs, this one fragrant and appetizing. Placing a plate in front of Medea and one in front of herself, she joined her friends at the table.

Ten minutes later, Corin came into the kitchen smiling cheerfully, buoyant in his step, though avoiding any verbal acknowledgement of his friends. He was the member of their family who had managed to hold onto his boyish youth, both in temperament and outlook, and in the mornings it clung to him like a fog so that there was no escaping the reminder they'd all been young not that long ago. After pouring a cup of coffee for himself and refilling everyone else's cup, he finally sat down at the table and waited, as was routine in the morning, for Jaren to bring up business.

"My sources tell me Caine is up to something really big this time. Top secret stuff. No one but the people closest to him even know what he's planning and even many of them are in the dark. We've got to do something. The new year isn't that far away and, from what I hear, that's when he's planning to move."

Corin replied first. "So, we're right into it this morning, are we? Just once, I'd like to have my coffee before Jaren makes me so nervous I feel sick."

"Well, Corin," Kale paused to take a sip of coffee, "if we waited for you to be up before we started our day, we'd never get anything done..." she let her phrase trail off and made the rest of her point with eyebrows raised and a devious smile.

Corin pretended not to hear her and instead turned to Jaren.

"So what should we do? I mean really?" Corin paused to look at each one of his friends but words weren't necessary. They all knew the truth. The rebel alliance was made up people mostly their age and, with less than a hundred members scattered across Berdune's cities and towns, they didn't stand a chance against Caine and his army. Sure, they'd caused Caine some trouble through sabotage but not enough to have a real impact. The people of Berdune needed to come together to stop him, and they weren't just going to pick up weapons and charge the castle without being forced to see the truth of what Caine was. That's what they needed to do.

No one answered right away. The silence instead stretched on, filled with the sad truth that they were still fighting for people unwilling to fight for themselves. If they were ever going to win, that would have to change.

Corin opened his mouth to speak and then closed it again. Stumped. He was the level-headed one in their little family, and he was the complete opposite of Medea in many ways. He was calm, clear-headed, and thought everything through multiple times before acting. Medea was always ready to act before she thought. In that and many ways, they balanced each other out.

"Corin," Medea looked at him as if annoyed, "you worry too much. That jerk, Caine, is no match for us. Let's just walk into that mansion of his and put an arrow through his heart, if you can find it that is." She made the gesture of firing an arrow but, as she looked around, she realized no one was impressed with her bravado. "Right then," she said putting her arms down, "anyone got any better ideas?"

That, of course, was a question with no immediate answer. Together they'd spent the last two years devoted to finding a way to stop Caine. The problem was he had few weaknesses, if any. He was heavily guarded by J'Kahl, and no one but them or his very inner circle could get inside the compound or near him.

United in their lack of faith in him and their deep sense of the injustice and cruelty he inflicted on the people of Berdune, they were dedicated to finding a way. All four had lost something to Caine, and they were unwilling to forgive him as a savior sent with a mission. All of Berdune, really, had lost something to the tyrannical leader. Yet very few were willing to admit they'd been robbed of it. Instead, most maintained they'd willingly given up their freedom because it would be returned to them when they were worthy of it. They waited for a promised land that Caine alone could deliver.

The rebels were trying to open the eyes of the common people and they weren't going to give up. Even as Caine fought unrelentingly to keep them closed, change was coming to Berdune. All four of them could feel it. They could be masters of it or victims to it, but they had to believe the choice was theirs.

SEVEN

Jaren and Corin had both hated the world after Caine's arrival, but neither one had considered that anything could be done to change their circumstances or those of the people of Berdune. The possibility that they would be a part of that change was once beyond anything either could have imagined. In their mid-teens, they'd only understood how to complain or despair about the way things were. Realizing even a single person had the power to ignite change came later, and after both had already lost far too much.

Corin lost his father when he was young and his mother had openly opposed Caine from the beginning. More than two years ago, she disappeared without a trace, and Corin still wasn't sure whether he hoped she was alive somewhere as a prisoner and slave or whether he hoped she'd died and was free from the horrible world they were fighting to live in and to change. What he did know is that he missed her and Caine was the reason she was gone.

Jaren's parents had disowned him. They were servants of Caine, deep within his inner circle of followers and unwilling to honor a son who didn't believe as strongly as they did that Caine was their savior. So many times, Jaren had wished his parents' absence in his life was because they'd died fighting Caine instead of serving him. At least, then, he could be proud of them.

Jaren never considered that he would find a way to fight back or find a way to put himself back together after his parents' betrayal had torn him into a thousand pieces. He never imagined he would be strong enough to show his parents that they were wrong and that Caine *was* evil. Just when he was ready to give up hope, he'd met Kale. He'd been standing on a street corner talking with Corin about how the world would never change or get any better, and a stranger had interrupted their conversation with a smile.

"Are you willing to give up so easily? You don't look like the type to just roll over and die."

When Jaren turned around to see who'd spoken, a witty reply ready, he found that the words got stuck in his throat. The girl standing before him was the most beautiful girl he'd ever seen. She was petite, more than a few inches shorter than both him and Corin, and yet she had a huge presence about her. So much so he actually took a step back as if trying to move out of its way. Her eyes and hair were both a shade of deep red in the sunlight and her skin was smooth and golden. When he looked into her eyes, he saw laughter and hope and...sadness, no, worse, sorrow. Something inside

Jaren stirred for the first time in a long time and he lost himself for a moment, never taking his eyes from hers.

He stumbled over his words, thrown off balance and feeling a little bit foolish for it, and finally she laughed and asked with a shrug, "I guess you're not used to being second guessed are you? Well, then, I don't think we'll get along too well, you and me. I'm Kale, by the way. And you are?"

She was still smiling. It was both mischievous and innocent, and Jaren couldn't help answering it with his own.

"Corin, nice to meet you," Corin said, extending his hand to her. "Mr. Speechless here goes by the name of Jaren."

"So, I don't like to eavesdrop but it sounds like you two don't think the world will ever change." Kale studied their faces and dissected their subtle reactions. Kale had been blessed with the ability to read people easily and quickly and right away she knew things about Jaren and Corin that they hadn't yet even learned about themselves.

She watched them intently and began to memorize their faces as she always did when meeting potentially new friends, or enemies. They could've been brothers, Corin and Jaren. They were both tall for someone of Berdune, though neither stood as tall as the feared Randall Caine, who, at six feet, stood as tall as the mythical Founders. Jaren had gentle grey eyes and wild blond hair that framed his kind face. Corin's eyes were blue and every bit as soft and passionate as Jaren's. His hair was a shade darker than Jaren's but not nearly as messy, as if Corin's neat personality grew out through the top of his head. Kale had instantly liked them both and, more than that, felt a kinship with them that birthed the friendships to follow.

"It's hard to imagine that the world will ever change," Jaren finally found his voice.

"Well, if you're serious about wanting to try changing the world on your own, I know some people who are taking matters into their own hands," Kale responded cautiously yet casually. Unlike the boys, whose eyes darted around nervously, she never looked away from them as if they were discussing nothing more dangerous than a summer storm.

"You mean the rebels?" Corin scoffed.

"I hear they're led by a child, and the only reason Caine hasn't disposed of them is because they aren't even a real threat," Jaren said with exasperation.

"Well, I'm not one to make decisions based on what other people say," Kale smiled playfully but something else swam in her eyes, "but I understand how two guys like you could be all talk. It was nice meeting you though. Maybe I'll see you around." Kale turned away from them and began walking away.

"Wait. Where are you going?" Jaren called after the intriguing girl.

Kale didn't stop but simply called over her shoulder while waving one hand dismissively toward them. "The child and her rebels are holding a meeting in just a few minutes. I've never missed one. I'm not gonna start now."

It was a dangerous thing to proclaim aloud. If the wrong people had heard, the J'Kahl, for instance, she could've been arrested on the spot. In those days, many of the poorer neighborhoods, like the one they were in, were much safer. The people were under much less pressure than they were just a few short years later, when people were so starved and desperate the possibility of a reward for reporting traitors to Caine could often be too hard to resist. The rebels would learn that lesson the hard way.

Corin and Jaren watched her for a moment and then ran after her. "Hey, we never said we weren't interested. Wait up." Minutes later, the trio entered an abandoned building that breached the tree line on Braedon Ridge's northwest point. Inside, the ceilings towered far above them, shrouded in shadows that couldn't be reached by the light of the candles and oil lamps that lit the room. The air was fragrant and sweet and both Jaren and Corin felt a little like they'd entered a dream as the aroma made their noses tingle and their heads swim.

"So, what do you guys think so far?" Kale watched them intensely.

"A little intimidating, if you ask me," Corin answered; he was a little unsettled.

"Kale, where have you been? Everyone is waiting for you." Medea had come up behind the boys and they both jumped when she spoke. She pushed between them and stood staring at Kale without taking notice of either of them. Despite themselves, neither could help studying her in the wavering dimness.

Medea was a plainer creature than they. She had the most common hair and eye color on Berdune; both were brown. Yet, she moved and spoke with a certainty of self that was both striking and imposing. Her features were bold, paired beautifully with her dark caramel-colored skin, and she was stunning in the flickering candlelight that lit the room and danced across her face.

"Medea, this is Corin and Jaren. They're here to see if we actually do anything of worth around here. They're looking forward to meeting whoever is in charge, though..."

Medea interrupted, "but you..."

Kale kept speaking, "What was that you said earlier? The rebels are led by a child...something like that anyway."

Medea began to laugh hysterically. "Oh, I'm already glad to meet you two. You've just made my day."

"Will you take these two under your wing, Medea? I have something to take care of."

"Oh, sure, I wouldn't miss this for the world."

Kale disappeared into the crowd, while Jaren and Corin stood nervously watching her go.

"Come on, you two, we'll sit over here and wait for the meeting to start." Medea led them through the crowd and people greeted them in varying ways, from smiles to looks of distrust.

"They really make you feel welcome, don't they?" Jaren whispered in Corin's ear.

"Are you trying to get us into more trouble than we're already in?" Corin whispered back, both annoyed and a bit fearful.

They found a spot to sit and, with Medea at their side, they watched the strangers who surrounded them with a mixture of interest and suspicion. The small crowd was comprised primarily of people near their age or a little bit older. It was obvious by the group gathered around them that the younger generation was most willing to oppose Caine. The mood in the room was buoyant, if not cheerful, and there was no mistaking the aura of hope that hung in the air. One both boys had long thought was a permanent casualty of the coming of Caine. Jaren and Corin were slowly starting to feel at home as people approached to introduce themselves and inquired about their lives. It was a strange and welcome feeling, those beginnings of belonging.

Suddenly, a hush fell over the crowd and all heads turned to the front of the room.

"Well, I guess we should get started. Has everyone met our two new friends, Corin and Jaren?" The speaker pointed toward them and smiled when she saw them turning red with embarrassment. "If there are any other newcomers with us tonight, I'm Kale. I like to think I'm in charge around here and mostly everyone lets me believe that but really we're all in this together, and every single one of us is as important as the rest.

"Now, our first order of business tonight is our reputation. It turns out most people think we're led by a child and the only reason Caine leaves us alone is because we're not a threat." Kale winked at Corin and Jaren and the color darkened in their cheeks. "This is great news. If Caine thinks we're weak, if he underestimates us, then we have a much better chance of stopping him. If we can, we should casually spread rumors of our own. We're not in this to be heroes. We're in this to change things. What other people think of us doesn't matter if it keeps us safe, and alive.

"Now, secondly, we have to find somewhere safe to store our arsenal until we're ready to put it to use. Sam, you said you had some ideas."

A young woman in the crowd stood and began to speak. The meeting went on like that for almost an hour. People shouted things out, people cheered, people laughed, people held hands and hugged. In that way, it was a place untouched by the rule of Caine. By the end of the meeting, both Jaren and Corin were contributing and it was obvious they now believed what they'd thought was impossible only a few hours before. The world could change, could be changed, and they could help change it.

"So, what did you think?" Kale asked them after the official meeting had finished.

Her real answer came a month later when they were all living together in Medea's parents' house in the woods, and she realized she finally had a family and that they were all fighting together for the same thing.

Jaren found it ironic that they were living in a house that once belonged to Caine's most loyal followers. The four of them were definitely the opposite of Medea's parents. He knew Medea felt like the only thing her parents had ever done right was to leave her their house. He also knew she felt deserted and betrayed by her old family and took pride in the fact that she could supply the home for her new one.

Jaren looked around the breakfast table at his friends. They were his home. Watching them talk, laugh, and argue, he felt a million emotions surge through himself. The predominant one was love, and he loved each of them differently. Medea was his little sister. She filled a hole in his life that had existed since childhood. Corin was his brother and his best friend. Words fell short of properly describing their bond or how much they depended on each other in a world slowly falling apart around them. And then, of course, there was Kale. Like most everyone who knew her, he loved her. He was closer to her than most. He got to see her in the mornings when she was steeped in hope, as if she'd been dreaming of another life, a life in which Caine did not exist. He saw her after the Mission, when she tried to bottle her rage and loathing so that no one else would see it and think her weak or out of control. He saw her all day, every day. He saw her in every mood she'd ever known and ever would. And yet, and yet somewhere inside himself, he understood that he'd never really seen her at all because you couldn't see something that wasn't really, wholly, there.

He didn't completely understand it, but he knew it just the same. He knew it the same way he knew that soon, far, far too soon, the fight they'd been preparing for would be upon them and the people he loved, like him, would have to fight and maybe die. The prospect of his own death didn't scare Jaren. He woke every day into a world that boasted of death and destruction and the possibility that it might be your last. But with the acceptance of his own ineffectual passing, came the apprehension that those he loved would face the same fate, and that scared Jaren more than he would ever like to admit.

He'd never loved anyone as much as he loved his new family. They were all he had in a sad and broken world. They gave him hope. They made him believe the world deserved to be a better place and that they, together, could make it better. Before them, the future had seemed to be a bleak and dreadful thing, something he'd wished to avoid, and something he'd dreaded the inevitability of. His friends had changed all that. Kale had changed all that. The gratitude that worked its way through him for everything they'd given him, for what she'd given him, ran so deep he sometimes thought he might drown in it.

"Jaren!" Medea shouted. "Did you hear me?" Jaren was startled out of his thoughts. "Honestly, Jaren, sometimes I wonder how you're supposed to be the competent and organized one. I mean, I've never known anyone whose mind wanders more than yours." Medea shook her head disapprovingly.

Jaren smiled, sheepishly. "Sorry. Just trying to come up with some ideas. And just for the record, Kale is much more distractible than I am. Now, what were you saying?"

Medea smiled and looked excited enough for Jaren to start worrying. Most ideas she had were dangerous or far too bold and more often than not, over the top crazy. She had an overwhelming desire to live a life of adventure, like many, but like few she often sought it out, dreaming and longing for its conception. Had she known that over the coming weeks adventure would hunt her down, hunt them all down, alongside danger, anguish, and pain, she might have given up hoping for a life of adventure. Life rarely grants us opportunities like that...to forgo the things we might regret. Life, too often in Caine's Berdune, was a series of regrets laid end-to-end, long and lasting in their bitter truth.

"Well," Medea paused for effect, "I say we go in. Undercover. Get as close to the man, the monster, as we can. It's time to get more aggressive with our tactics. What do you say?"

Kale was shocked. She looked away from Medea hoping she wouldn't notice how taken aback Kale was by her idea. It wasn't that Kale thought the idea was horrible, it was that she was going to suggest the very same thing. Except Kale knew something Medea didn't, the perfect person to go undercover and infiltrate Caine's organization, and she already knew how.

Far away, the ocean sighed against the shore. It was a sound of familiar lovers, that returning, that lying down of one body onto another, so sweetly. A million tiny suns danced upon the surface of the waves. Just above them, the salt wind hurried over the surface like a song heading towards the horizon, carrying secrets whispered to it over and over again as if no one could hear. It was a new day, a new dawn, and the friends could sense it. The time for action was finally upon them. They could feel the hope they'd been speaking of for years starting to become a reality, as it rallied around them and their willingness to begin the real fight. Not a single one of them could suppress their excitement even if it was accompanied by fear.

They were ready. They always had been.

EIGHT

Derin stared out of his bedroom window and tried to let the bright sunshine warm his mood. Once, not even that long ago, it would've been uncharacteristic for him to suffer from such a ridiculous affliction as unhappiness but, lately, it seemed to seep into every minute of every day. It showed up in the most trivial of moments and made its way into every one of his contemplations. When he worked, trained, or moved through any of the innumerable tasks of the day, he could feel it, an anchor not yet grounded, trailing along behind him, slowing him down with its weight and implications.

He'd generally been a happy young man whose faith had illumined how he looked at life. Like many people of faith, his truths were few and simple. He believed in Caine and in what he stood for, as he always had, but something had changed. No, not something, someone; Caine had changed.

When Caine first arrived, Derin was only six-years-old. He was an orphan with no memory of his family and no idea what the future held. Derin had come a long way since those days, as had the people of Berdune. Like those who wondered with longing what other life could've been theirs had the Scriptures been untrue and Caine not come to fulfill the Prophecy, Derin had begun to sense the possibility of another kind of life.

He could see that Caine had the power to change life on Alpha Iridium, to change life for the people of Berdune. He hoped with everything he was that the Prophecy would prove true and their planet would finally know peace. Except... except aside from arriving and taking over, Caine had done little else to play the role of savior. He had instead used the title of savior as a shield behind which he hid and laid his plans for greater power and domination.

Once Derin had been sure of his role in the new world, in Caine's Berdune, but recently that role was beginning to feel like a lie. He'd begun to find fault in Caine's ways and to notice inconsistencies between what he said he stood for and how he acted. Too much space was opening up between the truth and what Caine said or promised, and Derin was finding it more and more difficult to ignore the lies and injustices that stalked around him daily. *If not at Caine's side, then where could Derin possibly belong?* That question was just one of many posed by a conscience he sometimes hated because of the discomfort and uncertainty it marshaled into his life.

Derin's adoptive father encouraged him to follow his dream of becoming a great warrior and leader. Some days, Derin felt unsure of whether this was really his destiny, but his fear of disappointing his father always brought him back to the truth. Under his father's tutelage and with the help of the other J'Kahl, Derin had learned to become a greatly respected warrior and had gained the trust of all those who worshipped Caine. Even at the age of nineteen, it looked as though Derin was going to make a proud and powerful leader. And yet, in what war was he to be a warrior? And more unsettling still, was he truly fighting on the right side?

At first, Derin never even silently questioned Caine's actions. His heart and eyes had been so filled with pride for the leader that he couldn't see the horrors Caine inflicted upon the people of Berdune. He'd never once doubted the great ruler until recently. Though the horrors had been ever existent, it was a change he'd noticed in Caine that had sparked his concern and Derin began paying attention in a way he'd avoided for much of his life. There was a dark wilderness that grew within Caine and it had begun to show in his eyes when he spoke of the future, as if he were really seeing it, as if he were being shown somehow what was coming. There was strangeness in the way he carried himself, as if he was carrying an invisible weight, something you couldn't see but was there nonetheless. Most frighteningly, there was madness creeping over the corners of every smile and looking out through his eyes to the world around him.

Even though he idolized Caine, Derin was starting to notice that the way he treated the common people was without love or compassion. His actions had once been accepted by Derin as those of a vengeful god, but recently they seemed more like the actions of a small and demented child who tore the wings off bugs to watch them suffer and turned ants to fire with a magnifying glass to revel in their burning. Before Caine, the people of Alpha Iridium, of Berdune, had known little of Gods, saviors, and their ability to deliver hope or salvation. Now, they had hope and it seemed to Derin that Caine was slowly, painstakingly, stamping it out and using it to toy with and torture them.

Derin felt guilty for betraying both his father and his leader in thought and spirit. He wondered if the great Caine would know he was faltering in his faith. Ashamed, he wondered if instead of being confronted by Caine, he would just disappear one night while he slept, as so many others who'd lost faith in the Great Leader.

Derin immediately pushed the mutinous thoughts from his mind. Caine was great. Caine was their savior. Caine was god. If Caine was treating the people roughly, it was because he had a plan. Whatever he was doing, it was for the better; it had to be. He couldn't know that not all hearts were like his, true and pure, and willing to give anything for those cradled within it.

## NINE

Kayla walked slowly through the streets of Emery. As always, instead of drinking in the sights she passed, she ignored them. She'd lived there for three months now and she could hardly believe it had been that long since her mother had sent her away. She'd come to Emery to live with her mother's sister, her Aunt Helen, and her Uncle Chris. They were wonderful, kind, and caring people, and Kayla despised them.

Since coming to Emery, Kayla had done little more than walk around the beautiful seaside town. She was without the will to do much else. Despite the fact that she'd walked the tiny city a million times over, she'd never actually taken a good look at it. She spent much of her time down by the ocean watching the waves come and go, come and go, and there, by the sea, found the only comfort she knew. It never stopped. It never faltered. The tide came and went as promised. The waves hurried up the beach and then retreated down it, only to begin again. This, she could count on. This, she could be certain of. Yet, somewhere deep inside, it surprised her every time it happened. Every time the waves washed up again and drew themselves close to where she was seated on the sand, relief rose within her. It was as if she were always expecting something to change, to disappoint her, to let her down, and as if she knew within herself how misleadingly certain it all looked but how truly fragile and fleeting it all was.

Kayla came to the cliffs that towered far above the ocean at the edge of town. She could hear the angry waves slamming the rocks below, as if they were trying to shake the earth and send her tumbling down toward them. She stood with her toes hanging over the edge and dared the wind to toss her from the perch. Below, the rabidly foaming waves tempted her to join them. *I'm not afraid*, she thought defiantly, as she took a few slow steps back from the edge, and then she hurled herself forward and leapt into the air.

The wind tossed her sunlit red hair in all directions. She could feel the salty spray soaring all around her like a hurricane rocketing upwards from the sea below. She screamed. She felt exhilarated and filled with joy. It seemed like forever since she'd felt so alive, free, and whole. It felt like forever before she hit the waves, but when she did she had to wonder why she jumped.

The water was icy and her entire body went numb with shock and fear the moment she hit the angry torrents. Almost all of the air escaped her lungs the second she went under and it was only because of the immense pressure that she didn't immediately inhale salt water. She sank quickly, drawn downward by an unseen force, unable to kick or swim for the surface or maybe just unwilling to try. She calmed and stilled. She was strangely at peace. Sinking slowly, she let the last of the air out of her lungs and waited. For what, she did not know. She knew it would be upon her quickly and then all would be calm, quiet.

In those last moments, she glimpsed it, the truth, that place that pulled at her from the inside out. If she could just give in, surrender, in a few moments it would be hers and she would be whole.

The weightlessness among the waves began to rock her softly to sleep. She became certain she'd died when she felt herself floating upwards. Toward heaven, toward her unknown fate, up she went. She felt coldness caress her face and neck and saw bright white light all around her. She was home. She was safe. The pain, anguish, and loneliness were over. She was sure of it.

Kayla let herself be dragged into the afterlife, welcoming it as one would welcome an old friend. It was like going home, a kind of returning. It was like waking up. Only, it was truly like waking up. Kayla could feel her lungs burning with icy fire. Angry frozen flames tore through all of her muscles. She felt heavy, sore, and sick. Her head throbbed and what she thought was the white light of heaven stung her eyes. Her lungs shook with violent spasms as the warm air choked its way down her throat. When she finally stopped moving, she lay still for what seemed to be an eternity, retching salt water out, while the angry rocking of the ocean clung to her. She was unable to move and too confused to try.

Above all else, she was scared. She wasn't afraid to die. She realized that she wasn't ready either. She allowed herself to hope with everything she was that she wasn't dead. She prayed that by some miracle she was dreaming and she would wake in her aunt and uncle's home. Yet, this was far too real to be a dream.

She blinked violently, panicking, needing to know what was happening. Finally, her vision began to return and she saw someone leaning over her.

"Are you an angel?" she croaked, and the weakness in her voice frightened her.

"Today, I guess I am," the stranger gave a short, skeptical laugh, and then asked. "Are you all right? Can you sit up?"

Kayla gathered every ounce of strength she had and rose to a sitting position. She leaned against the stranger and stared up into his beautiful face. If he wasn't an angel, he looked like something very close. He had eyes the color of a calm and wishful sea, so light blue that she imagined she could look through them into the bright day beyond. His black hair, clinging to the sides of his face and head with salty water, framed his angelic face like a midnight halo. *Too intense*, she thought of that connection she felt when looking into them, and so she quickly looked away, embarrassed and confused.

Kayla looked around and saw that she was sitting on the sandy beach to the south, far below the cliffs.

"What were you thinking?" the angel scolded. "You could have killed yourself?" He paused and then ventured worriedly, "Were you trying to kill yourself?"

Kayla couldn't help but smile at the stranger's concern.

"Trying to kill myself? God, no."

His face relaxed, as did his protective, fatherly grip.

"So then, what were you thinking?" He managed a perfect combination of puzzled and concerned which made Kayla laugh.

"Thinking, that's no fun."

The exhilaration returned, just a memory, but still she could feel her heart begin to pound a little fiercer in her aching chest. She could hear the rush of blood in her ears and her entire body tingled with longing to repossess the daring she'd lived only moments before. Somewhere inside a voice she didn't recognize whispered, 'when you dare to die, you dare to live.' She shivered, casting the thought away.

"God, what a rush," she laughed again, "wouldn't mind doing that every now and then. Keep life interesting, you know. I would have to ask you to come along, of course. Seeing as you like to play the hero and all."

Kayla stared at the guy beside her, noticing the worry in his face, recognizing the annoyance for her recklessness. His blue eyes were riddled with concern and when she looked into them they reminded her of the icy waves that had almost taken her life. Again, she felt a rush of adrenaline and she blushed though she wasn't quite sure why. She began to take in the details of his appearance again, as if he'd changed since she'd looked at him the first time. His hair was a curious shade of black so dark it shone blue in the remnants of the golden day. She watched as a tiny piece broke form and tried to tickle his forehead though he seemed more concerned with her than the rogue strand of hair trying to get his attention.

"Do I know you?" he asked, changing his demeanor, a puzzled look now resting on his face.

"I don't think so," she replied. "I'm Kayla. I moved here three months ago when...to live with my aunt and uncle. I haven't really been out much. I mean I haven't really had a chance to meet people, you know."

He frowned. "Maybe I've just seen you around or something." He shrugged. "I'm Max. And, I guess you owe me one, huh?"

She laughed. "Yeah, something like that."

"Can you walk, Kayla? It's going to get dark soon, and cold. You should probably get out of those wet clothes. I'll walk you home if you like."

She tried to stand along with his help. Wobbling and uncertain, she made her way to her feet like a fawn in its first moments of life.

"Are you sure you don't want to give it a go, Max? I'm telling you, there isn't anything else like flying."

He held her arm to make sure she wasn't going to fall over and replied with a smile, "I'm an angel, remember. I fly all the time."

They walked companionably, arm in arm, chatting as they went. Kayla was so comfortable that more than once she'd almost handed over truths about herself she rarely shared. Max had a calming effect on her. He brought about a kind of ease she hadn't felt in a long, long time, and Kayla found herself wondering over and over again if she wanted to feel this way with another person or if she shouldn't begin the process of closing herself off and shutting all her truths and secrets in. When they got to her aunt and uncle's house, they stopped and stood together for a moment in silence.

"I'll see you 'round?" Kayla asked suddenly shy and uncertain.

"Yeah, something like that," he said with a smile as he turned away from her.

He walked down the drive and disappeared into the night. Even though she couldn't see him, she could hear his heavy steps echoing through the dark. Kayla caught herself smiling, but she didn't stop.


TEN

A few hours later, after her aunt and uncle were settled in their room for the night, Kayla was back by the ocean. This time, she sat down on the beach letting the cool wind dance around her playfully. She thought back over the day and was somewhat reluctant to let the joy she'd found take hold of her completely. She'd known so many years of misery that she wasn't ready to trust that they could be ending. Nor was she ready to hope that they were.

Kayla, sitting on the cool damp sand, letting the song of the rolling waves soothe her soul, couldn't remember ever feeling so lonely. Of course, she couldn't remember ever not being lonely at all. The loneliness had to it an ebb and flow.

Much like the ocean she loved so much, it was a thing eternal. There had always been a coming and going of loneliness in her life and so long had it cradled her in its certainty that the possibility of one day being without it was unsettling.

The night was calm but her thoughts were wild. She opened her journal and began to write. She wrote often in her journal. Almost every day she found herself filling the pages with her thoughts, worries, and speculations. Some days, she filled entire pages with nonsensical ramblings that questioned the very fabric of reality and proposed theories to the purpose of all things, of life. Other days, she would write a single line or two with factual precision; a statement bold and true about herself or the world. Some days, though these were very few, she would tell the truth of her life and all the terrible things that had happened to her and that she'd done. These days were the saddest because she could write with so much detachment for the horrors she'd endured that she became acutely aware of how her life couldn't possibly be entirely her own. Those days scared her and yet, she seemed most herself on those days. That scared her even more.

*What's wrong with me?* she thought. She worried, not for the first time.

She longed with everything she was, but she had no idea for what and that's what drove her mad. *What is it that I'm waiting for?* Some days, she filled pages with that question, posed a hundred different ways.

Kayla convinced herself at a young age that knowing you were waiting for something was all you needed but she'd come to question whether that was truly enough. Her impatience had grown steadily. Waiting for the life she was meant for was unbearable. Finally, one day, she'd given up and broken. She stopped waiting and started defying the destiny she'd once been certain she was meant to fulfill.

Attempting to banish the oncoming memories, Kayla stood and walked along the shoreline, letting the cool ocean water tickle her toes as it came and went, came and went. Stars started to jump into the night sky and the moon had risen to the east. She loved the night. You could be alone in the night but it was a unique kind of loneliness, one she relished. When it was only her and the great, big vastness of the universe above, when the sky became dark and it seemed that there was no barrier between the Earth and all that was beyond it, she shivered, but the night did not chill her; the past did, as again it tried to sneak through her well-built defenses against it.

Almost nineteen years ago, Kayla was brought into a family waiting for a savior. There was her dying grandmother holding onto life so she could, before she died, hold onto the granddaughter she already loved more than anything else in the world. She was certain her granddaughter would be someone special who would one day change the world. Three months after Kayla's birth, when she was certain she could see the hope and determination in Kayla's eyes that had dimmed from her own, her grandmother left the world of the living.

Kayla's life hadn't been different from that of most children. She was at a young age obviously intelligent. She spoke early. She walked early. She learned early to observe the world around her and take its lessons for her own. She had two loving parents who adored her as much as any person could adore another human being, if not more. As Kayla grew older, and it was not long after she was born that it began, she came to be more than adored; she was revered. The people around her who admired her couldn't pinpoint what it was about her that made them love her so overwhelmingly, but they felt that way just the same. That was when Kayla began her life, high up on her pedestal, as the perfect child, a child who was somehow more than the others around her, and therefore far out of reach.

Though Kayla loved the attention and enjoyed proving people right in their high hopes for her, she soon found that reality didn't permit such things as perfect people, and the one person for whom she always wanted to be perfect never even noticed. Instead of faltering in her perfection, she strove harder to portray it, hiding away the weak, confused, and rather real person she was inside.

She found ways to punish herself for her humanity and surrounded herself with people who couldn't see past or her perfect façade. Slowly, through the years, she floated upwards farther and farther away from the real world. Becoming so obsessed with perfection, she could barely communicate with anyone for fear of betraying the truth with every word she spoke and every breath she took. Smothering in her loneliness, she became angry, bitter, and longed for the world to know she was just like they were—scared of who she was really and always searching for the place that she belonged.

When waking from a restless sleep and still aware of the lingering sights she saw while dreaming, Kayla was certain she'd found her peace, but she was never sure how to return to it. She became obsessed with the worlds of make-believe she dreamed up in her head, certain that if she could never belong anywhere at least she could feel like she did.

She came to despise herself quite adamantly during her teen years. She hated that she didn't have the courage to defy what had been imposed on her, unable to see that the perfection she thought the world demanded of her was really the perfection she was afraid to rebel against. *If she wasn't perfect, then who was she?* Over and over again, she found that question easier to avoid than to answer.

Throughout her life, Kayla had been plagued with the questions of the universe. Her first memories from childhood were those of questioning time, space, and existence itself. She could stare up at a star clad sky, as she still could do now, and feel awe sweep through her so strongly she ached. Tears would well up in her eyes and spill down over her cheeks as she longed to hear the answer *yes*, as questions such as, *are there others like us out there*, and *will I ever reach them*, chimed over and over again in her mind.

She became fascinated with death because it seemed like a great and unknown journey. And so, Kayla found herself longing for it out of both curiosity and a desire to escape the monotony and pain in her life. It seemed like a much greater adventure than living and a much safer thing to reach for.

Many nights, Kayla found herself longing for that final rest, praying it would come and steal her away from the world of the living, convinced it would rescue her from the turmoil that raged inside her heart, mind, and soul, and hoping that she would leave the world of the living while sleeping as she watched the shifting darkness in her bedroom and wished she was seeing it for the last time.

By her mid-teens, Kayla came to an impasse. The confusion inside of her was overflowing and she was ready to buckle beneath its weight. Had she been brave, she would have faced it, but instead she redirected it. Kayla, still haunted by the night she gave in to her cowardice, remembers it perfectly.

When on the verge of screaming and letting the whole world know she was hurting beyond belief, she swallowed a tiny pill that changed her world forever. That's when Kayla made her first real friend. That's when Kayla found what she thought was where she was meant to be. In a small capsule no larger than a Tylenol did she find the freedom, peace, and wonder she'd longed for. Crystal meth was the thief that she would soon hand her soul over to just so she could stop trying to understand or deserve it.

Kayla was sixteen when she first found crystal meth, an age at which she was both far too young and far too old all at once. She fell in love with it right away. It became her sanctuary in a world she felt misunderstood her. It became the answer to most of what plagued her in the waking world. She could not be perfect if she was a drug addict. Life could have no point or purpose if it was that easy to throw it all away. No one could love her if she became a monster.

Kayla couldn't help but feel strong and safe when she was on her drug; it made everything around her disappear. When she was high, all else became obsolete and she became invincible. The drug made her forget. All the pain and anguish that had been with her since childhood became a mere shadow of the truth. The girl she was became extinct just as quickly as the horrors she had endured. She fell in love with the meth and never wanted to look back. Looking forward wasn't an option either. The drug gave her only 'the now.'

Most addictive was the sense of adventure she gained from it. Being a drug addict was, in her mind, exotic, romantic even. Hanging around dangerous people, drug dealers, gang members, prostitutes, where things changed every minute of every day, was exciting and exhilarating. One minute your friends were all around you, the next they were gone for one reason or another. Some were stolen by overdoses, some left to save themselves or sober up, some were driven out, others died, but it never mattered why they left, it just mattered that every moment was treated as your last. Kayla thought it was beautiful and wonderful. She loved the unknown. She loved being a part of something completely contrary to the mundane routine that haunted everyday life.

The problem was that she'd merely moved from one nightmare into another. By the time she realized it, she was far too in love with the crystal meth to give it up. A battle raged inside of Kayla far more brutal than she ever could've imagined or foreseen. She dove deeper into the nightmare because submitting seemed like the easiest route to take. She longed for rock bottom, certain that once she hit it, she would be able to make her way back up to the surface of her life. But down she sank and there she lingered. Lonely on the murky bottom of the ruin that she called home and frustrated enough to start digging for any escape, she stayed there for a long time. She was drowned and forgotten, abandoned by the people she'd abandoned first. Then, it felt like forever, and now it feels like not long enough ago, while tomorrow it might finally seem like yesterday so that she can begin moving on.

Kayla spent more than a year in her self-proclaimed hell of drugs and adventure, loving it and hating it all at once. She wasn't sure how to escape or even if she really wanted to. She wasn't sure how to say good-bye. She was horrified by the thought of giving up the one place she'd belonged even if it was destroying her. She'd seen the world of drugs through star-filled eyes. Once engulfed by it, she found it wasn't what she thought it would be and Kayla was too proud to admit she could've been wrong and too lost to believe there was a way she could be found. She was desperate to continue believing that the place she thought she would fit in wasn't a horrid place full of betrayal, heartache, and death.

Nearing the end of the eighteen months she spent in a daze high on meth, she watched as people she'd grown to love died. The worst deaths were those of the soul. The shell, the body, remained but the person inside had vanished.

Corroded by the dangerous effects of the drugs they took, often in lethal doses, that was the way that Kayla died. A year after getting sober, she'd yet to be reborn; but for the first time since she gave in to the drugs, she realized she really wanted to be.

Now, as the darkness whispered to the wind around her, and as the serene tumbling of the waves lit by a solitary moon called to her nerves to calm, Kayla felt like she was taking her first steps away from that horrible choice she'd made so long ago, in what seemed like another life. Things happen. Sometimes, they happen for a reason and sometimes they just happen, but they happen just the same. It's the choices you make that define you. Kayla was finally starting to figure that out.

There'd been a long road back after she left the drugs and Kayla was still travelling it now. The choices she'd made and the life they'd handed her weren't easily escaped or forgotten. As she closed her journal, she tried as best she could to dismiss the weight the memories settled over her like a heavy blanket. She was never without it completely, that heaviness, the truth of what she'd done and been. That part of her life was an echo that would not fade. It followed her everywhere. The only time she was free was while she slept and though she was grateful for the freedom, she was yet to be convinced that dreaming, though satisfying, was a healthy and viable escape. *Hadn't dreaming been part of the problem in the first place?*

She loved her dreams and the perfect fantasy worlds she created in her mind but she knew, though reluctant to give them up, that sooner or later she'd have to find satisfaction in the real world if she was ever going to live in it. More than that, she knew that she'd have to fall out of love with the dreams before she could forsake them. She didn't merely have to want to belong in the world, she had to choose to. She'd have to learn to be someone real, someone whole, who could live her life flawed and grateful for her imperfections. Perfection had no place in the real world, and the person she'd tried to be perfect for had left her almost too many years ago to bother counting anyway.

Kayla stood again and paused. Seated for so long on a blanket of sand, her legs tingled and she swayed a little before she could steady herself. She'd been on the beach for over five hours and she couldn't believe how quickly the night had passed. The dawn was fast approaching and she longed to taste it before anyone else did, but her aunt and uncle would wake shortly after the sun came up, and she knew they checked in on her every morning.

The walk home was slow but peaceful and, as she entered her temporary home, instead of feeling resentment and rage, she felt acceptance. A small but significant shift, a pang of guilt swept through her as she realized how awful she'd been to her aunt and uncle since coming to stay with them. She realized that maybe it was time for that to change as well.

Lying in bed, she could see the early morning light pressing against her blinds and, though she wasn't witnessing the dawn, she felt for the first time in a long time that she was finally seeing it.

She slept. Her dreams were real and horrifying, but she was finally ready to see them and finally ready to begin understanding. She was not alone in this hope. On a tiny planet on the other side of the universe, there wasn't a single person, whether they understood it or not, who didn't sense that the new day they were waking to was a little different than all the ones that had come before it.

Change was upon them all. Where it would lead them was beyond anything any of them had dared to dream.

# Part Two
Dreaming

ELEVEN

On the western shore of the continent known as Samnar, a tiny community buzzed with excitement. The people were preparing for change and after the more than thirteen years they'd endured, change was a welcome thing. A journey was about to be made. A long and dangerous trek southward towards the sea, then just beyond that. A man, a monster, was waiting to be stopped; and they were going to help stop him.

Alex stared out at the rolling crystal waves and let out a deep, troubled sigh. His mother had loved the ocean and, every time he stared out at it, he remembered her both fondly and with a deep and aching sense of loss.

At twenty-four, he was the oldest of the Founders' children. He had ice-blue hair, eyes that same piercing shade, and olive skin, making him look most like his father, Dellerim. He also had a delicate face and a huge presence like his mother, who was the only one of the six perfect beings, known on Alpha Iridium as the Founders, who'd disappeared on the night Caine arrived. She was also the only one of the six perfect beings who'd lived a life on Earth before journeying to Alpha Iridium.

Almost fourteen years ago, the Founders had gone to sleep to stop Caine's coming. Five of them never woke. One of them, Alex's mother, disappeared without a trace. Their children, without the power to read minds or project themselves in dreams like their parents, presumed she was dead, just like the sibling each of them had lost.

"You okay, Alex?"

Alex looked up from the waves and away from his troubled thoughts. Beside him stood another of the Founders' children, Joachim and Arianna's daughter.

Arin was twenty-one and stood an inch taller than Alex. Her eyes, like her mother's, were cherry-colored. Her hair was deep red and sparkled like a precious ruby in the sun. Her skin was light olive-toned and was smoother than silk. She was beautiful, something Alex had never noticed. For him, life was always about the day they would save their parents and return them to the waking world. He had no time for anything but planning, preparing, and waiting. When he wasn't doing that, he was taking charge of their small group, leading as best he could. None of it had afforded him the time or ability to be young, carefree, or happy. Alex didn't care. Since that first day when they'd woken and realized their lives would be changed forever, Alex had accepted that his role would be to lead and to one day undo what had been done, somehow. For Alex, there was also that one shadow hanging over the possibility of waking their parents; unlike the others, he had only one parent to wake, his father.

"I'm fine, Arin. Just thinking, that's all." He forced a smile.

"Lots to think about. I just said goodbye to Mom and Dad. Joah is upstairs with them now." She paused and looked out to the ocean. "Do you think we'll get them back, Alex? Do you think we can do this? I mean we're not really special like they are. We can't do any of what they can."

"We can read the stars," Alex said looking up to the morning sky as if the stars should remain just to clear his conscience.

"The stars." Arin shook her head. "Half the time the stars tell us what we can't do, half the time they speak in riddles." She took a deep breath and sighed it out, "Do you really believe we'll make a difference?"

"Honestly, Arin, I don't know. All I see is struggle, pain, and loss on the horizon when I look to the stars. I just hope it isn't us who do the suffering."

"I just want my parents back, and I want to help those people if we can. I hope we're not too late, Alex."

Alex smiled sympathetically and patted her gently on the shoulder, always ready to play the father. Entirely unaware it was a different role Arin wished him to play.

There'd been eight children born to the Founders. Alex was the oldest by a year. In the days after Caine's arrival, their parents comatose, three of the children missing, his mother gone, he learned quite fully that time could be a strange and slippery thing. Once, a year had seemed like just a moment of time between him and the two children next in age to him, but it had quickly become a vast stretch of space between them that could not be bridged. Alex had to grow up fast and leave a lot of things behind in those first few weeks and years. Innocence had been one of them. Having a life of his own had been another.

"The stars say we act now, no sooner, no later. Have some faith, Arin. Think of what our parents overcame."

From behind them, someone spoke and they both turned suddenly, startled by the interruption.

"Come on, you two sound like you're ready to lose this thing. Am I the only one here who is sure everything is going to turn out fine?" He smiled casually and walked to where the two friends stood.

"Actually, Joah, you're the only one who doesn't worry." Arin put her arm around her younger brother's waist and shook her head disapprovingly, though her smile gave away how fond she was of her brother's casual approach to life.

Joah placed a kiss on top of his sister's head. It was easy as he stood more than four inches taller than her. As Arin resembled their mother, he resembled their father. He had light brown skin accented by a mane of snow-white hair. His eyes were emerald green and, like his father's, they were welcoming and drew you in. They did nothing to hide the carefree and playfully mischievous person he was at his core. Like all of the Founder's children who'd survived, he teetered on that edge between youth and adulthood, so that he was sometimes still a boy and yet, too, often a man.

"I don't worry because we have nothing to worry about," he said casually. "We're about to take a trip, a vacation, if you will. You two need to learn to loosen up just a little." Joah gave them a stern and reproachful look before bursting into laughter.

Arin rolled her eyes. "Are you sure we all have to go, Alex? I mean we could leave Joah behind to make sure everything is okay here."

"Arin," Alex began.

"Yeah, yeah, the stars," she said with playful annoyance.

"You know Arin, you're more like your brother than you know...or will admit to." Alex had to bite his tongue to keep from laughing.

"Thanks, Alex, you always know just what to say to make me feel better. Come on, let's make sure we're all ready to go." Arin took her brother by the hand and led him away from Alex and back towards the house. As they walked away she leaned into him, and he into her, betraying a deep and loving trust that flowed between them freely, a willingness to lean on one another that Alex couldn't help but envy as he watched them walk away.

Alone again, Alex returned his attention to the waves and to the parents he'd grown up without. He felt a lot like them in his journey. They'd arrived on Alpha Iridium as adults physically but in their first moments of life. They were children in a way, forced to grow up quickly to survive in order to overcome everything they went through those first days and weeks on Alpha Iridium. Some days, he wished they'd never decided to travel to Berdune and create people to cure their loneliness. If they'd never done that then they'd still be with him, and Caine would never have come to Alpha Iridium. The past was written in stone, and though the future was written in the stars those could change. Alex didn't feel helpless when battling the future like he did when fighting the past.

"Mind if I interrupt?"

Alex was again drawn away from his thoughts. Beside him stood yet another of the Founders' offspring, Kendra and Kiernan's son, Beran.

"Not at all," Alex replied. "Just thinking about the past, probably shouldn't be though, we've got more important things to think about right now."

"Oh, I don't know about that. The past is why we're standing on this very spot. If you ask me, we should make sure we keep it in mind at all times." Beran smiled and Alex was reminded of Kendra and the way she'd looked when happy so many years ago. He was also reminded of Kiernan's thoughtfulness and hope. The way everything had seemed like a puzzle to Kiernan; there was always a solution and sometimes you just had to be willing to find another point of view.

Beran was taller than Alex by almost three inches and three years younger, making him twenty-one. His skin was deep brown like his sister's, though neither was as dark as their father. Beran's hair was jet-black and his eyes were the colour of gold; both features were gifts from his mother. His sister, Arwyn, who was the older sibling at twenty-three yet younger in so many other ways, looked more like their father. Her eyes and hair were both silver and when she smiled, a quiet intelligence swam over her face. It was much the same way Kiernan had looked when happily coming up with a good idea that he knew everyone would be impressed with.

"Where's Arwyn?" Alex asked.

"She's with our parents. She's having a hard time saying goodbye," Beran answered, following Alex's gaze out to the ocean.

"We all are. I guess we don't know what we'll be coming back to." Alex turned to watch his companion's face, but Beran didn't turn toward him.

"If we get to come back...it'll be home," Beran finished, finally turning toward his friend.

"Well, Beran, I hope home is what we want it to be."

"Alex, either way we've got to do this. We have a debt to settle."

"Oh, I assure you, Beran, our debt to Caine will be paid in full." Alex turned to the ocean again but this time he didn't see the sparkling waves. He saw the face he'd seen almost fourteen years ago when his parents had been dreaming a defense and Caine had arrived. Somehow, that night, he'd crept into the Founders' sleep and saw the face of the man who'd taken his mother from him. Even after all this time he could recall the face in an instant. It was Caine's face. When Alex killed Caine, he wanted his face to be the last thing Caine ever saw.

"It's time, Alex."

"What?" Alex looked toward Beran, shaking himself a little, until he realized where he was and what Beran had meant.

"It's time," Beran repeated and this time Alex smiled.

TWELVE

"Kale, there has to be another way. You always volunteer for everything. I thought we all agreed two of us would go!" Jaren exclaimed indignantly. He looked worried, Corin more so. Only Medea scowled slightly.

"We've been over this a million times, Jaren, and I'm the only one who can go. Jaren, you'd be recognized right away. Corin," Kale paused here sensing her friend's discomfort yet pushing forward just the same, "well, we don't know where his mother is, so we don't know how safe it is to send him in. Medea owns this house and we can't afford to lose it if we get caught. It's the only way. I have to go alone."

Plans had dramatically changed since Jaren's contact had informed him that Caine was planning to move in a month, on the eve of the new year. He had no idea what Caine was planning, and as far as he could tell only a few key people did, but it was something big and the rebels couldn't afford to wait and see without acting. Something was coming, they could all feel it drawing nearer, and though they'd originally thought there was lots of time to figure out a course of action, it simply wasn't the case anymore. They had to act.

"What about one of the others?" Jaren offered.

"I'm not willing to ask someone else to take this kind of risk. They've already risked so much for us. I can't ask for more. I won't. And really, as much as I don't want to say it, I don't know who we can and can't trust. Why take that risk? If I go in alone, none of the others even has to know where I've gone. This is the safest and best way. Now would you all stop worrying and help me figure things out? We don't have much time. If your sources are reliable, Jaren, we only have until the new year."

The atmosphere in the kitchen was strained. It wasn't that they weren't ready to act, it was that they weren't ready to let Kale take such a huge risk. So many things could go wrong and it felt like they were tempting fate.

The four friends sat in silence for what seemed like an eternity. Three of the people searched within themselves for an alternative, while one of them looked forward to starting out on the road to Caine's destruction, one she was certain she was always meant to travel.

"Well," Kale broke the silence, "if there are no further objections," she smiled, "then let's get on this. I've got the name of your contact, Jaren, but I won't use him unless I'm in trouble or we're ready to take the next step. You guys can't try to contact me unless something has changed. This is dangerous enough as it is. I can't leave Caine's compound once I'm in except if we're ready to take him down," Kale paused. "Anything else?"

"I think we're all forgetting something here," Jaren said, frowning, "we still haven't figured out how to get you in there, Kale? All of a sudden you're giving us a couple of days to figure out what should take months. How do you expect to just walk in there and get close enough to not only figure out what he's up to but figure out what his weaknesses are?"

Corin, Medea and Jaren were all nodding.

"He's right, Kale," Corin added, "maybe we should think this through a little more. We could even ask the others if one of them would volunteer to go in with you. Empris isn't that far from here. They could be here in a day or two at the most and we could be set to go a few days after that."

The nods became more vigorous, but Kale had yet to join in.

"This is happening whether you guys like it or not," Kale said sternly. "We've waited long enough. It would be different if we hadn't found out he was going to move, but we did and we don't know what he's up to. We're running out of time and luck. We have to stop him, now. Besides..." Kale took a deep breath and looked down at her hands crossed tensely in her lap. "I already have a way into Caine's compound."

The deep and ringing silence that followed lasted only a moment. Then, all three of Kale's friends tried to speak at once. Finally, Corin and Medea stopped trying and let Jaren speak.

"Kale, what the hell are you talking about? This is serious..."

Kale interrupted him. The anger in her voice weighed down every single word so that they landed like heavy stones in the center of the room, piling the truth up in front of them.

"I know this is serious, Jaren. No one knows that more than I do, alright? So, you have two choices. I go in alone and you guys help me, or I go in alone and you don't. Pick one."

Corin spoke next. "This is stupid, we shouldn't be arguing right now. Kale, we're just worried, that's all. Not a single one of us wants you going alone, but if you think you can get in there, seriously and safely, then let's hear it."

Kale relaxed a bit and waited for everyone in the room to do the same.

"I'm going to join the J'Kahl."

Kale didn't waver in her seriousness, but Medea, Corin, and Jaren burst out laughing in unison. As much as Kale didn't want to let them make her angrier than she already was, she couldn't help it. She was frustrated and annoyed.

"Kale," Medea spit out during a heavy fit of giggles, "you can't just join the J'Kahl. Everyone knows that. You have to be picked, chosen by Caine himself. You're crazy."

"Yeah, Kale," Corin put in, "I don't often agree with Medea but she's right. If you volunteer, he'll know something's up right away. You wouldn't get farther than the front gates."

Kale, hurt and annoyed, waited for the laughter to subside before she spoke again.

"I don't have to volunteer," she paused and again looked down at her intertwined fingers. *This is where everything changes forever*, she thought to herself, and then she spoke again. "Caine has already invited me to train with the J'Kahl. In fact he's offered me the opportunity to join him in any way, and I can take him up on the offer whenever I please."


THIRTEEN

The next morning, Kale was seated at her regular spot at Sunshine Bay waiting for the sun to rise and feeling as if her father was with her.

"No games this morning, Dad. It seems to me the time for games is past."

She thought back to the night before, drawn by the absurd idea that she didn't know how serious all this was when she'd given up everything for it already, and would give up more before the end of it all. The wind picked up and lightly kissed her cheeks and she couldn't help feeling like somewhere locked in that intimacy was a good-bye.

"I told them, Dad. They know everything though they don't get it any more than I do. I wish you'd just told me the whole damn truth. Maybe then I'd understand what I'm supposed to do and why."

Kale tried to keep the shaky note from her voice even though no one but the wind and the sea were around to hear her falter. She'd always been ashamed of being asked by Caine to join his ranks. She'd never told her friends because she thought it would weaken their belief that she really meant to destroy him. She had no more insight now than she'd had the day he'd approached her and made the offer. She'd never bothered to consider the possibilities because it was her way into the castle and very quickly she realized his affection for her would one day become a weapon she could use against him. What she'd failed to consider was that the reason he was so fond of her might have mattered, too. That truth was a weapon as well, and she wasn't holding it, nor was she even aware it might be raised against her.

It had all started one morning not so long ago. A morning Kale wished had never come, a morning Kale wished she wouldn't have to remember for the rest of her life with vivid clarity, it was that same morning when her life had changed that she'd made destroying Caine her personal mission.

She remembered perfectly where she was when she found out her parents had died; she'd been at home, alone. They'd only been working in Caine's inner circle for a short while, but an accident in one of his mines had claimed their lives. The irony was that unlike the slaves he put to work there, Kale's parents had been there to oversee the work. In doing so, they were condoning the slavery that Caine built his empire on. Kale had trouble believing her parents were capable of that kind of insensitivity and cruelty, but that's where they'd been.

Over the months they'd spent in his inner circle, a gulf had opened up between Kale and her parents. That space had filled with strain, anger, and resentment; and it distressed Kale to have to face that she didn't know who her parents were. She never had. Having them support Caine had been one thing, but knowing they could commit horrible acts as his loyal servants was another.

That morning, Kale returned from Sunshine Bay alone and awaited her parents' return. She met Caine for the first time that morning though Kale was unaware he already knew her. He'd arrived at the door weeping for his loss and hers and despite herself Kale had been touched by his sorrow.

She was invited to stay with him, but refused. The thought of leaving the home she'd shared with her parents was unbearable, even after all their betrayal. He offered her a place in the ranks of the J'Kahl, and she refused. He pleaded for her to join him in any way but she knew no matter how difficult life became she would never be able to accept. Lastly, he assured her that she would have enough money to survive each month and the only condition would be that she visit once monthly to dine with him. This condition she accepted. Though he made it clear she could ask for anything else he'd offered at any time and he would give it to her. She'd never visited him once but the money never stopped coming and much to her satisfaction she used every dollar against him.

That day, sitting in the wake of sorrow, Kale came upon the full force of rage and hatred toward Caine. In hindsight his sorrow seemed insincere and Kale was convinced that her parents had died by Caine's hand or by his will and not by accident. She had always opposed him before her parents' deaths but it was that day, while seated back at Sunshine Bay with tears still drying on her cheeks, that she pledged her life to making him pay. It was just a matter of time before she would take him up on his offer; she'd always known that.

Much to her surprise after telling all these things to her friends, they'd become more worried and skeptical than before. Kale thought by telling them that she had a way into Caine's castle, they'd be happy, but they thought that Caine's behavior was strange and out of character. They thought she was taking a bigger risk than they'd bargained for. The bottom line was that she didn't care, and she was done waiting. Changing the world, fighting for a world better than the one Caine had delivered, was worth anything she could give, including her life.

Kale wasn't sure why Caine had wanted to provide for her so generously. She assumed it had something to do with what her parents had done for him. What scared her is that it made all sorts of horrors pop into her mind about all the terrible things her parents might have done with her ignorantly standing by. She also considered that it might have had something to do with Caine's guilt, if he was indeed capable of such an emotion, but she really didn't care. She had an invitation into the dragon's lair and she was ready to accept it, no matter what it cost her.

She did understand that after she went into Caine's castle, everything would be different, including the relationship she had with her departed father. Kale wasn't sure how she knew, but she did. It made her feel guilty that she was willing to throw it all away if it meant destroying Caine, and she felt a deep and unsettling longing for a time when things were simple, before rebel alliances, before Prophecies came true, before she learned what real heartache was, before Caine.

As the golden sun peered over the mountains to the east, it seemed to Kale the day was reluctant to break. She thought back over all the wonderful mornings she'd spent with her father and hoped that though she was choosing a different path than his, he would be proud of her strength and determination.

The morning was crisp and cool but Kale took no notice. She was about to begin the part of her life that demanded she be at her best. She needed to compose herself. She had much to do before she could set out for Caine's compound. She had to be ready; there would be no turning back.

Saying goodbye to her father that morning, Kale realized she'd reached the point where all the games ended; what began she still did not know.

## FOURTEEN

Derin pulled his hood high up over his head and lifted himself up over the window's edge and down the other side. He held tightly to the rope ladder he'd hung from the small ledge and prayed silently that it wouldn't break. He wasn't afraid to die. As a J'Kahl soldier, he'd been trained for that, too. He was afraid of having his father find his body, sneaking out into the night without permission or reason.

Derin was grateful his window faced the back of the building where no one would be around at this time of day to see him climbing down or be able to watch as he snuck off into the woods and towards his borrowed freedom.

The sun had just appeared to the east as a sliver of gold above the horizon yet to warm the day, but Derin didn't care. He relished the moments he thieved, no matter when or how. He didn't sneak away often and it was usually when no one else was awake. All he really wanted were a few moments in which he could breathe without feeling like he was a warrior, a son, or under someone else's watchful gaze. If only he knew he was always being watched. No one was free in Caine's Berdune, not even in the early hours of a new day.

Derin sometimes used the time he stole to reflect on his life, a pastime that used to give him some relief from his obligations and stresses. Lately, he found that even *that* was frustrating. He was a warrior, but he was without a war. He was a loyal follower but loyalty was harder and harder to hide behind as the cruelty and violence the common people suffered at the hands of the J'Kahl and Caine became harder to ignore. He was a thinker and a leader, but he'd begun to feel starved of the ability to choose his path and make his own decisions, trapped by the expectations of those who looked to him to both lead and obey. He didn't understand the point of life, his life, nor did he understand the means to make it whole. Derin wondered if most people his age felt this way or whether he was simply being weak, something his father had drilled into him over and over again when it came to being uncertain of your place in the world.

As Derin ran across the huge lawn cloaked in the last shadows of night, he pushed all thoughts from his mind. He ran to escape, if even for an hour. He ran until his lungs ached and painful breaths escaped him and he no longer wandered through troubled thoughts. Only when he heard the rapids of the Craden River did he slow his pace.

Once, a few weeks ago, he came upon a path leading southward towards the sea and after some time he found himself at Sunshine Bay. He loved the ocean though he knew he hadn't been near it since before Caine's arrival. He couldn't really remember anything before that, but he knew he loved the sea and longed to swim in it. He'd forgotten what it was to stare at the beauty of it with the eyes of a person and not those of a servant and warrior, but a few weeks ago his love had been renewed.

The dawn, on this particular morning, called to Derin to be at peace. He lost himself in the empty, reassuring calm that settled over his mind, and for the first time in a long time he was able to forget who he was.

The last time he'd left his home he'd intended to turn south towards the sea and seek his solace there again on the bluffs at Sunshine Bay. The breaking of twigs underfoot tore him from his thoughts and made him stop dead in his tracks. He was always a soldier on guard and ready to act.

He watched as mere feet from where he stood a young woman seemingly lost in her own thoughts and following the rapids northward, hummed quietly as she made her way past him. Derin had never in his life seen anyone like her. His life as a warrior left little to no room for friends male or female and he was certain that if the time came he would marry a girl of his father's choosing. Many of the J'Kahl spent time in the surrounding areas carrying out Caine's work but Derin hadn't yet been permitted to take on a mission outside of the castle. He was beginning to wonder if Caine doubted him and his abilities. Why else would he have been kept from venturing out into the world to carry out a soldier's work?

The young woman had red hair that couldn't have really been that colour but looked so in the early morning light. Her skin was tan and she was honestly the strangest and most beautiful girl that Derin had ever seen. She wasn't beautiful in any conventional sense but it was true just the same. She seemed out of place, as if she didn't belong somehow, and along with her commanding presence and self-certainty, she had an air of innocence and fragility about her that was striking. He didn't know why but, before he realized what he was doing, Derin was quietly following the young woman, his hike to Sunshine Bay quickly forgotten.

As they'd entered the city of Braedon Ridge, Derin checked his hood to make sure his face wouldn't be revealed. He walked slowly through the city, trailing behind her like the tail of a kite, always within reach. He watched with a growing mix of awe and apprehension as the people greeted the stranger he pursued. Almost everyone, especially in the poorer sections of town, greeted the girl whose name he could never quite catch. Some walked up to her with wrapped parcels in their hands, offering them over with whispered words or smiles. Many hugged her and he could see her whispering words in their ears as they embraced. One child jumped into her arms and she carried the young girl on her hip as she walked. The child, too thin and pale, was giggling and her blond curls bounced like she did, even as they were weighed down by grease and dirt. A few feet later, she put the child down but never lost a step. The little girl waved after her.

Derin had seen only one other person treated this way in his entire life, Caine. There was a difference in the admiration Caine received and the admiration the beautiful young woman was receiving then. When Caine received admiration, especially among the common people, it was adoration offered up in servitude and fear. Even the wealthy and powerful of Berdune seemed to treat him with respect because that was the appropriate thing to do. What Derin witnessed that morning was nothing like anything he'd ever seen before and he couldn't believe his eyes.

Derin knew he shouldn't have followed her any further, but he couldn't tear his eyes away from her, and he felt so compelled to be nearer to her, drawn like a moth to a flame, he simply couldn't resist. Even the danger of it couldn't deter him. He could understand why the people seemed to adore her; there was just something about her that drew you in, as if she had her very own gravitational pull. She was a star, and anyone close enough to be caught by the force of her would be drawn into that waltz, round and round, forever.

She seemed sad, though who wasn't in Caine's Berdune? She also seemed sure, strong, kind, powerful, and full of hope and promise. It was an intoxicating combination and all at once he saw in her what Caine could never be. Derin's world shifted. The change within him was small and yet so violent and real he stumbled before he caught himself.

"What is she whispering?" he muttered under his breath as he followed her, almost unknowingly, drawn deeper into the city by a force he could neither resist nor understand.

Maybe it was instinct, maybe it was just luck, but Derin could feel someone watching him and scanned the crowd to see who it was. An old man Derin didn't recognize was looking him over with complete disgust and loathing. Could he have known who Derin really was even without his soldier's uniform?

On this morning, he was dressed as an ordinary person, though his clothes were new and clean unlike most of the people in the crowd. He never walked among the common people, his father forbid it, and he'd yet to go on a mission that brought him among them so no one should've recognized him; but it seemed that this man did. The man was only feet from the girl he'd been following and, as Derin turned to walk away, a woman bumped him and his hood fell down around his neck.

"I'm sorry, sir," she smiled up at him, "it always gets a little crazy when she comes down in the mornings."

The woman kept walking before Derin could even form a reply, and when he turned back to see if the man still had him in his sights, he saw he did, and in his arms was the young woman. Derin froze, aware that he should run but strangely wanting, needing her to see him. As she let go of the man, she casually turned and scanned the crowd, then smiling let her unsettling gaze rest on Derin. When their eyes met, Derin felt it happen, felt a shift deep within that left him stunned and off balance.

She held a hand on the shoulder of the scowling man and mouthed a single word that made shivers race down Derin's spine. 'Go.' And so he did. Turning in a daze and walking back through the bustling crowd, Derin's mind was once again blank. He felt confused, as if walking out of a dream instead of walking down the street.

He wandered home in that state and didn't stir from it until he realized he'd walked in the front door of his home without being certain no one had seen him. He scolded himself silently for his lack of precaution and told himself he wouldn't leave again for a month just as punishment. He walked up to his room and ran into no one, yet still he told himself he wouldn't leave for a month. He'd made it a week, and though he was ashamed that he was incapable of disciplining himself when it came to the strange young woman, he had to see her again.

Full of shame, only one week later, yet unwilling to turn back, Derin walked steadily toward Sunshine Bay with his heart beating fiercely in his chest. When he came to the cliffs and saw her seated alone staring out at the ocean, speaking to herself it seemed, he was flooded with relief that he'd found her.

"This is where we say goodbye for a while. This is where all the games end," she spoke softly and every word made his ears tingle, as he strained to both hear and understand.

Before Derin could stop the words, he was speaking, "Can I interrupt or is this a private conversation?"

Derin approached Kale as she jumped up and spun around to face him. When she reached her feet, they were standing only inches from one another and Kale stared up into his face with a mixture of curiosity and embarrassment. She smiled the simplest smile and Derin found himself leaning just a little closer to her as he returned it. He fought with himself to find something to say to the beautiful girl, so near to him he could smell the gentle scent that emanated warmly from her skin. It was sunshine mixed with stars with a hint of salt and sand. His head began to swim and he had the strangest feeling running through him as if he might faint or fall over.

Kale recognized the guy who'd surprised her right away. The last time she'd seen him he'd been following her through town. When he saw the startled look on his face, she was instantly drawn to his awkwardness. Now, as she stared up at him, she found other things about him that intrigued her.

His eyes were a shade of blue she'd never seen. They were so lightly coloured that the morning sun glittered off them as if they were tinted diamonds. His hair was black, which was normal among the people of Berdune, but in the light it shone blue and looked softer than silk. She wanted instantly to reach out and see how soft it really was. Instead she spoke, curling her hands into fists to keep them at her sides.

"Hey, I'm about three inches from stepping off this cliff. You mind?" She pushed past him and Derin finally found his voice again.

"I'm so sorry. Are you okay?"

"Me? Never better. You?" Kale sat back down and stared out at the new day and the ocean sparkling in response to it.

"I'm fine, just a little out of breath," Derin said though he sounded a little skeptical of his own excuse.

"You can sit down," Kale suggested casually. "Best view on all of Berdune." She stared up at him and Derin couldn't imagine saying anything but yes.

After a moment's hesitation, he sat down beside her and stared out over the ocean.

"This is the first time I've seen it at sunrise," he said as he drank in the sight and awe filled his voice.

Red touched the waves, painted there by the arrival of the sun. The sky was a glorious rainbow so subtle in its radiance that it was breathtaking. The ocean, calmer than the new day, stretched on and on to eternity and Derin couldn't help but wonder what places it reached to out past that arc of the horizon.

"It's really beautiful out here," he said sounding like a wide-eyed child.

"Yeah, I know. I come out here every morning to watch the sun come up. I haven't missed a morning in years." Kale smiled fondly obviously being drawn away from the day and into pleasant memories.

"Every morning?" Derin asked surprised, and he turned to meet her eyes. "Usually, a routine that dedicated has something greater behind it."

"You're very perceptive." Kale returned his gaze intensely. "And what kind of routines do you follow, other than following strange girls through town?"

Derin felt colour come to his cheeks. "Oh yeah, the other day. God, I'm really not making a great first impression, am I?"

"Not the best. No," Kale laughed.

"I don't know what to say," Derin paused. "I'm not really from around here, you know?"

"Yeah, I figured that. I know most everyone around here and you I've never seen before."

"Well, my father keeps me really busy. I have to sneak out just to get some time to myself. He has a whole plan for me and he's just really strict though I know he means well." Before he could help himself the truth poured out of Derin. Somehow she'd shaken it loose. "He wants me to be something that some days I just don't feel like I'm meant to be. So, sometimes I feel like I'm living someone else's life, you know?" Derin turned away from Kale and looked back out over the seemingly infinite waves as they began to turn blue with the day's arrival. Suddenly, he regretted having revealed so much about himself to the stranger at his side.

"You sound like someone looking for himself. That's good though, some people haven't even figured out they should be looking." Kale smiled and without thinking placed her hand gently on top of Derin's. "If it makes you feel any better about it, I feel the same way sometimes as if I'm alone in the world and most alone when I'm surrounded by people because then I'm trying to be what they expect or need me to be."

Derin turned back to her, and when he spoke his voice was filled with appreciation, "That's exactly it, most alone when I'm surrounded by people. I can't believe you just said that, so strange."

"I had a feeling you'd get it." Kale smiled again and Derin could feel the warmth from her hand slowly creeping up his arm. When she finally noticed her hand there, she pulled it away, too surprised at herself to be embarrassed.

"Sometimes, when I feel alone I like to sit by my window and watch the stars. I guess that's my little routine." Derin smiled. "I guess that's where I find my answers sometimes.

Isn't it weird that you can be so easily comforted by something like the stars or the sea, yet people just seem to stress you out?"

"So if that's your routine, then what's behind it?" Kale asked; her eyes and tone playful.

"Would it surprise you if I said I don't know?" Derin let out a short laugh, but couldn't resist turning inward in search of the answer.

"These are the days of Caine. Nothing surprises me," Kale began.

"Oh, my god, I have to go. I've already been gone too long." Derin stood up abruptly. Fear slammed into him. It was much stronger than the desire to stay seated next to her while the day unfolded around them. Kale, despite her instincts, stood up as well.

"Hey, you have to go right now?" she asked with a hint of exasperation.

"I can't stay. If I get caught, I'll be in a lot of trouble." He moved swiftly, soldier's reflexes kicking in, beginning to hurry away from her, but then he paused and turned around just as Kale caught up with him.

"Can I see you again? Here, at Sunshine Bay?" he asked her.

"I'm going away for awhile. I don't know when I'll be coming back," she said.

"Tell me, where I can find you then?"

Kale paused, trying to figure out what to tell him, and though Derin's instincts screamed at him to hurry he couldn't make himself leave her without knowing he would see her again.

"Please, tell me where I can find you," he pleaded.

"Ask at the Mission in Braedon Ridge. Tell someone you're looking for the rebels and they'll bring me to you." Right away Kale regretted saying it but something about the attractive young man, and the strange but powerful connection that already seemed to tie them together, made her forget all logic.

Horror raced across his face. "You're a rebel?" he asked with a hint of disgust though Kale took no notice.

"The rebels are a rumor, a myth, don't you know anything." She laughed as she always did when stating that well-known fact. "Just tell them that and they'll find me for you. Now, you better go. I don't want you to get grounded." She smiled playfully but Derin simply turned and took off running through the woods, propelled by the fear he'd be found out.

"Hey," she called after him, "you never told me your name."

"It's Alex," he called, saying the first name that came to mind. "What's yours?"

Kale couldn't see him any longer but she could hear him and was sure if she yelled he would hear her. She tried to think up a name to give him because something told her she should lie. Instead she just stood, watching the woods where he'd disappeared. The strangest ache she'd ever felt was forming inside her. For a few more moments, she could hear him crashing through the brush and then he was gone and all was silent again around her. She found herself strangely disappointed he hadn't waited to hear her name but he knew how to find her. Maybe in the world after Caine, which Kale believed they could fight for and find, there'd be room for whatever it was she was feeling.

"Kale," she said quietly to herself, "my name is Kale."

Slowly, she made her way towards the town of Braedon Ridge to visit the Mission and say her good-byes, unaware that things had been set in motion that none of them would be able to escape.

FIFTEEN

"Lord Caine, you wanted to see me?"

Caine turned from his window and smiled.

"Derin, I told you, it's still 'Father' when we are alone. No matter how old you get, you don't grow out of that obligation, my son. Only address me formally if the situation requires it."

Derin stopped a few feet from where Caine stood.

"Of course, Father, I just understood this was a formal meeting."

Often Derin faltered when addressing his father. Caine had adopted him almost fourteen years ago and had truthfully been a good parent to Derin, but there were still times when Derin felt more like a servant and less like a son.

"Not today, Derin. I'm just checking up on you, that's all. How is everything?"

Derin shuffled uncomfortably under his father's gaze. There were certain times when he spoke to him that Derin felt Caine knew something he didn't and this was one of them.

"Fine. Everything is fine, Father."

"I hear your training is going well. You'll be ready for active duty soon, I think. I'll need you right up at the top, Derin. I need someone I trust. I know you're young and it's a lot for you to handle but I want you at my side." Caine paused. "Oh, I almost forgot. We'll be having company soon, a new trainee, and I want you to train her. Her name is Kale and she is a very special case. Do you think you can handle that, Derin?"

Derin, taken aback, didn't answer right away. He'd never encountered a special case before nor had he been asked to train someone personally.

"Do you?" Caine repeated.

"Of course, my lord," Derin stuttered, the time for formality having returned without warning.

"Good, I'll inform you once she has arrived." Caine paused and turned away from Derin staring again out the window. Not turning he raised a hand and waved his son away absentmindedly. "That is all. You can go."

Derin left the room, disturbed. He walked slowly, trying to block the worry from his mind. Was he just imagining that Caine was acting strangely or had things really changed? As Derin trudged through the gloom, he knew which one he hoped it was. *Please don't let him know I'm no longer sure*, he thought, *just don't let him know.*

He walked through the halls, longing for his thoughts to return to the beautiful girl who'd brightened his morning and spoken his thoughts aloud. *She's a rebel*, he reminded himself, *or associated with them.* The rebels weren't really something they took seriously, of course, but it still meant they were on opposite sides. It could never happen. It surprised him that his heart ached under the weight of that realization. Though he really knew nothing about her, he'd felt such an intense connection with her. He felt empty when he realized he would never be able to see her again.

He forced his thoughts back to the task at hand. *Who could the new trainee be and why was she a special case? The name was familiar somehow,* he knew that much. *Who was Kale?* He turned the name over and over again in his mind but it remained a mystery. *No worry,* he thought, *I'll know soon enough.* At that, he cleared his mind of all thoughts wanting once again to cease questioning his father and leader and be the soldier he was meant to be.

## SIXTEEN

The sun had been up for well over an hour and Alex found himself annoyed that they'd yet to pack up camp and be on their way. He was anxious, restless, and wanted to push forward. The journey across half the continent would only take two days if they traveled swiftly and for as long as the sun was shining but now, that the time to act was upon them, he felt that pull toward Berdune, Caine, and whatever else awaited them with a force he'd yet to feel in his entire life.

When they came to the southern shore, they would stay there on the beach for one night. After that they expected to journey by sea for well over a week before arriving on Berdune's northernmost tip. Then, they didn't really know what was next except that they would be travelling by foot southward for at least a week unless the stars changed and told them otherwise. The stars could change nightly and the new year was a month away. That's when they were certain Caine would make his move. All they could do was move forward and continue to trust the stars. Hoping that the oncoming Darkness, creeping across the universe, consuming worlds and species unworthy of prevailing against it, would meet its match in them, and the savior, whoever that was.

Alex walked over to the edge of their camp and sat down. As much as his heart raced with both anticipation and fear, he knew he had to remain calm and patient with his friends. They'd all lost something when Caine had arrived and they would all gain something in his destruction. It was just a matter of time, he knew that much.

Alex let his mind tumble back to his youth when both his parents had been with him, when all their parents had been around and not a day went by without the certainty their joy would last forever. Forever, as is too often the case, had turned out to be only moments.

Alex loved to think back to the fireside stories Joachim would tell of the-one-they-called Froste, of how Froste had brought them to consciousness and led them to Alpha Iridium to start a new life. Originally, Alex's mother hadn't been in the plans. Fate, and love, had changed all that. It was Alex's favorite fairytale.

His mother was his closest friend even still. This said a lot about how much space Alex kept between himself and the other children of the Founders, his friends, his family. His mother had never been able to match the powers that the other five had. She'd spent too much time as a regular person on Earth. Yet, she never minded this. She was always happy and always grateful for what she had, but it always made her a little different than the rest of them. Alex felt connected to her because he too was a little different being, the only one of the remaining children who was now an only child. Joah and Arin had one another. Arwyn and Beran had one another as well.

Being the oldest, he'd fallen easily into the role of leader, just as his father had in days long past. And because destroying Caine had come to consume him, he accepted this role willingly and gave up any kind of life or happiness he could have had in pursuit of that end. He not only had four friends he couldn't disappoint but five sleeping parents who needed him to succeed, and an entire continent of people completely unaware of how their fate hung fragile and undecided in the balance of dark and light.

What he didn't understand, what he would never quite admit, was that he wasn't sure what the stars were telling him to do. They wouldn't reveal the savior to him, except of course to tell him it wasn't Caine. For all he knew, it was one of them meant to step forward when the time required it. Alex had no idea how he was going to figure everything out. What he did know was that he intended to succeed or die trying. That was his destiny now. He was sure of it.

Behind him, he heard someone emerging from a tent and was relieved that his thoughts were distracted from the darkness that plagued him. He stood and shook the dirt and grass from his clothes and then stretched. Finally, the day was beginning.

SEVENTEEN

Kale, lost deep in thought, walked through the woods that led to her house. Again, when she came to the ridge shaded by the dense canopy above, she felt strange feelings wash over her. She stopped and turned around, suddenly certain she was being followed. The woods were empty when she scanned them and she let a nervous and embarrassed laugh escape her.

"I'm losing it," she said quietly to herself as she turned around, and then she screamed.

The strange woman she'd seen before in that very spot was standing before her once again. Her large brown eyes were laughing kindly and though nothing about her was menacing, Kale felt chilled just the same.

"I'm sorry I frightened you, Kale. This seems to be the only place I can reach you."

"What are you talking about? Who are you?"

"I assure you I intend you no harm. I just want to help if you will let me." The woman watched her intently, waiting patiently for Kale to say something.

"I don't need any help," Kale said defiantly.

"Kale, your father…"

"My father is dead," Kale interrupted. "Now, if you don't mind, I have somewhere to be."

"Forgive me. Let me explain. I was born the same place you were, Kale. And reborn…" The woman began but she was interrupted again.

"Kale," Medea called from somewhere through the trees, "Kale, answer me. Are you okay?" Medea's voice grew louder and instinctively Kale turned towards it when she answered.

"I'm right here, Medea. I'm fine." When Kale turned back around, the woman was gone. She scanned the trees briefly but Kale knew better than to expect to see the woman anywhere. She'd vanished. Kale didn't want to admit it but she was beginning to wonder whether she was under too much stress. Through the trees, Medea came running toward her. Worry was painted all over her face.

"You screamed," Medea was panting. "What happened?"

"Nothing. I'm fine. I was just startled by a bird. I'm a little too wound up that's all." Kale smiled mischievously. "You're not one to worry. What's up with that?"

Medea immediately became defensive. "If you must know, it was Corin who sent me running out here like a maniac." Medea turned and started towards the house.

"Hey, I'm just teasing." Kale hurried to catch up with her. "Sometimes I think we've just got to find Corin a girlfriend so he'll stop worrying about us two."

"You got that straight," Medea added, her annoyance already forgotten.

As they walked, Kale's thoughts returned to Alex, the guy who had sought her out on the cliffs at Sunshine Bay. She could still see those crystal blue eyes and how within them there were so many conflicts, questions and insecurities, certainty and resolve. She missed those eyes, which unsettled her. She missed the way they'd looked at her. And because for the first time in her life she felt herself looking back in the same way, she felt a little bit grateful that she wouldn't have to see him again until all this was over, if they made it through it all and destroyed Caine.

"And just what are you smiling about?" Medea had stopped and was looking at Kale suspiciously.

"What?" Kale stopped walking and tried to keep from smiling but she failed miserably. "I'm not smiling. Why would I be smiling?" She looked away from Medea. "I'm not smiling," she repeated.

"You met someone!" Medea shouted accusingly. When she saw the horror on her friend's face, the dismay, even she couldn't quite believe what came out of her mouth next. "You're in love."

Kale turned to face her friend abruptly, horrified. "Shhh, don't say that so loud. I'm not in love, don't be crazy. I'm about to join the J'Kahl. We're about to do the most dangerous and important thing in our lives. Everyone is counting on me. I'm not in love."

Medea was smiling widely. "I won't tell the guys, just tell me who it is, please."

"I will not tell you who it is." Despite herself, Kale relaxed a little.

"So there is someone. Kale, come on. I've never known you to have that look on your face, in your eyes. Who cares what we're about to do. You've never had a life outside of the rebel alliance. All you've ever cared about is destroying Caine and I've watched that almost destroy you. Who says you can't have a life? Who says you have to give everything up? Who says you can't fall in love?" Medea looked at Kale with such heartache and hope that Kale couldn't bring herself to block out her friend's words. She knew it was all true and wished she knew why.

Kale smiled, resigned, giving in for the first time to the fantasy of a life after Caine. She'd never really indulged the idea of an ordinary life once her parents were gone and she'd vowed to stop Caine. Maybe it was that she was about to risk it all, do the most dangerous thing she'd ever done, and possibly not survive any of it, but she indulged herself and her best friend for a few moments. Maybe because deep down somewhere she believed she'd never really get a chance for anything more. "If you must know, he's got beautiful blue eyes and jet black hair that glimmers blue in the sun." Kale began walking as she spoke but Medea was too shocked to follow. Kale continued, "He's got a wretched father who keeps him locked away. And when this is all over, he's going to come looking for me. Sounds kinda like a fairytale, so I won't hold my breath. Now, can we drop this, please?"

Kale wasn't sure why the guy she'd met made her behave so out of character, so giddy, so hopeful about love, but right after she'd opened up to Medea she wished she hadn't. *I'm not really that girl*, Kale thought sadly, *I'm not a princess and he's not the prince. The purpose of my life is to destroy Caine and what comes after that isn't my concern until it's all done.*

"What's his name?" Medea was fighting not to burst into a joyous chorus of giggles as she ran to catch up with her friend.

"Alex. Now can we stop this, please?" Kale pressed down the anger trying to bubble up and cover her longing, for what she did not know.

"You are truly terrible at the girly-bonding stuff, you know that, Kale?'

"Yeah, well, out of all the things that have been thrown at me in this life, that's the one thing I'm glad I've avoided so far." Kale smiled at her friend mockingly.

"Well, who knows, when the new world gets here maybe anything will be possible and we'll make a girly girl out of you yet."

"Don't hold your breath, Medea, the new world is supposed to be better, remember? Why would me going soft be an improvement?"

"Why wouldn't it be?" Medea answered and went in the front door leaving Kale standing on the front porch searching frantically for a witty response.

EIGHTEEN

Just before the sun went down at the end of that day, Kale was sitting on the very spot where Medea had left her speechless that morning. She sat beside Jaren trying to find a way to say goodbye. So far the silence was enough between the two friends but Kale knew sooner or later one of them would have to break it. She watched as the sky slowly reddened as if rabid fires were burning beyond the tree line.

She knew the stars would be jumping into the night sky within the hour and for just a moment she thought of Alex and how he loved to look at them.

"You know, I wish you weren't going to do this, Kale."

Kale didn't turn her eyes away from the blazing sky but she turned her attention toward Jaren. "What we wish and what we get are two totally different things, Jaren, we both know that."

"Don't. Don't do that, Kale."

Finally, she turned toward him. His short blond hair was disheveled, as if he'd been running his hands through it repeatedly throughout the day. His grey eyes were solemn, full of fear and something else that was always there, but that Kale could never quite place.

"Jaren, my whole life has led me to this. The last few years have forbidden me from turning away from what I'm supposed to do here. And frankly, we're out of time. What do you want me to say?"

Because he didn't know how to tell her the whole truth, the one his heart begged him to share, he told her what he could. "How about you'll be careful? How about you won't do anything crazy to stop him? How about you'll think before you act? How about you'll come home..."

"Okay, Jaren, I get it."

Again, silence enveloped the friends. Kale was a little angry. This wasn't how she wanted to say goodbye. Why were her friends treating her so strangely when all she wanted was to be reminded they'd miss her and that they believed in her? Finally Jaren spoke, "You know, Kale, I still remember the first day we met."

Kale laughed. "You mean when I took you to meet the child who led the rebels."

Jaren shook his head. "You'll never let me forget that, will you?"

"Not in this lifetime."

"Well, what *I* like to remember about that day," Jaren took a deep and thoughtful breath, "was how a girl I hardly knew and who couldn't have been a day over sixteen made the world seem beautiful again. How a world I thought hope had abandoned finally became solely about fighting for, and with, hope. How I finally stopped talking and started acting and somehow I was important again because of that. What I felt was important, and what I believed was important. That's what I remember."

Jaren looked down at his hands and Kale left him for a moment with his thoughts and memories. Finally, she took one of his hands in hers.

"You know what else I remember from that day, Jaren?"

"What?" He still sounded tired and sad.

She giggled before speaking. "I remember the look on your face when you found out who I was when the meeting started. That was priceless."

Both Jaren and Kale began to laugh. Somehow, as it always seemed to be with shared laughter, the mood lightened as it chased the darkness away. When they were both able to stop laughing, Kale spoke again.

"Jaren, this is it, this is the great adventure of our lives and the most important thing we'll ever do. Honestly, I can't think of anyone I'd rather have living it with me than you guys. We're going to be okay. We're going to make a difference. We're going to change the world somehow. We're going to stop him. And then we're all going to settle down and have families and lives and grow old together."

"God, Kale, I hope you're right."

"When am I ever wrong, Jaren?" she asked, because she couldn't quite speak the truth, that there was a voice inside her whispering that the life she spoke of, the one she dreamed for after Caine, didn't really feel possible, for her anyway.

"Never," Corin said, as he walked out onto the porch to join them.

Jaren stood, as did Kale. They hugged fiercely for a long time, before Kale finally let go.

"Back before you know it, Jaren." She smiled reassuringly as she spoke. "If we're lucky, there will be no need for the backup plan and I'll be home in a few weeks."

Jaren headed for the door and pulled it open slowly. Before he walked through it, he stopped but he didn't turn around.

"I love you, Kale," Jaren said, wondering if he'd ever get to tell her that again and make her understand it. At that, he walked through the door and let it slam behind him. Neither of them aware that though they would see each other again before the new year arrived, everything would be different and nothing as they planned it to be.

"Don't you just hate goodbyes?" Corin asked.

"We're not saying goodbye, Corin. We're just saying, 'see you in a little while.' Am I the only one who thinks we're going to make this work?"

"No, you're just the only one who is so sure that there isn't an ounce of doubt in you. And that's enough for the rest of us. It will just be hard without you here. That's all."

"You know, Corin, this is the speech I expected from Jaren. You, I expected to be worried and to try to talk me out of this."

"Well, I'm glad I'm exceeding your expectations, Kale, but go easy on, Jaren. You must understand what this is doing to him. I mean because of how he feels about..." Corin stopped himself.

"About what? How he feels about what, Corin?"

Behind them, the door slammed shut again.

"How he feels about Corin keeping his mouth shut," Medea said and gave Corin a stern look. "Now, is it my turn to say goodbye or what? Kale has got to be on her way soon."

Corin and Kale embraced tightly. When they broke apart, they shared a knowing smile and nod. Then, he went into the house with his shoulders slumped slightly and his head hung low.

"Tell me you've got something cheerful to say, Medea? Those two are making me wish I'd just snuck away in the middle of the night."

"Kale, we're your friends, and you're going to do something really dangerous here. If it were one of us, how would you feel?"

"I'd be worried as hell, I guess. It's just making it a lot harder for me to leave this way."

"Kale, don't give me that crap. You can't wait to get in there."

Kale smiled mischievously. "Yeah, you're right."

"Let's make this easy on both of us then. Be safe. Be smart. And show those J'Kahl what a girl can do. I love you, sis. Come back to us okay."

Kale wrapped her arms around her best friend. She could feel Medea shaking and wished that there was something she could say to calm her. Truly, Kale had spent so much time focusing on what she was about to do that nothing at the moment could draw her away from it. In her mind, she was already in Caine's compound training to be a warrior while working towards his destruction.

Finally, the friends let go.

"Take care of my boys for me. Keep them out of trouble. It will all be over soon. One way or another, Medea, I promise you that."

"Yes, but how will it end?" Medea whispered as Kale bent down to pick up her bags.

She looked up and gave Medea an encouraging smile. "End? It's our turn to write the story, Medea, and this is just the beginning."

Kale turned and walked away, disappearing quickly into the trees now cloaked in the growing dark. Medea watched her go wishing she had Kale's faith that everything would work out well. She had faith in Kale and that would have to be enough.

From an upstairs window, Corin watched as the gloom enveloped his friend and he wondered what they'd gotten themselves into and why. *For a better world*, he reminded himself, as he let the curtains fall back into place to block out the oncoming night.

In his room, Jaren sat on his bed and tried not to become overwhelmed with regret. *How could he have let her go? How could he have sent her into the dragon's lair? He knew how, that she was more capable than the rest of them, and somehow if anyone could find a way to stop Caine, it was Kale.*

In the woods a little way from the house, Kale made her way anxiously toward her fate. She didn't think about her friends; she had to let them go to do what needed to be done. She didn't think about the guy she'd met earlier that day; love had no place in her world. What she thought about was

Caine and how much she would enjoy pretending to love and worship him while using every ounce of strength she possessed to destroy him.

Above her, the stars jumped into existence one-by-one-by-one, and, in more than one place on Alpha Iridium, people were watching them to see what the future brought.

NINETEEN

On a beach on the southern shore of Samnar, five friends sat around a blazing fire. They sat in the very same spot five of their parents had many years ago. On their third night on the planet Dellerim, Joachim, Kiernan, Arianna, and Kendra united for the first time since arriving on Alpha Iridium and spent their first real night together.

Now, five of their children were seated beneath the stars, feeling as close to their parents as they had when they were alive. In a way, as their parents had begun a life together from that spot, they were starting a life together in their journey to try to heal the world and deny the Darkness that was growing ever closer to their tiny world. The friends had endured much throughout their lives and, now, as they sat around the crackling fire in silence, this was the beginning of a journey towards a fight they had to win; their thoughts were much the same.

Before Caine had arrived, life had been a fairytale. Their parents had shared a love with one another that ran deeper than friendships or love affairs. What they endured together had forged a bond that could defy eternity. When the children arrived, the love and joy within their small community had grown exponentially.

As the oldest of the children, Alex had enjoyed eleven wonderful years with his parents actively in his life. Though he had none of their powers, he could remember almost all of that time. The days had been filled with games, laughter, magic, and always, swimming. Alex's mother loved to swim. Often, they slept out on the sand beneath the stars, imagining other worlds and what other people might be doing on them.

Alex's mother used to love to try and guess which twinkling point was Earth and, when she did this, she often fell into stories about Alex's grandfather, the man he was named after, Alexander Lascher. He was also the man responsible for all of them being here in many ways, though Froste was given all of the credit. They rarely spoke much of Alexander's work on Earth. Only when Alex and his mother were alone under the star clad night sky did she speak openly and fondly of her father.

Many nights they sat around a blazing fire and Alex's mom would tell them all stories about Earth; she was the only one of them who'd actually lived there. She told stories of her childhood and stories of any kind that entertained. And often, she told stories of both the beauty and the atrocities that littered humanity's history as far back as anyone had written it down. It was a warning about what we all could become if we forgot who we were and got lost in that drive for money, power, and the possession of people and things.

Many nights the story of how the people of Berdune came to be born was told. That had always been the favorite tale because it let the children marvel at the abilities of their parents. The night Caine had arrived that story had been told for the last time, just before the children were sent to bed, completely unaware their lives would be changed forever while they slept.

After that night, everything was different. With their parents trapped in dreamless sleep and four of their family members missing, the children were forced to grow up quickly. The games stopped. Laughter was less abundant. All the magic that their parents had woven into the fabric of their everyday lives seemed lost forever, except in memory.

The fourteen years since had been about one thing, waiting for the day when they would be allowed to mend their parents' innocent yet life-altering mistake.

Feeling closer to their parents than they had in years and sitting below the very stars that not only led them southward but that allowed them to finally pursue Caine and find answers to the questions they'd had for almost fourteen years, the Founders' children spoke of hope and other things.

"It feels weird being here without them." Arin's cherry eyes blazed in the firelight and, though she spoke softly, her anger for what had happened was revealed in their depths. "I always figured when we finally came to this spot, it would be with them." She stared into the fire, as if trying to see right into the past.

"Why didn't they ever bring us here?" Joah wondered aloud from beside his sister. His white hair was iridescent in the firelight.

"You know, I never even thought about that until now." Beran was seated right beside Arwyn, who leaned against him, drawing strength from her brother. "Do you think we were supposed to be here tonight for the first time together?"

"Maybe," Arwyn shrugged. "God, I wish we were more like them sometimes. If they couldn't fight the Darkness, how can we?"

"We don't have a choice," Arin said. "Do we?" She added skeptically.

"Of course, we have a choice." Every one turned to look at Alex who had been silent until then. "This is where the choices start, don't you see? Our parents were taken from us, and we had no choice. We grew up alone and defenseless. We had no choice. We had no one to teach us or care for us or guide us. We had no choice. Now, all of a sudden, we can choose. We can stay at home and let things run their course, or we can go and try to help because for some reason we can or we're meant to, but it's our choice. This is the first time in our lives we get a say in what happens to us. Good or bad, we decide." Alex looked around at his friends and they all sat in silence for a long time. Their thoughts were on similar paths. Finally, he stood. "I'll be back. Bathroom break," he said and walked away from the fire and down the beach into the dark, his footfalls lost to the sound of the sighing waves.

"Is he okay?" Arwyn looked around expecting an answer in one of her friends' faces.

"Of course, he's okay. It is Alex we're talking about. But this is literally all he's thought about the last fourteen years. He just wants us to take it seriously, too." Arin pressed her lips together as if she'd betrayed Alex somehow with what she'd said aloud.

"We are all taking this very seriously," Joah said indignantly. "Well, you guys are. I'm not too worried but that's just my way." He offered a laugh but, when no one joined him, he stopped. "Sorry. I'm just trying to lighten the mood."

"Joah's right," Arin said from beside him.

"I am?" He asked with surprise.

"Well, I hate to admit it...but, yeah. We've got a long way to go and maybe this is going to end badly. We don't know. What we do know is that we're seated right where our parents were seated all those years ago. Maybe that's something. Maybe it means something. They escaped the Darkness once. We can do it again. We need to stop worrying and believe."

Around her, the friends began to smile and nod. Further down the beach, Alex watched the tar-like waves and thought much the same thing. Looking to the stars, he forgot they held the future and saw through them to the past. One of the tiny sparkling stars gave birth to the Founders. The one he was sitting on had become their home.

It comforted Alex to realize that if Earth disappeared from the heavens, he would know. They would all know because a missing star would change their fate. So maybe, in the grand scheme of things, one tiny world did matter. Maybe one single person on a tiny world mattered, too, and was important because one person had the power to destroy it? If so, then one person had the power to save it. *We'll be okay*, Alex thought, as he began walking back to the campfire. It was time to tell a story, as they used to every single night. It was time to admit that hope was only a luxury if you believed you deserved to live without it. They were fighting for hope, for each other, and for so much more. It was time to start believing it.

## TWENTY

Kayla woke with a start and the dream came with her. Her first awareness of the waking world was that of crippling fear, literally. She tried to lift her head from her pillow but couldn't. She could feel the nightmare clawing at her to return to it and tried with all her strength to fight against it. She was unable to move, pinned down by fear or something else. If not for the terror, she would've been frustrated by her inability to move or fight back; to be free of what it was she'd seen while sleeping. It was as if she was in between the waking world and the dreaming world, caught in a strange sort of limbo, where the physical world didn't exist.

Slipping back into sleep, Kayla pleaded with herself to be strong enough to escape, to fight back, but she wasn't. She fell into the nightmare. She spilled over herself into that familiar story of heartache and hope, fear and fighting, and always the sting of loneliness, too certain to be set aside.

## TWENTY-ONE

*In a sea of dreams, I float aloft my longing...*

Kayla stared at the journal page and searched for the words to describe what she was feeling. She had the nightmares before but they'd never been so frequent. Kayla had been dreaming of the same place since she was a child and only recently had she come to realize it. The dreams coming often enough that she'd begun to notice a pattern and shape to it all.

As far as Kayla remembered, as a child, the dreams had come infrequently. She couldn't recall if all those years ago when they'd first begun she'd woken paralyzed and haunted by what she'd seen while sleeping. She wasn't sure if she'd always needed to struggle to free herself of sleep, only to realize that fighting only heightened the fear and never saved her. She did remember when the nightmares had become a major part of the waking world. She knew exactly when.

After weekends of partying and stretches of up to a week without sleep, Kayla found herself experiencing strange things. While lying in bed, she would feel waves like gentle pins and needles rolling over her entire body. While lying there, Kayla would feel like she was physically being tossed about as if she'd set sail on a stormy sea. Sometimes, she could feel herself floating up and away from her body, completely and totally out of touch with the physical world. At times, it was exhilarating, and other times, it was horrifying.

Those experiences always preceded the nightmares. Kayla would find herself in the same place and would always be fighting against one force to overcome and prevail. She was always scared beyond belief and never ready to face her fear. The dreams were more real than anything Kayla had ever experienced. She was always startled by her utter awareness in them, her ability to think, feel, and look at things from her own point of view.

When she woke from the nightmares, there was always an evil presence in her room taunting her inability to face it. She could always sense it in the dark, in her periphery, but still just out of sight. Waiting, mocking. Creeping ever closer. She ached with everything she was to face whatever it was, but she wasn't strong enough, and she knew it.

They came often, the dreams, while she neared the end of her year-and-a-half of drugs. They added to her distress and weighed her down with crippling anxiety. Yet, in a way, the horrible things she experienced while sleeping were part of what saved her. It had all become too much and either Kayla had to break or she had to give in.

Looking back now, she was glad she'd given in and surrendered. She let go of the chains that bound her and began to want to live again. Kayla often wondered how different life would be if she'd given up instead. *Would she even still be here?*

*In a sea of dreams, I float aloft my longing and there I see the truth of what it is to be.*

Kayla shut her journal and lay back down on her bed. The nightmares always exhausted her. As if she'd spent the whole night running a marathon instead of sleeping. Within instants, she found herself in the midst of normal sleep. She welcomed it. She resented it as well.

## TWENTY-TWO

Kale woke in a stranger's room, in a stranger's bed, and felt her stomach knot with alarm. As she sat up, her memory of the night before returned instantly.

She'd approached the gates of Caine's compound passively, as an able and willing servant of Caine. First, she'd have to convince the J'Kahl on night watch at the front gates who she was and what she wanted. It took only a minute to contact Caine for approval, and she was permitted to enter. It had been that simple. Kale had known it would be. She was meant to destroy Caine, and she knew it. It was time.

After being escorted to her room, Kale had been informed that Caine would call for her in the morning. She would be taken to meet with him and her training schedule would be laid out for her. Kale couldn't help but feel excited about the days to come. Even though she was here under false pretenses, the prospect of training and fighting, of getting stronger and becoming a warrior, pulled at her in a way not many things had.

Kale stared around the room that was, as she understood it, her home until she did what she had to do. Caine understood it was her home indefinitely, as she'd claimed to pledge her life's service to him. Kale couldn't wait to show Caine how foolish he really was.

The room in which she sat was not at all what she'd expected. She knew most of the J'Kahl slept where they trained, in another building inside of Caine's compound. When Kale had entered the compound the night before, she'd been surprised when she was escorted inside the main castle.

Her bedroom was huge, opulent, and extravagant. It seemed more like the kind of room a fairytale princess would reside in rather than a soldier. She kept wondering if Caine was trying to impress her, but that was irrational, and so she brushed the thought aside over and over again. The room was bright and decorated in warm tones from the ruby red drapes that hung over the large windows, to the royal blue sheets she'd slept under, to the citrus cornucopia that made up the rug covering the floor.

Kale almost wished she'd been thrown in a dark and forbidding little cell so that she wasn't feeling so comfortable. It threw her off guard and tempted her to forget how dangerous things really were and how much work she had ahead of her.

The only strange things about the room were the bars covering the windows. Those alone seemed to block out the brightness and beauty of the world beyond and hinted at the fact, maybe, Kale's motives for being there weren't as secret as she thought. Looking around the room unenthusiastically, she began to miss her own room and her own bed. Though it made her feel weak and uncertain, she had to admit she missed her friends, too.

She thought about them and wondered what they were doing while she sat in a room fit for a queen. She was more alone than she'd ever been and acutely aware of it. One, if not all three of them, was at the Mission. Maybe they'd eaten a breakfast of burnt eggs Medea had made and then headed off together. Maybe they were taking care of other things pertaining to their mission. Maybe they missed her. Kale let herself hope so.

TWENTY-THREE

"No, she hasn't run off to get married, Mr. Carlson. She's just gone to visit some friends in Empris. She should be back in a couple weeks at most. I promise." Medea watched Mr. Carlson walk towards a nearby table and wondered if there was anyone in Braedon Ridge who didn't love Kale.

Medea knew her best friend well enough to know she didn't know everything about her. She was also certain she knew more than most. Kale had layered versions of herself one on top of the other so that what you saw was never entirely the truth. Medea had known her long enough to know that Kale's fear of love and intimacy ran all the way back to her childhood. She wasn't even sure if Kale knew just where it had all begun. The only ones who'd ever really been close to her had been her parents. The betrayal she'd suffered when they'd joined Caine's inner circle and then left her to continue on in life without them, had left Kale with an aversion to love and being loved that Medea had yet to see her move beyond. Still, Medea knew what many people didn't, that no one could really love Kale because she wasn't a real person, not a whole person anyway. She handed over pieces, fragments, and no one had yet received the whole puzzle to put together and truly love. And yet, she drew you in with a magnetism few could ignore. The part of her that was so afraid and tucked safely away, that's the part you fell for first. Everybody did because that's the part that made you want to save her with your love. Medea smiled to herself as she thought about her best friend and wondered how she'd become so lucky and unlucky all at once.

Kale was a force, an imposing figure in both presence and personality so that she was often the center of attention whether she meant to be or not. It took a lot of confidence to stand in her shadow day after day and not whither in that shade. One of the reasons Kale and Medea got along so well is that Medea had never been insecure. In contrast to her confidence and certainty of self, Kale was actually the most insecure person Medea had ever met, though few people were aware of it. It was always as if Kale hadn't quite found her sure footing in the world, like she hadn't entirely figured out who she was, which was strange seeing as she was a leader to so many people. Medea also knew that Kale's strength was often reserved for everyone but herself. She could cross a vast ocean for her friends, for the people of Berdune even, but, in all the time she'd known her, Medea had never seen her take up action for herself.

"Mr. Wilson, how are you this morning? You look tired. Don't tell me you were partying again last night. I thought I told you no partying unless I'm invited."

Mr. Wilson reached out and took Medea's hand in his and then kissed it gently.

"Is she gone?" he asked.

Medea nodded.

"Then, it has started?" he asked grimly.

Medea nodded again.

"When I was a child, they told stories about the days to come. We would sit under the stars, a fire burning in the night, and someone would whisper about the coming of Darkness unlike anything we could imagine, and a light that could beat it back." He paused, his gaze trained on days far gone but not forgotten. Goosebumps had broken out on Medea's arms but she waited quietly for him to go on. He shook his head, once, twice.

"Are you kids going to be okay? You know what you're doing?"

"I hope so, Mr. Wilson. I really hope so," Medea replied quietly as if speaking more to herself than to the kind old man with the twinkling, youthful eyes of a child.

Almost everyone at the Mission asked for Kale. Her absence had a presence all its own. It prowled around the room, felt by all, and even though the mood was bright like most mornings, there was a current of worry running through it, stirred up by that predator and a sense that things were shifting underfoot. There'd been other mornings that Kale hadn't made it to the Mission but they were few and far between. With her speaking openly in recent weeks about the need for them to watch for their chance at freedom, people began to wonder if change was coming. Though none of them loved living in Caine's world, the unknown of the world that came after him was a scary thing just the same.

On her way home, Medea stopped to check in on Emily and her mother who had again not been at the Mission, and then she stopped in with some friends.

"Medea, you're either a day late or six days early," Samantha said as she hugged Medea and then stepped aside to let her into the house. "We said Saturday, right?"

The foyer they were standing in was huge with vaulted ceilings that reached at least fifteen feet above them. A huge twinkling chandelier hung above their heads. The floors were marble and the massive stairway that curled upstairs was decorated with beautifully crafted wrought iron railings. The Hughes' were extremely wealthy and they'd done well for themselves because they supported Caine. Though Sam's parents were not in Caine's inner circle, they were passionate and loyal followers and did what they could to donate to his cause. They owned factories and properties across Berdune and benefited from Caine's love of free labor. If Sam's parents had any idea of what their children did to oppose Caine, they would have disowned them both and turned them over without a second thought. Loyalty in Caine's world was unyielding. He forgave nothing, not even a parent's love for their child.

"How's your mother, Sam? Doing better, I hope," Medea said, following the striking blond girl through the house as they spoke.

"Oh, she's great actually. Don't tell her I said so, but I think that fight with my father was more the problem and not her stomach." Sam had dropped her voice to speak but raised it again when she continued, "Ryan's been waiting for you. Is everything okay?"

"Everything is fine actually. That's why I'm here. Kale said she came by the other day..." Medea paused, "is it safe to talk here?"

Sam looked around unnecessarily, "Yeah, my parents are both out, but let's go downstairs anyway. I think Ryan will probably want to hear this."

Medea followed Sam through the impressive hallways, the huge kitchen, and down the back stairs to the basement. Everything they passed attested to the fact they were in a home that was thriving under Caine's rule. Seated on the couch reading a book was Ryan. His wild mane of blond hair hung over his face and, as he looked up, he tossed it back out of his eyes. When he saw Medea, he returned all of his attention to the book without saying a word.

"So that's the reception I'm getting now? Well, it isn't the worst you've given me so I guess I can be thankful of that," Medea waited, but he continued to ignore her. "By the way, I saw you with a girl yesterday. Who was she?"

"You know very well I was not..." Ryan objected as he threw her an indignant look, his book quickly forgotten. Medea was smiling; devious and delighted. "I hate it when you do that, Medea. You know that, right?"

Still smiling, she answered, "That's why I do it. You still mad at me or what?"

"Yes, I am still mad at you. I'm very mad." Medea tried to look hurt but the game was over. Ryan was already smiling and said, "I don't know why I put up with your crap, you know that."

"Cause you adore me that's why," she answered and sank down onto the couch beside him.

Ryan and Medea had known each other for years and had dated off and on throughout them. It was a casual relationship governed mostly by Medea's involvement with the rebel alliance and what it demanded of her week-to-week. Having been intensely busy for the last few weeks, Medea hadn't even been by to say hello. Because Ryan loved Medea, as she loved him, it worked, even if it wasn't entirely what he wanted from her. Like many things in their lives, the relationship was often set aside with the promise that the world after Caine would have a lot of time and space for it to thrive.

Ryan worried about her immensely. Both he and Sam were in danger because of their parents but they were so wrapped up in Caine that they didn't even notice their children were running weapons out of the house. Medea, on the other hand, was on the front lines and Ryan often worried that she was going to get in over her head, if she hadn't already.

Since Kale's desire to destroy Caine had become an obsession, Medea had put herself nearer to danger than ever before. Originally, Sam and Ryan had used their connections to provide weapons of protection to the people of Braedon Ridge. Over the last year, Medea had placed increasingly larger orders for more complex weaponry and technology and Ryan had finally confronted her about their future use.

After much arguing and persuasion, Sam and Ryan had been let into the loop. As much as Ryan hated Caine and what he'd done to the people of Berdune, he was reluctant to admit that action against Caine was a good idea, let alone that a bunch of twenty-something kids were the ones to stop him. He would never admit it but he was relieved that Kale had been the one chosen to go undercover. He could just imagine the fight that played out with Medea trying to be the one to take that risk.

"Is Kale...?"

Medea answered before he could even finish his question. Both her demeanor and her answer gave away the worry she was feeling.

"She's in...for now. All we can do is wait, really, and get ready."

"You wish it was you, don't you?"

Medea frowned, "Yes and no. You know I never like to miss a chance for excitement and adventure but this is bigger than all that and much more dangerous. I have to admit that Kale is probably the right one for this job."

"Yeah, well, I can't say I'm disappointed." Ryan put an arm around her protectively.

"Hey remember, this is low key. There aren't many people who actually know where Kale is. We're not sure who we can trust so if anybody asks she's gone to Empris for a few days, okay?"

"Who am I going to tell?"

"I'm just saying."

On the other couch, Sam sat quietly listening but not bothering to participate. She was practically invisible. She didn't mind, as that's when she got the most information. When Ryan and Medea were together, everyone else seemed to disappear.

For a relationship that wasn't meant to be serious, anyone who saw Medea and Ryan together could see things didn't get more serious than that. Sam had always found the couple grating. She couldn't understand how her brother let himself get treated so poorly, so forgotten every time Kale or the alliance called. It drove her crazy. Unlike his sister and her sharp edges, Ryan was soft, in all the best ways. He was kind, loving, and empathetic. He could see the good in everyone he met. Every time Medea left him hanging, Ryan was able to see and understand why she'd done it, forgiving her over and over again. Surviving Caine's world meant sacrifice. Destroying it meant setting everything aside to reach that all-consuming goal. Ryan understood all this. Sam had a much different point of view. She watched them banter now, baffled, annoyed, and rolled her eyes. *Fools*, she thought. *If they didn't learn to pay attention, they were going to get themselves killed.*

"So, I have another list for you Ry. I really need this stuff, and soon."

"So that's it, right down to business then? I'll say it again, 'I don't know why I put up with your crap,'" Ryan paused shaking his head. "Give me the list."

After going over things and talking for a few short minutes, Medea stood to leave. "I really do hate to do this but we have a lot to take care of. I'll be back soon though, I promise, and not just to pick up my stuff. We need you guys right now."

Ryan hugged Medea. "Ask for whatever you need. We're always here for you. I'm always here for you."

"Why don't you come by tomorrow? We'll have dinner." Medea smiled. "You can even stay the night," she added with a knowing look.

"So now we see what this is really all about."

"Ryan, are you ever going to give me a break?"

"Are you ever going to settle down and stop all of this craziness?"

"You like the world we're living in, Ry? Oh, I guess you would. Your house is filled with marble and your pockets are lined with gold."

"Hey, that's not fair. I don't like the world we're living in. I just don't like knowing my friends and the girl I love are the ones taking all the chances. This is Caine we're talking about here. Think of how he deals with traitors."

"You love me?" Medea asked with a smile.

"You have your moments."

"So, dinner tomorrow or what?" She poked him in the side playfully.

"Sure. But I'm only coming so I can try and talk you out of whatever great, big crazy you've got planned next. You know that, right?"

"Hey, whatever it takes to get you over my place is fine by me."

In the background, Sam scowled bitterly.

Medea kissed him briefly on the lips. "Tomorrow, then. See you later, Sam."

Sam smiled. "See you, Medea. Be safe."

"Me? Not unless it's more fun than chasing danger," she called over her shoulder as she went up the stairs.

Walking home through the wealthier section of Braedon Ridge, Medea realized the absurdity of it all. The world was a crazy place. You could either admit it or try and ignore it. Or, she realized, fight to change it for the better. She wondered where her friends were right then. *Were they as excited as she was? Were they as worried? Were they as scared?* She knew one thing for certain, they were all in this together and somehow that made everything okay.

When she arrived home, Corin was seated at the kitchen table staring down at the cup of coffee he'd poured for himself over an hour earlier. He didn't hear her come in and didn't look up until she sat down across from him.

"What have we gotten ourselves into, Medea?" He raised his head slowly as if the questions and worries within it weighed a thousand pounds collectively.

She sighed deeply before answering, "I keep asking myself that, too, you know. But there really is no turning back, and why would we want to? We have to try and stop this, even if we are just a bunch of kids. Caine's up to something really big. I can't imagine what could be worse than what he's already done, but I think that's what scares me the most." She paused. Their eyes met and the truth danced back and forth between them.

"It's only a matter of time before he finds us. Even if we didn't oppose him openly, we sure don't support him. We're doomed to be slaves or to die trying not to be."

"And what if we have to go to the backup plan?" he asked grimly.

"I have to say, Corin, you really know how to drain the fun out of this whole thing, you know that?" Medea tried to muster a smile.

"You know what this is?" Corin said, opening up one of his hands to reveal a gold chain with a twinkling moon pendant on it.

"Sure, it was your mother's."

"I found this in the front hall of our house the night she disappeared. She never took it off. When I found it, the clasp was broken as if it had been torn right off of her neck."

"Corin, you never told me that before."

"She opposed Caine. Now, she's gone. It isn't supposed to be fun, what we're doing. We might not make it through this, you know that? We could end up as memories, as necklaces, favorite books, or photographs that other people carry around to remember us by. We might fail. We might die trying."

"Are you saying you want out, Corin?"

"No. I'm saying I always knew what I was getting into but I forgot I was getting into it with the people I love. I rarely told my mom how much I loved her because I always thought she'd be around forever. I never told Kale how she's changed my life and now she's living with Caine and for all we know we'll never see her again. I never tell you or Jaren that I couldn't imagine a better life than the one I have with you guys and what if Jaren doesn't come home this morning? What if you disappear in the night?" Corin looked back down at his hands. "I'm babbling, sorry."

"Corin, I'm going to tell you something I would never tell anyone but you," she paused and took a long, slow breath. "I'm really scared too."

"You are?" Corin looked up, a little shocked.

Medea let out a short but delighted laugh at his surprise. "God, I'm terrified. I know you guys think I don't worry, that I don't care, but that's just how I get through all this. My parents were taken from me, too. We all have a score to settle here and we all have people who are counting on us. And yes, we're taking a lot into our own hands. And yes, this is pretty much an impossible mission that's going to get us all killed. But what I tell myself every day is that I can be proud of this life if this is how it ends." The rest of the words tumbled out of her in a single breath, carried on a wave of fear, too long ignored, "And this is probably how it will end 'cause this is all a long shot and we have no idea what we're doing." Finally, Medea stopped and took a deep breath. Again she laughed, a bit embarrassed but relieved to be free of the truth. Corin joined her for a moment and the tension in the room dissipated.

"If we don't make it through this, Medea, then I'm glad it was you at my side; all of us I mean. Who knew a guy like me would live a life of adventure, huh?"

"I knew the moment I met you, Corin. We wouldn't be here without you."

"Thanks," Corin said and closed his hand over his mother's necklace. "Too late to turn back so might as well enjoy the ride, huh?"

"Exactly," Medea paused, relieved that they could set aside their fear and worry once again. "By the way, you gotta cook dinner tomorrow night. Ryan is coming over and I've never cooked anything worth eating before."

"Sure. No problem. I like Ryan. Why would I ask him to eat anything you've cooked?"

"Now that's the Corin I know." Medea stood and walked around the table. She wrapped her arms around Corin's neck and hugged him tightly from behind. "While I've got you in the position," she stood but kept her hands loosely around his neck, "you plan on telling anyone I told you I was scared?"

"Oh, no, not yet. I plan on saving that one up. It might come in handy later on in life."

She let go of his neck and made her way out of the kitchen calling casually over her shoulder, "Oh, I'm not worried about that. I have a few photographs that may convince you to keep my little secret." She disappeared up the stairs laughing to herself.

"Pictures?" Corin whispered suspiciously. "She's bluffing," he said to himself though he ran out of the kitchen and stood at the base of the stairs. "What pictures?" he called. The only answer she offered was more laughter.


TWENTY-FOUR


Kale stood in the center of the large room, her heart beating furiously in her chest. Small beads of sweat broke out on her forehead and it took all of her will not to reach up and wipe them away. It was a sign of weakness and she was sure not to display this early on. She didn't want to fear Caine but he was an impressive and imposing man, and the things he'd done and was capable of doing made him worth fearing. He was tall enough that he towered far above her and his long limbs and slender frame accentuated his stature. His height was the only thing that convinced her he was not of Alpha Iridium. The people of AI were at the most 5'6". If the Founders did exist, they were the only known beings on the planet who were taller than that.

Caine's eyes were dark and, though she was loath to admit it, there was much more than evil swimming within them. He was indeed a man of hidden depths.

He was an extremely handsome man and Kale realized that because he put so much ugliness out into the world, it always surprised her a little. Kale hated keeping her eyes fixed to his because he made her squirm, but she couldn't break his gaze. There was something about him and the way he looked at her that made her shiver. She could swear that through his eyes, along with him, all the dark and awful things in the universe were peering out at her, waiting, for what she could not know.

Caine always emitted an air of absolute power, yet had a playfulness about him that bordered on madness and was frightening in its unpredictability. He rarely stayed still. Stalking through his large office like a predator ready to take a meal, he prowled around her and Kale often had to turn to keep him in her sights; she was certain that, if she didn't, Caine would strike. She was annoyed and angry that she felt like the prey and not the hunter.

When at last he came to rest at the window, Caine spoke. "I knew your parents well, Kale." He laughed as if he'd made a joke and when Kale didn't return the laughter he pressed on, "They were loyal servants and dear friends of mine. I was extremely surprised and disappointed when you turned down my offer to take you in sooner."

Caine turned his back to Kale and stared out the window. She felt certain Caine was playing some kind of game with her but she couldn't figure out the rules.

"I was young and foolish, my lord. I hope you can find it in your heart to forgive my ignorance and insolence and allow me to show you what a true soldier is made of," Kale said and bowed her head reluctantly. She had a feeling that, though Caine couldn't see her, he would sense she was lying and wouldn't be fooled.

"Normally, I would not choose to be so forgiving, my child, but your parents served me well." Caine turned from the window, and Kale saw malice in his eyes as well as a wild and untamed madness that he was yearning to lash out with. There was something else there as well in amongst all the darkness and turmoil. It was a strange hint of pain, loss, and heartache that Kale instantly wished she hadn't seen. *Compassion will make you weak*, she told herself and looked away.

"I have arranged for your first training sessions to begin this afternoon. It's nothing serious, just a tour of the military compound and an idea of what you will be up against during your stay. If you need anything, you will come to me. We will meet for dinner every day. If my memory serves me correctly, you owe me quite a few meals together." He smiled.

"Of course, my lord."

"I wish you all the best, Kale. I know you will make me proud," just as Caine finished speaking there was a knock at the door.

"Enter," Caine said and smiled to himself as the door swung open behind Kale's back.

She didn't turn. She was too intrigued by the expression on Caine's face. It was a mixture of delight and something more sinister, but she couldn't quite figure out what.

"You called for me, my lord?"

Caine's smile broadened. "I have that new trainee here I was telling you about. I want you to show her around and show her the ropes. I trust you are still up for the task?"

"Of course, my lord," the young man said with both confidence and conviction.

Kale finally stood and turned around. When she did, something inside her broke a little and her breath caught in her throat. A moment later, she realized with deep and aching certainty that she was going to die by Caine's hand and most likely within the next few moments.

"Kale, this is Derin, my son," Caine paused for effect. "He will be training you. He's the best we've got here. You are very lucky to be working with him."

Kale saw by the look of shock on Derin's face as he stood in the doorway that he'd already guessed why she was really there. She couldn't believe her luck. She'd already failed. She'd let her feelings weaken her and now she was going to pay for it. *How could she ever live with herself after this? Would she even get the chance to try?*

## TWENTY-FIVE

Kayla stared down at her journal and ached. She'd dreamed of the guy again. When she dreamed, in amongst the horror and the struggle, there had arrived the beginnings of a love beyond anything she had known in the waking world. It left her feeling empty, alone, and restless. She wondered if she would only ever know love like that in her dreams, in that world of make-believe that continued to draw her further from the life she was living.

When she woke, his face had lingered in her mind, she'd seen it clearly, but as she stirred, the picture of him slowly faded even as she fumbled to hold onto it. Now she could only feel him. The space that opened up between her and the truth of him set off a yearning in Kayla she'd never known before. It had all felt so familiar, so real. How could it only be a dream? Deep within, she was certain she'd known who he was, but that's how she felt every time she woke with an image lingering in her mind from that other life she lived while sleeping.

She closed her eyes and reached out with her mind and heart in search of his memory, of any memory of that dream world that could bring so many fulfillments, and yet left her so sad and sorry once she'd woken. She reached out but as always the longer she'd been awake, the further away from her that other life drifted. Angry and frustrated, she gave up.

*Why did that other life satisfy her so much more than this one*, she wondered with a deep and troubled sigh.

It had to be that sense of belonging. Kayla wanted nothing more than to belong somewhere, to someone. She just didn't know where and couldn't imagine to whom. When she woke from the dreams, sometimes terrified, sometimes content, there was without a doubt a sense that she'd belonged, that the other life had been what fulfilled her and where she was meant to be.

Downstairs, the doorbell chimed, interrupting her thoughts, and she wondered bitterly what happy and loving neighbor had come by to visit her aunt. Kayla immediately felt ashamed. She knew she shouldn't hate people just because they were happier than she was. *I should be trying to understand them*, she thought as the voices from downstairs wafted into her room. *Is that the answer?* She wondered.

"Kayla, you have company," her aunt called up the stairs as Kayla's stomach lurched with a mixture of excitement and dread. *Could it be him?* she wondered, thinking back to the guy who'd saved her life. Kayla found herself smiling stupidly as she stood and opened her bedroom door. "Coming," she yelled back and went into the bathroom to make sure she looked okay.

When she finally came down the stairs, nervous and a little off balance, Kayla saw Max sitting in the kitchen with her aunt, talking enthusiastically. When she entered the kitchen, they both stopped talking and looked toward her. Kayla was certain her aunt was smiling hopefully at her. She was also certain that her aunt would be on the phone to her mother within minutes, just to tell her that a guy came by to see Kayla.

"Hey, Kayla. Just thought I would stop by and see how you were doing after the other night."

Kayla's aunt raised her eyebrows and asked, "The other night? What happened the other night?"

Kayla panicked and her mind went blank.

"Oh, um, Kayla twisted her ankle and I had to help her home," Max answered before Kayla even had to think up a lie. "That's how we met actually," Max offered and smiled, satisfied he'd saved the dangerous situation he himself had created.

"Oh," Kayla's aunt looked from Max to her. "You should have told me you were hurt. We could have iced it up or something. Are you okay?"

"I'm fine, Aunt Helen. It was nothing really. Back to new in the morning. Honestly."

"Well, all right then," Aunt Helen paused, a mischievous smile playing across her lips. "Listen, could you run by the store for me, Kayla? I need some things for dinner tonight. Maybe you could show her around the town, Max? I'm pretty sure she's doesn't even know where the store is."

Kayla interjected, "I know where the store is."

"I don't mind taking you." Max smiled. "I mean if you don't mind hanging out with me."

"Oh, I wouldn't say no to the kind of guy who likes to rescue girls." She smiled at him playfully, surprised at herself, enjoying that they were sharing a secret.

Kayla asked for the list of items her aunt needed from the store and then left her aunt happily marveling at the change in her niece. One she'd been hoping for, for a long time.

Walking down the street next to Max, Kayla couldn't let go of the certainty that she really didn't deserve to be enjoying herself, that she hadn't yet earned the right. Still, she indulged what was growing inside her and began to take notice of the world. The sun was bright and warm on her skin. Birds flitted through the trees lining the street, delighted with a world all their own. She noticed flowers, both wild and tame, and even spotted a bumblebee or two drifting amongst them. The whole world seemed vibrant and at peace.

Inside of Kayla, the storm raged. She wondered if it was too soon to forgive herself, and didn't know.


TWENTY-SIX

"It's nice to meet you...sorry, what was your name?"

Derin stared at the beautiful girl whose name tasted so sweet on his lips though he'd only spoken it inside his head.

He wasn't sure whether he could even find the ability to answer her. There were a million thoughts travelling through his mind at lightning speed. Shocked and dismayed, he could barely find the will to stop one of them long enough to try and understand it.

"This is Derin, the best soldier we have and I say that with no bias even though he's also my son. He'll be showing you around and supervising your training, Kale. How does that sound?" Caine looked like he was thoroughly enjoying himself.

"Well," Caine spoke again. It seemed both Kale and Derin were unwilling or unable to break the silence. "Why don't you two get acquainted? I have business to attend to. You're excused."

The duo turned and left the room swiftly. Neither wanted to remain in Caine's presence any longer than they had to, not after all that had just been revealed. They walked in silence for a long time, Derin leading the way slowly through the dark and winding hallways. Each of his footfalls was heavy with the truth.

Finally, it was Derin who spoke. "You're a rebel. What the hell are you doing here? Are you trying to get yourself killed?"

"The rebels are a myth, like I told you before."

"You and I both know that's a lie."

"A lie? Let's talk about lies, *Alex*," Kale raised her voice, anger mixing with fear.

"Why are you here?" Derin interjected.

"I'm here to try and change the world," Kale said defiantly yet honestly.

"I saw you in town, Kale. I saw you with those people. You're not a loyal follower of Caine's. I know that much about you. I have no choice but to turn you in to Caine."

"Don't you mean 'Daddy?'" Kale said angrily. The truth of it stung in a way she couldn't understand.

"You should leave here while there's still time," Derin said, managing to sound both pleading and severe.

"I'm not leaving here until I've done what I came to do," Kale retorted.

"And just what is that?"

"Train to be a soldier."

"More lies," he hissed.

"Look, *Derin,* I don't expect you to understand what it's like out there. From what I can tell, you've only seen the outside of this place a handful of times. I'm trying to help those people. I may have made some decisions throughout my life that were wrong but I've come to see the best way to change things is to try from the inside. So, I'm here to train, and I'm here to see if I can change the way the common people are treated. They can no longer be pushed aside. I'm just trying to do my part, alright? Now, I'm sorry if you can't believe that but it's not my fault the people that you call friends and family have made you distrustful."

"This isn't about me," Derin said defensively.

"I think it is, and honestly I'm tired of it already. I have no interest in your personal problems and, if you really think I'm a traitor to your dear old dad, then go ahead and tell him. Make it quick though because, if I'm going to die, I'd like to do it before lunch and just get it over with."

"You're sure I won't turn you in, aren't you?" he asked with exasperation.

"No, I'm sure I don't want to play games," her voice softened, pleading, laying out the truth for him. "So, what is it, Derin, do we train or do I die? Pick one."

They stood locked in a stare, the air electric between them. Each one was waiting for the other to back down. Derin knew Kale was lying but the girl he'd spent a sunrise with at Sunshine Bay was still with him. So was how she'd made him feel. He wrestled with it to set him free. That girl did not exist inside Caine's compound. Derin could see it in her eyes as if she were two different people. The one standing before him was a stranger. *He'd have to tell Caine,* he knew that much, *but how?*

Derin ached. He was so overcome with conflicting emotions that he thought he would buckle under the weight of it all. Everything he'd felt for her at Sunshine Bay and, all the thoughts and emotions that had lingered, crashed up against the truth of who and what she was. Overwhelmed and ready to be set free, Derin backed down. His shoulders slumped and he dropped his eyes to the ground.

"Let's get on with the tour then," he said softly.

Slowly turning, he began to make his way down the hall and Kale was close behind him. *Please, let him believe me*, she repeated over and over again in her mind, a mantra she would return to more than once in the month that followed. She was happy Derin's back was turned so he couldn't see how badly she was shaking.

## TWENTY-SEVEN

Derin dragged his feet as he walked, reluctantly headed towards the stairway that led him ever-nearer Caine. He could feel the magnitude of his task pressing down upon him. He'd have to turn in Kale out of loyalty to his father and to his fellow J'Kahl. He kept searching for an escape but, no matter how he looked at it, he couldn't see a way out. He actually considered just leaving the compound and walking away, walking until his feet ached and his mouth burned dry with thirst, walking until he no longer had to worry about any of it, his obligations, his loyalties, or the truth.

Derin slowed his pace even more, searching desperately for a way to free himself of his task. When he finally arrived at his destination, with no answer to save or stop him, he placed a hand on the door, slightly ajar, intending to push it open.

He paused for a moment, two, his loyalty wavering and his decision on the verge of crumbling. Just as he began to turn away, he heard voices inside and both, instinct and a kind of fear he often pushed aside and ignored, told him to stop and listen.

"My lord," it was a woman's voice, "how would you like us to proceed?"

"Terminate them," Caine hissed.

"But my lord, they've done nothing wrong."

"Do you dare question me?" Caine bellowed.

"No, my lord, I just mean they are innocent and loyal followers."

"Their ignorance is crime enough for me. Terminate them."

"Yes, my lord. And the young man?"

"Let him live. I have a feeling that shortly a time will come when killing him will be more pertinent and far more enjoyable."

"As you wish, Lord Caine."

"How are our other preparations coming along?"

"Everything is in place as you requested. We will be ready."

"Wonderful."

Derin was unable to listen any longer. His head was spinning. All he wanted to do was to run and forget everything he'd just heard. His father had authorized the murder of innocent people. He tried to tell himself he'd heard wrong and that his father wasn't a murderer but, somewhere inside, he knew it was true. He'd always known. It was the same truth he'd been running from for a long time; his father had within him the ability to be an evil man. The truth had finally pinned him down so that Derin stood frozen to the spot, facing it.

It wasn't the first time he'd heard things. Truthfully, he'd heard so many things he was suddenly astounded he'd let them go unnoticed for so long. But now, it was too much and Derin turned from his father's door and stumbled away filled with an uncertainty and fear he'd never before known.

He walked through random hallways not sure where to go or what to do. His head was spinning, a whirlwind of anger and regret. *If he'd only chosen a different route to get to Caine's office, if only he hadn't noticed the voices in the room and just barged in, if only he hadn't gone to see Kale at Sunshine Bay. If only...* seemed to be the only thought Derin could grab hold of and yet, even though he wasn't quite aware of it, that thought was the beginning of Derin taking a stand and facing what he'd avoided for far too long. *If only...*


TWENTY-EIGHT


Kale sat on her bed waiting for Caine or his soldiers to arrive and tell her that her cover was blown. The turmoil

Derin had been in was unmistakable but she was sure that in the end he wouldn't betray his father. She hadn't missed the sadness and regret in his eyes when he'd left her after their tour, but she'd also seen that all of it was overshadowed by his loyalty.

The tour had taken only a few hours. Despite the fact that Derin was certain she was a traitor, he'd acted otherwise. They'd left Caine's castle through the east-facing front doors. The front gates were to the north and were left unattended during the day so no guard stood watch as they walked.

Derin had led her west around the back of the castle and they'd walked side-by-side, as he'd spoken enthusiastically about what they did and how they trained. He spoke passionately and animatedly about his training, which was a stark contrast to how he spoke of Caine's leadership or their work on Berdune, and his voice became monotonous and dull, rehearsed even. She remembered their conversation by the bay and realized that was probably the most honesty she would ever get out of him and for some reason that made her really sad. She was sad in a way that was new and unsettling to her so that she brushed it aside.

Circling the back of the castle, they'd turned east, following the trees that grew inside the outer wall and leading to the only other structure inside Caine's compound.

"What's that?" Kale asked as they'd neared the strange square building.

"That's where we're going. It's our training facility and where many of the J'Kahl reside. Most new J'Kahl and those who haven't earned Caine's trust yet stay there. There are also...well, here, I'll show you."

They walked through the towering front doors that faced westward. Once again, Kale felt excitement and worry turn within her. She momentarily forgot she would probably not get to train and instead lost herself in the idea of learning to fight like a soldier within these walls.

Inside, the ceilings shrank out of sight and, in the dimness of the space, Kale could barely see them. She found herself standing in a large foyer. Covering the walls were pictures of strangers Kale had never before seen. She glanced over the pale, frozen faces and couldn't help but wonder who they were and what they'd done for Caine. *What had their lives been like? Where were those strangers now?* Then she wondered the only thing that mattered, in the days and weeks that followed, *would they be allies or enemies in the fight to save Berdune?*

Staring around the large space, she saw that there were only three places to go. Directly in front of her, a large black door stood slightly ajar. To her right, another door stood and written on it in bold golden letters was a single word, RESIDENCES. The door on her left was plain and bare, and Kale noticed that, unlike the others, this door was bolted shut.

Seeing Kale look over the locked door, Derin spoke, "as you can see," he pointed to the door marked residences, "in there is where the trainees and some of the soldiers live. Straight ahead, here," Derin motioned for Kale to walk through the door in front of them, "this is where we do most of our training."

Kale quickly forgot the bolted door, as she walked into a large hall with ceilings so high she found herself dizzy while staring up at them. As she looked around the large square room, Kale again felt excitement surging through her. *This is where I'm going to train*, she thought.

Circling the perimeter of the room was a track. Lining the walls were areas covered in large cupboards and, when she asked about them, Derin told her that they contained training equipment and some of the weapons they used to practice or train. He made a point of telling Kale that none of the cupboards were accessible without a key and that a novice wouldn't even know how to use the weapons anyhow. Kale ached to put him in his place, to tell him she could pick locks and that she'd used almost every weapon found on the continent. But that was her ego talking and, if she managed to get through this day alive, she would need to keep it in check or it would most certainly get her into trouble.

There were matted areas used for training, sparing, and wrestling. She watched as soldiers of all ages and skill levels engaged each other in differing kinds of combat. They moved skillfully and so in sync with one another that some of them seemed more to be dancing than fighting. Before joining the J'Kahl, she'd never really entertained the idea of learning how to fight 'properly' but standing there, awed and even inspired, it's all she could think about.

She could also see an area at the very back of the large room that contained workout equipment, weights, and another area reserved for target practice. She longed with everything she was to get started right away but Derin informed her that had been enough for her first day and led her out of the training facility.

Walking back towards the castle, Kale's anticipation for training was swallowed up by her certainty that Derin wasn't convinced she was there to train. Doubt started to bubble up inside her, then worry, then fear. She tried many times to coax him into conversation but Derin was lost deep in thoughts he was unwilling to abandon or share. All the way to her room, he met her attempts at conversation with silence or single word answers. Finally, Kale began to face the prospect of not being able to fulfill her mission.

Of course, she could stop him, or try, but there was a big difference between ending Caine's life for the betterment of Berdune and ending Derin's life because she'd screwed up. She cursed herself silently. She'd worked so hard to get here, to get close enough to stop Caine, and now her heart had betrayed her. Again.

Their time had been short together but Kale liked Derin. He was strong, smart, and extremely attentive to the questions she asked with sincere enthusiasm. She felt drawn to him for reasons other than those as well. Derin had an undercurrent of sadness running through him. He seemed out of place somehow in the compound, in the castle, in his life. He always had that look of someone who is lost, even in amongst all the confidence and ease. For some reason, it drew Kale to him more than she'd ever been drawn to anyone. He reminded Kale of someone she knew or had known but, no matter how hard she struggled to remember, she couldn't figure out who.

He made her forget that he was Caine's son. He was so gentle, kind, and careful with her. Yet, he was the young man Caine had raised and so, if he stood in her way, if he stood by

Caine's side, he was an enemy of Kale's. At the end of the day, she would have to be able to destroy him if it meant Caine's destruction would follow.

Now, sitting in her room, waiting, she thought again of Derin and wondered if, in a different life, they could have been friends or more. Kale wondered if the sadness that swam in his eyes had been with him always. She wondered as well, somewhat guiltily, if there was any way to cure it. She felt ashamed for thinking of Derin when she should have been thinking of the friends and people she'd failed and put in danger because of it.

She decided then she would try to find a weapon and kill Caine now, before it was too late. She would be killed, of course, but there was a small chance she could get to him. If he thought her so insignificant that he'd let down his guard for a few moments, it might be enough. *There's a chance*, she thought, getting to her feet, ready to find anything she could to use against him.

That's when the quiet knock came at her door. She sunk back down onto the bed and tried to sit straight and tall. She was too late. "Come in," she called. Her voice sounded small and scared.

The door to Kale's room opened, slowly, and, when she saw who was there, she was both surprised and fearful.


TWENTY-NINE

Kayla sat beside Max and felt her insides mimic the rolling waves. Max was three years older than she and had lived in Emery his entire life. He was extremely intelligent, exhaustingly kind, and infinitely compassionate. As much as Kayla noticed all the differences between them, she couldn't help but want to find out if there was anything they had in common.

They'd been seated in comfortable silence for a long time, staring out at the ocean, Kayla enjoying the tranquility that it washed over her, Max watching the waves, as if hypnotized.

"Why did you really jump off that cliff the other day, Kayla?"

Kayla was silent for a long moment, trying to recall what she'd felt, what she'd been thinking, when she'd leapt off the cliff. When the answer came, she finally spoke, "Have you ever forgotten how to love life?"

He smiled at her. "I guess I have, but I never threw myself off a cliff because of it."

Kayla smiled. "That just happened to be where I was when I decided I wanted to remember loving life again, that's all. I didn't really think about the consequences of jumping off the cliff. I was thinking about the consequences of forgetting how to live. Do you know what I mean?"

Max didn't look like he did but replied anyway, "I think so. Maybe."

"I know I don't know much," Kayla continued, "but I think I've figured out that life is about fear. Fearing death is what makes life so exhilarating. Like people who jump out of planes or climb mountains...maybe they've just become bored with the fear of death that accompanies everyday life. Maybe they're just looking for more fear. I guess I just wanted to be afraid again, so I could want to live, so I could enjoy living."

Max gave her a searching stare as if he hadn't expected that answer from her.

"How did you lose your fear then?"

"I gave it away," she replied, "I sold it to feed an addiction I didn't even know I had." Kayla looked down at the twinkling sand and felt herself slipping back to the place where she went when she was sad. It was a lonely place that only existed in her mind and her heart but she visited it often. The day began to swim out of focus around her. She found herself afloat on her loneliness, a sea of solitude where she couldn't be reached. She could hear the distant crashing of the waves and somewhere someone was speaking her name.

"Kayla? Kayla!"

She was snapped back to the warm day and blinked furiously in an attempt to banish her confusion.

"What? Sorry, just thinking back. Remembering."

Kayla's sadness was more than a feeling. Present since as far back as she could remember, her sadness had become a place, and she wasn't sure whether she would ever forget the way there.

"I asked you what you were addicted to."

"Oh," Kayla replied trying to find the words to explain, "I was addicted to being perfect." Kayla looked up from the sand and into his shining blue eyes. She hadn't noticed before how much they resembled the sea; deep, mysterious, constantly churning. "You look confused, Max."

He smiled at her in a way that made Kayla sure he wanted nothing more than to understand her no matter how confused he looked. "I thought you were talking about a drug or something, that's all."

"Actually," she paused and in that instant realized that it was the first time ever she was speaking about what she'd gone through. "I was addicted to a drug, but that was long after I found myself addicted to perfection." Kayla laughed, "Now you really look confused."

Max, still smiling, reached down and took her hand in his. It was the simplest and most intimate gesture she'd experienced in a long time. "I just want to understand."

Despite the warmth that the touch of his hand brought to hers, Kayla remained calm and cool.

Max said nothing more. He just sat there holding her hand in his and watching the waves. Kayla wasn't sure how but she knew that he was waiting for her to tell him the whole story. He nudged her heart open a little with that kindness of him waiting for her to be ready. She wondered if she was. It had been a long time since she'd left the drugs but, most days, it felt like only moments. She knew that's how time worked. She'd lost count of how many awful moments in the past few years had stretched on and on as if infinite. And, the good moments were too often gone in the blink of an eye.

"I was born perfect," Kayla said and fought off the euphoric feeling that came to her when she spoke about herself, her secrets. "My whole life was perfect. I loved it and hated it all at once." She stopped. Staring off towards the horizon with what seemed like conviction and watching her,

Max was sure she was staring farther than his eyes could see. She went on.

"I guess I just needed not to be perfect anymore, you know? I just wanted to be a normal person. So, I started doing things a perfect person would never do. I started partying and drinking and doing drugs. It was great, not being perfect. It was so wonderful."

"How is a person born perfect?"

"Well, that's just what my parents always thought. I could never do anything wrong. I was the most perfect creature the world had ever seen in my father's eyes. He always told me I deserved the world laid down at my feet. When he left a few years ago, I didn't want to be that girl anymore, his girl."

Kayla's voice had taken on a strange tone and Max couldn't at first figure out what it was. Soon, he realized that Kayla was ashamed but he didn't know whether it was because of the drugs or something far more profound and out of reach.

Kayla went on, "I just wanted to be normal. I didn't want to become a drug addict but somewhere along the way that's what happened. I was so in love with the idea of the lifestyle and so in love with the idea of not being my father's daughter." She paused, breathed deep. "It all seemed so romantic from the outside looking in. But, when I found myself inside that life, it was nothing like I thought it would be. And before I could do anything about it, I'd replaced one addiction with another. I guess I just got lost. No, I was always lost. It was never me. But I stopped looking, stopped trying to find myself."

Max could feel her pulling slightly at his hand. He'd not for a moment looked away while she was speaking and he'd seen the fear and regret building in her like a storm.

"Don't," he whispered. "Don't run away from me, too."

Kayla stopped, astounded. *Had he really understood what it was she'd become? Had he understood what she still was because of what she'd endured and brought down upon herself? Had he understood she hadn't wanted to run? That's just all she knows how to do.*

"So, how did you get away from the drugs then?" he asked.

Looking directly into his eyes as if abandoning the fear that had held her back for so long, she answered him honestly, "Fear."

Max let the silence stretch out between them. He wanted to give her space and time even as he yearned to find out more about her. He wanted to keep from scaring her away, but he also had this sense that there wasn't a lot of time to be had with Kayla, as if she was slipping away from him somehow, even as she opened up to him and began to bridge the space between them. Max didn't know what it was, but it nagged at him. It was strange and unsettling and left him feeling off balance.

There was a distance in Kayla. No matter how badly he wanted to get to know her, something about her, some strangeness he'd never come across in another person before, made him certain she was one of those people who disappeared out of your life without a trace. Someone you always fell for, loved even, desperate to be their anchor, she was someone who always left and, in their aftermath, you were never really sure if they'd ever really been there.

Max found himself worrying as he never had before. He'd always been confident and sure of himself in most matters, dating being one of them. He was far from arrogant but he knew when there was chemistry, and when there wasn't. He knew when to try and turn on the charm, and when to accept defeat. Yet, Kayla threw him entirely off balance. She was a kind of storm he'd never come across before, she'd thrown him off course, and he wasn't quite sure if he'd get his bearings back again. He'd just met her and knew almost nothing about her but at the same time he knew it meant something that she was confiding in him. He wasn't sure what, but he knew what he hoped it was.

He was drawn to her in a way that undid him a little. She seemed both fragile and strong so that in one moment he wanted to lean on her for support and in the next wanted to scoop her up and protect her. She was strong, stronger than she knew, but still seemed breakable, as if you needed to handle her with care or she'd slip through your hands and shatter. She confused Max and he wondered how it was that he'd never met another girl as strange or wonderful as Kayla.

"Kayla," Max waited for Kayla to look up at him and meet his eyes, "what were you so afraid of? I mean, shouldn't you give yourself more credit? You've been clean for how long now?"

"Clean for a year and, no, I don't deserve an ounce of credit. I went mad and somewhere within my madness, in a rare moment of clarity, I realized I'd given myself to a drug instead of having found myself. I realized I was nothing and even less than that because I'd emptied myself out to make room for my addiction. I knew it was killing me. That I wouldn't make it much longer if I kept at it. I finally got scared. Scared of dying. Scared of so many nameless things I can't even now tell you what they are. Scared that my father would never pay for all he's done, and I would never get to be the person to make him pay."

Kayla let go of Max's hand and he watched her eyes glaze over as if she'd memorized these lines and was simply reciting them.

"I am afraid of nothing more than letting my father win. Nothing," she repeated to make her point. "So you see, my reason for quitting was not one of strength or conviction. I was a coward." She spat the words out and, as much as Max wanted to contest them, he could tell Kayla was unable to see any differently.

"I was ready to get better and I wanted to get better, that's true, but I just wasn't strong enough to get better...not without the fear and my hatred for him."

Again, silence enveloped them and it seemed the ocean took its turn in the conversation. The waves slammed into the shore as the tide began to turn. The foaming water crawled up the beach toward them, then sulked back down and away to rejoin the rabid sea, leaving them untouched.

Looking at him again, Kayla spoke. The haze had finally lifted from her eyes. "So, enough about me, tell me about yourself."

Max let out a short laugh. He hadn't drunk in nearly enough of her, but he could hear in her voice and see in the heavy slump of her shoulders that she'd emptied herself out as much as she could for the time being.

"I don't know if I can tell you anything more interesting than what you've told me, but I'll try," he said and paused, bit his bottom lip, an enticing habit that drew Kayla's eyes towards it for just a moment before she caught herself. "Let's see," he said, and then he went on.

As Max spoke, Kayla studied him closely. A mixture of interest and regret moved within her. His black hair was being tossed wildly about by the wind. Every now and then she would look from him to a stray strand bouncing erratically with the breeze. It seemed to her as if it danced wildly in front of his eyes trying to get his attention, but he took no notice. He spoke of how he hadn't left Emery to go to university though he could have. How an ailing mother had kept him at home willingly. He spoke of how he'd had a scholarship to more than one school and, how every once in awhile, he did regret passing it up though he hated himself for that regret.

Max spoke with sadness when he mentioned rekindling his desire to return to school and get a degree. His mother's illness would soon steal her from the world and she'd made him promise he would go. He hated to look forward to it for even a moment because then she'd be gone. Max told Kayla things he would never have said aloud to another human being, not even the friends he'd had since childhood. He couldn't help it but, with every passing minute, he'd revealed a little more of his soul to Kayla, the girl he was absurdly certain would break his heart.

Kayla couldn't help herself. She enjoyed his company and already felt a deep and unsettling bond with him. He was the first person she'd felt comfortable enough with to divulge her thoughts and some of her secrets to. A weight had been lifted from her and she felt she owed that in great part to Max.

Still, there was sadness. She was certain that she could never become what he'd want her to. Kayla had never had a boyfriend. She'd never known how. She'd spent so much time throughout her life pretending to be someone she wasn't, and she was terrified she would love someone enough to be everything they needed her to be. She still couldn't trust herself to be herself because Kayla had yet to figure out who that was.

As the sun traced its path through the sky, Kayla listened to Max, rapt with attention. She couldn't know that he felt much the same about her. And yet they were different in one fundamental way. While Max was thinking about how to keep Kayla around, Kayla was thinking about how she would get out of the situation without a broken heart and without breaking one in turn.

Kayla was afraid. She'd said fear was life so maybe she was finally living. The question wasn't simply, 'would she like it once she'd tried it,' but 'was she even right about fear and living?'

THIRTY

"Kale, come with me, please."

Kale stood and swayed a little. Only now when the time had come for her judgment to be passed did she realize how scared she really was. Walking through the halls, she felt like she was walking through a dream. Her legs felt weak and strange, and it took all of her energy to put one foot in front of the other without stumbling. Everything around her looked glossy and yet blurred, as if she was seeing it all from far away but also through a pane of glass. She focused her attention on the stone floor in front of her, afraid to look up, silently wishing she had the strength to get through what was coming.

They went out the front doors of Caine's castle and headed towards the military training compound.

"Look," Kale finally said hoping she sounded braver than she felt, "where are you taking me?"

"It isn't safe to talk in the castle, so we're going for a walk."

They passed the training compound and headed for the trees and as they walked Kale began to hope that today her life would be spared. She stayed silent as long as she could but once through the tree line Kale spoke again.

"Look, you're only here for one of two reasons, so which one is it?" She felt bolder and braver now that she'd been allowed to live this long but she was still uncertain and needed to find out fast what was going on. If her cover was blown, she wanted to know.

"I know you're not here just to join the J'Kahl. I saw you with those people in town Kale. There is no part of you that belongs in the service of Caine. I've never in my life met a person who seems to belong to no one as much as you do," Derin said and stopped himself and took a deep breath before beginning again. "So, we're at an impasse here, aren't we? I know you're not here for the reasons you say you are and I doubt you're going to trust me with the truth, so I'm going to tell you what it is we're going to do."

Kale was again contemplating her luck and this time how it might have turned in her favor. She couldn't help the wave of gratitude that washed through her for Derin and what he was doing for her even as she realized it made her weak. Worse, it changed the circumstances of her mission. For one thing, she was now in his debt. For another, she'd come to respect and like him, but she'd have to deceive him. It actually made her feel a little bit guilty, both knowing she'd have to do it, and knowing she'd be able to.

"You're going to leave and we're going to forget we ever knew each other." Derin composed himself hoping that his eyes didn't betray what he was actually feeling or thinking.

"I am not leaving!" Kale said angrily. "I've worked too hard to get here." Panic started to creep over her but she did her best to hide it. "I'm not leaving, you can bet on that. You'll have to turn me in first."

"Kale, you're not safe here. Whatever it is you're up to, you screwed up before you even got here, so why don't you quit while you're ahead? Do yourself a favor and go home."

"If you're so certain I'm here for the wrong reasons, why are you letting me go?"

"Because I'm not certain and I don't believe in killing innocent people like..." Derin let his words trail off.

"Go ahead, Derin, say it, *like your father*," Kale's voice was full of malice. She hated Caine more every minute and, knowing Derin was his son, made her hate him even more. "I'm not leaving."

"Give me one reason why I should let you stay...and live?"

"Well," the malice and contempt might have been gone but Kale spoke with a confidence that told Derin she already knew he wouldn't turn her in, "because I think you and I might be on the same side, that's why."

"You're wrong," Derin said, "I am a loyal follower of Caine's. I am..." he let his words trail off because he just didn't believe them anymore and he didn't have the energy to lie.

He thought back to when he'd stood outside of Caine's office and what he'd heard. He thought back to all the times he'd overheard other things or seen things that made his stomach turn but that he'd forced himself to ignore. He wasn't sure whether he could forgive himself but he knew for certain he would never forgive Caine.

"Derin," Kale stared at him intensely, "why am I staying in the main castle when most J'Kahl, especially the new recruits, stay in the training compound?"

Derin stared at Kale wide-eyed with shock. For a moment, it felt like the whole world dropped out from under him. He was so accustomed to trusting everything Caine did that he questioned nothing. But it was all starting to come together, a truth that had been right in front of him but that he'd been unwilling to see or face. Kale's question, what he'd heard Caine say earlier that day, and all the things he'd pretended not to see over the years, all came crashing together and Derin's world came tumbling down around him. It was enough to make him understand he knew nothing about his adoptive father except maybe that he was not to be trusted.

"I don't know Kale, but it's definitely a first. I remember your parents and they were in his inner circle for awhile but they weren't that close with Caine. I'm not sure I understand what's going on here but let's not wait to find out. I'm asking you to leave. You're not safe here. Caine will kill you if he finds out what you're really doing."

"And, what is it you think I'm really doing here, Derin?"

"I don't know," Derin sighed deeply and let his shoulders sag with defeat, "but I have a feeling that whatever it is you're doing is a lot better than what I've been doing."

Derin turned away from Kale and started walking. He had a heavy weight on his shoulders that hadn't been there moments before. Derin paused and looked up into the night sky, newly arrived. He sighed again. When he spoke, Kale could tell he was speaking less to her and more just to hear his troubled thoughts aloud. "Darkness is coming. For many people, this won't end well. Things are really going to change. I can tell."

"Derin?"

"Do what you want, Kale. I'll come to get you in the morning to take you down to breakfast. If you're smart you'll be long gone. If you're not, then we'll start your training tomorrow."

Kale stared after him as he began to disappear into the darkness of the forest.

"So, that's it? This is all forgotten then?" she asked skeptically.

Derin stopped and turned and Kale wished she could see his eyes so that she might have understood what was going on behind them.

"No, that's not it, but I don't know what's next. And, Kale," he paused and took another deep breath, "he's still my father. If you try to hurt him, I will stop you any way I can. Goodnight."

Kale waited until she could no longer hear him making his way back towards the castle through the woods and then she let her breath out. Shaken, she stood for a long time wondering what she'd gotten herself into. She couldn't help smiling to herself as she thought of her best friend and wondered if Medea would be having fun in her place. *Probably*, Kale thought, *no, definitely*.

Before moving, she looked up to the night sky and drank in the stars. "Things are really going to change." That's what Derin had said and Kale believed him.

Walking back to the castle alone, Kale considered that she really wasn't sure what she'd gotten herself into. She definitely hadn't figured Derin into the equation and whether she wanted to admit it or not he made a difference in how she proceeded.

Later, lying in bed, Kale thought back over the day. A week ago she never would have imagined that she'd be laying in a bed inside of Caine's castle, waiting for sleep. She thought about the training she would be starting the next day and felt a surge of excitement go through her. She would never have told her friends but she was looking forward to learning the ways of the J'Kahl. She planned on learning as much as she could as quickly as possible.

The last thing that tumbled through her mind, as sleep came, calling for her, was Derin. She was thoroughly intrigued by him. Before coming she'd actually known quite a bit about him. What her parents hadn't told her years before, Jaren's contacts had filled in. She wished she'd known what he looked like. She could have avoided their morning talk at Sunshine Bay and thus avoided having him suspect her motives, avoided as well the strange but palpable connection that had formed between them almost instantly and threatened to derail her plans. She refused to try and understand or acknowledge how she felt about him, but it made her weak and vulnerable none the less. She needed to be strong and she knew it. Yet, as she slipped off to sleep, Derin's face lingered in her mind.


THIRTY-ONE

Kayla woke up to bright beautiful sunlight and for the first time in what felt like forever it matched her mood. Talking openly about some of the things she'd gone through had brought to her a kind of peace she'd thought was lost forever. The fact she'd talked about them with Max, well, that washed a different kind of peace over her, one she hadn't known before.

Thinking about Max, she smiled. She couldn't wait to see him again. She closed her eyes and let the picture of him hover behind the black of her eyelids. It wasn't until the irresistible smell of pancakes and coffee drifted into her room that Kayla got out of bed and followed her nose downstairs.

"Well, you're up early this morning," her aunt greeted her with a smile as she walked into the kitchen. "Sleep well, Kayla?"

Kayla smiled at her aunt and perched herself on the counter. "I slept better than I have in a long time actually," she replied.

"Coffee?" her aunt asked her.

"Oh, god, yes."

Kayla's aunt poured her a cup of coffee and handed it to her. Kayla set it aside and jumped down from the counter then took a seat at the table. Sipping her coffee, Kayla sat silently leafing through the paper her uncle had left on the kitchen table. She did this both out of curiosity and out of habit. Always looking for something to distract her from any kind of intimacy that might lead places she wasn't yet ready to go.

"Anything good in there?" her aunt asked, putting a plate of steaming pancakes in front of her.

"Nothing but bad news really," Kayla replied, "always bad news. The world seems filled with darkness." She shivered, a deep and chilling sense of foreboding snaking through her for just a moment before it was gone.

"Well," her aunt said, "some things never change." Sitting down at the table across from her, she added, "then again, Kayla, some things do."

Kayla sensed a lecture coming on but waited to let her aunt speak. She'd learned, in the two years she'd partied and done drugs, once you'd unleashed a slew of disappointments on people, you owed them the courtesy of letting them tell you how it made them feel. It was easiest as well. That heavy piling on of guilt and shame so that the other person could feel lighter and vindicated.

"Kayla, I know you've been through a rough time. You've always been a special person and sometimes life throws the most crap at special people. You're unique, and that's not an easy thing to be. But, your mother and I both love you very much so just try and remember that. Try and remember that you belong to someone..."

Her aunt went on, but Kayla had stopped listening.

The dream.

Kayla often had her nightmares during the night and woke full of terror trying to escape them. Many times, she was sucked right back into that dream world and woke in the morning completely unaware of what had happened. Most days, that's how it was. Only when she woke during the daytime from her nightmares did she remember them right away. Usually, she remembered the dreams later. A single word or smell or even a specific colour could jolt her memory. Today, she was unable to grab hold of the dream long enough to understand it. She'd been very scared within it, scared for her life. She knew that much.

As her aunt's voice echoed through the distance, she fumbled for the memory of the nightmare she'd had the night before. She reached for it and tried to grab hold so that it didn't slip back into the oblivion of all that had come and gone and lay forgotten. Frustrated, with herself, with not understanding why it was happening and what it meant, she gave up. The harder she struggled, the further away it drifted out of reach. It was the same every time. She knew that much. There was always a chance the dream would return to her later on. She hoped so. The more frequent they became, nightly now, the more certain she was it all meant something, if she could just find a way to understand and put it all together.

Despite the fact she could remember nothing about it, the dream lingered. It pulled at her, haunting. A longing to reclaim it washed over her and she had to struggle to draw her focus back to her aunt.

"Just don't be afraid to ask for help or advice, okay?" her aunt was finishing. "If you need to talk, if you don't want to talk, just remember, I'm here for you, okay, Kayla?"

Kayla smiled at her aunt gratefully, "I will remember that, I promise. And Aunt Helen," Kayla looked down at the half-eaten pancake on her plate.

"Yes, dear."

"I'm sorry if I didn't act like I already knew that, okay?"

"No need for apologies, Kayla. Fresh start, okay?"

Sitting at the table across from her aunt, Kayla finally believed that she was loved. She felt no nearer to her mother or her aunt, she would never feel any closer to them because Kayla would always be somewhere else in a sense, ever hovering just out of reach. She finally felt comfortable knowing people loved her despite what she'd chosen to become only two years before.

Kayla felt happy and, for the first time in a long time, she welcomed it, just breathed it in until she was full of it. She still toiled with thoughts of whether she deserved to be happy or not, but it felt so right that for now she simply accepted it.

THIRTY-TWO

Medea woke in her bed with the morning sunlight prodding at her gently to start her day. Her first awareness, of Ryan's strong arms wrapped firmly around her, drew a sleepy smile to her lips. Lying next to him, she felt like the whole world made sense and that somehow everything would work out because there were still things were worth living and fighting for. She immediately thought of Kale, alone in Caine's compound, not that far away, but out of reach. Medea wondered what her best friend was doing, how she was feeling, and if she missed any of them or if like always she'd become completely focused on the task at hand at the expense of everything else. If she did, it wouldn't have surprised Medea. Kale was the one out of all them who fought the hardest, and yet she was the one who kept the most distance between herself and the world so that in a strange and ironic way it seemed she had the least to fight for.

As Medea blinked the haze of sleep out of her eyes, mind weaving its way towards darker thoughts, Ryan stirred beside her. He turned his face towards hers and smiled as he opened his eyes.

"Good morning, beautiful."

"That's just what I like to hear when I first wake up. Be careful, Ry, I might ask you to stay more often."

"Good. I like this. I like feeling this close to you. I wish I felt this way more often."

"I wish you did, too, but..."

Ryan interrupted, "Don't. No talk about Caine or this crazy mission, or any of it, okay?"

"Crazy mission, huh? Too much danger and adventure for you?"

"Danger I could live without, yeah, sorry. If living in Caine's Berdune has taught me anything, it's that danger is one step away from a life snuffed out. Now, I do like adventure. Loving you for example is one hell of a crazy adventure and for some reason I just can't resist."

"Love is an adventure?"

"The greatest adventure of them all," he said with a sly smile.

"Well, I was talking about what we're doing to stop..."

"Medea, please, not that, not now. This is too perfect to ruin."

"You're right. I'm sorry. How often do we get some time all to ourselves when the rest of the world doesn't quite matter?"

"Actually, I think this is the first time ever, so we're going to enjoy it. If I have anything to say about it, we're going to stay in bed all day."

"Right until the sun goes down?"

"No. Until it comes up again tomorrow."

They both laughed, a delightful sound in a world that didn't hear enough of it anymore. They were free, for a little while at least, from their everyday lives and worries. Ryan leaned over and kissed Medea gently on the lips. It was a perfect moment, interrupted almost immediately.

Downstairs, the front door flew open and slammed against the wall. Startled, Medea sat up in bed and was out of it a moment later. In a panic, she pulled on the pair of jeans that were lying on the floor next to the bed.

"Ryan!" Sam's voice came hurtling up the stairs. "Ryan! Ryan!"

"Sam, what's wrong? What is it?"

As Medea was throwing on a shirt, she could hear Jaren already questioning Sam downstairs. Ryan already had his pants on and was running out the door. Medea was just a few steps behind him, a lump in her throat and a sinking feeling in her stomach. When they got down the stairs, Sam threw herself into her brother's arms sobbing hysterically.

"Oh, Ryan. Oh, Ryan," she let out between sobs.

"What is it Sam? What's wrong? Tell me."

"I found them. I found them, Ry. They looked so scared. God, it was awful."

"Who? Who did you find, Sam?"

"Mom and Dad. They're dead. I found them just now. I came right here," Sam looked at Jaren and then Medea. "I came here. I didn't know where else to go. Oh, god. Oh, god." Words, rapid fire, like bullets from a gun continued to burst from her, "I saw them. They looked so scared." She repeated herself.

Corin appeared at the top of the stairs, rubbing his tired eyes. "What the hell is going on?"

"You're here?" Medea scolded. "My god, you could sleep through the end of the world."

"Medea. Not the time," Jaren said sternly as Corin made his way down the stairs.

When Corin saw Sam sobbing and Ryan holding her tightly in his arms as she rambled, he stayed quiet, his eyes bright and awake as his mind began to assess and plan.

Jaren gave out the orders, "Ryan, why don't you take her into the living room and see if you can calm her down. Corin, will make you some coffee? I'm going to make some calls and see if I can find out what's going on here." Medea looked to Jaren who was motioning her into the kitchen. Corin followed.

"Something isn't right about this," Jaren offered as soon as they were in the kitchen. Neither Medea nor Corin disagreed. They were both thinking the same thing. Coincidences were the worst thing to come upon when you were hiding something and Sam and Ryan had been hiding a lot from their parents.

THIRTY-THREE

Kale woke to the sound of birds chirping outside of her window. Once again, when she rolled over and found herself in a stranger's bed, she panicked, completely confused. First, she remembered where she was. Then, she remembered all that had happened the day before. *If so much had happened in a day, what could be next?* she thought with a mixture of excitement and concern.

She got out of bed, got dressed, and then sat down to wait for Derin or whoever it was coming to get her for breakfast. Kale's mind went instinctively to Sunshine Bay. She already missed her morning meetings with her father. She longed not only for the days when she spent the early morning hours at the bay talking to the memory of him but the days when he'd actually been there with her. It felt like so long ago when things had been right. In only fourteen years, Berdune had become a place Kale no longer recognized. She thought of the Mission and wondered if her friends were getting on okay without her. She wished she could stop in at Emily's and see how she was doing. She wanted to laugh with Mr. Wilson and Mr. Carlson. She wanted to visit the Westons and see if the medicine she'd taken them was helping. Kale wanted to go home but not as much as she wanted to destroy Caine. Nothing had or ever would be more important than that.

It had been this way as far back as Kale could remember. Even as a child, she'd harbored a deep mistrust of Caine. She'd always been able to see, when looking at him, the kind of man who would betray those he swore to love and who could hurt anyone who stood in the way of his quest for power and control. She'd never bothered to question why she reacted so strongly to him, why his destruction had come to consume most of her life and energy, but sitting on her bed in the castle, drawing so close to a goal she'd dreamed of for more years than she could recall, she let her thoughts wander that way.

When someone knocked at the door, Kale let herself be drawn back to the moment and the task at hand. Her thoughts were quickly forgotten. As she opened it and greeted

Derin, all she could think about was her training and finding out what Caine was up to in the here and now.

"Ready for breakfast, Kale?" Derin asked. His voice betrayed the disappointment he felt finding her there. Truly, he'd known in his heart she wasn't going to run and save herself like he'd pleaded with her to do. There was a part of him that was relieved she was still there. He'd lost sleep the night before trying to imagine what his life looked like both with and without her, and he'd had trouble imagining both.

"I've been up for awhile actually. I'm a morning person. I usually get up early..." Kale stopped herself. It had only taken a moment to forget that if she wanted to be successful it meant keeping distance between herself and Derin despite that strange magnetic pull that demanded otherwise. Far too much was at stake, she reminded herself.

Derin didn't ask her to finish what she was saying and Kale offered nothing more. She followed him out of the room and they walked in silence down towards the dining hall. Kale noticed that Derin always stayed a few feet away from her and never looked her way unless he had to. She tried not to be charmed by his discomfort around her but Derin continued to tug her away from common sense and reason. A warning began to sound deep inside her that she would have to do something about it or risk losing everything she'd worked for.

When they entered the dining hall, Kale felt all eyes shift their way and then follow her and Derin as they made their way towards the head table. Voices hushed and conversations stopped. She wondered if this was the normal reception he received or if it was she who'd drawn the eyes and attention of the entire room.

"Kale, my dear, so good to see you. You will join me at my table of course?" Caine phrased it like a question, but Kale knew it was an order. She had the urge to tell him to drop dead but instead answered him with a bowed head.

"Of course, my lord."

Kale and Derin followed him over to his large table and sat down. Immediately, Caine began to make introductions.

"Kale has just joined the J'Kahl, and she will be staying here in the castle while she trains." Eyebrows were raised at this comment but Caine went on, seemingly unaware. "I believe you knew her parents well," Caine turned and addressed the two other people seated at their table.

"Ah, really?" one of them asked.

"Yes," replied Caine, "this is Kale Pitall. You remember the Pitalls, don't you?"

Kale again had the feeling of being toyed with. Looking at Caine, she saw that same childish grin on his face. *I know something you don't know*, it seemed to say, and Kale wanted nothing more than to remove it with her fist. *Soon*, she thought, *be patient, Caine, I will destroy you soon.*

"I'm sorry," Kale said, "I don't know who you are." Even as she said it, she began to see the similarities. "Should I?"

Caine laughed airily, delighted with whatever game he was playing. "I have forgotten my manners, not a morning person really." He gestured toward the two people sitting to his right, "Kale, this is Mason, and this is Lauren, the McLevys, but we're all on a first name basis here."

Kale hoped that the shock that ran through her didn't show before she'd managed to compose herself. As she sat down to eat her meal, a thought ran through her mind for just a moment before she dismissed it, that Caine was a man she'd underestimated. Throughout the meal, she glanced nervously toward the McLevys as often as she dared. They couldn't know who she really was but she knew all too well who they were. Kale had heard often of them because she knew someone who hated them deeply. She knew someone who hoped one day to destroy their faith in Caine in particular. She knew them only because they were Jaren's parents.

THIRTY-FOUR

Kayla sat on the sand and stared intently at her journal. She knew what she wanted to write but every time she brought her pen to the page her hand began to shake uncontrollably. All she'd managed to put on the paper so far were a few shaky scribbles.

*This is silly,* she thought, *it's time to face the past so I can finally move on.* She held her pen intently, wanting to convince herself she was ready to remember what it was she'd forgotten for so long. Finally, she was ready, and so she began to write.

Kayla wrote first about how a father who'd never really seemed present had finally left altogether when she was fifteen, almost four years ago now. She wrote about how that rejection had scarred her deeply and how it had pushed her to find a way to numb the pain and defy the man who'd created it. She wrote about her mother and how she was unable to acknowledge that her daughter was hurting in light of her own suffering. When she'd approached her mother in hopes of sharing their pain, the gap between them had only widened even though Kayla had thought, or maybe just hoped, that it would shrink.

When she later tried to open up and told her mother about the drugs and why she thought she'd fallen victim to them, her mother couldn't believe that Kayla was that weak or that willing to give up hope. When she'd spoken about the long bouts of depression she'd endured growing up, her mother refused to believe that Kayla had been anything but a happy child. She'd been happy, it's true, but the sadness running through her is a river born further back than she can remember. In a way, Kayla had revealed herself in hopes her mother could help carry her pain but she'd had too much already to carry on her own.

Shortly after telling her mother the truth, Kayla was sent away. Her mother claimed Kayla needed to heal away from her and the life she'd chosen. Kayla left without a struggle because she was too weak to stand up for herself and too hurt to want to be near her mom.

Kayla had always thought her mother didn't love her; blaming Kayla for the fact that her father had left. As Kayla wrote, seated on the shore, purging herself of her past pain and anguish, she realized her mother had always loved her and what made her hurt was that she would never understand who or what her daughter was.

The hurt and anger between them was a wound reopened again and again, now unable to heal. The past can be set right if you simply lay it down and move along. What they'd both needed, what her mother had given them, was time. What she'd forgotten to consider was that the only certainty there was about time, was that it always running out.

All Kayla had ever wanted was to be the daughter she was expected to be, to make her parents happy and proud, and to not have it be so hard. It was time to set herself free.

Kayla looked up from her journal and out into oblivion, beyond the waves, beyond the horizon, beyond the golden day. Again, her sadness took her and she floated away from the world into her loneliness.

She wondered where her father was. It had been so long since Kayla had heard from him and she like everyone else had come to believe he might be dead. She wanted to be angry with him, but it was hard to be angry with someone you worried about and missed so much. He'd been a selfish and selfless man all at once and Kayla both adored and despised him. She wished he'd never left them. As much as she was unsure whether they were better off without him, she couldn't help but think the world would be a different place if he'd stayed.

Her ears began to ring with the sadness welling up within her and it soon began to spill from her, first through her tears and then in muffled sobs. She shrank into a ball holding her knees to her head, trying to hide her shame. No one was around to see how weak she was, but she knew it, and that was enough to make her angry. *If I ever find you, Dad, I will make you understand what you've done to me.*

The sound of the ocean crashed around her as her grief crashed within. Her open journal lay forgotten on the sand, the pages rustling in the salty breeze. The journal had been a form of healing for Kayla as she spilled her thoughts and feelings onto its pages with devotion. Now, it was time for a deeper healing. It was time to let go.

THIRTY-FIVE

"Derin, you can meet Kale in the training facility. I have something I would like to discuss with her before you get started."

Derin frowned but turned without speaking and left the dining hall. Caine rose and Kale did the same. He turned from the table and began walking towards the door, and Kale trailed along behind him hoping that was what she was supposed to do.

She'd already come to dislike Caine, the man, as much as she hated Caine, the savior and ruler. He treated everyone like they were slaves, even those he claimed he loved. Kale couldn't figure out how no one had noticed he was more human than most men. He was selfish, immature, rude, uncaring, vengeful, petty, and egotistical. He hid it all under an intimidating veneer of arrogance. Kale struggled to understand how anyone believed he was their savior, the chosen one.

Caine led Kale down dimly lit passageways and narrow hallways, turning this way and that with no sense of purpose, and she was certain he was again playing games. Finally, they came to a towering foyer and Kale saw that lining the walls were pictures of Caine himself in different poses. *I hate him*, she thought, *god, I hate him.*

"This is where I come to think, Kale. This is where I find some of my peace. Have you found yours yet, peace, I mean?" Caine turned to face her, and she saw a wild and seething madness in his eyes that made her frightened of both him and what he was capable of. She was still certain that Derin hadn't betrayed her, not yet, but what she wasn't certain of was what Caine wanted with her.

"I have taken a liking to you, Kale." He watched the look of shock that leapt onto her face and laughed, "I don't really understand it myself but it's true." He paused and began pacing the room before he spoke again, "Have you ever had the feeling that you've known someone forever?" Kale had experienced the feeling but it had never been toward Caine. She had one emotion reserved for him and that was hatred, as old as the first moments of his arrival.

Not waiting for her reply, Caine continued, "Maybe you're so much like," Caine took a deep breath, "your parents," he paused again, "that I can't help but take an instant liking to you."

Caine sneered unconsciously and Kale pretended not to notice. *What the hell is going on here?* she thought, panic rising up inside her.

"Maybe it's that you remind me of someone I knew long ago." Suddenly his demeanor changed and Kale saw a weak and lonely old man instead of the Caine she'd come to despise. "I had a daughter once. Did you know that Kale?"

"No, my lord, I did not?" Kale was confused. She didn't understand what Caine was getting at. She knew he must be playing games, but he seemed so vulnerable and so sincere all of a sudden.

"She would be grown by now, married, maybe even have a family I imagine. She's almost twice your age now." Caine brought a hand to his face and swiped at the tears that were threatening to fall. She was surprised that she found herself wanting to reach out to him as pity and then revulsion swam through her.

Caine continued, "You're a lot like her, you know. I remember when you were young." Caine looked off into the dim hallway, but it was obvious he was looking far into the past. He smiled and made a sound almost like a purring kitten wrapped in complete contentment. "You used to ask so many questions. No answer was enough. You wanted to know everything. You hated being treated like a child. You hated being answered like a child." Caine paused and, despite the fact she didn't want to participate in the demented scene taking place, Kale couldn't stop herself from speaking.

"You knew me as a child? You knew my parents way back then?'

"What?" Caine was drawn back to the hallway, the past long forgotten. He took one last swipe at his moistened eyes and then composed himself, "No. I didn't know them that far back. That's how they spoke of you later on. They were quite fond of you. They thought you a gift from god." Caine paused. "I tire of these memories quickly." He gave Kale a stern and unforgiving look as if she'd instigated the conversation.

"I'm sorry, my lord. I didn't mean to offend you."

"No bother. I just want you to know that I am giving you a chance I would not give most, so don't take it lightly. This kingdom, my kingdom, will be the greatest in the universe one day soon, and if you play things right, you will be a part of that. I'm offering you the world, Kale. I haven't met a single person who turned it down and did not suffered for their ignorance. So, be warned, betrayal will only end one way. Do not disappoint me, as this chance, this choice, will not present itself to you again."

Kale wasn't sure whether she should speak or wait for him to go on.

"Do you understand me?"

She bowed her head submissively, "yes, my lord, I understand."

Caine smiled lazily, and it seemed whatever game he was playing was over for the moment. "Good. Now, get over to the training facility. Derin will be waiting for you. I will see you at dinner." Caine again turned his back on Kale, and she understood this to mean she could go.

The whole way to the training facility, Kale's face burned with rage. Coming into this mission, she'd assured her friends she could keep herself under control in Caine's presence but she was beginning to think she'd been wrong. Something about him drove her crazy and the only image that flickered through her mind was one of wiping the smug and arrogant smile from his face. But, today, and even since arriving at the compound, she was seeing a side of Caine she thought impossible for him to possess. He was truly mad or he was merely a puppet and all Kale could wonder through her anger was that if that were true, then who was pulling the strings?

THIRTY-SIX

She stormed in to the training facility and, when she entered the main hall, she looked around for Derin. She spotted him in one of the back corners sparring with another guy who couldn't have been any older than she was. For a brief moment, Kale forgot her anger. Watching Derin move, the elegant and powerful agility, the strength, the speed, it stirred something in her so that she could feel a fluttering in her stomach and a pull that both delighted and confused her. Before she could shake the moment away, Derin's gaze shifted away from his opponent and met hers. Electricity and something else much deeper and more frightening passed between them. Kale gasped inaudibly. The other guy dropped low and swept Derin's feet out from under him. Derin hit the mat with a grunt and lay there as the other fighter beamed.

"Hey, that's the first time I've ever beaten you, Derin. You think I'm getting better or what?"

Derin sighed, "You didn't beat me, Symon. You just got lucky. Overconfidence will get you hurt or killed." With one swift motion, Derin kicked his feet in a windmill motion and the next second Symon was lying on the mat and Derin had a hand at his throat. "Hurt or killed," Derin repeated. He stood and walked over to the side of the ring to grab a drink. It gave him time to compose himself before he had to face Kale and whatever it was she shook loose in him. Kale made her way intently over to the sparring ring and stood waiting, suddenly restless to have a turn.

"You're one to talk about overconfidence," she said tauntingly.

Derin let out a short laugh, "Me? Do you know anything about yourself?"

Kale ignored the comment. "Ready to start training?" Kale smiled at him confidently. "You should have stayed down on that mat because I'm going to put you right back down there in just a few moments."

Derin laughed dismissively. Kale could feel the tension building and wanted nothing more than to spar. Behind Derin, Symon got to his feet and moved away from where they stood.

"Kale, I don't think you're ready for one-on-one combat training yet. I was thinking something more like some laps and some weight training. I mean, honestly, I don't really think you stand a chance in here," he spoke condescendingly and, though Kale knew he was baiting her, she took it just the same.

"You don't want to find out, Derin. There's a good chance I'm about to embarrass you."

Kale couldn't help it, she was thoroughly enjoying herself. She jumped into the ring with an agility that surprised both her and Derin. Eyes locked intently, they moved slowly to the center of the ring. Circling each other, the tension slowly grew until Kale thought she would scream if she couldn't hit out at him. She wasn't sure why but he was able to get under her skin with the smallest effort, in a way no one else had before. Just when she thought she would burst with anticipation, Derin struck out at her and, though she was sure he was holding back when the punch connected, she couldn't stay on her feet.

A moment on the ground was enough to make her realize she didn't want to end up there again. She jumped to her feet and within an instant Derin swung at her with lightning speed. Kale wasn't sure how but this time she avoided the punch. It was as if there was some kind of instinct deeply ingrained in her and only now was it waking up. She was far from as agile or as talented as Derin, yet she was quickly proving she could hold her own in the ring. She could see Derin was surprised by her skill but he wasn't nearly as surprised as Kale.

They fought for more than twenty minutes. Both of them drained completely yet unwilling to relent. Finally, an older man with graying hair at his temples came over to intervene. He would later introduce himself as Mike, one of the senior trainers in the J'Kahl, and someone Kale already knew through Jaren.

"Don't you think that's enough sparring for today, you two." It was not a question and both Derin and Kale heard the warning in it. The fight stopped.

Kale had to bend over to catch her breath. Her entire body burned with a fire that oscillated between aching and exhausted. Though she was ready to stand, she wasn't sure she could without passing out so she kept her hands on her knees and took deep, rasping breaths.

"You okay there, Kale? You're not looking so good. Maybe you should go back to your room and take a nap or something," Derin was speaking in between gasps for air and he'd yet to stand up entirely either.

Kale finally stood and fought hard to keep from losing consciousness. Black spots appeared in her line of sight and she squinted, frantic to gain control of herself. "Me. Ha. You fight like a girl. If you didn't look so pathetic right now, I'd kick your ass again." Kale was amazed at how ready she was to keep going, even if her body wasn't. There was something exhilarating about combat one-on-one, about that dance around the ring with Derin that made her wish she had it in her to keep going.

They stared at one another, both of them still bent over slightly and swaying. Something passed between them, some unspoken understanding, and simultaneously they began to laugh. It was another unguarded moment between them. When the magnetism was set loose, they landed perfectly in sync.

When the laughter died out, both Kale and Derin sat down in the ring and again made eye contact. Kale was unnerved. She'd yet to meet a single person with whom she felt so comfortable and with whom she felt so connected she didn't always need to speak. 'It makes you weak,' a voice inside her whispered, 'he makes you weak,' and she believed it.

Derin sat up and then stood slowly. He reached his hand toward Kale to help her from the ground but she ignored it. Derin smiled down at her but she didn't return it. She stood, slowly, on her own.

The world came back into existence around them and with it the awareness of how inappropriate their display had been. Those in the room who weren't staring at them disapprovingly were obviously making an extreme effort not to. Kale became instantly annoyed, then angry, both with herself and with Derin, wondering, if again, she'd wounded her chances of getting close to Caine.

Derin composed himself and spoke loudly so that as many soldiers as possible would hear him. "I think that's enough for now, Kale. We probably overdid it a bit. Let's get you back up to the castle for a break and some lunch, and we'll continue your training this afternoon."

Kale didn't respond. She merely followed Derin from the training hall and out the front doors. She was relieved to be away from the heavy stares of the other J'Kahl.

"That can't happen again, Derin. I have to make a good impression here. I want to do this right."

Derin stopped walking and turned towards her. "Do what's right, Kale? What is it that you're really doing here? I mean, I've been training Symon for over two years now and not once have we fought like that." He shook his head, mystified. "Where did you learn to fight like that?"

"I don't know," she shrugged, and he realized she wasn't just being modest.

Derin watched her with disbelief.

"I swear. I mean my father taught me to fight years ago and it just came back to me, I guess." She smiled. "And maybe making you look bad just suits me."

Derin suddenly felt awkward and vulnerable. He was reminded of the people he'd seen in town wanting to touch her but probably never really getting close enough to do it. "Why are you really here, Kale? Tell me, please."

Kale stopped smiling and asked, "You want me to trust you, son of Caine?"

"My father is dead," Derin spat and turned away from Kale to keep her from seeing the anguish and confusion that must have shown in his face. The silence stretched on around them, full and ripe. "I didn't mean that. I just meant...Damn it." Derin paused and took a few long, slow breaths. "Caine is a murderer. He kills innocent people just because he can. He's my father. He's raised me since I was a child. But sometimes he does things that I just don't understand, that scare me, and I've known all along. I've known all along what he was and I never tried to stop him. I never stood up to him and I knew he could be a monster."

"Do you remember your real parents, Derin?"

"I don't think so. I feel empty not knowing who they were. Like all the things I feel and want are part of who they were and, since I don't know them, I don't know myself."

Derin turned to Kale and she saw his cheeks were streaked with tears. Large watery bulbs hung on his lower eyelids poised to fall.

"I've never told anyone this," Kale began, "but I'm adopted, too. When I was five, just around the time you were."

"Really?"

"No one knows. My parents died with the secret but while they were alive they made me promise never to tell another person, ever. I don't know why they cared so much, but I was forbidden from ever mentioning it."

"So why are you telling me?"

"Because I know what it's like to feel like you're the only one on the entire planet who feels what you feel and who is going through what you're going through. I know what it's like to be alone in a crowded room, remember? And I really don't think you deserve the life you're living."

Kale had drawn slowly nearer to Derin as he stood fragile and shivering in the midday sun. She thought it was strange to see such a proud and strong warrior be reduced to such a vulnerable state. Yet, it made her like him even more. She realized that Derin was only nineteen and he'd been through far too much for a nineteen-year-old. It came to her then, possibly for the first time, she wasn't nineteen yet, and maybe all that she'd been carrying was far too much for her to admit. When finally aware of her own sorrow and solitude, standing there helplessly in front of Derin, seeing her own secret world reflected in his eyes, Kale felt weak and helpless too, and yet finally not alone.

That's when she kissed him. At first, it was a timid, gentle kiss, a kiss of kindness, a kiss of comfort. But then, the same electricity that had gripped them during their sparring match grabbed hold again and they both found themselves completely swept away by the current. Kale couldn't get enough of him and every time his hands traced a new path across her arms, back or hips, she felt herself dive a little deeper into wherever he was leading her. Derin felt like he couldn't catch his breath. Everywhere she touched him lit up as if coming alive for the very first time. The last thought he had before his mind went blank and he surrendered entirely was that she was bringing him to life somehow, in a way he'd never known was possible. Her lips traced a path across his jaw, down his neck, but always hurried back to meet his again. There were no thoughts, no words, just that certainty for both of them that home was a place you were meant to drown in.

Neither knew how long they stayed there locked in the embrace but at some point they found themselves merely clinging to one another fiercely. Two lost travelers in a violent and raging storm, trying not to get washed away. When the fiery passion that had first gripped them burned itself out, they felt danger quickly prying them apart.

"Damn it," Kale whispered, breathless. "We've got to be more careful Derin. That shouldn't have happened. That can't happen again." Kale stepped back from him and felt her body sway with a mixture of exhaustion and adrenaline. Looking into Derin's aching blue eyes she felt herself ache in response but still she began to pull away from him, letting a space open up between her heart and the world that felt both familiar and safe.

"Lunch," she said. "I think we've both had enough for today."

He took her hand in his and lifted it to his mouth, kissing her palm gently, before closing her fingers around the invisible gift. She let him, despite herself, one last chance to taste a little bit of something she knew in heart she could never have. After a long, drawn out moment she pulled away from him again. Standing just a few feet apart they walked back up to the castle to eat lunch, both trying to suppress what it was they were feeling. Neither did that very well. There was a storm raging between them and, if they weren't careful, the wreckage left in its wake would be worse than either of them could imagine.

In a window far above them, Caine watched. A demented and playful smile sat on his lips. "Perfect," he whispered gleefully to himself, "perfect."

## THIRTY-SEVEN

The next few days passed quickly and without any great incident. Kale found herself overwhelmed with training and she devoted all of her energy to it. All of the J'Kahl were impressed, awed even, at how quickly and effortlessly she learned to fight and shoot. She became obsessed with learning as much as she could as fast as she could. It was an honest reflection of how intensely she undertook most things in her life. It also became a way to avoid all thoughts of Derin, and the way he pulled at her so that she always knew where in the room he was even when she couldn't see him.

Derin spoke to Kale in public only. He was certain that if they were alone he'd be tempted to confess to her how she made him feel. He found himself watching her often and worrying about her constantly. Caine had taken a special interest in Kale which bothered Derin. More and more often, Caine treated Derin like a stranger as he became increasingly distant. Derin saw him at meals only when and if he did show up to eat. On a few occasions, Caine would go the whole day without being seen, and Derin found his mistrust of the great leader growing with each passing day.

It was one week after Kale had arrived at the compound that things changed.

## THIRTY-EIGHT

Kale was seated on the cliffs at Sunshine Bay overlooking the rolling waves that stretched on to eternity. The sun was high overhead, and it seemed as if a million tiny diamonds were scattered across the water's surface.

Suddenly, Kale became aware of a presence at her side though she'd heard no one approach. When she looked beside her, she saw the same woman who'd visited her before, the petite figure with the jet-black hair and the golden brown eyes. This time when she looked at the woman, she saw her in a different light. She looked more familiar and reminded Kale of someone else she knew. *That's silly*, Kale thought, *she's not real...is she?*

"Kale, you are so alone," the woman said sadly.

"Who are you?"

"Does it matter?"

"I guess not." Kale turned her attention back to the waves as did her companion.

"Kale, you have lost sight of your path. You are putting people in danger. You are endangering yourself. You are forsaking the mission."

"How would you know about my mission?" Kale asked angrily without looking at the woman.

"I know everything about you, Kale. I see everything you see and more. Time is thin, Kale. The new year is swiftly approaching and with it comes Darkness. The end or the beginning? If you forget that, all will be lost. Your friends will perish, Derin will perish, innocent lives will be lost, and Caine will prevail."

Kale looked to the sky that had too quickly become dark with night. Millions of stars flickered above and, out of the corner of her eye, Kale saw her companion turn her face upwards.

"They're so beautiful," the strange woman sighed deeply. "It's been so long since I've seen them, really seen them." She paused, turned her head this way and that. "Which one is home?"

Kale's skin crawled as she broke out into goose bumps.

"What did you say?" she asked.

"A game," her companion laughed. "A game I used to play long ago on a different shore."

"Is this a dream?" Kale asked quietly.

Her companion turned toward her and smiled sweetly, lovingly. "Are you ready?"

"Yes," Kale answered, though she didn't really understand the question.

"Wake up, Kale."


THIRTY-NINE

Kale sat up in bed and stared around the dim room. Outside, she saw the dawn was only moments from arriving. She'd been dreaming, dreaming of the strange and alluring woman she'd seen twice before.

It hadn't seemed like a dream, Kale realized. It had all seemed so real, the ocean, the glorious sun upon her skin, and the warning. Kale shivered. The warning.

She'd been at the compound a week and had accomplished nothing except maybe convincing everyone she was a loyal follower of Caine's. Kale's stomach lurched. How could she have lost sight of her mission and her promise to her friends? How could she have allowed herself to lose track of time and of everything she'd worked her whole life to accomplish? How could she let herself come to enjoy being a servant, while doing nothing to stop Caine or find out what he was up to? She knew exactly how, Derin.

Kale got out of bed and looked up into the fading night sky. She saw only one star that lingered in the dying night. She wondered if Derin was up yet looking to the stars for answers as he liked to do. She thought back to all the times with her father when they would look to the last night star right before the dawn broke and they would make a wish.

Kale took one last look at the twinkling body far above then closed her eyes to make a wish. When she opened them, the star was gone. *What kind of sign could that be?* she wondered and turned away from the window ready for whatever the day held for her.

## FORTY

When the boat hit land, Alex was torn from his troubled sleep into the waking world. Instantly, he was aware of the cold chill that still ran through him. After only the first day soaring across the rolling ocean waves and having the frigid air whip and beat them relentlessly, the five travelers had found themselves cold and weak and sick. Their parents had made the journey in far less time, having had the powers to propel the boat with their minds and sustain immunity to illness. The children, unlike their parents, were bruised, ill, and exhausted. They'd been at sea a week and, though they'd first approached the voyage with enthusiasm and excitement, the violent and angry sea had shown them no mercy. Day after day, it took from them their joy and comfort as payment for passage. They stopped speaking, they stopped laughing, and they rarely looked to the stars. In a way, they felt betrayed by their guides, as if they should have been warned more seriously about the perils of sea travel and the journey ahead.

Only a week into their journey to stop Caine, they were already being shown how difficult the road ahead would be. How could they possibly face and defeat Caine, if the ocean could beat them down so easily? They could feel how far they were from their parents, a big part of the reason they'd found the strength to journey south in the first place. They could also acutely feel that deep loss of three of their siblings, a girl and two boys lost the night Caine had come. With these wounds exposed anew, raw and aching, the group succumbed to their first bout of hopelessness. They were lost on a sea of uncertainty and growing despair. When the boat finally hit land, one-by-one the exhausted travelers tumbled from it onto the shore, in search of something underfoot that felt solid and safe.

Yet, still they rocked, the raging ocean clinging to them in the only way it could. Even in their haunted sleep that night, the rolling waves found them. Alex couldn't wait for the dawn when they would leave the ocean far behind, and hopefully their misery, and travel into more welcome yet dangerous terrain.

## FORTY-ONE

After breakfast, Kale was summoned to Caine's office. She felt oddly uncomfortable in his presence after their conversation the other day. Again, Caine paced around his office like an animal stalking its prey. Again, Kale squirmed, wishing she could be anywhere but there.

"Kale, I understand your training is going quite well. I hear from the senior officers you have exceeded their expectations and in doing so exceeded mine."

"You flatter me, my lord."

"We are making some very important preparations for the new year, Kale." Her stomach knotted instantly and her mouth went dry in anticipation. Caine continued, "I have big plans for this planet and big plans for its people. We are venturing into a better and bolder world, Kale, and I think your talents would be put to better use elsewhere."

"My lord?" she asked, trying to sound confident. All the while certain she'd been betrayed or exposed.

"Unfortunately, I cannot give you any details as of yet. You must understand the need for secrecy, especially now." Caine cocked his head to the side as if he was listening for something but Kale had no clue what. Then, after a dismissive shake of the head, he went on, "but I would like you to head up one of our task forces. We are hoping to smoke out the rebel alliance before the new year arrives, and I have a feeling you are just the person to lead one of our teams."

"I am honored that you would ask me, lord Caine," Kale said but remaining very still, afraid the slightest movement would betray her thoughts. Her mind was spinning and her vision blurred. *This makes no sense*, she thought wildly, *this just makes no sense.*

"Am I really worthy of this though?"

"If I say you're worthy, then you are. Take the day to consider the request. All great decisions are thought out beforehand."

"Thank you, my lord. I will have your answer in the morning."

"I will have your answer by sundown," he corrected. "You're excused."

Kale stood and bowed her head. "My lord," she said and then left the room in a daze.

She tried, as she walked through the halls, to understand what had just happened. Caine had asked her to accept more responsibility and felt she deserved it; at least that's how he'd made it seem. What she wasn't sure of was what it really was.

Kale thought of the classic rule, *keep your enemies close*, but dismissed it instantly. Caine didn't live by that rule. Caine terminated his enemies. He'd never done otherwise. Maybe she'd really earned the promotion. Maybe her parents had earned it for her. All Kale cared about figuring out was whether she would have a better chance at taking him down as a J'Kahl or as part of Caine's mystery mission. For all she knew, it would send her farther away from him and ruin her chances at destroying him. She wasn't yet sure and needed time to think, to figure it out. Though she knew she should be headed to her morning training, when she left the castle, she made her way towards the trees instead.

FORTY-TWO

Around lunchtime, Kale was still seated in the woods leaning against a tree trying to figure out what she should do. At first, she'd realized she should accept Caine's offer. Whatever he was planning he would have to tell her about it, and that was her best bet at stopping him. Her thoughts had then turned to the curious nature of Caine's feelings toward her. She couldn't figure why she was getting preferential treatment. Was it about her parents or something else? Sometimes he behaved as if he would hand her his whole empire if she asked. Maybe she would ask. Maybe he did want to share his kingdom with her. Despite her intentions, Kale wondered what that would be like.

"Where the hell have you been? You can't just skip training."

Kale looked up from the dying leaf she'd been focusing on and felt her heart drop when she saw Derin standing over her. "I can do whatever I please."

"Kale," he sat down across from her, "what's going on?"

"It really isn't any of your business, Derin, is it?"

A shadow of hurt crossed Derin's face, but he quickly chased it away. "None of my business? I'm sorry, I thought we were friends. I thought maybe..."

Kale interrupted, "You thought what, Derin? We were going to settle down and have kids one day?"

"That wasn't what I was going to say, but what's wrong with that? Don't you want a normal life one day?"

"Derin, I don't have the luxury of thinking of one day. God, Derin, don't be such a fool. One day? Look around you, there isn't any 'one day' inside of this compound and there definitely isn't any 'one day' for me."

"So, we can't even be friends? We can't look out for each other?"

"Don't you get it? I don't want that. I have more important things to worry about. And since you haven't noticed, here's a tip, I'm not the safest person to be around right now. So, why don't you do yourself and me a favor and stay away from me?"

"What the hell is wrong with you?" Derin stood up abruptly and, despite her instincts, Kale stood as well.

"Derin, I'm sorry. That's just the way it is," she said it with a softer voice which somehow only deepened the sting.

"You're lying," Derin stammered.

"No, I'm not," Kale said coldly.

"And what about the other day?" he asked taking a step toward her, as she took two steps away from him.

"Can we not do this? I don't want to talk about it," Kale said dismissively.

"What about the other day?" He said pleadingly.

"I thought you could get me what I wanted, so I kissed you. It usually isn't hard to get what you want from a guy when he thinks you really like him." Kale's eyes were stinging and she fought hard to keep control of her voice. "It turns out that I don't need you anymore. I've already got what I wanted. I'm done with the J'Kahl. Turns out, I've earned myself a promotion, and I don't think I'll turn it down."

"You're treading on dangerous ground here, Kale. What makes you so sure I won't turn you in right now? Caine might still be interested in your real motives for being here."

"My motives have changed. I'm getting used to this lifestyle, and it seems Caine has dangled an offer in front of me that I can't refuse. Power tastes much sweeter than kindness, Derin, haven't you known that your whole life?"

"Kale, please."

"I get it. It would have been a bit of fun, but the thing is you're soft and weak and that's not really what I'm looking for, if you get my meaning."

Derin winced, amazed at how deeply she could wound him. He stared intensely into her eyes, looking for what he wasn't sure. The possibility of a truth he wanted to hold onto maybe. She was lying. She had to be. Finally, when it seemed he wouldn't find in their depths the truth he longed to see, he dropped his eyes from hers. A moment later he walked away, leaving her standing alone in the warm sun.

When Derin was well out of sight, Kale let herself fall to the ground. She managed to keep contained the sob she'd been afraid would escape her only moments before. However, amongst the sorrow, she felt relief. She was back on track and Derin was out of the way. If she was going to do what she'd come here to, she needed to be focused. She needed to be strong. Kale was certain that Derin made her weak.


FORTY-THREE

"So, what does this mean? I don't understand."

Jaren, Medea and Corin sat on the front porch trying to understand the information Jaren had just shared with them. His contacts inside the castle kept him apprised of Kale's progress. They weren't entirely surprised to hear how well she was doing in training. She'd already managed to match the abilities of many who'd been training for years. The fact someone who hated Caine so much could become just what he would expect her to was part of why Kale had been the right person to go undercover. She'd proven time and time again that stopping Caine made her capable of anything.

The troubling news being the more recent events and Caine's behavior leading up to them. What Jaren had told them was the strangeness of Caine's interest in Kale. They'd discussed it in depth and couldn't think of a reason for him to be treating Kale the way he did. She'd taken up residence in his castle from the first night she arrived. He insisted that she join him for meals and often met with her privately, to discuss what no one knew.

They'd all decided that though his behavior was strange it indicated one thing for certain, that Caine didn't know who Kale was. Caine had killed traitors before; they'd all seen it done at one time or another because he loved an audience. It meant striking fear into any who doubted what he was capable of. He didn't distinguish between women, children, and men. Traitors were animals in Caine's eyes, a lower form of life, and he could order them killed without a second thought. If he'd known Kale was a traitor, she would've been killed right away and they all knew she was alive and well. In fact, she was so well it worried them.

Somehow Kale had received a promotion just the day before. The exact details of it were unclear and the job she'd be performing even more so. They should've been happy that Kale was so close to Caine already but something seemed off. It all seemed too easy.

"I don't get it any more than you do. I can't figure out how she did it but she seems to have won his trust. She's running some kind of secret project that not even my contacts know anything about. They're sure it has something to do with the new year, but all Caine is saying is that something big is going down and that they should all be ready. He's smart anyway, not trusting anyone," Jaren took a deep breath as he stared off into the woods.

"So what are we supposed to do?" Medea asked.

"All we can do is follow the plan as long as nothing changes. If Kale doesn't send word that she knows what he's up to, then we attack two days before the new year at dawn. Kale knows she'll have to move on the inside. She's close enough now. If she has to, she'll kill him. Everything is in place."

"Remind me, again, why she doesn't just kill him now?" Medea asked.

"Because, we don't know what he has planned. Killing him isn't the answer, stopping him is."

"I still think those are the same thing," Medea said, unable to hide her annoyance.

"No, they aren't. I wish they were. The people have faith in him. If we just kill him, someone will take his place and all this will start again or, even worse, we'll make a martyr out of him. We have to show the people that all this is wrong."

"I'm really struggling to believe that speech these days, Jaren. Maybe you should mix it up a bit, you know, change it around a little." Medea's words might have sounded playful, but her voice hid nothing of the worry and fear that had begun to take root.

"I still can't believe we're even trying this. So many things have to go right for this plan to work out and the odds are stacked against us so blatantly," Corin scowled. "We should've just killed him somehow. Instead, we've all put ourselves in danger, for what? You know what, Kale. She convinced us to do this. She's had it out for Caine since she was a child."

"Corin, don't say that."

"Look," Corin began, "I love Kale with all my heart. She's like a sister to me, but I just can't help feeling like her desire to destroy Caine has clouded all of our judgment on this one. If it wasn't for Kale, would we even be trying something this ridiculous?"

"If it weren't for Kale, would we even have a chance?" Medea shot back.

"A chance at what, Medea, that's what I'm saying? We barely have a plan. Kale's living with Caine, for what? What did we think she would find other than danger or death even?" The words began to stream out of Corin unedited and filled with fear. "And we're out here just waiting, to either be found out and killed or to stage an attack on his compound that will most likely fail while Kale is inside, trying to kill Caine but most likely getting killed, or caught herself." When he stopped, he took a deep breath, a gasp really, and shook his head as if trying to shake off the weight of all his worry and fear.

"And what are we supposed to do? Just wait around until Caine does whatever it is he's got planned? Wait around until he makes us slaves and the whole world goes down the drain with no hope of ever getting better? Give me a better idea and I'll go with it, Corin, I swear." Medea reached out and put a hand on Corin's arm.

"I'm sorry. I didn't mean any of that," Corin paused and began to run his fingers through his uncharacteristically unruly hair. "I just feel so helpless and this all feels so useless. How are we ever going to change things?"

"Hey, maybe we won't. Maybe in a month we'll all be dead and this world will be in ruins and no one will ever even know we existed. Honestly, I'm okay with that if we tried. But maybe there is something we can do. Maybe Kale is onto something and maybe she'll find out in time for us to stop it. If she doesn't, maybe our raid on the castle will succeed or at least show people we don't need to be pushed around anymore. Maybe, maybe, maybe, Corin. Don't you get it? We just have to decide how we want to live this life, whatever is left of it, and do it." Medea looked from Corin to Jaren, who'd been quiet during the whole exchange while his mind poked and prodded at the mystery of Kale's relationship with Caine. He knew Corin well enough to know that he would always arrive back at his certainty they were doing right thing. It wasn't the first time fear led him to panic.

Silence enveloped the three friends. Somewhere far away, a bird cried out. It seemed a sorrowed sound in that moment.

"We've all lost so much," Corin whispered. "We're not losing anything else without a fight."

"Good. So we're back on track," Jaren finally spoke.

Suddenly Corin began to laugh. "I'm sorry," he spat out, while the laughter bubbled out of him, taking with it the last of his worry and fear. Before long all three of them were laughing, hysterical, though no one knew why. When the laughter died out, the silence that followed it was ripe with hope. There was still joy to be had in the world, and they'd just stolen a few moments of it. If there was joy, then there was something left worth fighting for.

"No one can say we lived boring lives," Corin said with a smile.

"That's my boy," Medea said putting an arm around his shoulder. "We'll make a superhero out of you yet, Corin."

"Now that is impossible." Again Corin laughed, "So what do we do now?"

There wasn't much they could do. The plan called for patience. All they could do was to wait, and hope Kale knew what she was doing.


FORTY-FOUR

Three hours later, Medea walked through Ryan's front door. "Hello?" she called, as she made her way into the impressive home.

"We're up here," Ryan called from upstairs. "In my parents' room." Medea heard his voice quaver as he said those last words and she hurried up the stairs to find Ryan and Sam seated on the floor embracing. Sam wiped tears from her eyes when she saw Medea enter.

"Hey, Medea. Sorry about the mess," Sam said pathetically, as if it mattered somehow. Then she forced a smile.

Ryan let his sister go and rose to greet Medea. She took him in her arms and he began to weep quietly as he leaned into her, giving in to the weight of his grief. When he was finally able to compose himself, he stepped back and wiped the tears from his cheeks with the back of his hand.

"How you holding up?" Medea asked.

"I was fine until we started sorting through their stuff. I just don't understand who could do something like this."

"Sure you do," she said firmly.

"I can't believe it. All this time, I never really believed it was possible. We've been helping with the weapons I know, but I never really understood what it was we were fighting for. I never saw how much of a monster he really is."

Medea bit her tongue. He'd grown up with the privilege of being sheltered from Caine's violence and cruelty but now wasn't the time to point that out.

"Hey, at least you're on the right side, Ryan. We're going to get through this. We may not be able to make this right, but we'll make him pay."

Again, the couple hugged. Behind them, Sam had abandoned her tears for a scowl, watching them with disdain. Neither Medea nor Ryan saw either before she stormed out of the room without a single word.

"Is she okay?" Medea asked.

"I don't know. She's...weird."

"What do you mean?"

"It's nothing. I mean our parents were murdered, why should she be normal? I don't think I've ever even cried before this."

Ryan took her hand and led her to the large satin covered bed and they sat side-by-side. At first, they sat in silence, one ripe with possibility, and Medea was sure Ryan was getting ready to tell her something very important.

"I'm in," he said after awhile.

"Ryan, you were always in. You guys have been taking care of the weapons for awhile now."

"Yeah, I know but that's not enough, not anymore. I have a personal tie to this now. If I was smart, I would have realized I always had a personal tie to it." He leaned over and kissed her on the forehead. It was such a sweet and sincere gesture that it caught her off guard and at first she didn't know what to say.

"Well, that's me, underappreciated far too often but always willing to put up with it...and always willing to forgive." She smiled up at him and he returned the smile.

"So, what's next, Medea?"

"We just wait. There are two plans. Both are crazy as hell and probably going to get us all killed."

"Can I take back my decision?"

"No way, Ry. We're the good guys. We're supposed to win right? Who cares if the odds are stacked against us? That's where all the fun comes in."

"You know sarcasm is a defense mechanism, right."

"What have I gotten myself into?" Medea said rolling her eyes.

"The adventure that it's all worth it for," he reminded her, drawing her into a kiss. They were, as always when lost in each other, able to forget the world was a crazy place, if even for just a moment or two. In a world where any moment could be your last, sometimes, a moment or two was enough.


FORTY-FIVE

The next two weeks were a test of patience and resolve for everyone. The children of the Founders journeyed ever-nearer Empris as the stars had directed them and each day passed with only a change in scenery. Their restlessness grew as each night the stars revealed to them nothing more than they had the night before. The journey threatened over and over again to dampen their hopeful hearts and upbeat spirits. All that kept them going was the slim chance they could make a difference, the desire to see their parents awake again, and the knowledge Caine had once stolen four from their ranks and he would have to pay.

Ryan moved in with Medea, Corin, and Jaren so that he could be at hand when they were ready to take whatever action they needed to take. They solidified plans to be ready to move when Kale indicated they should, and Sam journeyed to Empris to make sure all was ready to go with the weapons they'd been storing. Mostly, it was a game of worrying and waiting as reports of Kale's progress came in almost every day. She'd stopped training with the J'Kahl and spent almost every day in Caine's company. Doing what no one knew.

Simply put, they talked. Kale grew increasingly impatient with her newly appointed role as it seemed to her what she'd really been appointed to be was Caine's new best friend. The more they spoke, the more Kale realized he was a man on the edge of madness, teetering this way and that, depending on his moods. When she inquired as to their plans or actions for the new year, she could never predict his reaction. Sometimes, Caine would laugh airily, waving away the question, and comment on how Kale worried too much. Other times, he would turn on her, furious she didn't trust him, and he would send her away for the remainder of the day. At other times, he was calm and calculated, and when she met his eyes in those moments, she saw a Darkness there that reached deep down inside her and made her very afraid of what was coming.

"All plans are in place, my dear. When you need to hear them you will. I do promise that you will be pleasantly surprised and equally shocked at the wonderful things I have planned. Truly, I can't believe I can even keep it a secret," Caine would squeal like a child at this point and Kale would be reminded of his madness.

She saw Derin only at meals and never spoke to him unless formally. He made no effort to speak to her either yet he often found himself watching her when she wasn't looking and he inquired about her often. The girl he'd met at Sunshine Bay was no more. She'd disappeared into Caine's shadow and Derin found himself detesting his father for taking from him the only beautiful thing he'd found in the world. Though Derin never left the compound, he often sat beneath the stars at night watching them intently. He didn't know why he did this but it brought him comfort just as much as it filled him with dread.

There were others in the compound who watched the stars out of instinct. They watched to find out what would happen next. They watched and they waited; the same thing they'd been doing for fourteen long years.

On Earth, Kayla found herself happy more often than not. It was hard for her to face, the happiness, because she still wasn't entirely convinced she deserved it. Often, she found herself wrestling with horrible memories that she wished would set her free. She spent almost every day with Max but still kept her distance from him in many ways, her heart hidden safely out of reach. She had, over the few weeks they'd spent together, come to realize she was falling in love with him. The angel who'd pulled her from the icy waves was just that, an angel, whose love could heal and set you free of your demons. Kayla found that such a contrast to herself. Her love had never done anything but harm. She found herself thinking of ways to free Max of her. She was sure he would never understand why she was the way she was. Could anybody ever understand a person who didn't want to be loved? Could anyone understand a person who wasn't whole? Kayla didn't think so. The outcome was inevitable in her eyes and she knew if she didn't leave him soon she would end up breaking his heart like she had so many others before him.

Time is a funny thing. Eternity can pass by in the blink of an eye, and a moment can wrap itself around you so intensely that it feels like forever.

And so these two weeks passed much like that, in moments and eternities, strung end-to-end, with everyone left spinning in one way or another.

## FORTY-SIX

"If I've told you once, I've told you a million times, address me as Lord Caine," Caine was shouting and his face had begun to purple with rage.

"You are not *my* lord, and I will do no such thing,"

Caine circled the tiny woman in the center of the room and had to fight to keep his anger under control. The room they stood in was dark and smelled of must and moisture. The walls were covered with mold and somewhere in the shadows water could be heard trickling down that damp and slimy surface. In the center of the room, a beautiful woman was suspended horizontally three feet off the ground but, how, it could not be seen. She seemed to float in midair as if frozen in time and space.

She slept.

Her hair was jet-black and her skin was fair amber that seemed to give off light in a way that made her glow. Caine paced around the aura, always making sure never to come into contact with its shimmering light. When he spoke, he directed his words to the other figure in the room, the sleeper's twin in every way except that she was a mere apparition, transparent and without substance.

"I want none of your riddles," he spat out at her, "just give me the answers I'm asking for."

The woman, the apparition, smiled lazily. She was well aware of how she angered Caine. She silently scolded herself for being reduced to the level of enjoying his anger, but her pleasures had been few and far between for too many years now.

"I've told you everything I know. What more would you have me do, or is it that I've told you nothing that you want to hear?" Again, the woman smiled. A warning shot through her golden-brown eyes but she had no true power and they both knew it.

Caine paced angrily around the standing figure and finally he spoke, "I own your life. If you do not keep up your end of the bargain, I will decide I no longer have any use for the boy and you may not like what I do then." He turned and walked towards the door.

Behind him, the woman spoke. "It is you who is keeping up the end of a bargain, Caine. Your ignorance amazes me still. The Darkness will take its payment yet," She paused and sighed. Years of losing struggles with him took the fight out of her quickly these days. "I have told you all I know. You know I wouldn't risk his life."

Caine didn't turn or reply and merely slammed the door behind him and then used the key around his neck to lock it. Even with the door between them, he heard her warning and despite himself he was chilled. "When the Darkness has what it wants, it will come for you, too, Caine."

He shook the chill and the warning away before storming off. He was growing tired of the woman and her riddles. He was growing angry with feeling like she was playing with him and not the other way around. He was Caine. He was God. He would prevail.

In the room he'd just locked, the sleeping woman sighed but didn't stir. Her 'twin', that ghostly apparition was gone. The trickling water and that musty smell of places too long forgotten were her only companions.

## FORTY-SEVEN

Kale was having a beautiful dream. She was seated on a blanket of soft sand by the ocean and the rolling thunder was coaxing her to be calm. The day was bright, and overhead seagulls sang out in startled cries as if the beauty of the day surprised them over and over again. The sun danced upon the waves as they came and went, and all Kale wanted was to dive into them and be a part of that eternal dance. Beside her sat an angel with golden wings. She didn't look at the angel. She knew that he was there.

Then strangeness came down upon her, not from within the dream but from outside of it. Her angel took flight, rising into the sky in a panic, quickly becoming a tiny golden sparkle in the clear blue sky.

Kale became aware of being observed. A presence called her from her slumber and back into the waking world. Someone was in her room, instinct told her so.

She sat straight up in bed, instantly awake, and looked around her room for the reason she'd woken. Standing near the door, Derin watched her go from scared to angry in a few short seconds.

"What the hell are you doing? You scared me to death."

Derin stepped out of the shadows and smiled.

"I'm impressed you woke up so quickly. Not many soldiers are on guard even when they sleep." He couldn't help himself and chuckled.

"I'm no longer a soldier, remember?"

He took a few steps towards her. "Get up. We have somewhere to be."

The day had yet to wake as they walked in silence out of the castle and towards the training facility. Once inside, they moved quickly through the training hall and towards one of the storage facilities at the back. Derin unlocked it and they both went through the door.

"Are you telling me this couldn't wait until later on?" Kale asked in a whisper, unable to contain her curiosity another moment. He ignored her.

Derin reached the back wall and pushed a large pile of boxes out of the way, and Kale was finally beginning to understand. Behind the boxes stood a bolted door and, from his pocket, Derin produced a key. Within seconds, they were through it and found themselves standing in the woods.

"Just a few precautions," Derin said grimly, "I can never be too careful, not anymore, and especially around you, Kale." He offered nothing more and Kale was certain the time for questions had not yet arrived.

He led her through the woods and finally he stopped at the back wall of the compound and leaned against it. He stood there, resting for a moment, and Kale realized how exhausted he looked.

"Derin, what's wrong? Why are we here? Are you okay?"

"Like you care."

"Spare me the sarcasm. You woke me up, remember?" Kale had been mean towards him for so long now she didn't know how to be kind. If she let her guard down, she might falter and her new plans left no room for that.

"I'm leaving the compound today to go into town. Caine has asked me to stop in with some people and deliver some things. I was thinking if you wanted to give your friends any messages I could do that for you as well."

Kale was shocked. Time had passed so quickly within the compound and she'd become so wrapped up in her mission that she'd lost track of time. She hadn't sent them a message and she'd been away more than three weeks now. Though she knew Jaren's contact would be keeping them updated, it was strange not to even have thought of letting them know how she was and how their plan was progressing.

"My friends? What do you know about my friends?"

"Look, you're not the only one who knows how to get information."

Kale was horrified. "Why did you have to bring them into this, Derin? Do you realize what happens if anyone finds out they're associated with me?"

"I would have thought Caine's new right hand woman wouldn't care about a bunch of rebels foolishly trying to take on our savior and leader."

The hurt and resentment in Derin's voice stung but she pushed it aside. *Feeling anything about him, about any of them right now makes you weak,* she reminded herself, and having him angry was better than the alternative.

"Derin, this isn't a game. I don't care what happens to me, but you're endangering innocent people, and that's not right. You're endangering yourself."

"I'm just trying to do you a favor."

"Don't worry about me. You should be worrying about yourself," Kale replied, angry and annoyed. She'd never realized how much it bothered her when people acted like she needed help.

"Kale, this is me. You don't have to pretend you can do everything by yourself, not with me."

"I'm not pretending, Derin. I don't need your help. I thought we already went over this. I don't need anybody's help. Why don't you just leave me alone like I asked you to? Can't you take a hint?" Her words flew like daggers, Kale saw when they hit their mark, and Derin winced.

"You don't want me to leave you alone. I know you don't. What's so wrong with us being friends? What's so wrong with us being more than that?" Derin took a step toward Kale and she took a step away from him.

"I'm here because this is where I want to be. I'm here because I think I belong here right now," she paused and the resentment returned to her voice, "I'm not here to fall in love, or have fun, or..." but Derin interrupted her.

"Fall in love," he repeated quietly, turning the words over like a mystery. She made him regret it right away.

"Don't be ridiculous, Derin," she scoffed. Derin stepped towards her and this time Kale stood her ground. "Derin, you're losing it. There is no chance for you and I, ever, I'm not that kind of girl and you're not that kind of guy, though you seem a little confused about that lately."

"Kale, why are you so afraid of being loved?"

"None of your business. I gave you the wrong impression before and I'm sorry. Now, can we just leave this alone? You're wasting my time."

"You're not being fair." The pain in Derin's voice was becoming more than Kale could bear and she wanted nothing more than for him to leave her alone.

"You want to know the truth, Derin?" She didn't wait for him to answer because he had opened a floodgate and the contents it held were ready to spill out. "This is how I've been all my life. Love makes you weak, and it gives someone the power to destroy you. I don't want to love and I really don't know how. So, please, don't ask me to try. Please," the anger was gone from Kale's voice and now she looked weak and worn out, though her voice was still stern.

Derin took another step closer to her. When he spoke, he was only inches from her face. "Kale..." His voice came out in a whisper and it was so full of desperation that for a moment she almost faltered.

"No. I don't know how. Don't ask me again, please. It's too much."

"Kale."

"I'm sorry. Nothing is more important than what I'm doing here. Nothing...not even you." She let her words sink in. When she spoke, she'd composed herself. "I suggest you don't seek out the rebels in town. Lord Caine would not appreciate being betrayed by his own son, and I don't want to be the one to tell him." She let the threat and the fact that she meant it sink in.

Derin turned away from her. He'd lost her...she'd been so close but now she was gone. He knew then, in the deep and aching pain that settled into him, that in some ways she was right, that sometimes love gave someone the power to destroy you.

"Fine. I, uh, I guess I thought you were someone you're not. I apologize. It will never happen again." Derin moved away from her slowly. Kale knew if she wanted to salvage any of their relationship, it would have to be now. She held back her longing, instead grabbing hold of the truth of what she'd come to do, and what it would take for her to succeed.

She hadn't known there was anything left inside of herself to hand over to this mission, but as she watched Derin walk away from her, probably for the last time, she realized you could hand your heart over in a thousand tiny pieces one-by-one, and each jagged offering could tear you open over and over again.

## FORTY-EIGHT

Kayla stirred from sleep and knew instantly the dream was still with her. She panicked and tried with every ounce of strength she could muster to escape it. Her room was still dark and her eyes were heavy as she forced her lids open. He was in her room; she knew it. That dark and looming figure was ever present when she woke from her nightmares. That presence was lurking somewhere in the dark, watching and waiting. It was evil, she knew that much, and always male. She could sense him but never see him. He always managed to stay just out of sight, a monster that dwelled in the periphery of both her vision and her life. She wanted nothing more than to sit up and face him, to show him she wasn't afraid, but she couldn't.

She struggled under her sheets trying to convince her body to listen so that she could break free of the nightmare. It was always in these moments, when in between waking and asleep, that Kayla remembered the dreams vividly. Later, when she was looking for the memory of the dream, it would be that moment she was looking for, that clarity she was longing to dive back into.

The dreams changed but the place she found herself when in them was always the same. The story was always the same as well. It was her against everyone else. Sometimes, she had a few friends or allies but she could never recall their faces when she woke.

Now, as she struggled to be set free of the dreams and prove to herself that she wasn't a victim to them, the evil in her room swelled, surged towards her, and then swallowed her whole. The dream took her again. Once her journey back to that other life began, she stopped struggling and surrendered. Acceptance washed over her and carried her back to her dreamland. She was always more at home there than in the waking world anyway.

## FORTY-NINE

Derin stood on the edge of the poor section of Braedon Ridge and surveyed the strangers walking through its streets, while he gathered the courage to enter. He'd already done all that Caine had asked him to do but that business had been in a better and much safer part of town. The people here were gaunt, a sign of hunger, and most wore clothes that had seen better days. Derin kept an eye out for J'Kahl but the squalor in this part of the city seemed to repel them, and Derin felt ashamed for understanding why. It was unsettling to see people suffering in this way, even if you were part of the reason they suffered.

He saw a girl approaching through the bustling crowd and watched as she greeted many of them on her way. Her brown hair bobbed as she went and her eyes, the same color, seemed distrustful and yet daring.

Derin drew himself nearer to the girl and overheard as someone said, "Is she coming back to us soon?"

Happily the girl responded, "I don't know when Kale is coming back, Mrs. Doggart. I promise, as soon as I know anything I will let you know, okay?"

That was all Derin needed to hear. If she knew Kale, then she probably knew who Derin was looking for.

"Excuse me," Derin said standing directly in Medea's path, "I need to know how to find the rebels."

The smile dropped from the girl's face. "Who the hell are you?"

Derin lowered his voice, "I'm a friend of Kale's. She told me if I ever need to find her friends that I should come here and ask for the rebels."

"Don't you know anything. The rebels..." Medea began but Derin interrupted her.

"Yeah, yeah, I know. The rebels are just a myth."

Medea took hold of his arm gently. "Come with me," she said as she hurried through the crowd, no longer greeting people or stopping to chat. "How do you know Kale?"

"I've been training with her. I've got a message for her friends."

When they reached the tree line, she let go of his arm and stopped to look at him.

"How is she?"

"She's fine," Derin replied trying to keep all emotion out of his voice. "She's fine," he repeated lamely.

Medea stared at him inquisitively. "That's all. She's been gone for more than three weeks and that's it?"

"Listen," Derin interjected, "I'll tell you everything you want to know, but we can't talk here. If I'm seen with you, we're both going to be in a lot of danger."

"Fine," Medea responded and turned to lead him through the woods never pausing to consider Derin wasn't who he said he was.

Shortly after that, they came to the house that stood at the top of the hill. Derin was sure they were near the Braedon River because he could hear water tumbling somewhere off in the distance, hurrying around and over rocks to reach its destination downstream. Medea walked up the incline to the house and with Derin behind her she went inside. Derin could hear muffled voices from somewhere inside the huge home. As Medea led him through the house to the kitchen in the back, the voices became clearer. He could tell there were two people speaking and once in the kitchen saw who it had been. Two guys a few years older than he was sat at the kitchen table with paper and sketches littering the surface between them. When they saw Derin enter, both of them stood.

"Who is this?" one of them asked Medea while taking a step forward.

"He's..." Medea's words trailed off as she turned toward Derin.

"I'm a friend of Kale's. She asked me to come here and tell you how she's doing."

One of the boys laughed in disbelief, "Kale, ask someone to tell us how she's doing. Sorry, try again."

"Alright, alright," Derin began, "so she didn't ask me to come here but I'm worried about her and I didn't know who else to talk to."

Derin and Jaren were locked eye-to-eye.

"What did you say your name was?" Jaren finally asked.

"Derin."

It only took a moment for everything to fall into place for Jaren.

"Wait a minute," Jaren took another step toward Derin taking in his appearance, "Caine's son, Derin?"

"The very same." Derin's confidence was both intimidating and unsettling.

"Corin," that was all Jaren said, but Corin was already heading swiftly out of the room. "Medea, why the hell did you bring him here?"

Jaren looked away from Derin long enough to give Medea a disapproving and angry look. Medea talking about being reckless was one thing, but acting it was another.

"He knew the password," she said desperately, a mixture of regret and fear beginning to bubble up inside her.

"Can I sit while your friend fetches a weapon or would you like to search me first?" Derin asked with an air of arrogance.

"How nice of you to offer," Jaren said coldly.

"Jaren, I'm sorry. He knew the password," Medea repeated. "He knew where to find us," she stammered frantically.

"It's fine," Jaren said as he finished searching Derin. He placed the knife he'd confiscated on the kitchen counter. "You can sit now."

"Thanks," Derin said, sat at the table, and began to look around the room.

It was the kitchen of a family. Dishes, some dirty, some freshly washed, were stacked on either side of the sink. Food of all kinds covered the counter tops in a variety of containers. Posters and paintings littered the walls and while some seemed as if they'd been the work of children others looked like they were those of a professional artist.

Finally, Corin returned with a crossbow.

"You really know how to make a guy feel welcome. Kale didn't tell me you were all so friendly and fun-loving."

"Kale didn't tell you anything. So you might want to shut up until you're asked to speak. You'll live longer that way. Now, how many soldiers are with you? How many are on their way here?" he asked the questions, but somehow Jaren knew they weren't necessary. He'd seen something in Derin that made him certain the visit was not an attack but something else.

"I came alone. I told you I'm here because I'm worried about Kale."

Jaren looked Derin in the eye, holding his gaze. Though he volunteered nothing to his two friends, he decided Derin was telling the truth.

"Jaren, should we get out of here? What if he's lying?"

"He's not. Not yet anyway." Jaren sat down at the kitchen table across from Derin. His instincts and an ability to read people told him something he had yet to believe was true; Derin's loyalties had shifted. "Corin, keep that thing pointed right at him. If I tell you to, put an arrow through his heart."

Medea sat down between the two guys and watched and waited for whatever was about to transpire. For the first time since seeing Derin, she started to really look at him and something began to tug at her memory.

"So, have you and Kale become friends, Derin?" Jaren already knew the answer to this question but he wanted to see how honest Derin was.

"We were friends. We met a few days before she came to stay at the compound and we hit it off, I guess."

"How convenient," Jaren put in.

Derin knew from his training that there was a time to be the aggressor and a time to yield. If he wanted to accomplish anything during his visit with Kale's friends, he knew which tactics he would have to use. Truthfully, he wasn't really sure why he'd come to see them except that he wanted to understand Kale better and he thought maybe he could protect her if they just told him how.

"It's true. We met once before. We talked for awhile but I didn't know who she was and she had no idea who I was either. When she arrived at the compound, I was shocked but I didn't turn her in because, well, she has a way of getting what she wants."

"No offence, Derin, but I'm not quite buying it." Corin said, unimpressed.

"Oh my god," Medea spat out. The crystal blue eyes and the black hair, navy in the sun. She realized that this was the same guy Kale had told her about. The one she'd met at Sunshine Bay. It was definitely him. The impossibly light blue eyes like tinted diamonds. "Alex?" she asked accusingly.

"How did you know that?" Derin looked at her inquisitively.

"I knew it!"

"Alright," Jaren said with obvious annoyance.

Derin was smiling slightly but when Jaren looked at him he erased the smile instantly. Quickly, Derin began to speak again, before he lost his chance.

"We trained together for the first week. I thought we were friends but then Kale freaked out when my fath...when Caine promoted her. She promoted herself out of our friendship at the same time. Now I just see her around. We don't really talk all that much." Derin looked down at his hands and the three friends watched him intently and waited for something more about their friend.

"So, tell me then, Derin, how is Kale?"

"I don't know. That's why I'm here. Her training was going really well. She could've been a great soldier. It's ridiculous how quickly she learns. I think she just likes showing everybody up." Derin noticed they all were all looking at him with raised eyebrows. Jaren stared at Derin particularly hard and he found himself avoiding Jaren's eyes.

"He's been acting weird about her, Caine, I mean. I'm sure you guys have heard. He gave her one of the nicest suites in the castle. She eats at his table in the main hall. He asks about her constantly. And this was right from the beginning. Then, all of a sudden, he promotes her. No one knows to what, no one knows for what, not even me."

"Well, what does she do?'

"That's the thing. She spends all of her time with him. They walk around the compound. They talk. They laugh. If I didn't know better, I'd think they were friends."

"You're his son. Don't you know what's going on?"

"He tells me nothing. Since Kale arrived, he's barely acknowledged I'm alive let alone told me what's going on. If I ask, he gets suspicious."

"And, you don't know what these big plans are for the new year?"

"No one does. Not that I can tell anyway. I don't think he's told Kale anything. We're all in the dark."

Jaren was nodding solemnly. "Well, my contacts have been telling me the same things." Jaren looked at Derin as if to say, 'you should hear what else my contacts have told me'.

"Look, I don't know what I thought I could accomplish by coming here. She's not acting like herself."

"Like you know anything about who she really is," Jaren scoffed.

"I know everything that matters," Derin said softly, "and something's wrong."

Derin was quiet for a long time before he went on. The trio waited, sensing he hadn't quite finished yet. "She says her plans have changed because Caine offered her the world but I know that's a lie to keep me at a distance. But she needs help and she either doesn't see it or doesn't want it."

"And you're just okay with helping us..." Corin was about to say 'kill your father' but wasn't able to finish.

"Stop your father?" Jaren interrupted him quickly.

"Well you can believe me or not, it's your choice. I don't want to hurt him but this madness has got to stop. Something has got to change and, I guess, yeah, I'm ready to help change it." He sighed, annoyed he had to show his humanity in front of the strangers but it seemed like the only way they might trust him. "I'm just worried Kale's in over her head. I barely recognize her anymore."

Derin didn't recognize himself either. A month ago he'd been a reputable soldier, an admirable leader, and his father's pride. Now, he was a heartsick traitor chasing after a girl who wanted nothing to do with him and even worse he was visiting her friends to try and take care of her.

"Kale doesn't get in over her head," Jaren said.

Derin let his thoughts tumble away from him gratefully. "I guess I knew that," Derin paused. "Look, I just want to know if there is anything I can do to help her, or you guys? She won't let me help."

"The best thing you can do is act normal, like yourself, and stay away from Kale," Jaren finished, but Corin had words of his own to add.

"What I want to know, Derin, is how you're certain we'll let you leave this house alive?"

"I'm not actually. But make up your minds quickly because if you're going to let me leave, it has to be now. If I'm gone too long, it will raise suspicion and I'll wish you'd killed me instead of what will get done to me back there."

"You're free to go," Jaren said sternly, and Derin realized that Jaren was probably enjoying the only benefit of Kale's absence, he was in charge.

"You want me to give her any messages for you guys?"

"Tell her we miss her," Medea said.

"Yeah, tell her we can't wait for her to come home," Corin offered lowering the crossbow at last.

"I'll walk you out, Derin." Jaren stood.

"You mind?" Derin pointed at his knife still sitting on the counter.

"Take it."

Derin grabbed the knife and put it back in his belt loop where he carried it. It made him feel safe having it that close to his skin. He would always be a warrior in some ways, never looking for a fight but ready if one found him.

When they came to the front door, Derin stopped, expecting to say his good-byes to Jaren as well but Jaren pushed past him and kept walking. Derin followed him down the steps and towards the woods.

"So, she's okay?" Jaren asked. Derin had the feeling that Jaren understood a lot more about Kale than he would ever admit.

"Honestly, I don't know. I think so."

Jaren nodded. "So, son of Caine, I know you weren't a traitor a month ago, what's changed?"

Derin wanted to stop and collect his thoughts but Jaren kept walking. "Everything's changed," he admitted.

"She'll probably never let it happen, you know that right?" Jaren stopped to turn and look at Derin and so he stopped walking as well.

"I know."

"Do you love her?"

Derin didn't want to answer the question and he waited so long trying to figure out how to answer that finally Jaren spoke again.

"She probably doesn't know how to love you so why bother?"

"Did you, Jaren?"

Jaren stared at Derin, both annoyed and impressed.

"No," he replied, "I haven't bothered yet."

"Then," Derin paused, "I'm not the one you should be asking that question to."

"You hurt her and I'll kill you," Jaren said without raising his voice or changing his tone.

"I know," Derin replied and turned to walk off.

"Tell her I miss her, please."

Derin didn't turn or reply. The whole way into town thoughts of Kale and what she'd said to him earlier that day had run rampantly through his mind. Now on his way home, his broken heart and spinning mind returned to her again. He'd seen such a distance in her as if she was always far away even when she was right in front of him. Derin knew many people interpreted the distance as sadness. He also knew that Kale did as well. Only recently had Derin noticed a change in her that made him believe she was starting to get a little nearer somehow.

Over the weeks since he'd met her, Kale had become happier than he'd ever thought he would see her. He loved seeing her happy but hated that it was Caine who was making her that way. Derin had never been jealous of his father before but he was now, and along with all he'd seen in the last few weeks it was enough to make him wish the great leader nothing but ill.

Derin again thought back to where he'd been only a month before. He'd been a loyal follower of Caine's and a son to make a father proud, but he'd been blind to the realities of his father's reign. He'd been blind to fourteen years of disappearances and deaths and murders and slavery. He'd been blind to so much and he resented Caine for being able to pull the wool over his eyes. He resented Caine for making him look like a fool. And if he was being honest, he was ashamed of himself for refusing to see what was right in front of his eyes because it was easier and more comfortable to remain blind. He didn't want his father dead, he still had the unconditional love that fourteen years had built, but things had to change, and Caine had to be stopped. Derin was certain of that.

As Derin strode home, he wondered how he would face Kale after all he'd revealed to her that morning. He hoped he could be strong enough not to show her he was hurt or how deeply. He hoped he had the strength to keep Caine in the dark about his betrayal. He hoped most of all that he could be strong enough to protect Kale somehow; he knew she was far more fragile than she'd ever admit.

After a long while standing in the woods, Jaren began his walk back to the house. The conversation between him and Derin hadn't gone as planned. The last thing he wanted was to walk back into the house looking distraught. They were all worried about Kale and if anyone was going to break in her absence it wasn't going to be him.

He'd known before questioning Derin about the relationship that had transpired between him and Kale. He hadn't told Medea or Corin because he didn't want them to see how badly it had hurt him. He always knew there was a possibility she'd open up to someone, give her heart away, before he could act and tell her how he felt. For it to be Caine's son, the enemy, he still couldn't quite believe it. He was also pretty sure Derin would still be a loyal follower of Caine's, if Kale hadn't been the one under cover. *I guess we sent the right person in there after all*, he thought with a mixture of resentment and resignation.

Thinking about Derin and how he'd betrayed both a father and a leader for Kale, it made him realize how much they had in common. The only difference was that Derin was willing to tell Kale how he felt if it meant he might have a chance. Dismayed, Jaren wondered if that's all it might have taken and if maybe he'd missed his chance. He put his hands over his face to brood within that covered darkness.

Once composed, he was ready to face his friends. He wasn't sure why he'd gotten so angry with Derin. Kale had never once liked a guy enough to brave a relationship. Jaren could admit that, if it couldn't be him, he would like Kale to fall in love with someone just because he wanted to see her happy for once and know someone was taking care of her. For the longest time, the only man she thought about with any kind of intensity had been Caine. And now, from what Jaren's contacts said, it seemed Caine was the one who'd finally made her happy, and he couldn't understand any of it. When he arrived at the house, Medea and Corin were seated in the kitchen waiting for him.

"Jaren, are you sure we can trust him?' Corin asked right away.

"We don't have a choice," Jaren stated, feeling more worn out than he ever had.

"I don't know about this. It seems kind of weird. Why would he come here? Why would he risk so much?" Corin was looking more frightened than skeptical.

"God, Corin, get with it. He's obviously in love with her." Medea rolled her eyes.

"What?" Corin ventured with disbelief. He hadn't noticed.

Before anyone could say anything more, Sam's voice floated into the kitchen. "Medea!" she called. "Jaren! Corin!"

They stood and made their way into the front hall. Sam was standing in the doorway looking oddly gleeful.

"Hey guys, what's up?"

"Hey."

"I just stopped in with some updates. Ryan had some stuff to do so I volunteered to come. We're just getting so close to the new year it's hard to hold still, you know." Sam looked over at Jaren and gave him a long inquisitive look before speaking again, "So, should we sit down, and I'll tell you where we're at?"

"Sure. Let's go back into the kitchen."

For the first time since Derin's arrival, Jaren had the sinking feeling something wasn't right and that they were truly in for more than they'd bargained for. He wasn't sure if it was Derin who bothered him or something else. Jaren thought of Caine and his worry intensified. Something about Caine's behavior gave Jaren the sneaking suspicion that Caine knew what Kale was really doing inside that compound, but that was a completely ridiculous thought.

There was no way he could have found out about Kale. No way, he told himself over and over again.

Jaren silently cursed how swiftly time was working against them. In fact, they were almost entirely out of it. Because Kale hadn't sent word she'd discovered Caine's plans, they had no choice but to move forward with their back up plan. Sunrise four days from then, they would be attacking the castle while Kale was paying Caine a little visit. They'd gotten lucky so many times already on their mission Jaren hoped their luck would last until the new year. Pushing the inkling that something was wrong out of his mind, Jaren grabbed hold of that hope and held on tight.

## FIFTY

In the dream, so real, Kale walked through the winding corridors lost deep in thought. These days her mind raced with all that was weighing on her and she found little relief or escape. Day after day, Caine used up most of her time but informed her of nothing. Because she'd failed to find out what it was he was planning, the backup plan was now in place and she'd gotten word to her friends through Jaren's main contact inside the castle. In four days, she would have to find it within herself to kill the great Caine without having found any way to discredit him among the common people. She'd never doubted that she'd be able to do it, kill Caine, but she'd also never imagined getting to know him. He was a complicated and haunted man. He had within him, however small, the memory of a man whom she'd begun to like. It was only an echo, but it still rung inside him. Kindness, humor, compassion, the ability to feel shame or regret, all of it hidden far beneath a veneer of darkness and pain that she'd yet to understand the source of. Kale had come to learn that the madness and cruelty that drove him toward power and evil weren't the entire picture. It would have to be enough. Caine would die in four days and, Kale, whether it was a struggle or not, knew she'd be able to go through with it.

"Kale." She heard a voice drifting through the hallway of her dream and stopped. "Kale."

As her skin began to crawl and fear raised the hairs on the back of her neck, Kale looked around wildly. The strange voice had reached right down to her core and sent a chill racing through her entire body.

"Kale," the voice called again. "Kale, I'm waiting."

Kale was standing in the area Caine had brought her to what seemed like years ago. She looked around at the different Caines upon the walls. Again, she felt hatred swell within her, swallowing anything else she might have felt for the man. The faces jeered at her, some of them snarled and laughed tauntingly. 'What's going on here?' she worried, fear grabbing hold and squeezing her tight.

"Kale," it was a woman's voice and seemed to come from everywhere and nowhere all at once.

Kale looked around in a panic, ready to run, when she spotted a bolted door that she hadn't noticed before and her curiosity overtook everything else she was feeling.

She walked over and examined the lock only to realize there was no way she could get it open without tools. Her instincts told her something important was behind that door and she banged on it once, twice, her frustration landing in hollow thunks against the thick wood. When she turned to walk away, trying to avoid looking at the mocking Caines who hung on the walls around her, watching, she heard the lock turn and the door open behind her.

She turned swiftly, startled, and a little afraid, looking around for whoever had opened the door even though something told her that person was on the other side. The Caines had all stilled, but Kale was ever aware of their eyes, always watching. She walked slowly towards the door and then through it and wasn't surprised to see the same woman who'd visited her in the forest near her home.

Kale remained silent and waited. The woman looked deeply into her eyes making Kale shiver.

"What are you doing here?" Kale asked, sounding more certain of herself than she felt.

The woman stared at her so intently that Kale felt like she was being looked right through. As if her very thoughts were being heard, it was beyond disarming.

"Are you real?" Kale asked, her voice barely a whisper.

"Not here, I'm not."

Kale was silent for awhile, and the beautiful woman simply watched her.

"Ask your question, Kale."

"You're one of them, aren't you?" Kale didn't know why she asked. She didn't believe in the Founders and yet, in the world of dreams, it seemed that all you believed while waking could quickly become obsolete.

"Yes, I am. My name is Cyan. I come from Earth just like..." Cyan stopped and took a deep breath before continuing, "just like Caine," she finished.

"How are you in my dreams? Is this real?"

"I come to you like this because it's the only way I can reach you. The things you have read in the Scriptures are true. What you don't know is that, when Caine arrived, those whom you call the Founders were sent into a sleep from which we cannot wake. I have been unable to reach any of the other Founders, my friends, my family, or anyone else for the last fourteen years. I'm not sure why I have been able to reach you, I can only imagine, and the irony...well, this isn't the time for that now, is it?"

Again, silence enveloped the two women standing in the dungeon-like room. Kale became aware she was in the presence of someone who had many of the answers she was looking for.

"My parents?" Kale asked.

Cyan smiled gently. "I met them once, in a dream, a long time ago. I warned them of many things."

"Do you know how they died?"

"They died by Caine's hand," Cyan paused. "They were traitors."

Kale felt relief, disbelief, and shock break over her like a tidal wave. She stumbled and fell to her knees, gasping for breath, for reason. "How is that possible? Why didn't they ever tell me?"

"They were protecting you for more reasons than you could ever understand."

"But if they were traitors, why is he treating me so well?"

"The very same reasons he killed your parents."

Kale didn't understand and she wanted nothing more than to ask Cyan to clarify but she was speaking again already.

"Those things must be set aside for now though, Kale. The truth will be revealed soon enough."

"So, you know what will come of all this, Cyan?"

"I know some. If you can imagine that every single moment for all of eternity is, in a way, laid one on top of the other, on top of this very moment right here, then you can understand what it's like to be able to get a peek at it all, every once in a while. It's not always easy to make sense of all of it, you see..." Cyan had been staring past Kale, like she was seeing something far off and out of reach. After a long pause, she came back to herself and to Kale, and gave her a sad and sorry look. "But do not trouble yourself with those things."

"Then why are you telling me this? What does it all mean? Why do you keep trying to help me?"

"Because time is wearing thin. The Darkness is coming, and the real savior is yet to be seen. If Caine isn't stopped, all will be lost. Alpha Iridium and its people will be no more. Devoured, like so many other words, by the Dark they invited in themselves."

"What I am supposed to do?"

"Don't be fooled by his smile. Let him be fooled by yours. In three days, you may proceed with your plan. And pray that the savior finds the strength to fight with us or there is no hope."

"Do you know who the savior is? I mean can't we contact him or something?"

"I know, as does Caine."

"How does he know?"

"Because I told him."

"What? Why?"

"My reasons are not important. I'm sorry, but soon you'll understand everything. And remember, Kale, it is the choice that matters, not the outcome. You have to choose to be stronger than you've ever been. You have to choose to become whole so you can fight him. Choose wisely over the next few days, Kale. Choices are what define our lives. Goodbye and good luck."

Before Kale could say anything more, the room began to dissolve around her. "Wait!" she called out. "Cyan, wait!" but it was too late. Her bedroom began to come into focus around her and she realized she was still calling out. She sat up in bed panting and looking around wildly. When she was finally sure she was alone, she began to calm down. Had it all been a dream? She wasn't really sure. Was her subconscious simply finding ways to justify what had to be done or was something more going on? The woman had been so real. Her words had sounded so right. Was it all that easy? Kale didn't know.

Could her parents really have been traitors? All the mornings she'd spent asking her long dead father why he'd been a follower, should she have been thanking him for what he'd done? Kale's thoughts instantly drifted to Sunshine Bay and she longed to go and ask her father for the truth.

Rage welled up within her. It was a rising she couldn't stop and didn't want to. It was a rage toward Caine that burned more intensely and ached more deeply than ever before. Her vision swam in and out of focus and she felt her body begin to shake uncontrollably. Whether the dream was real or not, it had reminded her of what she'd come to do. In three days, she would kill Caine.

FIFTY-ONE

Kayla picked up the phone and dialed her old home number. After two rings, her mother's voice came on the line.

"Hello." Kayla heard but couldn't speak. "Hello?" her mother asked again.

Still, Kayla was silent, not sure she had the courage to go through with what she'd planned.

"Hello? Is anyone there?" her mother asked again.

"It's me, Mom, Kayla." Kayla could hear her mother smiling and it made her wonder how she'd let so much space open up between her and someone she knew so intimately, so well.

"Kayla, how are you?" She sounded far away and a little sad, despite the smile that remained in her voice.

"I'm okay, Mom, but we need to talk."

"Is everything okay, Kayla?" The quick shift to worry only a mother could manage.

"Yes and no, Mom."

"Are you hurt?"

"Mom," Kayla paused and took a deep breath, "just let me speak, okay?"

"Alright Kayla, go ahead."

"Mom, I know we've fought in the past about who I am and what I want out of life. I know I've let you down many times and I want you to know I'm sorry. I just wanted so badly for you to accept me for who I am that I tried to destroy the perfect image you had of me. I hurt you and I'm sorry, but you hurt me, too. What I want now is for none of that to matter anymore. What I want is for us to choose to move forward and learn to be friends again. I'm coming home, Mom, not for good just yet because I think that would be too much too soon. But I would like to be on the next bus out of here so we can talk face-to-face, so I can ask you to forgive me and have you hug me like you used to," Kayla's voice finally cracked, and the flow of words stopped. There was a deep and aching silence inside her and yet the void was a little smaller and a little less painful than it had been before.

"Oh, Kayla, forgive me. I just know what great things you're capable of, and I forget sometimes that doesn't mean you can't make mistakes. I'm so proud of you. I really am. We're just different people and sometimes we've forgotten to let that be a good thing. I love you. You know that, right? I have never in my life loved anyone as much as I love you."

Kayla felt relief rush through her like a long awaited tide. She hadn't expected her mother to deny her forgiveness but she hadn't realized how worried she'd been until after she'd said what she needed to say. Now Kayla found tears were tumbling down her cheeks carried by the anguish she'd held onto for so long. Her mother loved her. Kayla could finally begin to let go.

As much as she'd fought with her mother, she was still the person whose approval mattered most to Kayla. She sought it out with every decision, and every failure was a reminder of how surely she was incapable of finding it.

When she was young, it had been easy. As she grew older, she found herself a victim to the things that shook her certainty. Things like insecurity, self-loathing and even love. The latter of these was the greatest problem for Kayla. Love hurt. Love left you empty and alone. Love gave someone the power to wound you and leave you broken. If only Kayla hadn't learned the lessons of love from her father.

When Kayla was young, her father was rarely around. He'd been obsessed with work and unwilling to force himself to see that other things in life could be just as important. He'd adored his daughter and always thought his success in work would one day make her forgive his absence during her youth. Kayla never even had the chance to forgive him, one day four years ago he simply left and never came back. All of the love and approval she'd sought from him landed on her mother and yet Kayla had learned a lesson she would never forget about how weak and helpless love could make you, if you let it. So much the same in their broken hearts, yet still Kayla and her mother would be unable to share their grief. Kayla had begun to close herself off in order to keep her heart safe and whole.

It was a choice Kayla had only recently become willing to admit to, pretending to be perfect and whole because it was easier than being real. It opened up a gulf between her and the world yet still she grasped onto that performance, wore it like a shield. Perfect people didn't suffer pain, perfect people didn't come from broken homes, perfect people weren't abandoned by their fathers, and perfect people were never afraid of anything. Kayla didn't want to go back to that, and she couldn't. The thought of it terrified her.

The truth was Kayla was afraid of so many things she could barely keep track. Looming above her was the greatest fear of all; that she belonged nowhere and to no one.

Now as she said good-bye to her mother and told her she would see her in a few days, Kayla wondered if she was ready to believe something different. *Some things change,* she thought as she hung up the phone, *but can everything change?* Kayla didn't know but she was finally choosing to find out.


FIFTY-TWO

"Okay, so everything is all set. You guys are all packed and ready to go?" Jaren stood in the front hall of their home with a grim expression on his face.

Corin, Sam, and Ryan stood around a small pile of bags looking uncomfortable and worried. It was Monday morning and the first day their plan outside of the compound would take place. Corin, Sam, and Ryan were taking the train to Empris to meet up with the people storing their weapons. They'd made arrangements to use two train cars to hold all the weapons, and they had to be back by Wednesday in time for Thursday morning's attack. The rebels may have been a small group but they were still ready to arm themselves and anyone who would join them when the time came.

Everything seemed ready and the plan seemed flawless, but each of them knew there could be a lot of space between what seemed to be and the truth. They could all sense danger looming and realized there was no turning back, for any of them.

"So, this is it, huh?" Medea asked.

"You sound worried, Medea."

"Me, worried? You're damn straight." She moved closer to Corin, and they hugged tightly for a moment.

"We'll be back before you know it. Your biggest worry now is how bored you'll be while we're gone," Corin laughed and Medea forced herself to smile.

"You sound too damn calm, Corin."

"Yeah, well, I learned from the best."

He stepped over to where Jaren stood and the two friends hugged.

"Well, this is it. Did you ever think this day would come?" Jaren asked while they embraced.

"Mostly, I hoped it wouldn't but, now that it's here, it's full steam ahead. You take care of yourself. I'll see you in a few days," Corin said with an unusual air of cheerfulness.

"Of course," Jaren replied. They stepped away from each other, both smiling, if maybe a little strained. Though they were all approaching dangerous days, the last thing they wanted to do was say goodbye, which felt a little too much like tempting fate. They tried to keep the mood light but the longer they stood in the hall the harder that was.

"I'm going to stand out front. See you guys soon," Corin said at last.

"I'll come with you. I was never too good with good-byes," Sam said heading out the front door ahead of him.

Medea and Ryan hugged next.

"You scared?" Ryan asked as they hugged.

"It's no fun unless you're a little scared," she replied lightly but, as she continued, her tone showed how worried she was. "You just get back here safely, okay? We can laugh about how scared we were a week from now."

"It's a date," Ryan said finally pulling away from her. He took her face in his hands. "I love you," he said bending slightly to kiss her on the lips.

"I love you, too," Medea replied after he'd pulled away again. "Come back to me, okay?"

Ryan smiled at her before stepping over to where Jaren stood. The pair hugged briefly.

"I'll see you soon," Ryan said as he stepped away and picked up his bags.

"Yep. Be careful, alright?"

Ryan took one last look at them and then walked out the front door. As it closed behind him, quiet enveloped the house and the two friends. The silence was deep and ripe enough to reveal that some of them had seen each other for the very last time. It chased Medea out onto the porch and Jaren was just a few steps behind her. They watched as the trio disappeared into the trees without looking back. *That's right*, Jaren thought, *none of us can look back now.*

He turned and went back into the house leaving Medea to watch the trees where her friends and a piece of her heart had disappeared. She'd almost had enough waiting, restless for the final stages of their plan to unfold. She was hopeful they would all arrive on the other side of the new year unscathed, though somewhere deep down inside there was a whispering that they wouldn't be so lucky.

FIFTY-THREE

Kale walked through the empty hallways of Caine's castle feeling more alone than she ever had. She turned the dream over and over again her mind. The more she did the more certain she was it had held the truth. Though she was relieved at her growing certainty that her parents hadn't actually been servants of Caine, it made her realize that maybe she'd never really known who they were. 'That's how your friends will feel when you die,' a dark and quiet voice inside her whispered, before she could shove it away.

Thinking about her friends made her long for another time, one that hadn't happened yet, the one they were fighting for. It was that promise of peace and freedom after Caine. As she thought of Medea, Corin, and Jaren, Kale longed to have them with her, if only to make her feel a little more certain of herself. And then, she realized that maybe she owed herself and them much more than that. Maybe it was time to open up, to truly connect, and to try to let go of her fear of love and intimacy. She made a promise to herself then that once Caine was destroyed she would do better for the people she loved and who loved her. She would be better.

Despite all that hung in the balance, undecided, despite all that was coming at them at an undeterminable speed, Kale felt a weight had been lifted from her. Finally, she felt more in tune with what they were fighting for, not to destroy Caine but to build a better world...for each other.

She stopped, stood still, letting the truth sink in and settle. That realization, preceded by calm and quiet, took hold and she felt a shift deep within that made her tremble. A small smile tugged at the corners of her mouth. In her desire to destroy Caine and out of her personal hatred for him, she'd lost sight of the true reason for everything she was doing, but now she saw it again. The storm inside her, wild and raging, had finally blown itself out. All that remained was a crisp, cool clarity.

They were trying to make the world a better place, to overcome the Darkness barreling towards them, and that was far more important than Caine, and far more important than her. But if you weren't willing to embrace the light, to grab hold of all that was good, then what was it all for?

Kale looked up and around at her surroundings, as if she'd fallen asleep and was only now just waking up. When she realized where she was, she wasn't sure whether she'd sought out that specific door or whether it was coincidence that she'd passed by it on her walk. Either way a moment later, she knocked. The door opened.

"Kale, what are you doing here?" Derin stepped back into his room to let Kale walk through the door and then spoke again. "Kale, are you all right? You look strange. What's wrong?"

"Nothing is wrong. I just...I just..." She stood there, unsure of what to do or say next.

"It's safe to talk here," he urged but still she was quiet.

Derin couldn't help himself and drank in the sight of her, quenching a thirst he wasn't able to control or entirely understand. But, he couldn't be the one to reach out. He couldn't let her hurt him again. "I saw your friends," he offered instead of all the words his heart wanted to send soaring into the space between them.

"You did." Gratitude swept through her as she stepped in and let him close the door behind her. "And?"

"And, they're okay. They were a little suspicious of my reasons for going there though."

"I'm surprised you made it back here in one piece."

"Jaren and I came to an understanding."

"Jaren? Jaren trusted you? Medea, I can see, Corin maybe, but Jaren?"

"Yeah, we found common ground."

"Oh, really, and what was that?" Kale asked suspiciously. She was unwilling to question why but the thought made her squirm with discomfort.

"It's nothing you would understand," Derin said brushing her question away.

"Oh. I see."

Kale sat down in one of the large chairs by the window and looked out at the new day. She could sense the day was waiting for something but she couldn't imagine for what. Grey and white clouds bounded through the blue sky like cotton tumbleweeds, hinting at a breeze.

"Kale, are you sure you're alright?"

"You know my whole life I've felt like half a person, like I've always had to be extra special and extra good at everything just to feel whole. That doesn't make sense though, does it?"

"Kale, I know I don't understand but let me try. What are you so afraid of?" Derin wanted to reach out and touch her. Take her hand in his and comfort her. Never before had he seen anyone look so lost and alone. This was a part of the Kale he recognized. This was the Kale he loved.

As he tore through his mind for the right thing to do or say, Kale spoke again and spared him the effort, "Caine murdered my parents. I know that now for sure. My parents were traitors just like I am." She looked over at Derin and waited for his response. To her surprise, he laughed.

"Kale, I know that you're a traitor. Caine has been my father for almost fourteen years and I love him, but Berdune is hurting with him in power and crumbling under his will. I don't want any harm to come to him. Even though I know he's done horrible things, that's how I feel. But things need to change and we don't have much time."

"We?"

"If you don't trust me by now, that's fine, but I'm in this thing. I know too much. I've seen too much. And maybe, I can find out what we need to know."

"I spoke with one of the Founders," Kale said staring at him intensely.

"You what?" Derin interrupted but Kale kept speaking.

"She's the one who told me about my parents. She also told me Caine knows who the real savior is, and he's going to try and stop him from saving the people of Berdune."

"Hold on. Slow down. The Founders are a myth, Kale. Everyone knows that."

"A myth like the rebels?"

Derin paused, unsure where to go next. "Alright, say I believe the Founders are real?"

"You believe the Prophecy, don't you? Why don't you believe the Scriptures?" Kale retorted.

"Because no one has ever seen the Founders. They're supposed to have all kinds of power so, if they exist, why have they let things go on like this?"

"I don't understand most of it, really. I think they're in some kind of prison or something. This woman, she's visited me a few times, mostly in my dreams. She said something about the savior not being Caine and that he knows who the real savior is because she told him."

"Wait, what, your dreams? And why would she tell him that?" Derin said with exasperation and growing disbelief.

"I don't know. She wouldn't tell me."

"Well, how is it that she can talk to Caine but can't stop him?"

"I don't know that either. It doesn't make much sense when you put it that way," Kale paused and sighed deeply. "I don't know, but say this is all true. What if Caine plans to sacrifice the savior to save his own life?" Kale looked over at Derin and waited for his response.

"I guess that's possible."

For a long time, he was silent. And instead of listening to his mind, he listened to his intuition. He thought of knowing things that were going to happen before they did, even though he had no idea how. He thought of the multitude of unexplained or mysterious things that he'd dismissed as absurd throughout his life, and he thought of Kale and how all he'd wanted these past few weeks was for her to need him somehow, and now she did.

"If you believe it, then I believe it," he finally offered.

"Really?"

"Really," and he did.

Derin's mind was spinning. He'd never once considered that Caine wasn't the savior they'd been waiting for. Could the man he'd worshipped for so many years, that they all had in one way or another, be just a man? Had Caine deceived them all right from the beginning?

"If Caine isn't the savior, then who is?"

Kale shook her head, "I don't know, Derin. I don't know much of anything anymore."

"Kale?"

"Yes."

"Why are you trusting me, all of a sudden?"

Kale shrugged, "because you deserve it, I guess."

"And, us?"

"Maybe when this is all over, we can be friends, Derin," was all she was willing to offer. "Right now, the people need help. Caine needs to be stopped. My friends need to be protected, and I can't let them down. I can't abandon any of it."

"Kale, it isn't about abandoning the people who need you, it's about not abandoning yourself," Derin took a deep breath. "I know you think you're alone and I won't pretend to understand why. What I do understand is that there are people out there who love you beyond belief and, I'm sure that more than needing you to be strong, they want you to love them back."

Annoyed, Kale retorted, "How do you know that?"

Derin didn't answer her right away, and she turned away from him and stared out the window again. She watched the day brighten slightly with every breath she drew. *The day comes so quickly*, she thought, *it all comes so quickly.*

"So, what do we do now?" he asked instead of answering. He was letting go of everything else that was bubbling up inside him and that he wanted to hand her; offerings for a life that could be, if she'd just let it.

"I suggest that Thursday morning you make sure you're not in the compound anywhere, Derin. Until then, we should continue to stay away from one another. It's safer that way."

"You won't hurt him?" Derin asked.

Kale shook her head and felt a pang of guilt mixed with sadness weave its way through her entire body. Betraying him by killing his father would change everything, irreversibly so. But she couldn't permit herself to care what killing Caine might do to her and Derin's relationship. That couldn't matter. She wouldn't let it. That life she dreamed about, where there were no wars for her to fight, no monsters to face, no Darkness to vanquish, and love was possible, that life would never be real. What she wanted, what she needed, none of it mattered more than one simple and overwhelming truth, Caine had to be stopped and she was the one who was going to stop him.

"And you?" Derin asked watching her face for the answer rather than waiting for her to voice it.

"Me, don't worry about me," Kale said with a smile.

"Kale." He moved towards her and she stood, stopping him. The space between them was filled with that crackling electricity that had flowed between them so many times before. Kale knew if he reached out then she might falter, might just give in, too tired to fight that current that tried over and over again to sweep her away. Again, she struggled against it and won.

"The less you know the safer you are, Derin. I'm going to be fine. I've been ready for this for a long time. I'll let you know if I need any help, okay?"

Derin let out a laugh, "Nice touch but highly unbelievable. It'll have to do for now though." He smiled at her and Kale returned the gesture as brightly as she could manage.

"We better get down to the dining hall. We don't want to raise suspicion."

"You go ahead, Kale. If we show up together..."

Kale interrupted, "Of course, I guess I'll see you around."

Kale walked around him toward the door. When she opened it, she stopped and turned around. "Derin?"

"Yeah?"

The silence was filled with possibility. She let it stretch on and on until she finally gave him far less than she wanted to but all that she could, "Thanks."

She walked out into the hall and let the door fall shut behind her. Resigned, Derin smiled to himself. It was the most Kale could offer. He understood that. For now, maybe it was best. He was a traitor no matter how you looked at it and he was in just as much danger as any rebel if not more. He needed to stay focused. The world was going to change and Derin finally understood that he wanted to help change it instead of just going along for the ride.

As he walked down to the dining hall, at peace with his decisions, he felt relieved. He'd chosen a side, one he could live with dying on, if that's what it came to.


FIFTY-FOUR

Tuesday morning Ryan, Sam, and Corin were standing outside of the back entrance to the old building they stored their weapons in. Sam turned the key in the lock and they all went through the creaking door into the endless darkness beyond. Sam was the last to enter and after closing the door the sound of her locking it echoed through dark.

"Sam? Did you just lock the door?"

"You can never be too careful these days," she said flicking on the light.

"What the hell!" both Corin and Ryan said in unison, equally shocked, just a moment before being rushed by J'Kahl soldiers.

The pair shouted and kicked, confusion and terror spurring them on, but they were outnumbered and outmatched. The J'Kahl quickly and efficiently bound their hands behind their backs and then tossed them both to the cold and dirty floor. It didn't take long for the realization to dawn on both Corin and Ryan that things were far from what they'd expected. In the dimly lit warehouse, the truth crept toward them.

"Sam!" Ryan called. "Sam, are you all right? Sam!"

Sam's melodic laughter came floating toward them.

"Oh, I'm fine," she said stepping into view.

"Sam, what's going on here?" Corin demanded, panic and anger battling to dominate his voice.

Before Sam answered his question, Corin began to understand. With growing dismay, the truth closed in on him.

"Oh, come on, now," Sam's voice slithered through the gloom. "You two are smarter than that." She laughed again.

"Sam?" Ryan asked sorrowfully. By his tone, it was obvious he was barely clinging to his disbelief.

"Oh, my dear little brother, what a fool. What a pathetic fool you've been." She took a step toward them. "Stand them up," she ordered.

The J'Kahl forced Corin and Ryan to their feet and, what they saw when they stood and could see the entire warehouse, made them sick.

"I just didn't know what to do with all this space," Sam said calmly as she pulled a knife from her belt and used it to point around the room. "I know. I'm not great with decisions."

"I don't believe this," Ryan said, his voice full of heartache.

"Oh, you mean the weapons, or rather the lack of weapons," Sam laughed again. "I'll let you two in on a little secret. There never were any weapons. Not here, anyway. Your weapons are being stored in Caine's compound. Oh, I love the irony," she said gleefully. "The money you got from Caine you used to purchase weapons to use against him, but he stole those weapons from you and you had no idea. You really are in over your heads."

"Sam, I don't understand. What's going on here?" Ryan sobbed. He was begging his sister to tell them that they'd misunderstood and she hadn't betrayed them.

"My dear brother, I wish this could have all been different. We would have been great together, you and I. Oh, but you had to fall in love with that rebel whore and now you're in this whole mess even deeper. You're more pathetic than Mom and Dad, you know. They pretended to be loyal followers but they were just in it for the money."

"Sam?" Ryan whined.

"You should have heard them beg for their lives before I killed them. It was all rather disheartening really. Sadly, they died thinking we both had betrayed them. No matter though." Smiling maniacally, Sam walked over to where Ryan and

Corin were standing. "You can tell them the truth when you see them." Sam ran the knife along her brother's throat and a crimson stream made its way quickly down his neck and began to stain his shirt.

"No!" Corin screamed as Ryan fell to the ground beside him.

"Oh, one last thing, Ryan. Tell them I said, 'hi.'"

He couldn't hear his sister, he'd already started to drift off and away to the place that comes next. His last thought, as he wandered out of this life, was of Medea, and a love that would have to wait for another time.

The crimson pool swelled around Ryan's body, too still, and Corin shook uncontrollably beside him. "Oh my god" was all he could manage to say, his voice filled with revulsion and disbelief, "Oh my god."

"Has the other prisoner been fetched?" Sam asked one of the soldiers.

"Yes. She's at the train station with the others just like you told us she should be," one of them answered timidly.

"Perfect. Everything is going as planned."

Sam took one last long look at her brother's lifeless body and for a moment grief swept over her before she banished it.

"Leave the body," she said roughly before motioning toward Corin. "Get him to the train. Caine wants him for something else." The J'Kahl stared at her skeptically. "Let's go!" she screamed, and they set into motion right away.

Corin could do nothing to compose himself. He was completely unable to draw himself back to the gravity of the situation unfolding around him. He'd lost all sight of the larger picture. All he could do was shake uncontrollably at the shock of losing one of his friends. As they dragged him out of the building into the startlingly bright day, he had a moment where he wished they'd killed him, too. He had a feeling that what was awaiting him was far worse than death.


FIFTY-FIVE

"So, this is it," Alex said.

"Alex, this isn't right. Don't do this," Arin pleaded.

"We all saw the stars last night, Arin. This is where we part ways."

The five friends were seated in the same train car they'd slept in the night before. Because their appearances gave away their identities immediately, they'd decided to get on the train late the night before and stay there until they were ready to act.

The other decision they'd made, or rather the decision that was handed to them, was that Arin, Joah, Arwyn, and Beran were to make their way to Braedon Ridge undetected and try to address the people. They weren't sure what they were supposed to say, but what else could they do but what they always had, and that was willingly to follow the stars. It was a way of life so deeply ingrained in them that they rarely fought against it. Yet when the stars told them their group was to be split in two and that Alex's path forward was different than theirs, they found themselves unsure and beginning to struggle against the chains that had always bound them.

"Guys, let's not drag this out. This isn't goodbye. We all saw that, too." He looked around at his family and drank in the sight of them as if for the very first or last time. A deep wave of sadness washed over him as he was struck by the contrast between their strength and vulnerability. There was no room in his life to regret that he'd kept so much space between himself and them to do what was best, but for just a moment the regret snuck in with the sadness and pulled at him in a way that took his breath away. "You guys ready to do what we need to do?" he asked to chase away the ache that had started down deep.

No one answered.

"That was a question," Alex encouraged.

"We're ready," Arin responded. "Now, give me a hug and then get out of here."

Alex hugged her tightly for a moment and then hugged the others in turn. As he headed for the compartment door, he could hear muffled cries coming from the other side of the train yard.

"Damn Caine and all those who serve him! He's a monster! He's a murderer! Don't let him fool you! Damn Caine!" Corin's voice came squeezing through the small sliver of an opening in the train car door.

"That's my cue," Alex said, throwing the door open and disappearing out into the bright day beyond. Arin closed the door behind him and the darkness surrounded them once again. Through the tiny crack, she watched as Alex crossed the train yard toward a large crowd of people who'd gathered around the commotion.

FIFTY-SIX

"Damn Caine!" Corin screamed as he kicked and struggled against the two J'Kahl holding him tightly. "Damn Caine and all those who serve him! He's going to destroy us all! Can't you see that!?" He met the eyes of anyone in the crowd that had begun to gather. He wanted them to believe so badly. To see the truth of the world they'd all allowed to be built around them.

"I'm impressed, Corin. I really didn't take you for the feisty type. Medea would be very proud, I have to admit that much," Sam's words taunted. Before she could go on, her attention was drawn by cries of shock from the crowd that had gathered to watch the developing scene. All around them, people were bowing or falling to their knees. "They've returned," people kept whispering reverentially. "They've come to save us."

Sam was looking around for the source of the commotion and, even before she saw who was causing it, she saw a mop of ice-blue hair bobbing through the crowd. *Oh my god*, she thought wildly, *Caine said they would come and they have.*

Finally Alex broke through the crowd and stood only feet from where Sam had stopped. He was a stunning creature. His mane of ice-blue hair matched his eyes perfectly and he was the only person Sam had ever seen as tall as Caine. He was so striking and so beautiful that he seemed entirely otherworldly and even Sam had to shake herself to try and break his mesmerizing spell.

"What is his crime?" Alex said pointing toward Corin whose mouth had fallen open in shock.

Though Sam was frightened by both his power and his certainty, she tried not to sound it when she spoke, "He's a traitor to Lord Caine."

"Caine, that monster, that murderer, that imposter? Then your prisoner is a hero. Release him." Immediately, the J'Kahl holding Corin, let go.

"What the hell are you doing?" Sam screamed at them and they took hold of Corin once again though they looked ready to let him go again if Alex demanded it.

"What is your name?" Sam asked as forcefully as she could manage.

"Alex."

"Grab him," Sam ordered.

No one moved. The crowd was still on its knees in Alex's presence.

"You remember what Caine told us. These freaks would arrive and try to trick us. What's wrong? You think he's a Founder. Is that it? Has he shown us any magic? Has he proven himself to us at all? Look at him. He's practically a teenager. Now grab him before I report you to Caine."

Propelled by fear, the J'Kahl moved in on Alex. They braced themselves to be struck down by some kind of power but when they grabbed hold of him and nothing happened they were emboldened and quickly became more aggressive. Their certainty Alex was harmless grew with every passing moment.

"Get them into the train car now, and keep your eyes out for the other freaks like this one. Caine said there would be five of them."

The group made their way through the crowd back towards where Alex had come from. Corin was still silent but Alex began to yell.

"Damn Caine! He is a liar! He's tricked you! He's imprisoned the Founders!"

"Damn Caine and all those who follow him!" Corin joined in.

"The only way to stop him is if you rise up and fight back!" Alex shouted. And, they heard him.

"Caine is imprisoning a Founder!" one woman yelled out as she stood.

"Caine has lied to us!" came another voice.

Some people started to stand and push toward Corin and Alex.

"Let them go!" one man yelled as a soldier threw him to the ground.

"These men are prisoners of Caine's," one of the J'Kahl said defiantly. "Do you dare oppose Lord Caine?"

People were tossed out of the way and struck down as they tried to reach the prisoners but they never even got close. Corin and Alex kept yelling until they were tossed up the stairs into the train car with the other soldiers and Sam right behind them.

Only one thought turned through Alex's mind, *Caine knew they were coming, but how?* Alex wasn't sure.

FIFTY-SEVEN

Once Alex and the other prisoner had passed out of her view, Arin slid the door fully shut and turned back toward her friends. Their eyes had adjusted to the dark compartment and they could see each other well enough. They hadn't heard anything except the shouting at the end of the confrontation but they'd seen enough to understand what it was they could do once in Braedon Ridge.

Arin let her back slide down the wall until she was seated. Her chin dropped towards her chest, she let her eyes fall shut, and, for just a moment, let herself ease into a safer kind of darkness than the one they were fighting. Watching Alex be taken prisoner was the hardest thing she'd ever had to do. She had a sinking feeling the days ahead would bring many things much harder.

"They'll listen to us," Arin whispered into the darkness as she opened her eyes to face her friends and the task ahead. The train lurched forward and began to move down the track.

When she spoke again, her voice was clear and certain, "the people will listen to us."

## FIFTY-EIGHT

Corin and Alex were thrown side-by-side into a corner at the back of the car. The trains were used primarily for shipping and only one or two cars were meant for passengers. Though they were in a passenger car, they weren't given the luxury of sitting on one of the cushioned bench seats. The soldiers left them there, bound and unable to move, while they found seats as far from them as they could. Alex couldn't help but enjoy the fact he intimidated them.

Sam approached them with a scowl. "There's no way out of this train car that isn't through us. I'm not going to tie you up any more than you already are. I think Caine would like you alive and kicking. Try anything, and I change my mind." Sam turned and walked away. "Oh and Corin," she called over her shoulder, "we've got a little surprise just for you. You'll thank me later, I'm sure. It was all my idea after all."

"She's wonderful," Alex said sarcastically but saw immediately he'd taken the wrong tone under the circumstances.

"Sorry," he offered. "My name is Alex."

"Corin. I'd say nice to meet you, but under the circumstances..."

"Yeah, I know."

"Are you really one of the Founders? I mean you look like one. As far as the legend goes, at least."

"Kind of, I guess. My parents were Founders."

"What happened to them?" Corin was stunned. He would never have believed the Founders were anymore than a myth but here Alex was.

"When Caine arrived, they fell into a coma and they're still sleeping. That's why we've come."

"We?" Corin asked.

"The other children of the Founders. There are four others with me. We came to help."

"You're doing great so far," Corin said, unable to muster the light or joking tone he was aiming for. "Why don't you zap these soldiers or something, get us out of here?"

"My parents could do that stuff. I'm afraid us kids are a bunch of duds."

"So then, how exactly do you plan on helping? I mean all I've seen you do is get captured," Corin couldn't hide his annoyance for their helpless situation.

"So, I guess I'm making as much progress as you are."

"Sorry, Alex," Corin sighed, a deep and troubled sound. "I just watched that sociopath Sam kill her own brother, my friend, and I'm pretty sure I'm in for much of the same. My other friends are all in danger and I can't warn them because I got myself captured by someone I thought I could trust. I'm not exactly having a good day."

"I'm sorry, Corin. How did you get into all this anyway?"

"Mostly by thinking a bunch of kids had a chance against Caine."

"Well, we have something other than being prisoners in common then. Except of course I still believe a bunch of kids do have a chance."

"You do?" Corin asked hopefully.

"Would I be sitting here if I didn't? Would you?"

Despite himself, Corin smiled. It seemed the whole world was against them at that moment but, for some reason because it was 'them' and not just 'him,' Corin felt a little more at peace.

The new friends settled into silence as the train moved steadily toward Braedon Ridge and whatever fate awaited them. Not long into the journey, Sam brought drinks to them but they were given nothing to eat and had only each other for company and comfort. Before the train arrived at its destination, they were both deep in a drug-induced sleep. Neither of them dreamed.

FIFTY-NINE

"Why do you always try so hard to be what people need you to be?"

Kayla had never heard the question from anyone before and yet the answer spilled from her instantly, "I don't know who else to be."

Max and Kayla were sitting in his room on the floor. Night had fallen outside of the large bedroom window and their plan to watch a movie had been abandoned when they'd started talking. An hour later, they were still talking and much to Kayla's dismay the conversation had wound its way towards her unwillingness to let Max or anyone else into her heart.

"Do you love so little about yourself that you can't see all the wonderful things there are about you? Everyone who meets you loves you, Kayla, can they all be wrong?"

Kayla let this question sit and settle within her. She poked at it, weary. It was a thing that could come to life and strike out at her at any moment. She wondered if the answer was even within her at all, but it must be if she was so afraid.

"It's not that I don't like who I am. I just don't know who I am. So what?" Kayla became defensive. "I don't think I'm the only person that's a little confused about that."

"You're changing the subject."

"Max, I don't even know what we're talking about anymore."

"I love you."

Kayla didn't at first reply. She sat staring at the wall wishing she hadn't heard those words. They always seemed to signal that soon there would be pain. Even though Kayla couldn't remember being hurt as many times as she felt she'd been, the pain was present none the less. Sometimes, it was like remembering someone else's life. Someone else's suffering was layered on top of her own.

Max loved her.

Kayla thought about all the times she wished she could hear those words and truly believe them. She looked up into his twinkling blue eyes and realized that finally her wish was a reality. And yet, she wasn't ready to face it.

"What do you want me to say to that?"

Max took Kayla's hands in his. "You don't have to say anything. I told you because I wanted you to know. I told you because you deserve to hear it."

"Because I deserve to hear it?"

"Because you deserve to believe it."

"Thanks," Kayla said unconvincingly as she stood up. "I have to go home. My aunt will worry if I'm late."

"I'm sorry, okay? Stay with me tonight?" Max pleaded quietly as he stood, seemingly afraid of the question instead of the answer.

"Max, I..."

Max interrupted her, "I need you, Kayla. Just stay. Nothing will happen, I promise, I just want you to be near me, okay?"

After a long silence, Kayla finally said, "Okay" and let him draw her into the bed and under the sheets where he wrapped his arms tightly around her. All she'd learned how to do with love up until then was run from it. Even for her, hurt too many times to count and afraid of being hurt again, the possibility of staying still, of letting love catch hold of her even just for a little while, was too much to resist.

Lying in bed over an hour later, Kayla was still wide awake. She listened to Max's rhythmic breathing and found it just as calming as the sounds of the sea.

She wondered how she could have let him get so close to her. A month earlier, she'd been certain that loneliness would be her only companion for a long, long time; if not forever. She'd only just found the strength to get used to the idea of solitude and now the world had pulled it away from her and asked her to get used to something else.

Staring at Max as he slept peacefully beside her, propped up on one elbow so that she could look down and drink in the sight of him, Kayla wondered how she would ever be as great as he thought she was. She wondered how she was going to keep from letting yet another person down. Mostly she wondered how long it would be before Max realized he didn't love who she really was. *He'll find out,* she thought as she lay back down beside him. *They always do.* Max stirred and wrapped his arms around Kayla again and all she could think, as she let herself be drawn into his warmth and security, was how she never wanted to be lonely again.

"I love you," she whispered into the darkness, sleep nudging at her gently.

She slipped into familiar dreams almost right away. The same dreams she'd been haunted by since she was five-years-old. These were same dreams that distracted her from a normal and happy life, and the same dreams that called out to her to sleep forever and set them free.

## SIXTY

Jaren leapt from his dreams into the waking world with a start. He heard someone downstairs in the house and knew right away that something was wrong. He blinked once, twice, to adjust his eyes and saw by the clock that the night had barely begun.

Outside of his room, he heard movement and was relieved to hear Medea's voice come in a hush as she pushed the door open, "Jaren, someone's in the house."

"I know," he whispered back as he carefully and quietly got out of bed. Jaren grabbed the knife he kept in his bedside table and quietly made his way towards the door.

"Stay here," he whispered.

"No way," Medea retorted in a loud whisper.

Unwilling to argue, and somewhat relieved, Jaren crept out of the room with Medea right behind him. They moved slowly towards the stairs and the waiting darkness below. Each step felt like a loaded landmine. At any moment, a creak or groan could give them away to whoever was in the house. Adrenaline raced through them both, tense and ready to react. Weeks of stress and strain and worry waking up in both of them a kind of fear they hadn't known before. When the intruder finally stepped into the light of the foyer, Jaren let out the breath he'd been holding the whole way down.

"Emily," Medea stood frozen to the spot with shock. "Emily?" She repeated and this time it was a frantic question. "What are you doing here?"

As Medea took a step toward the child, she could see her face was streaked with tears and stained with either dirt or bruises, though she couldn't quite tell in the dimness of the hall. She knew immediately the situation was bad. Emily was shaking violently and terror swam in the depths of her eyes.

"J-J-J-J'Kahl," she stuttered, "th-th-they raided th-the Mission and the town. M-m-mom's g-gone. Th-they're all gone." Emily finished with a wail as she fell into Medea's arms. Medea held her tightly letting the small girl shake and shiver in her arms. *What the hell is going on here?* she thought as she looked toward Jaren for an answer to the question she'd yet to ask aloud.

A moment later, the front door swung open violently and Jaren instinctively jumped in front of his friend and the small child.

"Jaren! Medea!"

Standing in the doorway looking around frantically was a man Jaren met with often. He'd been a great help over the years and was always willing to pass on information in the fight against Caine. He was one of the senior trainers of the J'Kahl but, more importantly, he was invaluable in the gathering of information for the rebels.

"Mike, what the hell is going on?"

Mike turned abruptly towards Jaren and started shouting. "We have maybe two minutes to get the hell out of here. They're coming. They know who you are, and I'm almost certain my cover is blown. Let's go!"

"Damn it!" Jaren spat. "Get them out of the house, Mike...now! You know where to meet me. I won't be far behind you," he yelled as he ran up the stairs two at a time to get what little he could. He didn't mind losing his things but there were a few papers and documents in the house that could identify all of the rebels, and he didn't intend on leaving those behind.

"Jaren," Medea shouted up the stairs after him.

"Go, Medea! Go!"

With Emily in her arms, Medea ran out the back door followed closely by Mike.

She could hear her heart pounding in her ears and her chest burned for air. Branches whipped at her face and she was amazed that she hadn't lost her footing through the dangerous woods. While she raced through the darkness and a forbidding sea of fog, only one thought raced through her mind on repeat, *He knows. Caine knows about us.*

Back at the house, Jaren moved with lightning speed as he took what he needed to from his room. They lived their lives and ran the alliance as if at any moment they would need to erase what little proved who they were, who Kale was, and what they were doing. Yet, it felt like an eternity stretched on around him as he grabbed the handful of papers that could destroy them if they landed in the wrong hands. As he made it to the top of the stairs, Jaren heard the front door burst open once again. This time he was certain the visitor wasn't coming to warn him of danger but instead was bringing it. He turned around and darted back into his room. Moving into the darkness as quietly as he could, he hoped against hope that he would find a way out. Somehow.

What he knew in his heart, what had become clear to him the moment he'd heard Emily's fearful voice was that the role they thought they would be playing in the last days of Caine's fourteenth year had changed somehow. Not even Jaren could push his imagination to the truth and in many ways he didn't want to. He would soon find out and he was certain that when he did he would wish for any of the moments before this night when he'd been certain they would succeed without contest.

Walking quickly towards the window, Jaren saw beams of light sweeping across the yard and realized he was trapped. Pulling a lighter out of his bedside table he lit the precious papers on fire and held them by an edge until only the small piece between his fingers had yet to burn. It would give him away, the flickering light, but not the others and that was all he could do now. He had no idea if they'd all been compromised or not, and he wasn't about to risk his friends' lives to save his own.

"Put that down!" a shadow in the doorway screamed at him.

Jaren let the last few scraps of charred paper waft softly to the ground and waited.

The soldier was upon him in an instant and took only a moment more before he was fiercely binding Jaren's hands behind his back. The ropes bit into his wrists, making him wince, but the pain didn't reach past the shock of their failure. Jaren wasn't sure why, but he didn't struggle or try to wrestle himself free from the soldier's grasp. The J'Kahl kicked Jaren towards the door.

"Move," he commanded.

Jaren stumbled and hit the hardwood floor with a grunt. The soldier rewarded him with another hard kick to the ribs before pulling Jaren up and shoving him towards the doorway again.

Pain throbbing in his side, vision clouding with rage, and something else rising in him he didn't want to face just yet, Jaren could think of only one thing, *Kale, he knows about Kale, and she must be in danger.*

Suddenly, his rage flared up and he pulled violently loose of his captor and ran towards the stairs. Two more soldiers met him there and though in his heart Jaren knew it was too late to try and fight his way free, he struggled and kicked just so that he would never have to question why he'd gone without a fight.

Not far away, Kale slept peacefully. She was unaware her friends were in danger. She was unaware how much danger she was in herself. Jaren struggled and fought with that one hope, that if he could free himself he could warn her, but he was outmatched.

When the soldiers tossed Jaren out of the house and onto the front lawn he landed on his back, cracking his head on something hard. For a moment, he thought he might blackout but he didn't. Looking up, he noticed the midnight sky was unusually dark. No stars danced within the heavens above.

Darkness had come.

## SIXTY-ONE

Sam stood in Caine's office and beamed at him with pride. She'd done well for herself in the last month and she knew she would be rewarded for her dedication.

She'd always been in love with Caine. As a child, she'd indulged in silly childhood fantasies of Caine rescuing her from her dull and boring existence and making her his queen. As she grew older, she outgrew the fantasy yet her love for Berdune's ruler had never faltered.

He'd approached her a few years before though she was never quite sure why. She assumed that after spending so much time with him during the meetings he took with her parents he'd realized what a loyal follower she was, but the truth was a far darker and more sinister thing. She'd always despised the way her parents had cared more about money than the vision Caine spoke of. After years enamored with him and all that he promised, she hadn't really minded taking their lives for Caine. Her brother had been a different issue.

Sam and Ryan had been close since childhood and had maintained a rare friendship throughout their early teen years until he'd met the rebels. When Ryan had fallen in love with Medea, he'd lost sight of what Berdune really needed and he'd spent less and less time with his sister and more and more time with her. Sam's hatred for the duo had grown exponentially over the years and, though it did break her heart to have to take her brother's life, she relished denying Medea her one true love. She also knew Caine would never doubt her if she was willing to murder her own family in his name.

"I must say you have surpassed all my expectations of you, Samantha," Caine said with demonic pride.

"When I said I would do anything for you, my lord, I wasn't lying." She bowed her head submissively and as Caine approached her, a shiver of excitement ran through her entire body.

"Family is the deepest bond there is, Sam," He moved ever closer as he spoke. "You have served me well."

As she brought her eyes to his, she saw the truth in them even before he brought it upon her. The blade slid across her throat delicately but the damage was violent. Warm blood spilled from her throat, her eyes widened with shock, and she fell to her knees.

"I really did adore you, my dear, but you can't expect me to trust someone who would betray their friends and family as you have. I hope you can forgive me." He paused, mesmerized by the pool of blood that was spreading around her knees. "Of course, I'll be quite fine if you don't," he said with a dismissive shrug.

Choking on her own life, Sam fell onto her side. She wanted so badly to tell Caine to go to hell, to tell him she would see him there, but in a strange moment of clarity, the first one she'd had in a long, long time, she understood Caine was already there. Her last thought wasn't one of those she'd loved, or even regret, it was simply to wonder if Caine was luckier than most because he was willing and able to surrender to his fate, no matter how awful it was.

SIXTY-TWO

"Medea, keep moving. We're not safe until we're far away from here."

Medea had stopped again to look behind them, straining with her eyes and ears for any sign of Jaren catching up with them. They'd reached Sunshine Bay safely by way of the Braedon River and now they were heading eastward towards the towering mountain ranges that lined the eastern part of the bay.

Mike was carrying Emily and she slept fitfully in his arms. Despite the extra weight, he didn't let the child slow his pace. Like most nights, she dreamed of the sea but tonight it was turbulent and wild, tempting her to drown within its depths.

Medea could feel the cuts and scrapes on her face burning angrily and, each time she brought her fingertips up to inquire about them, she could feel moisture there. In the lamplight, Medea saw her fingers touched with blood and the sight made her shiver with foreboding.

"Mike, what's going on. Why did they raid the Mission? Why would they take innocent people?"

Without slowing his pace, Mike replied between ragged breaths. "Strangers showed up in town tonight, four of them. They were Founders. They started gathering people and speaking out against Caine. The people began to listen."

"Founders?" Medea asked with disbelief. "You can't be serious."

"I am. Caine was expecting them, too. He had soldiers watching the rally and everyone who joined in was arrested. I don't know where they took the Founders."

Medea had so many questions but she didn't know which one to ask first. She tried to clear her mind and focus, listening to the incessant crashing of the ocean waves. Suddenly, she thought of Kale. Kale could be sound asleep inside the walls of Caine's compound and completely unaware of the danger that was swiftly approaching and Medea, the one who was usually in search of danger, was fleeing from it.

Medea stopped and let the darkness consume her as Mike and the lamplight pressed on.

"Medea, please! I told you, Jaren can take care of himself. Let's go!"

Medea was rooted to the spot. She couldn't run away.

"Medea, what's wrong?"

Mike scanned the silent woods to their left hoping they'd not been found by the J'Kahl. He saw no sign of danger and looked back to Medea hoping she'd explain.

"I've got to warn Kale, Mike. She's in danger and she doesn't even know it."

Mike looked at her sympathetically but shook his head. "There's nothing we can do right now. We need to meet up with the others and get Emily to safety. Kale is going to be all right for tonight. We have to take care of ourselves."

"But..." Medea began.

Mike interrupted her, "Medea, you won't get into that compound. Getting yourself captured is not going to help Kale. Getting ourselves to the people who can help us will."

Mike turned and kept walking and reluctantly Medea began to follow. She had no idea where Corin, Sam, and Ryan were or if they were safe. She also had the sinking feeling that Jaren wasn't on his way to meet them. Her best and oldest friend was in the most dangerous place she could possibly be, and Medea was running to hide. These thoughts tore through her for only another instant before she spoke. "Mike," Medea pleaded and, as he turned to look at her, Medea bowed her head, both a show of regret and a show of submission. There was no escaping who she was or what she had to do. "I'm sorry, Mike, but I can't do this. Take Em to where we agreed to meet Jaren. I can't run away."

Mike walked over to Medea and took one of her hands in his. "Be careful, okay?"

She nodded and then turned away from him. She wasn't yet sure what she planned to do next but at least she wasn't running away.

Mike watched her go for a moment and then he continued quickly in the other direction. He was surprised at how far she'd made it without turning back to go find her friends. She'd never been one to hide or run from trouble and though now the circumstances were much more threatening, and what they had to lose was more than you'd ever want to, it seemed Medea hadn't abandoned herself. All Mike could do was hope they'd be okay. As much as he knew they could all take care of themselves, he was aware of how badly they all needed each other, whether they would admit it or not. Watching Kale this past month as she trained with the other soldiers, as she won them over along with Caine, determined to go it alone even when help was offered, had made that truth painfully clear to Mike over and over again.

It was hard to see how but, as he stumbled through the dark toward safety, Mike thought maybe they would all come through this all right in the end. The world they were living in was about to change, and Mike just hoped it wasn't going to leave them all behind in the dark.

## SIXTY-THREE

Medea followed the rapids north towards Caine's compound with no idea what she was going to do once she got there. She'd abandoned all logic for urgency and, as she left the rapids for the woods, she lost track of where she was. If Caine was moving already, then he would be ready for almost anything. Still, she'd rather die trying to save her friend than live knowing she'd run away.

From the woods to her left, she heard leaves and twigs crunching heavily underfoot and, when she stopped abruptly, she could hear voices speaking in a hush. She froze. Whoever it was had yet to realize she was there. *Maybe it's Jaren*, she thought hopefully as three figures burst forth from the trees.

Two large figures flanked another smaller one, and Medea could see that the one in the middle had his hands bound behind his back. Right away, she knew she'd stumbled on Jaren. They'd obviously circled through the woods instead of heading directly back to the compound. Medea had the feeling that was courtesy of her escape.

"Hey!" she yelled without thinking, running up behind the turning soldier and kneeing him in the groin. "Oh, that had to hurt," she said, kneeing him in the face as he fell to his knees. Despite herself, despite everything, she couldn't help being pleasantly surprised by her ability to remain sarcastic. It was comforting somehow, reassuring that some things were still certain in a world falling apart around them.

Jaren reacted right away. He swept the other man off his feet and managed to kick the crossbow out of his hands.

"Medea, the crossbow!" Jaren shouted as the fallen J'Kahl grabbed him around the ankles and brought him to the ground. Jaren let out a cry of pain and shock as his ribs connected with a large rock. Medea ran towards the discarded weapon but felt something wrap around her ankles and take her to the ground as well.

Looking behind her, she saw the soldier she'd kneed holding tightly to her feet as she kicked and struggled to break free of his grasp. Finally, she got her left foot loose and kicked out at the man wildly. He screamed in pain as her foot connected with his nose and he let go of her other ankle reaching his hands instinctively to his face. Medea jumped to her feet and turned, ready to run to where the weapon had landed but it was gone. She looked wildly around her, panic rising up so that she almost choked on it. Then, she saw him. The J'Kahl Jaren had been struggling with was holding the crossbow and pointing it toward her.

Medea looked into his eyes and the moment seemed to draw itself to the edge of eternity and back. In eyes that could not have looked upon the world for more years than her own, Medea saw fear and so much more than should have been in the eyes of a servant and a soldier in Caine's army. She saw compassion and humanity, regret and longing. She wondered if he was longing for love, the very thing he'd been starved of, serving a monster for so long. But it didn't matter whether she was right or wrong. What mattered was in her heart she could still see all the wonderful things they were fighting for, even in the eyes of her enemy.

*Light can win*, she thought wildly, *it has to.*

The moment passed. Gone as quickly as it had come upon her and Medea let it go, let it drift away from her without a second thought. She was in no position to pity the soldier. She needed to save hers and Jaren's life so they could finish what they'd started.

Had she been thinking, Medea would have stayed frozen to the spot, but she lunged toward the young man hoping she would startle him and get the chance to wrestle the weapon away. It happened in only a few seconds, but for Medea time slowed down to a crawl and again she felt as if she were eternity's prisoner, shackled to some awful forever. She heard Jaren from far away shouting, "No," as she flew through the air towards the J'Kahl. He stumbled backward in alarm and the crossbow, now empty, flew skyward as Medea landed on top of him with a gasp.

Her ears were ringing and she could feel a sharp stabbing pain in her right shoulder. Instantly, time caught up with her and as she rolled off the soldier, who she'd wanted to pity only moments before, she could hear Jaren screaming at her to run. She stood and swayed, her head pounding furiously, and then she fell to the ground again.

Medea tried to use her arms to prop herself to a sitting position and was confused when the only response she received was terrible pain in her right side. When she lifted her left hand to her right shoulder, she realized with growing dismay that she'd found the arrow that'd been loaded in the crossbow only moments before. Looking over at the wide-eyed J'Kahl with her mouth open, Medea saw the horror on his face.

"I'm sorry," he kept saying over and over while shaking his head, "it was an accident. I'm so sorry."

For the first time since seeing the J'Kahl, she saw a child instead of a soldier. Now, it showed in more than just his eyes. If she could have found the strength to reach toward him, she would have. They were enemies, true, but suddenly that was irrelevant. They were both just people, lost in a world that was drowning in darkness. Her vision began to swim and she realized with a sudden sense of urgency that, if she could just find the strength to ask the soldier, he would set them free.

"Don't be sorry, Symon. These two are traitors to Caine and we don't tolerate those kind of people," a liquid voice swam out of the darkness and Medea craned her neck to see who'd spoken. Wincing in pain and squinting through the night, Medea saw a monster standing before her.

He was tall and slim, an imposing figure, especially in the dark, which had come to life around him, coiled and pulsing like a hungry snake. His face was cloaked in shadows, menacing, lit only by the lantern Symon had dropped when he'd first fallen, but in that moment Medea was convinced that's how his face must look all the time. His eyes were bright with power and something else, madness so vast and sweeping it took on a life of its own. Medea felt a shiver run through her entire body.

It was Caine.

Jaren was stunned. Caine himself had come for them which meant they were in more trouble than he could have imagined. Caine approached and stood towering above him, his lips drawn back in a snarl.

"Get back to the compound right away," Caine said, as he pulled Jaren roughly to his feet, his hands still bound tightly behind his back. "Tell the McLevys the plan has changed slightly. Tell them to leave the boy alone. And, tell them, I've got a pleasant surprise for them. A little family reunion, if you will." Caine smiled gleefully just as Jaren winced at the mention of his parents.

As he stood, the J'Kahl Caine had referred to as Symon looked at Medea apologetically. She realized in that moment that she was seeing someone turn away from Caine and all he stood for and yet Symon could only stare at the two prisoners uselessly. What power did he have to defy the man, the monster, who stood between them? Finally, helplessly, he turned away from them, disappearing into the darkness behind the other soldier. Only the light of their lantern could be seen bouncing erratically as it receded into the night.

Caine reached down, grabbed Medea by her wounded shoulder, and lifted her effortlessly to her feet as if she were a small child. She cried out in pain, unable to stop herself.

"Don't touch her!" Jaren yelled as Caine began to laugh, delighted, and let her drop back to the ground, heavy and hurting.

"Jaren, I don't think you're in any position to tell me what to do. Besides, I'm not going to hurt her, not too much anyway, nor you for that matter. No, no." Caine began to pace, a predator in his element. Oddly, it was the first time Jaren realized how dangerous he truly was. "I've got bigger plans for you two. Ah yes," Caine continued as he began to laugh again, "big plans. Now let's get going, I want to check in with Kale at breakfast." Caine smirked, taunting and cruel. Both Medea and Jaren began shouting.

"Don't you dare touch her, you monster!"

"If you lay a hand on her, I'll kill you myself!"

"My, my," Caine went on, "what tempers. Let me remind you that if you hadn't taken up this mission and been loyal followers instead, none of this would be happening." He reached out and tore the arrow from Medea's shoulder as easily as if he was pulling a needle and thread through cloth. Fresh blood, almost black in the night, poured out and onto her sleeve. Medea screamed once, an exclamation point on the truth of how much trouble they were in, before she crumpled to the forest floor. Jaren kept repeating her name, trying to draw her back and away from the pain, but all she could hear was the rushing of blood in her ears, and all she could wonder was if it was the sound of her own dying.

"You'll wish you hadn't underestimated me. Now, let's get going. We have a savior to destroy." Again, Caine laughed maniacal and piercing. Then he led them, bound by rope, at a painful pace through the night, towards their doom.

Every step she took sent pain radiating through Medea's chest and arm, and she struggled equally to breathe and stay on her feet. Jaren's attention shifted between fear for their own lives and fear for those out of reach. He wondered if Corin was okay. If he knew the plan had gone south somehow and was safe or if he'd been captured, too. And he thought about Kale and about how he'd do anything to keep her from being hurt or killed, even while deep down a dark little whisper kept asking, *had she failed them, or had they failed her?*

That night, Kale slipped swiftly into strange dreams. She dreamed she lived in a world where Caine had no power. She dreamed of a world where she was a normal girl with a normal life and she had different battles to forge but no wars to win. She dreamed of a world where peace reigned and routine ruled all.

Kale dreamed, but the world around her moved forward just the same. The new day would bring many changes and she would wake unaware of them all.

SIXTY-FOUR

Wednesday morning, Kale got out of bed and walked to the window to study the day outside. The sky was unusually grey and muted. Like it had been painted with one giant charcoal brushstroke. Kale couldn't help but think of the Prophecy. Had Darkness come? In a strange way she hoped it had. Because then it was time to face it.

In twenty-four hours, their attempt to stop Caine would be well over. Her friends would have launched their attack from outside as she launched hers within. Her stomach lurched as she realized the time for action was bearing down upon her and for a brief moment she wanted to flee from her life and curl back up in bed and fall back into her dream world, the one where the battles were oh so different; softer and simpler somehow. But as she passed the mirror, pulling a shirt on over her head, she saw her reflection and the dream tumbled away from her and out of reach. She let it go. It was a nice dream but that's all it was and all it would ever be. Kale was destined for many things but none of them included a calm and normal life governed by routine and mundane joys. Not in Caine's Berdune anyway.

After getting dressed, Kale went down to breakfast and joined Caine at his table like she did every morning now. It surprised and unsettled her how easy it was to sit in his presence, to talk with him, to look him in the eye knowing the next morning she would be making an attempt on his life. Anger welled up within her, a fierce and fiery wave, for all that had become possible in Caine's Berdune that shouldn't have been possible at all. Her parents were murdered. Her friends had to become rebels and fighters. She was capable of murder. Young men like Derin served a monster and aided in unspeakable acts.

She looked around for Derin, but he was nowhere to be seen. Uneasiness began to gnaw at her. She watched Caine closely. He was uncharacteristically gleeful and a sneaking suspicion rose up in her that something was wrong, very wrong. She tried to dismiss her worry as paranoia, but her instincts told her things were not as they seemed. Caine couldn't stop smiling and he repeatedly glanced over at Kale. He was laughing at her. She was sure of it. As usual, the McLevys' eyed her with distaste but on this morning they smiled as well. Kale's discomfort and anxiety grew by the minute.

"How are you this morning, my child?" Caine finally asked and again she felt like the mouse to Caine's cat. *He's toying with me. Well, two can play at this game.*

"I am fine, my lord. I am eager to see more action though. When is it you will let me get my task force started?"

Caine nodded and pursed his lips, as if thinking her question over, but he made no indication he was going to answer her.

After a long silence, Kale spoke again, "Where's Derin?"

"Oh, he's off on some errands for me," Caine smiled widely baring his teeth at her. "It is too bad I had not known you were ready for action yesterday, Kale." Caine shook his head in mock disappointment, faking a frown.

"Why is that, my lord?" Kale asked innocently, uncomfortably aware that all eyes were on her. The McLevys watched her as if waiting for something specific in her behavior but she couldn't imagine what.

"Well, we raided the Mission and most of Braedon Ridge last night. There was quite a commotion, some kind of demonstration for traitors to Caine. Can you believe it? They would have been better to just turn themselves in. Fewer people would have been hurt and killed. No matter, it was a triumphant night for us, Kale. I'm sure you would have loved to be there."

Kale sat frozen to the spot. "Really, my lord," she said blandly, "that is wonderful news." She forced a smile and she could almost feel it hurt as her lips curved upward defying her heart.

"Isn't it?" Caine returned to his smile. "Interesting stuff actually," Caine laughed airily and looked towards the McLevys, "Mason and Laura here had the misfortune of finding out their son is a traitor. Lucky for them, I will not let that tarnish their reputation nor their position here."

Caine watched Kale closely and she was amazed at how composed she remained. "Really? That's terrible." She looked toward the McLevy's daring them to see through her façade. "You must have been horrified when you found out."

"Yes, we were. But it has been remedied," the McLevys both looked toward Caine and Kale followed their eyes.

"Yes, we captured him last night along with another girl, Meda, Media, something like that," Caine began. "Tragic, the girl was wounded and died sometime early this morning." Caine stared at Kale intensely. "One less worker for the mines or the factories is always a tragic day, wouldn't you agree, Kale?"

Kale could feel the blood rushing to her face and she tried to focus on being strong. "Tragedy seems to befit you these days, my lord," Kale said with a hint of defiance.

For the second time in her life, Kale faced the truth that a broken heart, no matter how devastating, was something you could live with. Jaren was a prisoner, and Medea, her best friend, was dead. If she'd only found a way to stop Caine sooner, her friends would still be okay. They wouldn't even have come this far in fighting Caine, if she hadn't encouraged them. It was all her fault. And when this was all over, she'd have to figure out how to live with herself and with everything else that came with the new year.

"Pardon me?" Caine asked accusingly.

"You mentioned more than one person has died. I can think of nothing more tragic than losing a slave, my lord, except of course losing two." Kale couldn't believe she'd yet to fall apart. Her vision was swimming with shock. Rage and heartache dueled within her and she wanted to scream so badly that her chest burned and her throat ached as if she was breathing fire.

"Yes," he replied with raised eyebrows. "No matter though, we raided Empris as well. A rather successful night, if I do say so myself."

Kale didn't think her heart could ache more than it already did but, at Caine's most recent comment, she thought she could feel it crumbling with guilt. If her friends had followed the plan, then Corin was in Empris, or more likely Caine's custody, if he was still alive.

"Empris?" Kale asked lightly. "You must have captured many useful people there as well." Kale waited hoping Caine would take the bait.

"Yes, yes, many useful people. I like the way you put that, Kale. Useful." Caine stood and began to pace behind his chair. "Actually, we had a hugely successful night. I don't know what I was thinking letting you sleep through it. Forgive me."

"There's always next time, my lord."

"I assure you, Kale, you won't have to wait long," Caine smiled lazily.

The entire table was watching Kale and many eyes throughout the dining hall were turned their way as well.

"I look forward to it. Now, if you'll excuse me, my lord, I have some things to attend to before we start our day." Kale stood.

"Of course, my dear. In fact, I have some business to attend to as well, as you can imagine. Why don't you take the day off, get some fresh air, clear your head?"

"Your generosity is too much my lord, thank you. I will see you at dinner then."

"Until then," Caine replied as Kale left the table as quickly as she dared.

When she reached the sanctuary of the hallway outside the dining hall, Kale braced herself for her anguish. Pretending not to hurt while in front of Caine had altered her pain somehow so that it was a gentle breeze when it found her, instead of the violent storm she owed her heart and her friends. She felt more alone than she ever had. Even more than alone, she felt less than human, like fighting off her pain and pretending it didn't exist, had taken her one step further from being like everyone else.


SIXTY-FIVE

Kayla woke in the morning completely refreshed. Sleeping next to Max, she'd found the most peaceful, dreamless sleep she'd ever known. Rolling over with a big smile on her face, Kayla was disappointed to see the bed beside her was empty. She looked at the clock through the haze of sleep that still lingered and saw she'd slept late. She wondered with a welcome pang of longing if Max had gone out already.

She rose from bed and walked toward the window to study the day outside. The sky was a pale yet resilient shade of blue that stole her from the present and carried her back to days long past, days when, in youth, joy was not a luxury but a constant and unfailing part of every day. Days when she would wake from sleep afraid of dreams she couldn't understand, fearful and alone, only to be wrapped up safe and warm in her father's love when he hurried to calm her back into blissful slumber. Days so numerous no one would have even dared to try and count them. For the first time in a long time, Kayla remembered that joy clearly because now it had begun to visit her again.

She'd regained some of that joy in Max, and she couldn't help feeling a sense of warmth at the thought of him. It moved through every cell in her body and being until she felt like she was steeped in it. As much as the prospect of having someone to love her frightened Kayla, her heart still swelled knowing someone in the waking world did. That realization drew her instantly to memories of her dreams, strangely absent the night before, swallowed by a Darkness void of anything. *Could she match the love she'd dreamed of out here in the world?* she wondered Kayla wasn't sure, but she thought maybe she was ready to try. Max was special. She'd never met another guy like him. She wanted to give him just an ounce of what he'd brought to her life already.

When Kayla heard movement behind her, she turned around and saw him standing in the doorway. He smiled at her, his gaze intense and piercing, as if framing her in his mind, as if he'd seen a little piece of what she was feeling and he wanted to keep a snapshot of it perfectly inside his memory. It was a smile that dreamed of forevers and yet one that knew maybe there was no such thing.

"Always deep in thought," he said moving towards her. The fondness in his smile was teasing and playful.

"Regret or happiness?" he asked as he kissed her gently behind one ear and then the other.

"Both, I guess," Kayla said smiling up at him.

"Well, I'm not letting go."

"Well, you'll have to Friday."

"Friday?"

"I'm going home to my mom's for the weekend, remember?"

Max sighed deeply and looked out the window. He watched the day beyond with an intensity that made Kayla uncomfortable. He wondered how long she'd known she was going home, and a dark and quiet voice inside him whispered, 'is she ever coming back?' No matter how badly he wanted her to, he wondered if she'd ever trust him, if she'd ever really open up and let him in.

"Don't tell me you can't handle having me gone for three days?" she asked with a touch of annoyance.

He sighed again, "It isn't that."

"Then what is it?" she asked with growing irritation.

"You, Kayla. I don't get you sometimes," Max's voice was both pleading and resigned.

"I warned you" was all Kayla offered him in return. Already, she was angry and distant, beginning to close up her heart to keep it safe, locked up far away and out of reach where it belonged.

"See. That's what I mean. Do you even care about me or am I just a cure for your small town boredom?" he wished he could take back his words, but he knew she wouldn't let him.

"I should have expected this," Kayla said, moved away from the window, and began searching for her things.

"Expected what? That I wouldn't be satisfied with you keeping me at a distance like you do everyone else? That I would expect more because I deserve it?"

Max watched her, waiting for an answer. If he couldn't back out, then he might as well dive in headfirst. As much as he wanted to give her space and time, he deserved to be believed. He wasn't playing at loving her.

Silently, Kayla finished packing up and headed for the door. Max intercepted her and lightly took hold of her arm.

"Kayla, please."

"Max, I told you what I was capable of. I warned you."

"Kayla, you don't need to come with a warning. I know you. I like you just the way you are."

"Max, don't you get it," Kayla said opening the door and pulling away from him. "If you really knew me, you wouldn't be surprised."

Kayla walked out of the room, chased by her fear, and Max didn't follow. He wanted to scream and to yell at Kayla, tell her to let go of her anger and fear, to just open up. He also wanted to scream at himself for letting his fear that she'd run away from him turn a happy morning into a silly, pointless fight. He went back to the window to watch the day outside. To marvel at the wonder of the universe was far less vexing than to try and understand the girl he loved. He wouldn't have been surprised by her behavior a month ago but he'd hoped she'd changed; that he'd changed her. That love had set her free.

## SIXTY-SIX

Kale fled the castle and headed straight for the trees. She walked slowly but her heart was racing and her mind was turning at an immeasurable speed. For the first time since she could remember, Kale found concrete doubt swimming through her.

A long time ago, she'd waged a personal war against Randall Caine. He was a man posing as a god, a false savior preying on the people of Berdune and their belief that they weren't capable of making the world a better place on their own. Kale had known very young that Caine needed to be stopped. Something deep down inside her recognized him, the kind of man he was, and the kind of monster he was capable of becoming. Somewhere along the way, she also became certain she could be the one to stop him. She'd spent years dreaming of the day when Berdune would know freedom from Caine's reign of terror. She'd spent years trying to find a way to stop him and convince people there was a way forward without him. She'd never given up believing that the Darkness that was Randall Caine would bow down before them when at last they confronted it.

Looking back, it was beginning to seem a little like a life filled with delusion, one in which her obsession with Caine's destruction had allowed her to put her friends in danger. Now, more than being in danger, they were discovered. Medea was already dead, Jaren would be soon, as Corin would be if he wasn't already and, if she was being honest with herself, she had issued that sentence.

She fell to the ground, gasping, trying to catch her breath, and keep the panic and heartache at bay. She needed to let the reality of her situation sink in without losing control or losing her way. Mourning her best friend was a luxury she didn't yet have. She had to find a way to discover where Jaren and maybe even Corin were being held. If she was lucky, they still had a chance.

*Focus*, she thought, *there's always a way.*

She would ask Derin. There was a chance he could find out. There was a chance he might already know. If he didn't, she would be putting him in danger, another selfish decision, but she brushed that truth aside. Even if there was no chance in saving them, Kale had to try.

She stood and composed herself. The day tried to wiggle away from her. Spots leapt and danced in and out of her vision, but she fought to stay. All was not lost. Cyan had spoken of the savior and maybe that was too much to reach for, but Kale didn't know what else to grab hold of other than that dwindling hope. It was all she had.

Slowly, she started back towards the castle to find Derin. She hated involving him again, especially when it looked like anyone who joined her would suffer for it. Over and over again, she repeated the mantra that led her to Derin to ask for his help and that would put him in danger, 'I have no choice, I have no choice, I have no choice.' Just like she would have no choice when the sun rose on the following day but to be standing over Caine, blade in hand, deciding which part of his body she would drive it into first. *Not his heart*, she thought wildly, a vision of Medea coming to mind, *that would be too quick a death for him.*

SIXTY-SEVEN

Derin stood in his father's office and waited for him to return. Kale had asked him to find out the location of the captured traitors, her friends, and though Derin didn't think it would work, he never even considered refusing her. This was life and death. The world would change in the next couple of days. He needed to decide who he wanted to be and why.

To Derin's surprise, Caine had agreed right away to tell him where the prisoners were being held. He thought it was a wonderful idea that Derin's first moments of active duty would involve disposing of traitors and shipping the others to the mines and factories in the northwestern regions of Eirnan. Caine had gone immediately to fetch the paperwork for Derin; the lists of names and the people's locations.

"So much going on I can barely remember if I've eaten," Caine exclaimed jovially while he'd left the room only minutes before.

Now, the door opened again and two J'Kahl walked through it who Derin had been training with since he was a child. They eyed him suspiciously, as two more soldiers entered the room after them.

"Hey, where's my father?" was all Derin was able to ask before they jumped on top of him.


SIXTY-EIGHT

Kayla was seated on the beach staring out at the beautiful rolling waves. The only thoughts that wandered through her mind were those that chased the sound of the ocean. When she saw Max coming down the beach toward her, she didn't bother to wave or call out and neither did he. When he reached her, he sat down. Side-by-side, together, they let the ocean be their peacemaker.

"Do you want to be happy?" Max finally asked, tossing a piece of black hair to the wind like some bizarre offering.

"What is happiness anyway?" still afraid, she wanted to sound aloof, uncaring. Instead, she sounded like she felt, too tired to want to talk about anything but far too tired to resist.

"You first, Kayla."

"You know those dreams that you wake from, and you may remember them or you may not, but they're still with you somehow, the feeling of them?"

"Yeah," he said wondering what point she could be trying to make.

"Well, usually...no, always, with the good ones, I close my eyes and try to hurry back to lose myself again in them. I always go back, always."

"What does this have to do with happiness?" Max asked mostly to let her know he was following what she said and that he would follow wherever she led him.

"Well, when you can wake from the most blissful of dreams and realize that you don't need to run back to it, I mean you stay awake because life is just better in so many ways. Well then, that's when you know you're happy. When you want to be awake more than you want to lose yourself in dreaming."

In the silence that followed her pain and poetry, the world began to shift.

SIXTY-NINE

"Father? What's going on? Why have you brought me here?"

Randall Caine had just walked through the dungeon doorway and let it slam forcefully behind him. He stood tall and proud and looked so much like a monstrous predator out of a nightmare that Derin flinched when they made eye contact.

"I'm not locking the door but that's because someone is fetching your surprise."

Derin watched Caine's face and the hatred that burned in his eyes was disturbing. Derin had always known that Caine was a man made of many men. Derin had loved his father, the man he'd known most of his life. Derin had respected the leader who was able to guide and inspire anyone who would listen. The man standing in front of him was a dangerous and hate-filled creature whom Derin barely recognized and truly didn't want to. This was the man who had inflicted so many horrors on the people of Berdune, and he looked stronger and surer than he ever had before.

"Father, what is going on? I don't understand."

"Derin, do you think me a fool? Did you think I wouldn't find out?"

As Caine moved toward him, Derin held his ground, but it was becoming all too clear why he'd been removed from Caine's office that morning and thrown in the dungeon.

"Why did you do it, Derin? Why did you betray me?" again another Caine spoke, one hurt and disappointed.

"I don't know what you're talking about?"

Caine continued, "For love, I imagine. I had hoped you and Kale would join me, and instead you try to destroy me. I would have been prouder if you'd done it for power instead of trying to save the pathetic world you all seem so proud of. How weak you turned out to be. I should have known. No true child of mine would have faltered as you have."

Caine stood still, thoughtful and quiet for a long moment. Then, he began to laugh. "How ironic that during my life both of my children betrayed me."

Derin didn't understand what Caine was talking about but the great leader gave him no time to figure it out.

"I'm starting to think it might be me," Caine's laughter rose to a roar, a brushfire out of control. Derin felt fear coursing through every cell in his body.

"Father, I don't know what…"

Caine interrupted, "Let's drop the father façade, shall we? I gave you a father's love, Derin, but I will not extend to you a father's forgiveness."

Derin's mind was reeling. He wasn't sure how everything had gotten so out of hand, and he longed for just a moment where he could feel that he was in control. He was trained to be a warrior, he was trained to notice everything, yet somehow in the last month he'd failed to see the truth. He'd not only failed himself but in betraying his father without worrying about the consequences, he'd failed Kale, and all of Berdune as well. Darkness was coming, Derin could feel it, and he could see no way to stop it.

The dungeon door swung widely open and a stranger was tossed to the ground. He was badly beaten and looked to be barely conscious, but those things all took second place to his striking features.

"Look familiar, Derin?" Caine asked with a smile.

The young man had a messy mane of ice blue hair and, though one of his eyes was swollen shut, the other hung open slightly and Derin could see it was an iridescent ice-blue and eerily like the eyes Derin saw when he looked in the mirror.

"You never had a true chance to live together. That was my fault, I apologize. To make up for it, I will let you die together," Caine said and made his way towards the door. "I will of course let you spend some time together first. Makes it a little more bittersweet. Not to mention more enjoyable for me."

Caine stopped in the doorway and faced them again. The sheen of insanity twinkled brightly in his eyes. Somewhere deep in his mind, the ever-present whispering rose to a roar, demanding he end the lives of the young men crumpled before him, demanding he stop playing games and sparing those who could destroy him and halt the coming of the Dark. Caine wasn't listening. He kept telling himself it was because he had plans of his own, but there was another truth churning deep within him. He just hadn't glimpsed it yet.

"You will wish you had not betrayed me, Derin, and I'll hear you say it before you die." Caine walked out of the door and then closed and locked it behind him, leaving Derin and the all-too-familiar stranger by themselves.

SEVENTY

Jaren opened his exhausted, stinging eyes and immediately became aware of his aching body. Slowly, every pain, both dull and sharp, brought him back to the reality he'd hoped had been a terrible dream. Looking around, he saw the room was dim and, as his vision swam into focus, he began to remember clearly the events that had landed him there.

"You're up early this morning."

Jaren squinted into the darkness for the source of the familiar voice.

"Corin?" he rasped, realizing that his throat was sore and swollen, and his mouth was painfully parched.

"Right here, Jaren," Corin said as he appeared out of the shadows and helped his friend to a sitting position.

Jaren saw by the bruises on his face and neck that Corin probably felt just as terrible as he did. Corin sat down next to his friend and they leaned up against the cold damp wall. A pair united in their peril and their pain. It was strangely comforting, being together again, no matter the circumstances. And for that first minute, huddled in the damp and dark together, they found solace and escape in the familiarity of their friendship.

"Where are we?" Jaren finally asked in a strained voice.

"I'm assuming we're somewhere in the castle," Corin looked around as if the slimy walls held confirmation of his statement. Pain shot through his neck. His vision blurred, stilling him for a moment. Then with a grunt, he brought a hand first to his neck before dropping his forehead into it with a sigh.

"Great bunch of heroes we turned out to be, huh?" Jaren said, slowly leaning his head back to rest on the wall.

"There's still a chance, Jaren. What about Kale?"

"If he knows about us..."

Corin interrupted, "What about Medea? There's still a chance she can get us out of here."

"You mean Medea isn't here?" Jaren asked, his voice filling up with panic, as he looked around frantically, ashamed he hadn't noticed her absence right away.

"No. See what I mean? There's still hope."

Jaren's face crumpled in pain and he brought his hands up to cover it before he composed himself and spoke again, "Medea was captured with me. She was shot and hurt really bad. I don't know where she is."

"What do you mean you don't know where she is? She's got to be in the castle somewhere then, right? She's okay though, right?" Corin forced the words out though his throat had begun to tighten with a pain far more intense than any of his physical wounds could inflict.

Jaren didn't bother answering. The two friends sat silently against the wall for a long time. Only the sound of trickling of water mated with their labored breathing.

"Well, old friend," Jaren began, hopeless and hollow and unable to hide it, "I guess this is how it's going to end."

"Hey, we tried, right?" Corin laughed a little but it was a pathetic sound and echoed sadly through the darkness. "Great bunch of heroes we are indeed."

Corin scowled bitterly into the darkness as silence slipped around the two friends. Both of them retreated into thoughts of how differently they'd believed things should have gone.

"Jaren, we're not really giving up, are we?"

"Of course not, we're just a little behind schedule."

This time when they laughed there was a little more enthusiasm behind it, though the darkness devoured the bright sound almost instantly.

The darkness had indeed become a thing, real and palpable.

"So, what's the new plan then?"

"There's still the savior," a woman's voice, strong and sure, came wandering through the dark.

Jaren turned towards the shadows where the voice had come from, squinting, and when he could see no one he looked back towards Corin inquisitively. Corin was smiling slightly and, though his fat lip made the gesture a little ghastly, Jaren welcomed the hope it floated towards him like a life raft in a troubled sea.

"Who is that?" Jaren asked, turning back toward the shadows and the figure slowly emerging from them.

"I know it's been awhile but I'd expect a little more from you, Jaren."

"Sarah?" He whispered with a mixture disbelief and awe. "Sarah," he repeated again, breathless with wonder.

"The one and only," Sarah said, finally stepping near enough for Jaren to see her.

"I don't believe it," Jaren said as he struggled to get up.

"Oh, don't stand for me," Sarah said waving for Jaren to stay seated. "Besides, I think I'd rather sit."

Sarah placed herself between the two of them and before leaning back against the wall, she gave Jaren a long and loving hug. Finally, as she settled against the wall, she wrapped an arm around each of them. It was a maternal gesture and suddenly, magically, like only a mother could manage, everything seemed safe and okay just then.

"It's been a long time," Sarah said.

"You look terrible," Jaren quipped. He let his eyes take in her thinning blond hair, streaked with grey and eyes that had once been a bold blue like her son's, now dulled by years of hard labor and deprivation. She was thin, so much smaller than he remembered her, and yet she looked strong and sure of herself despite it. His heart swelled first with love, and then the thing that followed it most often, hope.

"Have you looked in the mirror lately?" she replied with a rueful smile.

Jaren raised his hand to his face and winced as he felt abrasions across his cheeks and chin.

"Damn. How am I ever going to get by without my good looks?"

"If I remember correctly, you weren't doing so good with them," Corin said, leaning forward to smile at his friend.

"Well, we're all in rather good spirits for a bunch of prisoners, but this is going to get bad pretty fast," Jaren said grimly.

"Don't you mean worse?" Corin asked with an exasperated sigh.

Jaren ignored him and went on, "I can't believe you're alive, Sarah. I mean we hoped but we never thought..." Jaren let his words trail off.

"I missed you, too. Thanks for taking care of my boy," Sarah said, kissing Corin on the forehead. "Seems like he turned out okay without me around."

"Well, I have to say most parents don't thank the people who get their children thrown into dungeons, but I'll take a compliment wherever I can get it." Jaren leaned up against Sarah's side and closed his eyes. Without his vision, he became more aware of the aches and pains that wracked his body.

It was fine to joke, to try and stay positive and hopeful, but the reality was that sooner or later they would have to face the truth. With the truth looming, this awful thing coming at them too swiftly to escape, both Jaren and Corin were willing to leave it be for just a little while longer.

"So boys, how are we going to get ourselves out of this mess?" Sarah finally asked, loathe to break the silence but aware it had to be done.

"Do you really think there's a way out of here?" Jaren asked skeptically.

"Well, I never thought I'd see you two again and now look at us," Sarah's optimistic voice began to brighten the darkness around them. She'd spent a long time working as a slave in the mines prepared to die there. Yet, here she was, a prisoner, but still reunited with her son and Jaren who for a time she helped to raise. Despite the situation, Sarah couldn't help but be hopeful that things would work out. She could have given up years ago yet she didn't, and now she was with Corin again.

"And there are the Founders," Corin added.

"Corin everyone knows the Founders are a myth," Jaren said.

"Until yesterday, I would have agreed with you."

"And what could have happened yesterday that changed your mind?"

"I met one of their children," Corin said simply.

"That's impossible," Jaren said but there was a note of uncertainty in his voice.

"It's true. After Sam..." Corin stopped himself. "Oh god, Sam."

The memories came crashing into the Corin like a freight train. He saw again the moment where one friend betrayed him and the other died. The pain came back upon him like a hurricane and he was swept up in its fury, unable to speak or breathe.

"What about Sam?" Jaren asked.

"And Ryan, Ryan," he spat the words out between gasps for breath.

"Corin, what about them?" the fear in Jaren's voice was palpable.

"Sam's the traitor. She killed Ryan. Oh god, I watched her kill him and she didn't even flinch. And, if she knows..." Corin stopped himself.

"Then Kale is working on borrowed time," Jaren finished for him.

The truth rolled in all around them like mist on a cool fall morning. There was no way to sweep it aside. But something else nudged at Jaren and he couldn't quite push it aside either. If Caine knew about Kale, had always known, then how had they gotten this far, and why was she still alive unless he had some greater plan for them all?

"Well, we better find a way out of here because so are we," Corin added, interrupting his thoughts.

As the night progressed slowly around them, Corin told Jaren about the strange young man he'd been held prisoner with on the train ride from Empris. He told Jaren about the others who had journeyed with Alex to try and help stop Caine. They talked about the Founders and how they were amazed to find out they were more than a myth. If the Scriptures were true, maybe a real savior was going to appear to save them, maybe. Either way, awareness began to creep over them. There were greater forces in the Universe at work than either of them could possibly understand or even hope to. Maybe those powers would come to their aide. Maybe those powers, older than time, aware that moments and eternities weren't all that far apart, would sit by and watch as another world disappeared back into the oblivion of the Dark.

What they knew was that they weren't willing to sit by and wait to see which it was. They had to figure something out. They had less than two days until the new year, and giving up was not an option.

## SEVENTY-ONE

As the night marched forward, others were willing to join the fight against Caine and, in the bowels of the castle, heroes were waiting to be made.

Symon had only been fourteen when his parents were killed for being traitors to Caine and he'd been left homeless and alone. When a few of his friends had decided to enlist, the thought of a warm place to stay and food in his stomach every night was enough to overshadow the truth, that he was going to serve the very man who'd made him an orphan. Two years in training and he forgot about his sweet, kind and fiercely brave parents and began the journey towards being a loyal servant and soldier for Caine. But his heart, always a perfect mating of the loving and generous hearts that had borne it, had never forgotten the truth of itself.

"Are you sure about this, Symon?"

"James, we're not murderers. Open the door," Symon commanded.

James unlocked the dungeon door and Symon rushed through it into the darkness beyond.

"You!" the prisoner said accusingly.

"I'm here to help. We're getting you out of here," Symon whispered as he helped her to her feet. "Come on, we don't have much time. You have to trust me."

They made their way out of the dungeon and into the dimly lit hallway. James locked the door and watched them nervously.

"The other one, too," Symon said forcefully.

"If I get caught, he'll kill me, Symon."

"You won't get caught. Just stand guard until your shift is done at dawn, then get out of the castle right away, and don't stop for anything. Meet us at the house in the woods, the one I told you about. Just make sure no one sees you. Jet and Archer are taking care of the others. All you have to do is this."

"Are you sure about this, Symon?" James asked weakly.

He wanted to be a hero, but even more than that he just wanted to do the right thing. A boy barely twenty, he'd already seen enough terrible and wonderful things to last him a lifetime. Like many of the soldiers in Caine's army, he'd begun to see that there was a difference between enforcing rule and simply hurting people for no reason. Like Symon, he'd once believed they'd joined a movement that would save their tiny world and its people, but it had become harder and harder to deny that he'd landed on the wrong side.

"We've stood by and done nothing for too many years, James. It's time to stand up to him. Now, open that door or I will."

James went to the next door and unlocked it spilling light into the dreary room beyond.

"If you want to live through the night, you'll come with me," Symon said to the three figures hunched against the far wall. "Please."

## SEVENTY-TWO

"It's weird, Kedall, I feel so lost without the stars."

Milar gazed out the window as she spoke to her companion of almost fourteen years. Kedall usually marveled at how her silver eyes reflected the starlight, mirrors for the secrets they were whispered in the night. Tonight, they seemed grey, tired, and dark with worry, much like the night sky. Her skin had once been a deep brown but after years of life inside, it had faded to a sickly color, like rotting leaves. Her hair, once a startling black mane, was graying in spots and it lay limply around her shoulders. He longed for the days when Milar had been a striking beauty instead of looking like a suffering slave. She was nineteen, the same age as him, and looked at least ten, maybe fifteen years older than that. Time had not been kind to either of them in more ways than one.

Kedall watched her from the other side of the large room and wondered how many more days they had together in the tower they'd called home for so long. He could barely remember life before imprisonment, but he was certain it was far better than any day he'd spent locked away in Caine's castle.

"Do you think we'll ever leave this place?" Milar asked him, a question asked every day for almost fourteen years by one or the other.

"You saw the stars. We'll play our part still."

She turned away from the window and looked at her companion lovingly. "Will they really come for us, Kedall?" Milar asked worriedly.

"They will," he answered though he sounded less certain of himself than he wanted to admit.

Milar watched him for any hint that he may be lying, but she knew he would never try to deceive her. So many years together had left them with little. One of the only things they still had left was trust. His face, though flirting with uncertainty, held no place for lies, yet it drew her away from her suspicion and to quiet study, as it sometimes did.

She didn't always look at Kedall. Mostly because some days it broke her heart to really see what he'd become. Now, she studied him. She told herself that years from then, when he was strong, proud, and healthy again, she'd want to remember what he had looked like at that moment, reminding her they'd survived. The truth was she also knew the world was changing, for some of them irreparably so, and it could very well be the last night she saw him alive. She tried not to frown when she saw how ill he looked, how old and worn. When she realized she probably looked just as bad, the frown found her lips. Kedall's once vibrant cherry hair was faded and yellowing. The emerald eyes that used to twinkle in the light looked the color of dying grass, and they were sunken and dark. His skin used to shine as if he'd spent an entire month under a golden sun, but now it was a shade of grey Milar knew skin was not meant to be.

Anger coursed through her tired body. She thought about the long years they'd spent waiting for change, helpless to oppose the stars, helpless to escape, and giving Caine all that he asked for because he could use them against each other. That special kind of torture Caine enjoyed of hurting one of them so the other would speak. She still wasn't sure how he'd known they could read the stars but it had made the years more unbearable. Telling him what they had to, knowing they'd have to live with it, and never seeing any indication they would go free, until now.

"Sometimes I get so angry at them, the stars. We've been locked up so long. We don't even know what's become of our parents or our families. Not once have the stars changed in our favor. Not once have they given us good news. Even the most recent changes show us terrible things are still to come and there is no indication as to whether this Darkness will pass us over or whether we'll all perish and it would have all been for nothing."

"Hope is never for nothing," Kedall said no louder than a whisper and yet the words were heavy and ripe. "Milar, we just have to have faith."

"I don't want to have faith. I want out of this prison."

Before Kedall could give the speech of reassurance that he often offered her when she travelled down this road, despondent, they heard the door unlock and a soldier stepped through it. He wasn't much older than they were, and if he was twenty years old, he didn't looked it. He stared at them with a perfect mix of shock and hope.

"You're real," he said with wide eyes.

"Well, I would hope so. After almost fourteen years in this place, I would hate to find out I'm an apparition and I could have left long ago," Kedall said as he watched the young man suspiciously. "Who are you?"

"My name is Archer. I'm here to help. We're getting out of here."

"How do we know we can trust you?" Milar asked suspiciously.

"Do you have a choice?" Archer answered. "Now, come on. We don't have much time. If we plan on living through this night, we've got to get out of this castle, now."

"And how exactly do you plan on getting us two out of the castle unseen?" Kedall asked him, curious and afraid.

"Underground tunnels. No one knows about them," Archer started back toward the door. "Now either you're with me or you're not, but in ten seconds I'm locking this door and getting the hell out of here."

"Alright, alright. You're a little high strung, Archer, so you should really consider a different line of work," Kedall said following him out the door with Milar right behind him.

With their freedom dangling just out of reach, both Milar and Kedall hurried toward it. As Archer locked the door behind them, Kedall couldn't help but take a deep breath. *Freedom,* he realized, *that's what freedom tastes like. It's been too long.*

"Come on," Archer said heading down the stairway in a run, "let's try and make it out of this castle alive."

Though they were weak and tired, they kept up with Archer. When they reached the underground tunnels, he let them stop to catch their breath and then they were off again at a run. Neither Kedall nor Milar minded. Every step they took away from Caine's castle brought them a little more joy. It had been a long time since they'd felt anything like it.

## SEVENTY-THREE

"Medea! Oh my god, I thought you were dead." Jaren jumped to his feet and had to grab the wall to keep from passing out. He instinctively reached up to the large bump on the back of his head and winced.

"Me, dead? And let you guys see all the action still to come?" Medea forced a smile, but it was obvious by her face she was in a lot of pain.

"What's going on?" Corin asked as he stood and swayed. The effects of whatever drug they'd given him the night before had yet to wear off completely.

"I'm busting you guys out. I got me a hostage and everything," Medea smiled proudly.

"Really?"

"Well, I am busting you out, but this guy here is helping us actually." She motioned toward Symon.

"He's the one who shot you! He helped capture us," Jaren said angrily.

"Look, we don't have time for this. I'll apologize all you want later but, if we don't get out of here quickly, we'll have far worse to worry about than who shot whom."

"You shot her," Jaren corrected as he made his way toward the door.

He took Medea from Symon, holding her up as best he could. Corin quickly joined him and, with both of them supporting her, they followed Symon through the halls with Sarah only a few paces behind. They hurried through the corridors drowning in the hope they would make it out alive.

It was hard in those minutes of jogging through the winding halls not to imagine Caine or one of his loyal soldiers jumping out of every doorway or materializing out of every shadow. Thankfully, it was hard in those minutes to think further ahead than the next few steps. The journey they would have seen before them might have been so insurmountable they would've collapsed at the very thought of undertaking it. Before they knew it, they were safely stumbling into the underground tunnels so close to freedom it was dizzying.

When they'd been journeying through the tunnels for almost a minute, Jaren stopped them. "Wait. Kale? We have to go back for Kale. If we don't, she's dead," he said between ragged breaths.

Symon stopped walking and turned around to face them. "You can't go back. You don't even know where to find her."

"If Derin betrayed us, he's betrayed her, too," Medea couldn't hide the worry from her voice.

"Derin?" Symon was perplexed.

"Derin didn't betray us Medea..." Corin let his words trail off, unable to hand her the truth just yet.

"We're not going anywhere until we know Kale is safe," Jaren stated, both imploring and firm as he met Symon's gaze.

"Damn it," Symon said as he started to turn back. "Look, keep going, we're all meeting at Medea's house and then moving from there. I'll go get Kale, and we'll meet up with you later."

"I'm coming with you," Jaren said letting Sarah take Medea's arm and moving to follow Symon.

"No, you're not. If I'm seen in the hallways, no one will think anything of it. If you're seen, well, I think you get the picture. You want to help, get back to the house safely so we can get ready to finish what you started."

Symon sped up as he moved away from them but no one made any attempt to move. Symon turned around but kept walking backwards, "I'll get to her. Get out of here. Now."

Reluctantly, they turned away from Symon and continued through the dark, not knowing whether they were heading to freedom or speeding toward death.

SEVENTY-FOUR

Alex slowly began to open his eyes and immediately looked around in confusion. He pulled himself up to a sitting position, wincing in pain, and tried to figure out where he was and how he'd gotten there. The last thing he remembered was the train ride with Corin, the other prisoner, and then he must have blacked out. When the room began to swim in and out of focus around him, he realized he'd probably been drugged and wondered how long he'd been asleep.

"Finally up," Derin said approaching through the gloom and sitting down a few feet from Alex to lean against a rotting pillar.

"How long have I been out?" Alex asked as he leaned back against the wall and began checking his body for bumps and bruises. When he reached his face, he cringed.

"Don't worry, it looks worse than it feels," Derin attempted a joke.

"Thanks," Alex said sarcastically, dropping his hands to his sides and looking at Derin. First, he noticed Derin's blue-black hair and crystal blue eyes. Then some other kind of familiarity pulled at him and his head began to swim. His one unharmed eye widened with shock and he started shaking.

"You okay?" Derin asked, concerned.

"Under the circumstances, you mean?" Alex quickly tried to steady himself. "I'm fine, I just...what's your name?"

"Derin. Yours?"

It took Alex a moment to answer but the pause stretched out so long he was amazed how many thoughts were able to tumble through his aching head while it went on. He realized he must be dreaming. He must still be asleep on the train or maybe even back on Samnar still waiting to make the journey south. *How long have I been asleep*, Alex wondered, eying Derin suspiciously.

"It's Alex."

"Alex," Derin said thoughtfully. "Have we met before?"

Alex didn't answer. He'd toyed with the idea of some strange dream he might be starring in but he knew in his heart he was awake and who he was talking with. He may have always known the truth, all these years, and just kept it from himself for reasons that didn't matter anymore. He watched Derin with growing awe, his unharmed eye widening again in shock. For a brief moment, when happiness bubbled up, he tried to suppress it, afraid it had no place in the gloom. There was a chance he was wrong, but he was so sure he could taste it.

"How did you get here, Derin?"

Despite something about Alex making him uncomfortable, Derin began to tell him everything. He told him about the events leading up to his capture and his arrival in the dungeon. He told him about his doubts and his fears. He told him about Kale and why he'd finally been willing to betray Caine. As he spoke, he felt something inside himself soften and then settle back into place. When he was through, Alex sat quietly for a long time, contemplating the story.

Finally, Derin spoke again. "What about you? You're not exactly an average looking person."

"You mean you don't know what I am?"

"Well, I know what it looks like you are but those are all myths...aren't they?"

"My mother and father were two of the Founders who are written about in the Scriptures," Alex began and then paused, unsure for a moment how to continue. "There were six of them altogether. Three perfect pairs to begin life anew on a planet far away from the one that gave birth to them. There were eight children born between them. My parents had two sons." Alex looked off into the past, seeing days long gone, days that still pulled at him.

"So, it's all true then? Does Caine know, I wonder?"

Alex tumbled back into the present. There would be time again for the past. "He knows a lot of things he chose never to tell you, Derin." Alex watched Derin closely and asked, "Did he ever tell you who your real parents are?"

"No, I was an orphan. I told you that," Derin answered innocently, though the hairs on his neck had begun to stand on end.

"You're not an orphan, Derin. Your real father is alive, and you have a brother who thought he'd lost you forever,"

Alex's voice began to crack under the weight of all the emotions rising up in him.

"What the hell are you talking about? How do you know all this?"

"Because I'm your brother. Your real name is Froste. You were named after the being that led our parents here across the ocean of time and space. The night Caine arrived, you and two of the other youngest children disappeared along with our mother. We were young. We didn't know you were alive or we would have come for you sooner. I'm so sorry," Alex's face was wracked with pain. "I'm so sorry."

"Stop it. I don't believe you," Derin said, but his words didn't reflect what his heart believed. Alex looked just like him in so many ways and felt familiar somehow. More than that, Caine had told him. 'You never had a true chance to live together,' that's what he'd said.

"Froste," Alex whispered as if the name was magical.

"Don't call me that. Please, don't call me that."

"I'm sorry," Alex took a deep breath, "Derin, do you ever look to the night stars and see what's coming, like you're understanding some kind of unspoken language in the night sky?"

Derin didn't answer but his face showed enough for Alex to understand.

"That's what we do. Our parents were a lot more special than we are. We can't do anything they could do, but we can see stuff through the stars. Doesn't sound like much but it's more than nothing."

"We're brothers?" Derin asked, his voice full of wonder.

"Yes."

"I knew. I knew all along something wasn't right. I remembered stuff, too. Flashes of strange looking people, like the Founders, I thought I was just imagining things. I thought I was just dreaming it all up." He took a deep breath. "We're brothers," Derin said again and then stood.

Alex smiled. "Brothers," he confirmed.

Tears were streaming down his cheeks as Alex stood and made his way toward the brother he thought he'd lost forever. When they came together, they hugged fiercely. Years of pain and longing for his brother reduced the usually calm and emotionally restrained Alex to quiet sobs. Years of anguish set free at last. Derin held him tightly and realized he was crying as well. It was the sweetest sound either of them had ever heard.

As they embraced, they were unaware of all that was transpiring in the world around them. In that moment, none of it mattered. Though they had much to worry about, for now it was simply this, losing themselves in the fact they'd found one another.

A strange sense of calm washed over the brothers. The new year was swiftly approaching and both knew other horrors approached with it. If death was going to find them in the next few days, it would find them together, united. For the moment, it was enough to make them forget where they were and all that they'd suffered.

Later, in the dark and quiet of the night, Alex would make a promise to the Darkness and to the world. 'I will thank Caine for reuniting us, right before I kill him.'

SEVENTY-FIVE

"Symon, I suggest you stop right there."

Symon turned away from Kale's door slowly. That single moment stretched on and on as he searched for something to say before he faced Caine, who was standing only a few feet away from him. Behind Caine stood four J'Kahl Symon knew were not on his side.

"Lord Caine, I was just..."

"No need to explain, Symon," Caine interrupted with a predatory smile. He signaled to the soldiers behind him. "Kill him. Not here though, we wouldn't want a mess outside of Kale's door when she wakes up."

"Please, no," Symon wailed as they dragged him down the hallway. "My lord, please, I haven't betrayed you."

"God, sometimes I hate it when they plead," Caine said, heading back towards his room. He needed to get some rest before an early morning appointment.

"Kale!" Symon screamed as one of the soldiers clamped a hand over his mouth.

It was the last word he would ever speak. He would plead no more. Soldiers died proudly and that's how he'd been trained. Like his parents, he'd die a traitor, and one of his last thoughts was to wonder if like him they had no regrets despite it all.


## SEVENTY-SIX

Kale woke with a start. Her name was ringing through the air and, though sleep clung to her, she listened for any indication she'd been drawn out of it by something in the waking world. When all was quiet, she quickly convinced herself that the voice had followed her out of a dream. She sat up in the chair she'd fallen asleep in and was relieved when she turned towards the window and saw that it was still night. Kale couldn't believe she'd fallen asleep so easily knowing she had the early morning task of meeting Caine for the last time and ending his life.

She checked the clock and saw she still had a few hours until it was time. She thought of Derin who hadn't returned with the location of her friends. Maybe he'd been found out. Maybe, as she sat in her room, he was rescuing them. Maybe they'd all fled to safety and were readying an attack on the castle. She hoped so, but it seemed to her none of that could truly be possible. No matter how badly she wanted to know, to help, to find them, it would all be for nothing if she didn't see through this final task that had been handed to her by forces she couldn't even begin to understand, or hope to. All she knew is that it had been in her for as long as she could remember; the map that led her ever closer to Caine's destruction.

She would be able to worry about her friends when it was done. Somehow, after killing Caine, she would have to survive long enough to free them if they were still being held captive. Kale felt overwhelmed. So many years she'd relished being able to carry the weight of the world if that was what was needed of her. Now, she wished she had someone to lean on, if even for just a moment or two.

How would she ever do it all? How would she keep from letting people down and letting more people die? She tried desperately to quiet those thoughts. The same ones that she'd expected to keep her from sleep the night before. All that would have to wait until it was done. She just hoped there would be enough time and that she could find a way. Walking to her window, she forcefully pushed aside all thoughts of her friends. There would be a time not too far from then when she could mourn those who'd fallen. If all went well, it would be after she avenged them. If all went poorly, she would mourn them on her way to meeting them, in whatever place came after this life.


SEVENTY-SEVEN

"Whose house is this?" Arin asked impatiently as she tossed a strand of dark red hair out of her eyes.

Arin, Beran, Joah, and Arwyn were seated in the large living room with the J'Kahl who'd freed them, Jet. They'd had no choice but to follow him through the winding underground tunnels that led out of Caine's castle and into the woods, but now it seemed they had a choice whether or not they would sit in a stranger's house and wait with him, for what they didn't know.

"It's the same person's house it was when you asked me two minutes ago, Arin," Jet said defensively.

"*I don't know* is not an acceptable answer."

"It's the only answer I have," Jet got up and started pacing. "Where the hell is Symon?"

Joah stood up as well. "Arin, let's go into the kitchen and get something to drink."

"I'm not thirsty, Joah."

"I wasn't asking," he said calmly.

Arin huffed in objection, but she rose and followed him out of the room.

"She is one wound up girl," Jet said once he was sure Arin was out of earshot.

"Do you blame her?" Beran asked, his honey-colored eyes flashing. "We don't even know who you are or why you helped us."

"I'm someone making up for a lot of years being someone I knew I shouldn't have been," Jet said, finally sitting down on the couch.

"Look," Arwyn began, "we really are grateful that you helped us and risked your life to do it, it's just we don't know who you are, we don't know where we are, and we don't know who we're waiting for."

Before Jet could answer his distraught companions, the front door swung open and someone called into the house.

"Hello? Jet, Symon, it's me, Archer."

"We're in here," Jet called back sounding relieved. Everyone in the room stood in anticipation.

When Archer appeared in the doorway, his eyes widened. He stopped in his tracks and took in Beran and Arwyn who stood beside Jet. Tall, imposing and beautiful, both of them, they were quite the sight to take in together. Arwyn with her silver mane and Beran's black as night. Both of them with dark brown skin, rich and silky smooth. And Arwyn's silver eyes glinting in the light. He wasn't sure he'd ever get used to seeing the striking features of the Founders' children, no matter how much time he spent with them. Finally, Archer shook himself out of his trance.

"Maybe we should give these guys a few minutes," Jet said walking toward Archer and taking him by the arm.

At first, Arwyn and Beran panicked. Suddenly, it became clear they'd been led into some kind of trap and it was about to be sprung, but when Jet and Archer moved out of the way, the truth was a sweet and wonderful thing for once.

"Milar?" Arwyn managed to whisper as the younger sister she'd been without for almost fourteen years ran into her arms. Beran joined his sisters in the hug, leaving Kedall standing in the doorway unaware of what he should do next.

"Come here," Milar encouraged Kedall and waved him over, but before he could move someone else addressed him.

"Kedall?" a voice said behind him and when he turned and saw Arin and Joah, his siblings, standing in disbelief he ran to them and wrapped his arms around them both.

"We thought you were dead," Arin kept saying as she tried not to cry. "I thought we'd never see you again."

The hug was fierce and was filled with the full force of years of missed moments. Laughter, joy, tears, and comfort all collided. When the hug softened, some of the heartache wiggled its way in, but they simply wrapped themselves a little tighter around the truth of it all. At that moment, none of them could imagine there was any world beyond the safety of the living room or any time past the moment they were in.

In the kitchen, Jet looked through the fridge for something to eat. Archer stood beside him wringing his hands nervously.

"Do you believe any of this?" Archer asked Jet with a mixture of awe and disbelief in his voice.

"None of it has quite sunken in just yet to be honest."

"We did good though?" Archer wondered aloud.

"Yeah, but we're not done yet."

For a moment, they were silent and Jet returned his attention to the distraction of the fridge though he wasn't really hungry.

"Do you think this will end well, Jet?"

Jet stood and looked at his friend with a mixture of pity and sympathy. What Archer wanted to hear is that it would all end well. Like Jet, he just needed someone else to tell him it would whether they believed it or not.

"I think it might, Archer."

"Any regrets?"

"One," Jet smiled at his friend sadly. "That we didn't join the good guys sooner." He put his head back into the fridge and Archer sat down at the kitchen table pondering what his friend had just said.

Archer hoped with everything he was that the saying 'better late than never' was true and he would be able to redeem himself for the years of doing what he'd known was wrong. Like many of his friends, he'd joined Caine's army young. His parents had disappeared when he was thirteen and though he suspected they'd ended up slaves in one of Caine's mines, the temptation for food, shelter, and belonging was too much to resist. He'd been young enough to believe the lies he'd been fed but pure enough of heart to begin questioning them as well. Because neither he nor Jet had seen much active duty yet, their list of sins was much shorter than most but there were still things they'd have to live with and ask forgiveness for, even if they would both just rather forget.

Archer hoped that being a good guy meant you won in the end and everything turned out well, but he wasn't so sure. Though he had many doubts about where they'd be when the new year arrived, he was glad to be hoping again. It had been so long since he'd felt hope that as it began to put him back together in a way he'd forgotten about, as it began to make him whole again, he finally understood how much a part of a person's soul hope truly was. Even if his life were to end in the fight against Caine, as he understood many of theirs probably would, he felt whole and certain of himself for the first time in as far back as he could remember.

SEVENTY-EIGHT

Derin sat on the floor leaning up against the damp pillar and never let his eyes leave his brother. His back pressed up against the wall, Alex watched him back thoughtfully. He studied every detail of his younger brother's face trying to let the reality of their reunion sink in. Alex had foreseen so many terrible things coming and though he'd always believed they'd find a way to stop Caine, he'd never imagined he would find something he thought he'd lost forever.

Derin smiled. "You still can't believe it, can you?"

"Can you?"

"Hey, I thought I was an only child until an hour ago."

Derin smiled fondly. He had a family, a real family. He'd never questioned his origins before and maybe it was because in his heart he'd known who he really was. But now he had a brother, and a father, and a whole family back on Samnar, a family who celebrated life and each other daily; or at least they had a long time ago before Caine had arrived.

Alex had spoken of days long past when their parents had brought magic into every moment of every day, when they used to play on the shore and especially in the waves. He talked of how their mother had loved the sea and adored the stars and the mystery locked within the night sky. She'd loved that they'd all been a part of that mystery. It meant for certain they were special and part of the wonder that made up the entire universe.

As Alex poured out his stories, Derin began to remember things, little things, and warmth would wrap itself around him even in the cold, damp confines of their cell. More than once, moisture came to his eyes when he realized images he thought were fantasies he'd imagined in sleep, were really memories locked away in some deep and love filled place inside him.

Caine had been a good father to Derin once. He'd been a role model and Derin had looked up to him in many ways. It wasn't until Alex spoke of how loved Derin had been, that Derin began to feel the truth growing within him that he realized he'd never loved Randall Caine and had never really been loved in return.

"So, what do we do now? Do you have any idea what he's up to...Derin?" Alex still had trouble remembering to call Derin, Derin. He'd spent so many years remembering a brother named Froste that now it was hard to talk to that same brother with a different name. Of course, he wasn't the same and if they were given the chance to know each other again, Alex would have to learn all of the ways in which his brother had been rewritten by a life with Caine and the J'Kahl.

"I don't know, Alex. I just don't know."

"What about this girl, Kale, I keep hearing about?"

Instantly, Kale's face appeared in Derin's mind and he held onto the image with a troubling mixture of remorse and longing. The image of her began to lead him to a memory, tugging at him to wander back a little ways and remember. He recalled a conversation they'd had not long ago though sitting in the dungeon it felt like eons since that day.

"Our parents," Derin began, "Kale said she spoke to one of them."

"That's not possible. They can't communicate with us. They're trapped."

"That's what she told me. She said this woman came to her more than once actually and that she said Caine knew who the real savior was," as Derin spoke, his excitement grew. "The woman told her that Caine knows because she told him. I know it sounds crazy, but I believe Kale."

"Derin, you don't understand, our parents are comatose, I find it hard to believe that Kendra or Arianna were able to project all this way and talk to Kale. Not to mention that they wouldn't tell Caine anything and how would he even make them."

"I don't know, Alex. It fits though. He's been planning something for new year's eve. Something big. He knew the Darkness would come now. He's been waiting for it all along. So, what if he's got the savior? How are we going to stop him?"

"We wait."

"What?" Derin said, exasperated.

"The stars say to wait, we wait. Caine will fetch us when it's time and then we watch for the right time to act."

"That's your plan?"

"That's the way it has to be," Alex said with conviction.

"How do you know we'll live that long?"

"The stars never lie, Derin. I think you've known that your whole life."

That's when the dungeon door opened. Neither could have imagined what came next.


SEVENTY-NINE

"And you're sure it's safe to stay here tonight?"

"Tonight, yeah, tomorrow who knows?" Jet shook his head. It was nice being asked for all the answers, as if he was in charge, but it was frustrating having none of them.

"This is the last place they'll look for us, but they will check here eventually," Archer added.

Medea's living room had never had so many people in it before. The group was as diverse as any could get and though they were living through the worst times they'd ever seen, the mood in the room was one of hope and elation. No matter how dark the night, a promise of dawn, in this case that coming of the day when Caine was defeated, was a kind of hope on the horizon they were all beginning to watch for.

Kale and Symon had yet to arrive, but they were unwilling to consider that they weren't coming. When Jet and Archer told the group that Alex and Derin's whereabouts were unknown, the mood darkened. Symon tried to find out where they were but it seemed no one but Caine knew. Even though they hadn't been able to find or free them, they weren't ready or willing to give up hope yet. The group had yet to decide how they were going to proceed, but there would be time for that. For the moment, they were soaking in the little bit of good that had come their way.

On the large couch, Arin and Joah sat on either side of their younger brother Kedall. Though there was enough room for them to spread out they sat closely together and Arin held Kedall's hand tightly in her own.

Beside Arin, Sarah leaned against the couch. Exhaustion pulled at her eye lids and they looked as though they would slide shut at any moment. Still, she watched her son fondly and smiled gratefully every time he looked her way and their eyes met.

Medea sat in the large loveseat with Corin and he had his arms wrapped around her protectively. Her shoulder was heavily bandaged and she winced every time she breathed. There was a sadness that hunched her shoulders and wove its way around her and she was more aware of it than the pain that was harassing her.

Milar sat in between Arwyn and Beran on the smaller couch and they were squeezed so tightly together that there was still room for Jet to share the tiny space with them. Jaren sat in another chair on his own while Archer sat in a chair he'd carried in from the kitchen. It was a comfort to all of them to be in the presence of allies and to feel like their numbers were growing.

"I hate to do this, guys, but we've got to make some plans," Jaren said apologetically.

"Jaren, ever the leader," Medea mused.

"Well, someone has got to say it. Besides, the sooner we make a plan, the sooner we get some sleep," Jaren reminded them.

"You mean we're not going back for Kale?" Corin asked.

"And what about Derin and Alex?" Arin added.

"Arin, you know about Derin and Alex already. We can't break the rules," Joah cautioned.

"You know, Joah, of all the people to remind me of that, I'd expect it not to be you."

"Look," Joah began, his emerald eyes flashing wildly, "our parents broke the rules, look where it got them. I just want to get out of this alive, if that's even an option. And I'd like to see our parents again. I don't like it any more than you do, but let's just do this the right way."

"Excuse me?" Medea ventured. "What the hell are you two talking about?'

"The stars," Arwyn offered quietly. "The stars show us what will come, and we are forbidden from disobeying them. That's how we know Alex is still alive. He still has to meet with Caine on the eve of the new year."

"As far as we know," Beran corrected. "We can't see the stars anymore. For all we know, things have changed."

"And for all we know, they haven't," Joah added.

"And remind me how we know not to break the rules?" Arin asked. "I mean have we even bothered?"

"Yeah," Milar added, "what's the point of knowing what's going to come if we aren't allowed to change it?"

"I think that maybe this is the wrong time to be defying the stars or the way things are done, guys," Beran finally put in.

"Alright," Jaren said authoritatively. "We can't worry about maybes and the stars, we have to deal with what we know. Jet said those captured in the raids are going to die tomorrow at dusk. Caine's way of making sure people know he's not the kind of leader you want to oppose. What I suggest is that we figure out how to free those people. Then the six of you," Jaren turned his attention to the children of the Founders, "and Jet and Archer will get them to safety, away from Braedon Ridge and away from Caine."

"Well, we know where they're being held. But by then Caine will know you're all gone, so we're going to have to be careful and we're going to need a damn good plan," Jet added solemnly.

"And what about you guys?" Arin asked. "What happens while we're running for safety?"

"Well, from what we gather Caine is going to move Friday night sometime. There's still a chance Symon will get Kale out tonight. If not...well, we have to assume Caine's got her. He's known all this time what she was really doing there if Sam was the traitor. And Kale is involved in this whole thing, we're just not sure exactly how, or why Caine's let her stay alive so long. We will have to hope it's because he plans to keep her alive just a little bit longer."

"Yeah, we know all that. What are you going to do about it?" Arin persisted.

"Well, we're waiting until Friday, until Caine gets up to whatever it is he's up to and then we'll go get our friend."

"Friends," Arin corrected. "Don't forget Alex."

"And, Derin," Medea added hastily.

"Right. We're going to get our friends," Jaren finished.

"And what if they don't live that long?" Corin ventured, his voice filled with worry and fear.

"We all knew what we were getting into when we started this whole mission. Kale signed up willingly, just like the rest of us. There's no point in trying to rescue her and getting killed trying. We have a better chance if we're patient. And I guess," Jaren said smiling a little, "we'll have to have a little faith in the stars."

"Well, how about we have a little faith in the fridge?" Joah said with a smile. "I feel like I haven't eaten in years."

"Good idea. Then, I think we should all get some rest. We'll have to take shifts. Corin, you and I will take the first shift," Jaren said.

"Archer and I will take the sunrise shift. It could be the most dangerous," Jet said proudly.

"I'll take the second shift then," Medea volunteered.

"No, you won't. You're hurt, so you sleep through the night and that's final," Corin said sternly.

"Fine, but I'm not hurt. I'm wounded. Just to set the record straight."

"What's the difference?" Jaren asked playfully.

"Well," Medea began, "one sounds far more impressive."

"We'll take the second shift, Milar and I," Kedall said volunteering himself and his friend. "We haven't been outside in fourteen years, I think we've earned it."

"Second shift," Arwyn and Beran called simultaneously both wanting to be with the sibling they'd been without for so long.

"I'll take sunrise with the men," Joah said with a smile. "Fend off danger, protect the women folk, you know." Arin rolled her eyes and elbowed her brother in the side.

"If you don't mind," Arin said smiling shyly, "I'll take the first shift, too. I'm not quite ready or willing to sleep just yet."

"Sure, that's fine," Jaren said without looking over at her.

"And where does that leave me?" Sarah finally put in.

"In the same category as Medea, Mom. You need your rest if you're going to be up for tomorrow." Corin smiled over at his mother and she beamed when he called her "Mom." It had been so long since hearing that word, she couldn't imagine getting tired of it.

"Normally, I'd object, but I'm exhausted," Sarah said with a laugh as she stood. "But if you guys ask nicely, I'll cook you a meal you'll never forget before I head up to bed."

Suddenly, the room was full of energy as everybody answered to the longings of their aching bellies and one-by-one they followed Sarah into the kitchen.


EIGHTY

"Hey, aren't you going to eat?" Arin asked walking out of the house and sitting down on the porch beside Jaren.

"Not really hungry but Corin said he'd bring me out a plate when he was done."

Arin began to laugh. "Oh, I wouldn't count on that."

"Why, no food left?"

"No, Corin is sound asleep in the kitchen. Can you believe he's still sitting at the table with his head leaning over to one side?" Arin was laughing heartily and Jaren couldn't help but join in.

"It's been a long couple of days, weeks for that matter, he deserves to sleep."

"And what about you? Haven't earned a nap yet?" Arin smiled over at him.

She was strangely at ease with Jaren yet she was unable to tell exactly why. She'd barely spent any time with him but there was a commonality between them, she could feel it.

"You know I never would have believed it." Jaren said looking at her fondly. "That you guys, your parents, well, you know."

"Good surprise? Bad surprise?" Arin asked.

"It's good. Just strange to think that something so wonderful could have come before all of this you know." Jaren let out a short laugh. "Kale will probably have a heart-attack when she finds out. She was never one to believe in the strange and unusual, the Scriptures and the legends I mean."

"You're worried about her."

"Kale can take care of herself. If anyone will survive this it's her."

"She's really special to you, huh?"

Jaren laughed again, "Kale is special to everyone who meets her."

"And how about Kale? Is anyone special to her?"

"Caine, I guess. Stopping him, I mean. She doesn't really have time for anything else. She always said she'd have a life after all this was done. I don't think she ever once considered the fact we might fail."

"The sign of a true leader," Arin said looking away from Jaren and off into the night. "Alex is the same. He hasn't had a life since the night Caine arrived. He was just a kid but he was the oldest and he just ended up being in charge. Because his mother and brother disappeared that night, he's thought of nothing other than revenge since that day." She smiled, fondly remembering her friend. "It's hard though."

"You mean loving someone who can't love you back?" Jaren said following her gaze into the darkness.

"Well, that too," Arin said, as the space between them filled with that common thread of love unanswered and ignored. "But what I meant was not being able to love the people around you."

"So what you're telling me, Arin, is that we have the better end of the deal?"

"Whoa, where did all this 'we' stuff come from? I was just telling a story. We were talking about you, remember?"

"In other words, this conversation is our little secret," Jaren smiled and suddenly he became aware of how long it had been since he'd felt so lighthearted and free of worry. Like it was just a regular night and he was sitting with a friend talking about anything and everything and yet nothing of huge importance. How long had it been since life had been simple and easy. He couldn't even recall. He realized then that if they ever survived the days to come, and Caine was stopped, he would never again take for granted the simple little joys in life that could pass you by in an instant if you didn't stop to savor them.

"I like you, Jaren. You get me," Arin said matter-of-factly, turning toward him with a smile. "In the midst of all this horror, we've found some good things."

"Makes you believe it's all worth it, huh?"

"I always believed. It's just nice to be reminded."

They settled into a comfortable silence that surprised them both. A world running out of time could speed things up in the most astounding of ways. Jaren felt like he'd known Arin his entire life, like he was talking to a friend who knew every little secret he possessed and so he couldn't lie and really didn't need to.

"You really think we're going to get through this, don't you, Arin?"

"Yeah, I guess I do. What do I have to lose? It's going to end how it's going to end so I'd rather feel like I'm fighting for something instead of against something," she sighed deeply. "What about you? You think we're going to get through all this?"

Before Jaren could answer, they heard someone approaching through the woods. Instinctively, Jaren stood and placed himself in front of Arin. With one swift move, he had retrieved the crossbow from the porch beside his seat and he held it aimed at the night and whatever was coming through it.

"Don't shoot," the stranger said. "Please, don't shoot. It's me, James." James appeared in front of Jaren and he slowly lowered the bow.

"You're early," Jaren said accusingly.

"I was relieved early and placed on one of the teams being sent to Empris to guard the mines. I guess I'm not trustworthy enough to be around the castle right now." James was panting and it was obvious he ran all the way from the castle. Scrapes decorated his face and neck and his skin was damp and stained with dirt.

"Are you okay? Did you get out okay?" Arin asked worriedly.

James fell to the porch and tried to catch his breath. "Symon, he's dead. They killed him. I didn't know what to do. I wasn't sure if it was still okay for me to come here."

"Does anyone know you're gone?" Jaren asked, his voice laced with panic.

"No one knows. They think I'm on the train. They won't notice I'm gone for awhile. Caine sent a whole bunch of soldiers."

"Alright James," Arin said sympathetically, "just calm down. Let me get you in the house and we'll get you something to drink. Come on." Arin took James by the arm and led him into the house. Before the door could close, Corin walked through it yawning. Jaren had his face in his hands and when Corin spoke he looked up with a start.

"Did I miss much?"

"More bad news. We lost Symon. Kale is definitely on her own." Jaren sat down and leaned up against the cold wall setting the crossbow down within arm's reach. Corin sat down beside him and put his arm around his friend.

"Hey, we knew it would be mostly bad news when we signed up for this. She's gonna be fine. She has to be. You know Kale."

"That's the problem. She'll die trying to stop him."

"Jaren, we all would in the end."

"Yeah, but she's the one in there with him," Jaren said hopelessly.

"We're with her, she knows that."

"How did we ever get into this Corin?" Jaren asked. Still, a touch of humor wound its way into his voice. He'd asked Corin the question a million times and always received the same answer.

"It all started when you called Kale a child who led a bunch of people who weren't really a threat to anyone, and she decided to prove you wrong."

"So, you're saying this is all my fault?" Jaren asked with a touch of humor.

"No, Jaren, I'm saying thank you."

They both began to laugh first calmly then heartily then hysterically. Sometimes when grief, worry, and fear become too much to handle, the only thing to do is laugh. Not the laughter that comes with joy but the laughter that mocks the absurdity of it all. They laughed until they could laugh no more and then they sat in silence and let the simple fact of being together, alive, still, bring them the only comfort they would know that night.

Arin, James, Jaren, and Corin finished the first watch with no further incident. The night lay still like a predator in wait; no shadows moved, no stars appeared, and yet it was a living, breathing thing, that Darkness that drew in around them. When the third watch began, the dawn had yet to tease Berdune and the woods made not a single sound. It seemed as if they were afloat in the vast ocean of space with no escape or salvation to be seen across the deep.

EIGHTY-ONE

"I never thanked you before for helping us. Both of you. You really risked a lot for us," Joah was standing on the front porch watching the night beyond as if he expected visitors at any moment.

"We don't deserve thanks. We stood by for years and let people suffer and watched people die. We're paying a debt now," Archer said as he leaned against the wall looking both thoughtful and remorseful.

"You could have kept standing by. It would have been safer. Give yourself some credit, you joined the minority at the most dangerous time, you could have chosen differently."

"It doesn't change how terrible I feel though." Jet was seated with his back to the wall and he was intensely watching his hands as they played with a piece of bark.

"You saved a lot of lives tonight, and tomorrow we're going to save more. If you haven't redeemed yourself yet, then you're both well on your way."

"Thanks, Joah, that really means a lot coming from you," Jet looked up and smiled.

Behind them, the front door opened and Medea poked her head out smiling lazily. Her eyes were still hazy from sleep and she used her good arm to rub them absentmindedly.

"Boys night out, huh?"

"Aren't you supposed to be sleeping?" Archer asked watching her with a worried look.

"Couldn't sleep. Lots of bad dreams and a little bit of pain," she said patting her wrapped up shoulder. "I think I'd rather just sit out here for awhile. If you'd rather do without my company, then I'll leave." Medea smiled mischievously.

"Don't be ridiculous. There's a seat right here with your name on it." Archer motioned to the porch and Medea stepped out into the cool night and sat down with a grunt.

"I was actually going to check the backyard." Joah went to stand, but Archer put a hand on his shoulder.

"We'll go. We're not used to standing still this much. We'll check everything out back there and check in with you in ten minutes or so, let you know we're okay." Archer rose and stretched his arms high above his head.

"Men of action," Jet confirmed as he made his way down the front steps and started around the house with Archer right behind him.

Jet and Archer had both undergone visible transformations since rescuing them. Their freedom was a kind of drawing back to who they'd been before Caine had come to Alpha Iridium. Watching them leave, Joah couldn't help but notice the lightness in their steps as they bounded around the house and disappeared out of sight.

Medea and Joah sat in silence for a long time. Both had thoughts churning in their minds that they couldn't seem to still. When Joah realized he didn't want to chase his spinning thoughts any longer, he broke the silence. "How's your shoulder?"

"The truth or the nice version?"

"Let's try the nice version."

"Not bad at all. Don't even notice it's hurt. Feels like heaven," Medea smiled sarcastically.

Joah laughed, "And, the truth?"

"And the truth would embarrass me," Medea replied with a chuckle that turned almost immediately into a cough. He could tell by her face how much pain she was in but he gave her space, somehow aware she needed it. When she finally stopped coughing, she looked up into his emerald eyes and forced a smile.

"You okay?" he asked trying not to sound as worried as he was.

"Oh yeah, I'm fine. I'm a fighter."

"I've noticed."

"It should heal nicely. Probably leave a nasty scar though," Medea said raising her hand to her wounded shoulder once again.

"My father," Joah began, "he was wounded once. He almost died."

"But I thought the Founders couldn't be injured."

"Well, they can and they can't. Basically, they can heal themselves instantaneously. But their first day here, before they'd found one another, before they'd learned all their powers, my father hurt himself acting before he thought, acting without worrying. Sort of like I do all the time."

Medea smiled at him appreciatively, "Sounds familiar."

"Well, he almost bled to death on the beach all alone but somehow in his desperation he remembered how to heal himself because he thought about his friends, the other Founders, and he realized he couldn't die alone. He was so new to the healing that it left a scar on his leg. He could have gotten rid of it any time since then but he didn't. He kept it as a reminder of how lucky he was to be alive, to be with the people he loved," Joah's voice finally cracked and he could speak no more. Medea took his hand in hers and held it gently hoping that Joah would draw strength and comfort from her touch. He squeezed her hand reassuringly and finally looked over at her.

"You really miss him, don't you?" Medea finally said.

"I just feel robbed. Like it shouldn't be like this. They were just trying to do good. They were just trying to save people. Look where it got them."

"I'm not good with saying the right thing, Joah, but I do understand. My boyfriend, Ryan, he was the one killed in Empris yesterday, the one Corin told us about." Medea had to struggle to keep her composure as she spoke, yet still she went on, "He wouldn't have joined up with all this if it weren't for me. But I look back over my life after my parents were taken from me and I realize I would never have survived it if it weren't for Ryan, and Kale, Jaren, and Corin and this crazy mission. And I wonder if maybe because Ryan loved me, he understands," she paused, sadly shook off her mistake, then took a deep breath and went on, "understood, I mean, how much it meant to me that he was with us, because it all matters so much."

"I'm sorry. I didn't know," he said lamely.

"It's okay. How would you?"

"And you're still fighting?"

"That's the only way to make sure he died for a reason. It's the only way to make sure that all the horrible things we've endured were for a purpose. I won't stop fighting until we've won," she paused again and that deep and heavy sadness settled itself over her once more. "And maybe, just maybe if we end all this and I play a part in it, he'll forgive me, wherever he is."

Joah tightened his grip on her hand, a show of solidarity and comfort, the only thing he could offer her to ease even a little of her anguish. Medea wiped at the tears that began to fall. She didn't bother feeling silly or ashamed of her sadness.

That kind of love, the one she'd lost, was never anything to be ashamed of.

Joah saw Medea as if for the very first time in that moment. Living on Samnar, they'd faced different tragedies brought by Caine but now he was seeing how truly beautiful things grew out of horrors. Medea, her friends, the rebels, they'd all found ways to make something beautiful in the wreckage Caine had left in their lives. She was still doing it, sitting here with him, heartbroken and hurting. She was grabbing hold of the beauty of what she'd had, not the ugliness that was left after its passing.

They were silent for a long time, comfortably so, before Joah spoke again.

"Well, before we got all serious, I was just trying to say that you should cherish that scar. I think it will suit you."

"Yeah? You think it will make me look tough."

"Tougher," Joah corrected with a smile.

Once again, his emerald eyes twinkled with hope and Medea felt warmed by them. There would be a time when she would have to face all the losses they'd sustained against Caine, but for now it was time to get ready to finish the battle.

"All clear around back," Jet said as he and Archer rounded the corner.

"For now," Archer added. "I'm going to go back in a few minutes and stay out there. Better safe than sorry, right?"

Medea stood, wiping the last of the tears from her cheeks. "I hate to be the party crasher but I think I'm ready to try to get back to sleep. I want to be in top form tomorrow."

"Goodnight," Joah said warmly.

Medea turned before going in the house, "Thanks for the chat, Joah. Goodnight." And at that, she disappeared into the house.

"And what was that about?" Jet asked Joah with a teasing smile.

"Get serious. We were just talking," Joah defended.

"About what?" Archer asked him joining in the game.

"Medea and I just see a lot of things in the same way. But that's all it is." Joah's eyes drifted to the heavens and his thoughts once again to days long past.

## EIGHTY-TWO

Kale stood in the dark over Caine's sleeping body and didn't hesitate for a moment. She wished there was a moon outside the window so she could see it shining off the blade poised to take his life. She drove it downward into Caine's torso and felt him jerk, but he made no attempt to scream; only a muffled cry escaped him. She felt triumph wash over her as she twisted the blade once, twice, before removing it. Still, Caine made no sound. Kale felt disappointed that she couldn't coerce a wail from him, but she would take victory any way she could. It was over. Caine was dying.

Kale stood in the dark and searched within herself for an indication of what Caine's destruction truly meant. Her entire life had been leading up to that moment and she realized that it would be hard to figure out what to do next. Was she anything but Caine's biggest enemy? Had she sought any purpose other than destroying him? She thought about all the years she'd despised him and realized they were all the years she could remember. Her whole life had been about this end. She'd had her friends and family during those years, but in so many ways they'd taken second place to her obsession with ending the rule of Berdune's false god and savior.

It was strange to think that her life would have to have a different purpose. It was hard to imagine that she could be anything more or less than she'd already been. She felt, for the first time, entirely and oddly empty. She'd never expected to feel sorrow at Caine's demise but in many ways it marked her demise as well. What was left beneath the version of herself who'd lived for his destruction? So many questions, and all of them leaping through her mind as Caine bled, dying by her side.

Kale raised the blade high, ready to strike again, this time closer to his heart to make sure there was no chance Caine would survive. The lights came on suddenly, and that's when she screamed.

## EIGHTY-THREE

Kayla stumbled out of the dream in a panic. Both terrified and heartbroken, she tried to sit up, to physically flee the dream but again she couldn't make her body respond. Her eyelids were heavy and she could barely keep them open long enough to search for the monster stalking through her room.

It was strong this time. Stronger than it had ever been before, it slithered around her, an eel in the dark, taunting and ready to strike. Kayla tried to turn her head to see it. She wanted so badly to confront her demon but it eluded her every time she tried.

She felt the dream pulling her back. It was a wave washing back out to sea, and she began to panic anew as it took her with it. She would have wept, but the dream would not allow it. She could feel her heart racing in her chest and her muscles twitch and convulse in complaint. She pleaded silently to be set free. 'No more,' she begged, 'please god no more. I'm so tired of it all.' But no one heard her pleading, not in the waking world where her throat was frozen and she couldn't scream. Not in that other world where the unforgivable had happened.

Back she went.

Awake while dreaming.

## EIGHTY-FOUR

"My dear, your strength and determination make me so proud," Caine said with a tormenting smile. Kale didn't see it but she could feel it tearing through her.

She was looking down at Caine's bed to the place where he should have been. To the place where she thought he'd be. To the place where she'd driven the blade. She felt anguish flood through her, and something inside her broke, something she was sure could never be mended, when she realized she should've known. It had been too easy to get into his room. It had all been too easy, hadn't it, but she was too stubborn and too arrogant to think she could fail.

Eyes wide, tears spilling down her cheeks, she looked down at Derin and thought she would break entirely when she saw both acceptance and forgiveness in his eyes. In a panic she pulled the gag out of his mouth and began untying him all the while trying to avoid looking at the growing red stain below his ribs.

"Oh my god, Derin. Please, no."

"Kale," he whispered, tears spilling down his cheeks.

"Derin, don't you dare leave me. Look at me. Come on, focus," she shouted as his eyes rolled back in his head. "Oh god, I'm so sorry. I'm so sorry. Forgive me, please."

Derin forced a smile and his eyes closed briefly. "Just a scratch," he said bringing his arm to the wound. He opened his eyes and brought his fingers within an inch of his face staring blankly at the crimson stains across his fingers as if the blood were a curious and intriguing find. "Just a scratch," he repeated.

Kale grabbed the top bed sheet and tore at it forcefully. She pulled Derin up to a sitting position and began to wrap it tightly around his middle as he let out small cries of pain. When she'd wrapped it around him as many times as it would go she tucked the end in as tightly as she could.

"Stay still, Derin. Don't move. You're going to be fine."

"Kale, I need to tell you something."

"Don't, Derin. Don't say goodbye because I don't want to hear it."

Kale looked around the room in a panic though she wasn't really sure what she was looking for. She saw some of the J'Kahl she'd trained with enter the room and make their way towards the bed.

"Stay away from him," Kale said raising the knife in front of her. "Come any nearer and I will kill you. You know I can do it. I trained with all of you."

"Stand down, Kale," one of the soldiers said and when Kale took a step toward them to attack he threw a small blade that struck her in the arm. It barely scratched her but the distraction gave the soldiers enough time to jump on top of her and hold her down while the others got to Derin.

"Throw him back in the dungeon," Caine ordered. "Let him die with his brother by his side. If we can stay on schedule, I'll get down there in time to watch him do it."

Two of the J'Kahl picked Derin up and he moaned.

"Let go of me!" Kale screamed as she struggled against the soldiers holding her down and watched helplessly as Derin disappeared out the door.

"Caine, don't do this. Don't punish him because of me. Caine, I beg you, you've got me, let him go. I'll do anything."

"Kale, don't disappoint me now by begging," Caine said approaching her slowly. "You've almost made it to the end, your end, not to mention the end of your friends and all else you love. Really, my dear, you should try to finish it right."

Kale couldn't help herself. When Caine was within a foot of her, she spat on him. A smile spread across his face as he wiped it with the back of his hand.

"Better, much better. So much more potential than those cretins you called parents."

"Don't you dare talk about my parents!" Kale screamed.

"Did you know they were traitors? I imagine you know that by now. What a pity I didn't find that out before I killed them. I would have enjoyed it so much more."

Kale stared at him with wide-eyed shock. For the moment, Caine had her attention. She could feel rage growing within her like a storm and her vision began to swim. Still, she glared at him waiting for an explanation.

"That's right. I didn't even find out they were traitors until after they were dead. Figured it out with a little help from some of their friends. You knew them, actually. Your friend Medea's parents, they pleaded for your parents' lives and later a few other pieces came together and it all became clear. I killed them, too, of course, but it was far less enjoyable than killing your parents."

"I hate you," Kale seethed. "I hate you."

"It hasn't always been that way," he said with a knowing smile and she cried out as she kicked at her captors.

She was ashamed of her inability to keep her emotions from taking over but there was no hope of stopping them. Caine ignored her and began speaking again.

"I find it odd that you have been surrounded by traitors your whole life, Kale. I have to ask myself what kind of person you must be when your friends are traitors and your parents were traitors. Did you think you could just show up here and pledge your loyalty to me and think I would believe you?" Caine laughed. "It was fun though. I'd hoped I could change your mind. I was going to give you the world, Kale." For a moment, he seemed far away, even a little forlorn. When he spoke again, his voice had changed. It was deeper and softer and sad, "I was going to give you the world."

"How? How did you do it?" Kale fought hard not to weep.

"I'm afraid I don't understand." Her question drew him back and he sneered.

"How did they die?" Kale screamed. "How did you do it, you coward?"

"Tragic, your parents, they were great people, they were just too stupid to know which side to be on. Your father was brave. He didn't make a sound when I killed him. Your mother on the other hand begged for her life, and yours."

Kale was shaking violently and though every word Caine spoke pushed her to the brink of her rage, she had to know. She wanted to know.

"I became so tired of hearing her pathetic pleas that I slit her throat from ear to ear." Caine ran his finger across his throat from one ear to the next as if Kale would need a demonstration to fully understand what he said. "Messy, but she deserved it."

Caine's eyes glinted with madness. Kale stared at him but didn't see him, instead she saw her parents. Her parents who'd died by Caine's hand. Her parents who'd fought for a better world. Her parents.

"You lunatic!" Kale screamed and she spat in his face again. "You're not a god. You're a man who has never found one." Again, Kale tried to struggle free of the two soldiers holding her back but they were too strong and her anger was exhausting.

"My, my, Kale, what a temper. Runs in the family, I'd imagine. I wish things could have ended differently but you're out of time and chances. Tomorrow night you die with your friends and finally the new world will arrive." Caine made his way toward the door. Before going through it, he stopped, paused, and then turned around to face her one last time. "You should have been more afraid of me, Kale. Don't forget who I am."

"I'm not afraid of you! You're an imposter. You're nothing! Do what you want to me. The people will rise up against you. You will not succeed Caine and I promise you I will live long enough to see your downfall."

Caine turned and left the room and Kale realized how little she meant to him. Just another pawn in some game he was playing. She couldn't know the game was much bigger and older than all of them and they were all pawns in one way or another.

The soldiers knocked her down violently, kicking her repeatedly before lifting her off the floor just to knock her down again. They lashed out at her with all the bitterness and rage that had been poured into them for fourteen long years. Pain rang through Kale's entire body, but she hardly noticed it. Beyond it, there was something else. Something that was bigger than she was. *I don't care if I die today*, she thought, *but I'm not leaving this world without Caine.*

With a bloody nose and bruises covering her face, neck, and torso, Kale was dragged, limp and gasping, out of Caine's room and taken to a cell. She sat in the dark, wiping at her bleeding nose, wincing every time she did and fell into the kind of exhaustion that comes at the end of a life. In so many ways, it was the end. The life she'd known for fourteen years was drawing to a close. Her mission, all consuming for so long, was almost over. Whether it ended in light or whether it ended in darkness was the only unknown.

Kale thought of her friends in danger, or hurt, or dead because of her. They'd all believed in her and so far she'd failed them. *I can still do this*, she thought desperately, *there has to be a way, it can't all be for nothing.* And, as she tumbled into troubled sleep, Kale let dreams of a more peaceful existence wash over her once again.

Her body ached and her mind tried over and over again to return to the horror of that day, and to wondering what horrors might still be ahead. Yet for a short while she was someone else, in a dreamland with a different life she was never truly meant to lead.

EIGHTY-FIVE

Kayla woke with a start, fleeing the dream. Terror slammed into her with so much force her breath caught in her throat. She knew the monster was in her room perched at the foot of her bed, that dark and hulking beast, watching her with growing enjoyment. She struggled to break free of the dream yet she couldn't. This was the first time she'd woken twice in the same night with the nightmares. Again, she'd dreamed of being the sole member of an army. Again, the loneliness and fear had overwhelmed her. Kayla longed to repossess the dream as much as she longed to wake from it. It was how it always was. On the days she woke from that dream world, it followed her around, a fog settling over everything else so that only the feeling it left her with was real and clear.

The dream took hold of Kayla firmly, calling her to return, intent on drawing her back into that other world. She shuddered at the thought of it. 'No,' she wanted to scream, but there was only silence. 'I'm not ready to face him yet. Please god, no. Somebody help me.'

Kayla tried to tell her body to thrash and kick until she broke free of the nightmare, but her arms and legs wouldn't respond. It was as if they'd already accepted what she hadn't. She fell into the dream. Poised, as she always was when she realized there was no escape, to face the demon in her other life.

The morning was calm around her but in Kayla's nightmare the morning was everything but. With a strange sort of acceptance, she sank into the horror that pursued her, drawn back by her weakness and that ever-growing feeling of belonging.

## EIGHTY-SIX

And so the dawn broke over Braedon Ridge though it was a grey and tired sight much like its people.

Caine's castle was eerily silent. As he did on many mornings when the new day's light was creeping through the empty streets, Caine stood at his office window and looked down upon his kingdom. It looked sad and bleak, the world he ruled, and he wished for a time when he could regret all that had brought him there. Something strange was happening to Randall Caine. For a few moments on this morning, he felt like the man he'd been so long ago, like the past was pulling at him, calling him home.

Once, he'd truly wanted greatness, not for himself but for the people who admired him and had believed he could change the world for the better; be it Alpha Iridium or Earth. Once, he'd sought to do good in the world, in any world; but something had gone wrong and he couldn't even figure out what or when. Kind, caring, considerate, gentle, and incapable of doing harm, where was that man now? Where had he gone?

Randall Caine felt anguish wash through him. There was no turning back. He had to follow through with his plans. He could see no escape. He wanted more than anything to be the man he'd been so long ago and for a moment he wondered if he'd actually left that man back on Earth.

Somewhere deep inside a voice reminded him, 'that man was a lie. You are the truth.'

Secretly, he hoped that he would be defeated so it could all be over, so all the pain would stop, so all that dark and festering madness deep down inside would stop bubbling up and out and taking shape, and he could stop hurting people. Then, he would be free.

The whispering began again. That dark and incessant voice slithered all around his mind and heart and drove him to lash out at the world with all the awfulness inside. 'Kill her now,' the Darkness demanded, 'end this.' Randall Caine fought and struggled to silence it. To find refuge within himself, a place where even the tiniest bit of light remained. It was the only time he rebelled against that deep, dark that had gotten inside him long ago. When it asked for the one thing he still could not bring himself to do, 'Kill her!' it screamed inside his head so that he covered his ears and fell to his knees, buckling under the weight of its fury.

"I will," he whimpered, "when the time is right. Allow me this, please."

The Darkness grew quiet inside him. Randall Caine knew sometimes the silence could be worse than the noise, but he'd learned to bow down to whichever he was granted. He'd also learned we aren't meant to understand everything in the universe and maybe that's where he'd gone wrong all those years ago, trying to understand more than he was meant to and trying to find an answer to questions he wasn't meant to ask.

Getting back to his feet, he wondered if the same god that governed Earth governed Alpha Iridium, if there was a god, and whether that god would forgive him when he left his life. 'It will all be over soon,' the voice inside him whispered. *But how will it end?* he wondered in reply.

## EIGHTY-SEVEN

Shortly before sundown that day, Caine had forgotten his worries and his heartache, he'd traded them for outrage and disdain. Most of the prisoners being held captive in his castle had escaped. He was certain they would return for Kale which made the game a little more interesting, but he still hated being outsmarted and betrayed.

What later changed his plan was the attack that took place just before sundown. It was brutal and well executed. Fueled by a passion, the J'Kahl guarding the holding compound where the townspeople had been awaiting death could not match. The attack barely lasted twenty minutes and within ten more the tired yet grateful townspeople of Breadon Ridge were following their rescuers northward to safety. The rebels' plan was working perfectly so far, but soon it would change; whether for the better no one knew.

## EIGHTY-EIGHT

"Medea! Medea slow down and answer me," Mr. Carlson shouted and finally Medea stopped moving and turned towards him.

"Mr. Carlson please, we have to get you to safety. I'll tell you everything once we're sure we're out of danger."

"I'm not going anywhere until you answer me. Where is she? Where is Kale?"

Medea pulled Mr. Carlson over to the side and as quietly as she could she told him as much as dared. Kale was with Caine, hopefully alive and they were going to find a way to free her as soon as they'd gotten the people of Braedon Ridge to safety.

"Listen up!" Mr. Carlson shouted, while stepping up onto a large rock to make sure everyone could see and hear him. Before he continued, he waited for the large crowd to slow to a stop. Hundreds of expectant faces turned up toward him.

"Listen up everyone! These kids here have done quite a lot for us," he began as people throughout the crowd were nodding and smiling at the group of people who'd saved their lives. "But if you ask me they're in over their heads and too damn proud to ask for help. I know we're just a bunch of poor, old, sick and tired people but I think we should stand up for ourselves instead of letting these kids do it for us."

"We just barely got away with our lives. You want us to run back into town and try to lose them again?" a woman shouted through the crowd.

"We don't stand a chance against Caine. Why don't we just get to safety before those soldiers come after us and pick up right where they left off?" another man yelled.

Soon everyone was shouting. The realization that every second they spent arguing was a second closer they came to getting captured again wove fear throughout the crowd at lightning speed.

"Listen up, please!" Mr. Carlson shouted again. "He's got Kale. Do you hear me, Kale is in trouble."

The crowd went silent. Throughout it the children of the Founders, the J'Kahl turned traitors, and the three friends who in one way stood to lose the most, looked on with growing awe and anticipation. They'd always thought they were fighting for something worthwhile but they never imagined it would be anything more than a few against many. Now as the crowd started to respond to Mr. Carlson they realized that running for safety might be the wrong thing to do.

"What do you mean he's got Kale?" someone else shouted.

"She got some crazy idea that we all needed saving and that she could do it on her own. But who cares about that. He's got her. That monster has got her. Are we going to stand around and let him hurt her?"

"And just what can we do?" came another voice though less skeptical.

"I know some of us are too old, and some of us are too young, and some of us are too sick, and if those people want to head north to safety right now then no one will blame you. But some of us are strong enough to fight and I think that we should. We've stood by and let our people get killed and enslaved and ruined for a long time. All along we let it go because Caine was the savior but I haven't seen him doing any saving and now he's got someone we all care about, someone who did us all right at one time or another. I don't care what you all do, but I'm going to that castle to find Kale and I will tear it down brick by brick to find her if it takes me a hundred years."

Throughout the crowd, though silence prevailed, it was obvious by the faces staring toward him that Mr. Carlson had made an impact with his words. People were beginning to nod their heads in agreement and as they looked around their conviction grew.

"What about the children?" a woman called out with concern.

"I'll take the children north along with anyone else who isn't up for this," Sarah said taking Corin's hand in hers and smiling at him. "You go fight," she said to him. "Save your friend. Finish what you started and take all the help you can get."

She put a hand on Jaren's arm and looked him in the eye. What passed between them was much the same as what passed between a loving mother and her son. "I'll lead them to safety, Jaren. You lead them to freedom. Sound like a fair exchange?"

Mike had appeared in the crowd and as soon as Mrs. Blanchard saw her sleeping daughter in his arms she was upon them. Mike handed a soundly sleeping Emily to her mother but his eyes never left Jaren's in the hope he'd see the leader they all needed him to be.

"This is crazy," Jaren ventured. "It's too dangerous. We can't ask all these people to do this."

"We didn't ask you to start this but you did, for all of us. It's time we stood up for ourselves," Mr. Wilson said firmly. "It's time to fight back."

"We can get into the castle through the tunnels," Archer offered.

"If some of us attack the compound from the outside and the rest of us sneak in we could have a chance here. We know that castle better than anyone," Jet added helpfully.

"We already have an attack plan. Now, we've got more people," Medea put in hopefully.

All eyes were turned toward Jaren as he closed his eyes and rubbed his temples. He didn't want to put anyone else in danger but wasn't this what they'd always hoped for. The people had a right to fight for themselves, for their freedom. Maybe that was the key to surviving the Darkness that was stalking them all. Maybe it was time to let the people of Berdune choose their own future, come what may.

"Sarah, you better head out right away. The rest of us are heading back to town through the woods. We'll split into two groups when we get to the tunnel entrance. One will go in that way the other will attack outside. This isn't a game, they'll kill any one of us if they get the chance, so if you're not up for doing the same I suggest you follow Sarah north and don't feel ashamed for doing so," Jaren turned his gaze across the hundreds of hopeful faces looking back at him.

"Let's go. Tonight we take back Berdune!" People cheered and shouted and then the crowd began to move in two different directions.

Corin said goodbye to his mother; wondering if they'd been reunited only so he could say goodbye to her before he died. He knew that for the first time they were acting as one people and if they were going to fail it seemed more comforting to do so united. With their cover blown, Kale probably hadn't gotten the chance to kill Caine but maybe they could still rescue her, and could still destroy Caine and stop the Darkness from swallowing them all whole. It mattered that they were finally fighting together. It had to.

"What are you doing?" Jaren asked Medea as she made her way south.

"I'm coming to fight."

"But you're hurt. You should be heading north to safety." Jaren said with a hint of exasperation.

Medea scoffed before answering, "Jaren, have you ever known me to miss out on the action?"

"Medea, this could be it. This could be the end. Kale could be dead and the rest of us could be right behind her."

"If this is how it ends, badly I mean, then I'm where I'm meant to be and with the people I'm meant to be with. Look around you," she said looking around at the determined faces of the people heading south towards Caine's castle and whatever fate awaited them, "did you ever think they would fight back? We helped do this. We helped make them see that things could be better and that we deserve better. I signed up for the whole thing, right until the end. I'm not quitting now." She put her good arm around him as they walked.

"Medea, I just want to let you know, I mean before we get to the castle and..."

"Don't worry, Jaren, I know," she said emotionally, trying to keep herself from falling apart she stopped and took a few deep breaths. When she recovered she smiled up at him and he returned the gesture. Despite the worry that it would all be over soon, there came the comfort that it would all be over soon.

The crowd moved energetically south, toward whatever awaited them at Caine's compound. A river of hope and determination. A few days ago, most would have let the world move forward around them and just been content that it didn't leave them behind. They'd been willing victims for a long time and within them all rang the truth that standing aside was a far greater crime than Caine had ever committed.

Jaren, Medea, and Corin had stopped thinking about Caine and realized they still had a chance at saving Kale if she was still alive. Truly, it was a ridiculous notion to think they had a chance against a well-guarded castle and supremely trained soldiers but as they parted at the tunnel entrance, unsure as to what the night would bring and who would survive it, they were hopeful. Much like the people of Berdune, oppressed for too long, they were willing to die fighting if it meant they died free.

## EIGHTY-NINE

The first assault that came at the front entrance of the compound was a shock to the J'Kahl who were standing guard. Many of the soldiers had been sent to Empris at Caine's command so their ranks were thinner than usual. The people storming in the front gates met them with such rage and vehemence that many of them quickly fled like children from a summer storm. Those who chose to stand their ground cut down the common people easily yet they still didn't last long. For once, they were outnumbered and their power over the people of Braedon Ridge, born of fear, was no more. It left the remaining J'Khal with the choice to die fighting or to run away.

When the battle inside Caine's compound was over many had perished in the darkest night Berdune had ever seen. Many more were wounded and helpless in their pain yet they'd gained something precious, something they'd been without for a long time, their right to choose their own destiny.

While they helped each other up and cried out mournfully for those who would never rise again, they regrouped and made their way toward the castle entrance.

Arin and Joah led the way, hand in hand, warrior siblings, ready to do whatever it took to make their parents proud. Arin's left arm had been cut twice and a wound to her leg added a slight limp to her stride but she took no notice.

"We've come for you Caine!" she shouted as they entered the front doors of the castle. She stopped when they were greeted by an eerie echo. A chill swept through her as she became certain her voice was wandering through the halls of hell, and she was right behind it.

## NINETY

Inside the castle, Archer and Jet led Jaren, Medea, and Corin through the empty hallways with a growing sense of unease. The others who'd come with them had dispersed through the hallways yet there wasn't a single sign to indicate anyone was left inside.

"Something's wrong," Archer said. "Where is everyone?"

They checked every room, crashing through doors and bracing themselves to fight but they found no one. Each door led to emptiness and a mounting sense that things were not quite what they seemed. Some of the rooms contained recent followers of Caine's who'd taken their own lives and with each corpse they found the group realized that something was very wrong.

"What the hell is going on here?" Jaren asked as he swung open another door.

"Oh my god," Corin stammered as he stopped dead in his tracks and stared at the spectacle in the large room beyond. The space was dimly lit and two swinging shadows danced on the far wall reflecting the suspended bodies that hung in the center of the room. As Jaren stared at the two faces contorted with pain and horror, he sought out the satisfaction he thought he would find when his parents realized they were wrong. But seeing them then, so pathetic and so weak, he could only pity them.

"Cut them down!" Archer shouted as he ran into the room beside Jet and started to cut the ropes from which the

McLevys hung. They hit the ground with one thud and then another, and still Jaren stood in the doorway unable to move or even begin to comprehend what he was or wasn't feeling.

"Are they alive?" he finally asked in a whisper, making his way towards them.

"Your father is. Your mother..." Corin let his words trail off as he removed his fingers from her throat where he'd been searching for her pulse.

Jaren felt a wave of nausea wash through him and then a wave of anger so fierce and fiery he started to sweat. He'd wanted to hate them until the moment they died and now this, so sad, so sorry in their attempt to take their own lives. How could he hate anyone so pathetic?

"Let me speak to him," Jaren ordered and pushed Corin and the others out of his way. "Where is he?" he asked his father. "Where is Caine?"

"Don't know," his father wheezed.

"Don't you lie to me!" Jaren shouted and in so many ways he was confronting more than just the situation at hand. Jaren wanted years of lies accounted for but he didn't have time and he knew it.

"Tomorrow. Caine will prevail." Jaren wasn't sure whether it was a threat or a piece of information and the only person who could clarify that was only moments away from leaving the world of the waking forever.

"If you believed that, I doubt you'd be lying here like this, you coward," Jaren spat out, filled with rage and hurt and sorrow.

"Where is he?" Jaren demanded again. "Where the hell is Kale?"

"He left us. Don't know."

"Damn you! Tell us where she is." he begged, helpless, his anger starting to melt, leaving just heartache and pain.

"Code Red. Initiated. No time. Get out," Jaren's father rasped.

Before Jaren could request more information, Jet began to shout.

"We have to get out of here. Code Red is self-destruct. This whole building is about to go up. Let's go!"

Archer and Jet made their way toward the door quickly while Jaren kneeled beside his father, unmoving.

"Get everyone out," Jaren commanded. "Corin, you go too."

"What about you?" Corin asked worriedly.

"I'll be right behind you. Go!"

Corin took one last look at his friend and then left the room reluctantly. There was something in Jaren's voice he'd never heard before and it scared him, but he chose not to disobey his friend.

"Get everyone out of the compound now!" Jet yelled as they ran through the halls. "The castle is going to blow up. Get out now!"

The growing crowd began to run for the front exit hoping they would make it in time. Unlike the monster they'd come to destroy, they left no one behind. Within a couple minutes, they were standing in the cool night amongst the carnage that had taken place outside without them.

Medea kneeled down next to Mr. Carlson, laid out on the grass, slashed open too violently to have survived, and closed both his eyes so that he wasn't staring blankly up at the darkness above. She touched his cheek and thanked him silently, for the light he'd brought to every day including the one they were trying to survive, and for reminding them what they'd forgotten, that the people of Berdune deserved to fight for themselves, they'd just needed to be reminded why.

Inside the castle, Jaren finished what he'd waited so long to finish.

"You see now what he is, your fearless god and leader? He lets you hang yourselves while he's off hiding somewhere. You see now?" Jaren was shaking with rage and anguish. So many years stolen, the happy, easy life he'd never gotten to lead, it pressed in on him now and broke his heart.

"Go," his father whispered to him. "Save yourself."

"I will save myself," Jaren said as tears streamed down his cheeks. He rose and took a step back from his father. "And I'll give you what you gave me the last few years. Not a second thought." Jaren turned and walked toward the door.

"I'm sorry," his father called desperately after him. "I'm so sorry." Jaren wasn't listening.

He started running through the halls and prayed he wouldn't get lost within the monstrous building. He wasn't sure when the castle was going to explode, if in fact his father had been telling the truth, but he knew he didn't want to be in it when it did.

Jaren raced through the hallways, passing doors left ajar and dark corridors. He had no idea if he was headed the right way or not but he pushed himself as fast as he could go, until his chest burned with the mere effort of drawing breath. Turning one way, then another, he ran and fought to stay calm. When he reached the huge front hallway and pushed through the heavy doors relief flooded through him. He felt the cool night air on his face and took a deep and filling breath. He was barely down the steps when heat rushed passed him, lifting him off his feet and carrying him through the endlessly black night. The sound was like nothing he'd ever heard before. Stone tearing, the earth heaving, and in his heart he heard his father screaming for forgiveness.

Jaren felt the world tumble away from him as the blast continued ringing in his ears. His eyes began to burn, his vision fluttered and then slipped away from him so that all was dark. He thought nothing in that moment. Not of the people who needed him or those who still needed saving, not of the parents who'd shamed him for so many years, not of the leader and monster who still needed to be stopped. Not even of Kale. Jaren's world was silent and all he could do was surrender.

NINETY-ONE

And so the wounded yet finally proud people of Braedon Ridge returned to the Mission full of joy and certainty. Their numbers had been slashed by a third yet their spirits were high. They'd finally fought back and realized that Caine hadn't been their true oppressor, their willingness and ignorance had.

The children of the Founders nursed their wounds and tended to the wounds of others. They'd been prepared to lose any one of their friends and were relieved to all be alive.

Medea and Corin leaned over their unconscious friend and watched with worry as his furrowed brow lent beads of sweat to the cool night air.

"Jaren," Medea whispered, "Jaren are you okay?" She looked up in to Corin's worried face and he could only shake his head uselessly.

Jaren's face and arms were covered with scratches and bruises and every now and then words indecipherable in the waking world, would be carried from his troubled sleep. Finally he cried out in terror and woke.

"Jaren, oh my god, are you okay?" Medea asked while doing nothing to stop the tears that fear and relief wrestled out of her.

Jaren smiled as he tried to sit up with Corin's help.

"What a ride," he said as he let out a short burst of laughter.

"Damn it, Jaren, that isn't funny," Medea said indignantly yet she kept smiling at him gratefully. For a few moments ,the world slowed, stopped, and then disappeared around them. They found themselves in that perfect pause of time, a moment eternal, where it seemed like everything was okay.

Each of them could feel it, when time caught them again, dragged them back and held them down. Each one of them came willingly because the fight wasn't over.

"Do you think Kale was…" Corin began but his throat tightened and he couldn't even bring himself to finish his question.

"No, I don't think she was in there. He has other plans for her. I just wish we knew what they were," Jaren said letting his body droop with the weight of his worry.

"But she is…" Corin again couldn't finish his thought aloud and this time Medea stepped in.

"She's alive. I know it. The world doesn't just change like that without us noticing. Without us feeling it shift," Medea's certainty was palpable and he believed her.

What they needed to figure out was what they were going to do next. When they were finally able to sit down with six children of the Founders, Archer, James, and Jet, it seemed they were all willing to do what it took to keep the fight going and finish what they'd started. And so it was decided quickly that they would travel to Empris to attack the factories and mines to free the slaves and prisoners Caine had taken the night before. Everyone who'd fought beside them at Caine's compound was willing even though they were reluctant to leave without having rescued Kale.

"Are you sure about this, Jaren?" Arin asked him worriedly.

"My place is here. Who knows, maybe they'll show up and we can stop him or save Kale," he offered a smile but it was a tired sight.

Medea, Corin, and Jaren had decided that their part of the battle was fought. They'd given the people a reason to stand up for themselves, to fight, and now all they wanted was to find their friend and save her life. Arin and Joah wanted to stay and help, hopeful they'd find Alex and Derin with Kale, but after much deliberation and to Arin's disappointment it was decided they'd be more effective in Empris. The more Founders the people saw the more likely they would be to fight and win. Arin couldn't help feeling that deep and aching pull towards Alex, wherever he was, and the thought that she was undertaking any fight except the one that led her to him was hard to accept. But she knew he'd want them all to do what needed to be done. And so Arin pushed Alex out of her thoughts so that she could do what she had to despite what her heart begged, which was to find him and bring him home.

When the group parted, it was reluctantly and flavored bitterly with foreboding. Medea, Corin, and Jaren found themselves in a ghost town shrouded in darkness so deep they couldn't even see shadows. They walked without purpose at first, their lone lantern cutting through the dark erratically. They weren't even sure where they should start looking for Caine.

When hope had finally fled, their ideas had run out, and they'd searched every place he might be hiding, or so they thought, they sat huddled together in the dark of night, alone but together, if only to be reminded what it was they'd gambled so much for and why.


## NINETY-TWO

Dawn broke tiredly over Braedon Ridge on the last day of Caine's fourteenth year. It was barely light enough to see more than ten feet in any direction but it was slightly more welcome than the bottomless night they'd endured before it.

The people at the Mission were weak and tired yet their pride was now an un-extinguishable flame, still burning bright. They were ready to make their way to Empris to free the slaves Caine had put to work in his mines and factories. They couldn't know what they were facing, nor what demented game the great leader's insanity had led them all into. What they did know was that they still had a chance. Whether fate or the stars were fond of them was no longer the issue. The people knew they still faced hard times and maybe even worse when they met the J'Kahl guarding Caine's slaves in Empris. But they were strong and united, and willing to die fighting.

The children of the Founders along with Jet, Archer, and James were resting. They would make the journey to Empris with the others. They planned on hijacking the train set to leave Braedon Ridge in just over two hours so they would arrive just after dark.

Though Medea, Corin, and Jaren had no idea where Caine was or what he'd planned they couldn't bring themselves to leave Braedon Ridge with Kale's fate unknown. Whether their friend was alive somewhere or whether they were just going to end up waiting for the end wasn't important. They couldn't leave and keep from feeling like they'd betrayed Kale in some way. They'd given the people the strength they needed and now it was time to look out for themselves. Together, they made their way to just east of Caine's now ruined castle and sat by the Craden Rapids letting the hurried tumbling of the river keep them company.

Caine stood watch outside of his hideout and wondered what the new day would bring. He was impatient for the last night to arrive and if all went as planned it would not last long. He wasn't sure why he was welcoming the beginning of the end of Alpha Iridium so enthusiastically but from somewhere in his mind came an insistence that that is what he must do.

Inside the hideout, Kale slept fitfully in her cell haunted by dreams of a life she knew nothing about. With a mother who was healthy, and happy, and who loved her dearly. With peace around her in the world and no wars to fight, except for the ones within. No savior to seek, no fate to bow-down to or defy.

In another cell, Derin shook and shivered on the floor, coughing crimson spray when he woke confused and unaware of where and sometimes even who he was. Alex held him tightly, painfully aware the brother he'd just found had only a short while left in the world. If he couldn't hope his brother back to life, then he could only hope for one more chance at revenge.

The day would pass slowly and with no sun to watch crossing the sky it was hard to imagine the day passed at all. But the deepest darkness Berdune had ever seen fell upon them all that night and if the light that could defy it was truly a reality, no one would have believed it just then.

Staring upward, Jaren couldn't help but marvel at how dark the night sky was. He couldn't see a single star and he wondered if there was actually a cloud cover blocking out the twinkling bodies far above or whether the Darkness had indeed found them and devoured it all. He understood one thing for certain, they were in a lot of trouble and all he could do was reach for the possibility that the savior was as real as the tiny flame of hope that burned within him still. That burned, no matter how dim, within every heart except those the Darkness had already consumed.

# Part Three
## Awake

NINETY-THREE

She dove into the darkness. Awake.

Slowly, the nonsense slipped and tumbled out of reach. She gasped. Shaking. Shivering. The night had been waiting for her, and now she had arrived. She felt trapped within herself. Still trapped within the dream. As always it had followed Kayla into the waking world. A predator with only one kind of prey.

Waking, being torn out of that other life that clung to her more and more every day was disorienting. The evil was in her room again and she could sense it stalking her, though she couldn't see it. Every time that Darkness reached out towards her she shrank away from its ferocity, terrified. She longed with everything she was to sit up and shake away the horror but she was paralyzed. Frustrated, wracked with fear, Kayla wrestled with the waking world hoping to grab hold of it long enough to be set free.

From the hallway she could hear the purposeful steps of someone walking towards her room. Shoving aside her fear, Kayla calmed herself long enough to still, and listen. When the footfalls came to rest outside her door Kayla's terror wrapped itself around her throat and squeezed, tight, so that she had to gasp for breath.

Time slowed. Slipping by like a lazy river, shallow and unconcerned with reaching the sea. It might have been a moment, that pause, but it felt like an eternity trapped within her terror. Kayla's door finally swung slowly open and in the doorway, surrounded by a halo of light from the hallway beyond, stood a strange and beautiful woman. She radiated power. It was palpable enough that Kayla could feel it washing over her in waves so strong she began to dizzy. The woman's eyes were pools of knowledge, so deep that Kayla wondered if she would get lost within their depths.

She'd never been more afraid in her entire life.

Kayla knew she wasn't gazing at a monster but something worse, the truth. She felt the Darkness in her room falter as the woman began to speak in a voice not of this world. Kayla strained to hear her but couldn't. Still, she understood just the same. The words were a sea of truth, kind and careful, and she was finally willing to drown in them.

Kayla sat up in bed and all was calm. The demon in her room fled. She'd somehow overcome her helplessness. She looked towards the doorway where the woman stood and waited, for what she didn't know.

"Choose," the woman whispered and then she disappeared.

Kayla lay back on her pillow and stared at the ordinary darkness that swam through her room in the wake of the being of light. She realized that for the first time in her life she was ready to face her demons. The Darkness, she was sure was a thing real and terrifying, but the monster that had appeared to her had been a figment of her fear. Fear of truly living. Fear of repairing the remnants of a broken heart, the last thing her father had ever given her. Fear of facing herself. Fear of being whole.

In the last of the late evening light filtering in through her windows, so many truths that had evaded her before were lit up. Brightest among them her longing for perfection, an excuse not to face the realities of the waking world and in fact a lie, because like everyone else she was already perfect, exactly as she was. Perfect and beautifully imperfect, the truth and mystery of every human life, whole or not.

Kayla could feel herself wading through relief and felt as if she was tasting peace for the very first time. She didn't really understand what it was she'd faced or was preparing to face, but she understood that she was finally ready.

She thought of the strange words the woman in the doorway had spoken to her. She'd caught only one other fragmented phrase. "It's not the dream...it's the dreaming."

She turned the words over and over again in her mind but could make no sense of them. *It's not the dream. It's the dreaming.* She shrugged, baffled.

Kayla knew two things for certain, she wasn't yet ready to understand but she would be soon, and she'd experienced her last nightmare. Walking into the bathroom to shower, Kayla pushed all thoughts of the past from her mind. It was time to move forward. It was time to begin again.

## NINETY-FOUR

An hour later, just before eleven o'clock that night, Kayla was packed and ready to leave for her mother's house. Her Aunt called up the stairs to tell her Max had arrived to take her to the bus station and Kayla grabbed her suitcase and walked out her bedroom door. She stopped, remembering there was something she'd forgotten to pack, something she never went anywhere without. She dropped her suitcase and ran back into the room to grab it.

She'd forgotten her favorite book. It was an imposing volume over an inch and a half thick written in fine print. On the inside cover the author had signed an autograph and written a little note to Kayla. *"Don't ever forget how to dream Kayla. The answers are always found while dreaming."*

Kayla placed the book in her bag and went down the stairs to say good-bye to her Aunt and Uncle. Though she was only going away for a few days there were tears and hugs and best wishes before Kayla was on her way to the bus station. She had the strange and unsettling feeling as the shops and buildings of Emery sped by her window that she was seeing them for the last time.

When they got to the station, after loading Kayla's suitcase onto the bus, Max took Kayla into his arms and hugged her fiercely.

"I'm sorry about the other morning," she said sadly, leaning into him, feeling this deep urge to make things right before she got on the bus.

"Me too. It was a silly fight."

They moved apart just enough to come back together in the sweetest and gentlest kiss they'd shared yet. It was the kind of kiss that told entire stories. But would either of them listen.

"Why do I feel like you're never coming back?" he asked her worriedly.

"I don't know," Kayla faked a laugh. "But it's just a few days. I bet you won't even notice I'm gone."

"Kayla, what are you hiding from me?" Kayla was surprised by his question but answered it immediately just the same.

"I don't know. I wish I did."

The question tugged at her subconscious. A thought, long hidden, was asking to get out. She was hiding something from him, and herself. Soon, she would know what.

Max hugged her again and then stepped back and away from her.

"Come back," he whispered, "just come back to me okay." He kissed Kayla gently on the lips. "I love you."

"I love you, too, but don't spread it around okay?" Kayla said with an embarrassed smile. Trying her best to lighten the mood. "I'm still getting used to it."

Kayla got on the bus and stared out the window at Max who stood smiling and waving at her. The gesture, forced and practiced, made her feel a little sad and sorry. His hand moved stiffly and his smile twitched at the corners. Kayla waved back at him and thought irrationally, *I'm never going to see him again.*

She felt a great sense of loss press down upon her when Max turned away from the bus and started walking away. She wanted to bang on the window so he'd come back. She could tell him all the things she wanted to say to him but had always been too afraid. She wanted to get off the bus and wrap her arms around him tightly, tell him she was sorry for being her, sorry for making it so hard for him to love her, tell him she got it now and that she could let him in if he just gave her time. She wanted so many things and yet she simply watched until he was out of sight.

She pulled her favorite book out of her back-pack and ran her hand across the golden letters on the worn leather cover. She'd never realized how ironic not only the title of the book was but who the author was as well. Kayla thought that maybe for the first time since acquiring the book she understood what the title meant.

"Awake While Dreaming," she read aloud, "by Randall Caine."

The scientist Randall Caine had had many insights into the realm of sleep and dreams and the answers that they held. Kayla wondered if any of those answers had made his life better. She had a feeling deep down inside that they hadn't. As much as she found truth in the book, she couldn't help but question Randall Caine's understanding for his own words and revelations.

Kayla wondered where he was. His disappearance had gone unnoticed by many. Those who did address it felt he'd vanished by choice to continue his ludicrous research without criticism. Sometimes, Kayla thought he was dead.

'Where are you Caine?' she wondered as the bus began to move. Unaware she'd finally asked a question whose answer would find her almost immediately.

NINETY-FIVE

Sitting by the Craden Rapids where they'd been sitting for much of the day, Medea, Corin, and Jaren were still waiting, for what they didn't know. They felt like they'd been seated there for all of eternity and equally no time at all. They weren't sure where else to look for Kale. They'd searched everywhere they could think of and had found no trace of Caine, the J'Kahl, or any of his loyal servants.

It was a terrible feeling, that of knowing someone you loved very dearly was in danger and that you might not be able to save them. Even worse was the certainty they were Kale's only hope of rescue, so if they didn't figure something out all would be lost.

They sat in helpless silence, exhausted, letting their thoughts run rampant in search of a plan. If the Darkness came with purpose then with it must have come a glimmer of hope, a promise of light.

It was Medea who first noticed the bobbing light that approached them through the dark. She elbowed Jaren in the side to bring his attention to the approaching unknown and Corin joined them, observant and unsure, yet too exhausted to react.

"Hey guys. Having a party without us?" Joah said with buoyancy only he could muster under the circumstances. The lantern swung erratically in his hand as he held it high to shed light on all of them.

"What's wrong?" Jaren asked urgently making his way to his feet. "Aren't you guys supposed to be on your way to Empris?"

"Don't stand just for us Jaren. Nothing's changed," Arin said as she sat down beside Medea and smiled. "Everything is still going as planned. The train should be arriving in Empris on schedule. They're just two people short, that's all."

"We couldn't let you guys sit out on the party all alone," Joah said shaking Jaren's hand as if they were meeting again after years rather than merely hours.

"We just thought maybe you guys could use some company under the circumstances," Arin said trying not to sound hopeless. "And if there's any chance Alex is alive...well..." she couldn't quite finish her thought and Jaren reached out and squeezed her arm for support.

"I'm glad you came," Jaren said.

Joah and Jaren finally sat down and for a moment none of the group could think of anything to say. Finally, Arin broke the silence. "So it took us forever to find you guys. We've been everywhere."

"This place doesn't look like much in the dark," Joah added sounding uncharacteristically sad and sorry. Again silence enveloped the group and the quickly moving rapids grew thunderously loud while the seconds ticked by.

"So this is how it all ends," Medea stated with no hint of humor.

"You guys are always talking about the end before it gets here," Joah stated. "Nothing is over yet. We're just waiting for how the next fight begins."

Medea chuckled, "Words of wisdom from the joker."

"Hey, I prefer to be referred to as the comic relief. And I'm right. You guys look a little too sad for a bunch of people who just witnessed the world change."

"Do you blame us?" Corin asked.

"Well I'd expect more from a bunch of heroes," Joah retorted.

"Heroes?"

"We all knew this was going to get bad before it got better. Maybe it keeps getting bad. Maybe the world ends tonight. But did you see what went on in the last day? Did you see those people full of hope, and pride, and anger, finally willing to fight for themselves? You helped do that. You helped give them something they haven't had for a very long time. Even if it's only for a day and the world ends tonight. Eternities have unfolded in a day. That means something. That's more than they would have had if it weren't for you guys."

"If it weren't for all of us, you guys, too," Medea said with a smile.

"Now you're talking. I don't mind playing the hero every now and then. I'm very good at it you know," Joah said with a smile.

"Alright now you're pushing it, Joah," Arin said with the same smile that was slowly beginning to spread throughout the group.

They'd done something. They'd changed the world like they'd all wanted to, like Kale had made them believe they could. Some of it had changed without their consent and now it seemed as if they'd have to sit and wait to see what came next. Hopefully it was the dawn. Though in the oppressively dark night it was hard to imagine anything so bright and promising.


NINETY-SIX

On the mountain shelf high above Sunshine Bay, Kale stood with Caine at her side and hatred pumping through her heart so strongly that her chest was tight with it. From where they stood, it seemed as if they'd been sucked into a black hole. Not a single ounce of light could be seen across the vast ocean that lay beyond the cliff. Kale knew it was there only because she could feel it like she'd always been able to.

Alex and Derin had been brought with Kale and she couldn't fathom why or what plan Caine had to bring the Darkness. She watched Derin worriedly. He was lying on the cold ground unattended. The bandage around his middle was soaked in old brown blood and every time he coughed ruby speckles dotted his pale and parted blue lips. Beside him two soldiers held Alex tightly and kept him from running to his brother's aide any time he tried. Now and then Kale looked to Alex wondering if he knew she'd been the one to execute his brother. She wondered most of all whether Derin would forgive her even as she knew she couldn't forgive herself.

Around them, some of the J'Kahl that she'd trained with stood watching with a mixture of pride and helplessness. Kale couldn't help but pity them. In a way, they were victims to their ignorance and eagerness to be followers, to belong. In her heart Kale knew they were greater victims than she.

"Kale, I will ask you one last time to join me and we will rule this world and its people together," Caine said with a serpentine smoothness that chilled Kale far worse than the night. "I will spare your friends, even Derin if that's what you'd like. But you must stand at my side." He knew, if he could just get her to join him he could take back his rule of Berdune. The people would bow down willingly again, and her life would be spared. There would be time, after the Darkness won, for him to rule, to finish out his days in power.

Despite the scene unraveling before her, Kale found herself looking inward, searching for an answer to her life. Destroying Caine was what had mattered for so long and yet now she was another helpless victim with no defense in sight. She longed for the heavens to toss the savior down into their midst. She held her breath, waiting for the darkness to part. Waiting for someone to arrive who was able to destroy Caine and stop the Darkness. The heavens ignored her. There was no sign of light.

"I would rather die a million painful deaths than stand with you," she said defiantly. Unable to lie, even now, with so many lives in the balance and the Darkness swarming above, ready to devour them all.

What she knew was that the people of Berdune had finally risen up against Caine and that even though she'd failed in killing him somehow her friends had succeeded in making him a man in the eyes of the people.

She was surprised to realize she'd always expected to die by Caine's hand and now that the time had come it felt too familiar to disobey. Like a moment come upon her for a second time, all she could do was let it pass again. Medea was dead, Cyan was gone, Derin was dying and who knew how many other people she loved had left the world violently that day. It was simply her turn to meet her fate.

"Kale, I gave you the chance to join me but you refuse. You leave me no choice but to sacrifice you. You leave me no choice," he said sadly before the madness took him again. "Will you beg for your life like your mother did? I hope so, Kale, I really do hope so," Caine raised the blade to Kale's throat and smiled maniacally.

Unattended and unobserved, Derin rose to his feet and staggered towards Caine. Kale cried out, shocked, and stepped back dangerously close to the cliff's edge.

"No," she screamed as Caine drove the blade deep into Derin's stomach. Then he lifted the blade a few inches and twisted it summoning a cry of anguish from Derin. A perfect match to the one that Alex issued a few feet away.

Caine pulled the blade from Derin's stomach and let him fall to the ground without a sound. Kale was at his side in an instant. She could think of nothing to say though she was frantic to find the right words. Two more soldiers had to join in holding tight to Alex as he kicked and screamed to be let go. He used all of his strength and anger to try and fight off the J'Kahl but there were too many of them and he couldn't break free. He wailed, broken hearted. The brother who'd lived a whole life without him would leave it without him too.

Looking up at Kale with distant eyes, Derin tried to speak but the only things issued from his parted lips were ruby colored bubbles. The last offerings of a life too short. He heaved a huge sigh and in that moment of anguish it sounded to Kale like relief. She rocked his head in her lap stroking his cheek gently.

"Derin?" she asked quietly, but he couldn't answer, he was already gone.


NINETY-SEVEN

Kayla stared out the window at the sea that flowed far below them to the east. They were driving along the highest of the cliffs that fell to the ocean on their way out of Emery. Further back was the same ledge Kayla had plunged from not too long ago even though it felt like forever. Time was strange like that though wasn't it, she thought to herself.

She longed to be seated on the shore talking to the ocean the way she liked to. Listening as it spoke to her with that wisdom born of a timeless existence. For a few moments she let herself be drawn back into the memory of it but her thoughts were quickly interrupted by the scream of rubber tearing at pavement. She was thrown forward in her seat and felt all the breath get slammed out of her lungs. Disoriented and frightened Kayla listened in horror as the other passengers on the bus began to scream.

The bus swerved wildly to the left and Kayla saw through her window that they'd swerved to avoid a moose on the road. The lanky, awkward looking beast seemed unaware he'd just changed the fate of a bus full of people as he continued to the other side of the road.

The bus driver shouted out, wordless cries and curses, as he tried to turn the bus sharply back to the right but the metal beast lifted onto two wheels and after skidding sideways for a few breaths it dove off of the cliff towards its demise.


NINETY-EIGHT

Alex let out a wail full of so much anguish and fury that Kale's heart broke again. She stood, slowly, and turned toward Caine surprised he'd yet to make a move. In his eyes she saw madness but heartache as well. And his unwillingness to be just one man, the cowardice of it, made her hate him even more. Meeting his gaze with her own she spoke calmly.

"I will kill you, Caine."

Without giving him any time to consider her threat Kale lunged at him.

She slammed into him with so much force, he fell over and skidded a few feet, turning up clouds of dust and sending rocks skittering over the mountain's edge. Shocked, angry, he got quickly to his feet and stood to face her. He'd never looked more imposing than he did in that moment but Kale didn't care. She ran at him again but this time he was ready and moved swiftly out of the way. She came to rest on the brink of the cliff and had to lean back and away from the drop below to get her balance. Behind her, Caine spoke, "I wish it could have ended differently, Kale." Then, he pushed her.

She could hear cries of shock behind her but only for a moment. After that all she could hear was the rushing of air around her as she fell towards the jagged rocks below.


NINETY-NINE

The moment the bus began to fall something strange happened to Kayla. She became fully aware of another self, another her. Yet Kale wasn't simply another, but the pieces of herself she'd been missing for so long.

The entire life of her other half flashed before her eyes as the Earth prepared to reclaim her. She saw a strange world yet she recognized everything about it. She glimpsed friends, acquaintances, and a different set of parents that she'd loved dearly. She saw the adventure she'd longed to live and was still living now. She realized it had been awful and hard and heartbreaking too. Not glamorous like she'd thought it might be.

She saw that she'd been wrong. Life was not about fear, it was about love. That is what her heart, forever cracked in two, had been waiting for her to learn. She saw the love that surrounded her in that other world and she became a part of it. She let it fill her up and empty out all of the dark and lonely places she had hidden within her.

She saw with growing horror where Randall Caine had disappeared to and why; and though time was short she found within it the means to be repulsed by what he'd become.

She saw the beautiful boy with the crystal blue eyes whom she'd dreamed of often. The one she'd pushed away over and over again and yet still he'd fought for her. She saw that he'd been killed and that in many ways it'd been her doing. She felt hatred for Randall Caine well up in her so strongly the feeling of falling to the Earth was briefly washed away.


ONE-HUNDRED

Caine stood on the brink of the gulf and watched as Kale tumbled downward through the gloom and out of sight. He could hear someone screaming, horrified, and he realized that he was the one crying out in shock and pain.

Not far below him Kale tumbled to the earth aware of more than her approaching fate. She saw another life, her life in a way. A life she'd been born into and lived for five years until one night she'd mysteriously found herself in the Braedon woods on a ridge at the very same moment Caine had arrived. The moment she'd been split in two.

Kale saw she had a mother in that other life who loved her and who was still alive. She had a father who was barely that and absent throughout most of her life. She saw Max who'd fallen in love with her and whom she was afraid to love, though she did.

Mostly, she saw the pain she'd endured in that life and finally understood why she was the way she was in this one.

Falling to the earth, Kale was whole at last and even though she knew her time as a whole person was short she relished it just the same. She was complete, and nothing could change that.

In the distance, the darkness parted and through the gap tore the sun. *Sunrise,* Kale thought wildly, *bright, beautiful light.*

## ONE-HUNDRED-ONE

The last thing Kayla saw was where she was right then in that other world, that other life. She was falling there too. Toppling down from a frightening height to her death. 'I'm going to die,' she realized. 'I've finally found out how to be whole and I'm going to die.'

Then she remembered. *Choose. You have to choose.*

Kayla thought of her mother. So much pain and then finally forgiveness and healing and yet it was all just to mark an ending. She wished there was a way to explain to her mother what she had to do but time was not hers to bargain with.

Kayla realized that she could only choose one life to finish. There was no longer a choice to be made, she knew who she was and where she belonged if only as a memory.

And so the choice was made.

## ONE-HUNDRED-TWO

"Did you see that flash of light?" Joah asked excitedly getting quickly to his feet and pointing towards Sunshine Bay.

The group stood and followed Joah's outstretched arm. The night was still pitch black, with no indication it would be anything but for all of eternity, yet they sensed a difference in the deep. They stood still, waiting for a sign, hoping that the light that Joah had seen would come again, ready for anything, but nothing happened.

"Joah, are you sure you aren't just seeing things?"

"Yeah, we've been in the dark so long maybe you just imagined it."

Joah was shaking his head vigorously.

"Have you all got something more important to do than follow my hunch?"

The group turned back the way that Joah had pointed and squinted into the night for any sign of what he claimed he'd seen. Really, they'd been waiting for a sign all day and whether it was imagined or not it was time for them to choose how they were going to spend the last minutes of Caine's fourteenth year.

## ONE-HUNDRED-THREE

The last moments of Kale's downward fall were those of bliss. Her entire life she'd had questions roaming within her that she didn't even know how to ask aloud. They'd always been beyond her understanding. Now, though instants from the end, she understood everything.

When she was five years old, she'd woken in the woods south of Braedon Ridge near the very same ridge that brought familiarity every time she passed it. That was the same night that Caine had arrived and the moons had exploded in the heavens sending thousands of shooting stars across the sky and moon dust sifting slowly to the earth.

Caine hadn't left Earth until she was fifteen but time, ever a mystery, ran differently on Alpha Iridium. Hurrying to catch up with the rest of the Universe. Caine's fourteen years on Alpha Iridium had only been four of Kayla's on Earth.

And somehow Caine had traveled back to the very moment he'd realized what he could do. The night his five-year-old daughter had woken from horrible dreams screaming in her room.

On Alpha Iridium, her adoptive parents had found her in the woods that night staring up at the star clad night sky and the meteor shower. Kale had been giggling, full of glee and awe. They'd fallen in love with her instantly. What they never told anyone is that a Founder, Cyan, had visited them both in their sleep and told them where Kale would be. Told them that she would need them. That she would need their strength and protection. The same Founder had warned against telling anyone, especially Caine, how Kale had come to them. They were to protect that secret at all costs.

Being torn between two worlds had forced Kale to live half a life in both. Still, her fears and pains had flowed freely between them. Now she was whole. She'd made her choice even if she'd only chosen to die as one of those people.

She had chosen.

Kale tumbled downward waiting for the end to arrive. Time slowed. Moments stretched on and on. It felt like forever, that fall towards the end of her life. When she realized that she should've already hit the ground, Kale began to look around. Below her, as the wind tore violently past her toward the sky, she saw only blackness and was unable to tell when she would meet the last instant of her life.

The rushing wind slowed, then stopped, and Kale found herself suspended in mid-air. Cyan hovered peacefully mere feet from where she did and Kale wondered if she was dead.

"No, you're not dead." Cyan smiled. "We have been waiting for you Kale."

"Why?" Kale sounded so much like a curious, wide-eyed child that Cyan couldn't help smiling lovingly at her.

"The savior who is sent down from the heavens," she quoted from the Scriptures and then paused looking upward for a moment before continuing. "Not a single person, I think, but maybe three needed to fulfill a cycle."

"Three?" Kale asked, her voice full of wonder.

"But who?"

"Caine, that much I've known for a long time."

Kale could only shake her head in disbelief. "How can I destroy him if he is one of the chosen ones?"

Cyan kept smiling sweetly. "Inside each and every one of us there is a light borrowed from the spark that lit the universe. It's not through destruction that we conquer, Kale, it is in finding our way back to that light, *that* love, the beginning of ourselves and all things. Are you ready?"

Kale didn't answer. Too many thoughts swarmed within her mind, but there was no time to even consider them as she resumed falling and knew that the end was near. *Yes*, she decided, *I'm ready.* And so, she surrendered.

Then, she felt a tug as if the back of her shirt had been caught on something and she was jolted upwards. All awareness of mind and body vanished and Kale simply was. *I'm dead*, she realized but felt nothing. All the pain was gone. And for just a moment, everything went dark.

## ONE-HUNDRED-FOUR

On the mountain shelf far above, chaos was in command. Jaren, Medea, and Corin followed by Arin and Joah had finally arrived and they stood in stupefied horror, unable to voice their anguish or express it. They'd been informed by Caine, strangely solemn in his moment of triumph, that Kale was gone, that she'd disappeared over the edge of the cliff minutes before, and that they were too late.

Arin and Joah stopped dead when they saw the crimson pool that had formed around Derin's lifeless body. It seemed in a strange way as if his heart was bleeding sadness and they knew right away they'd lost one of their own, though it had been fourteen years since they'd seen him. Arin's heart broke when she saw the anguish in Alex's eyes, and she knew that this loss would carry him far away and out of reach for a long time.

Before any of them could react in time to defend themselves, the J'Kahl were upon them. They struggled, kicked, lashed out, but the fight and fire had gone out of them. All seemed lost and they were too tired and too shocked to resist. The soldiers finished tying their hands and forced them to their knees.

Caine was shouting in a strained and panicked voice, "Traitors to Caine you must die like your leader. I am the savior, the chosen one, and you have opposed me in hopes of bringing the Darkness to these people. Have you anything to say before I send you to join your friend." It was as if he was pandering to a crowd, and even the J'Kahl seemed confused and unsettled by his hysterics.

No one spoke. The shock was too much of a barrier for anyone to breech. For Kale's friends it was mostly that they'd never once seriously considered that she'd fail. And now she was gone. They wondered if they'd ever really known anything about the girl who'd tumbled to her death only moments before. How could they have if she'd done something they never thought she would do?

"You kids have caused me a great deal of trouble, but it was worth it. The immense entertainment you provided with all your blundering was truly enjoyable. I dare you to speak your righteous words now. Whatever will you say when all is lost to you?"

"If you will allow it, Lord Caine, I will speak for these people."

Heads turned left and right to see where the disembodied voice had come from. A muscle in the corner of Caine's eye twitched furiously as he scanned the crowd for an indication of who'd spoken, defying him.

"Who dares to speak to me in that tone? Who dares to speak to Lord Caine in such a way? I will have your head, or will you even dare to speak again?" Caine was smiling playfully but the madness and fear hadn't faded from his haunted eyes.

"You don't recognize my voice, Caine? It seems in both your lives you find it easy to forget who I am."

Murmurs and cries of shock echoed through the crowd as the J'Kahl gathered on the mountain shelf began to part. Caine could see a light moving through the stunned and frightened group of soldiers and despite himself felt panic rise up within him.

"What's going on here? What is wrong with you people?" Caine bellowed but he was no longer the focus of attention.
Through the final cluster of soldiers stepped a figure cloaked in silver light. The J'Kahl stepped and stumbled backward away from Cyan, the Founder Caine had kept prisoner in his castle for so many years. But it wasn't until Caine realized that it wasn't her who'd spoken, or was emitting the eerie glow that he began to really be afraid.

"Mother?" Alex croaked and the J'Kahl who were restraining him let go immediately and stumbled back.

"Alex," Cyan whispered as Alex staggered towards her and she wrapped her arms around him tightly.

His ropes fell instantly from his wrists and he could finally return the hug he thought he would never feel again. Tears spilled down his stained face carving rivers through the dirt and dried blood until they reached his chin and plunged to their demise. He lingered in the hug as long as he dared, then Alex reluctantly stepped away from her realizing they had much to finish and time was slipping away. The only chance for dawn would soon pass them by.

Alex looked over to his brother's lifeless body and then to his mother desperately. Cyan tried to hide the anguish from her face as she shook her head helplessly. Even years apart hadn't hindered their ability to speak without words. At the moment he'd realized his mother was alive, Alex had a glimmer of hope that she would be able to save Derin somehow. He saw in her eyes that she could do nothing and Alex realized the road ahead of them, even if they defeated Caine, could still be laced with pain and sorrow.

Turning away from her fallen son, trying as hard as she could to remain in the moment Cyan raised her arm and swept it in one fluid motion toward the prisoners. The ropes dropped from their wrists as Alex went to Joah and Arin's side. Arin wrapped her arms around his neck, so relieved he was alive she felt dizzy. Finally they broke apart but he kept an arm protectively around her.

It was then when everyone stood not understanding what came next that Kale stepped into view and the source of the silver glow was finally clear.

"What...how...you...I...I...you're dead. I watched you fall. I saw you... You're dead. You're dead. I saw you die," as he stuttered Caine stepped backward away from Cyan and Kale. In response to his stuttering, Kale simply smiled. It was Cyan who answered his questions.

"You knew, Lord Caine, not the entire truth because I kept it from you. It seems the Prophecies have been misinterpreted, but no matter. We find ourselves where they become real, the written word is of no circumstance."

"It's over. I killed her," Caine blubbered.

The irony that Caine tasted then was bitter. He'd never truly believed he was the savior and then, of course, he'd forced Cyan to tell him it was Kale. He'd used the lie to build his empire and had never once considered the complexities contained in the Scriptures. Executing Kale should have guaranteed that the Darkness would grant him full reign over Berdune until it devoured the planet entirely. Yet she stood in front of him then, alive, ready to fight, and in his heart Caine knew she'd returned with more than just power.

"Did you think defeat would taste so sweet? Did you think the Darkness would come so simply?"

Kale listened as if from far away. All eyes were on her despite the confrontation transpiring between Caine and Cyan. She could hear their words but couldn't really understand them; maybe she wasn't supposed to. Instead Kale felt instinct well up inside her. Like all those nights she'd stared up at the midnight sky on Earth and marveled at the vastness of what lay beyond that speckled cloak. Now she was a part of that vastness and there were things she was meant to do.

Kale felt all the years of longing to be special coming together in one instant of realization. She walked over to where her friends stood, mouths wide with shock and no voices to express what they were feeling.

Cyan kneeled at Derin's side, Caine no longer posing any real threat. Heartache welled within her when she realized that all the years of waiting and serving Caine in hopes of seeing her beloved son again were for nothing. He was dead and she couldn't heal him. She touched his cheek, a light and loving caress, and laid a gentle kiss on his forehead.

"Stop them!" Caine shouted, but the power and command were both gone from his voice. "If you won't stop them then I will!" he screamed and took a step toward them but one look from Cyan stopped him where he stood.

"Kale," Corin said hoarsely as she stepped up to him and wrapped him in her silver embrace. As she did so his wounds slowly healed. She stepped back from him and smiled.

"I always hoped you'd find your mother. I'm so happy for you. Didn't I always say you need a woman in your life?" Kale laughed and then stepped over to Medea leaving Corin in as much shock as he'd been in when she'd arrived.

The two girls hugged for a long time and just as Corin's wounds had healed Medea's did the same. When they finally stepped apart Kale spoke.

"I left a little scar, don't worry."

"Kale," Medea said softly.

"I missed you, too." She paused. "I'm so very sorry about Ryan."

Medea nodded, eyes filling with tears. Still she wasn't quite ready to face the full force of her heartache.

"My parents..." Medea began, tears slithering down her cheeks.

"Yes, they died for us."

"Thank you, Kale."

"It's the truth. It's what you've always known, deep down inside," Kale replied and then walked to where Jaren stood.

"Kale," Jaren whispered as she stopped in front of him, "Kale, I can't believe you're not dead. Oh god, Kale..." Jaren let his words trail off as the tears that had formed were threatening to fall.

"Jaren," Kale spoke softly as she reached out to him. She wrapped her arms around him and hugged him fiercely. The silver light enveloped him and when she stepped away his wounds were no more.

"Oh Jaren," she said sadly, "I never knew." She wiped his tear stained cheeks and then laid a gentle kiss on his lips. "We did good," she said after stepping back from Jaren and once more drinking in the sight of her friends as they stood there amazed and overjoyed. "You guys did great. What would I have done without you?"

Still the J'Kahl, Cyan, and Caine had yet to move as Kale proceeded to heal Arin and Joah's wounds as well. When she stepped up to Alex, she gave him a warm hug and again injuries were mended. She took his face in her hands and looked deep into his eyes. "It will be okay. This is the beginning of a different kind of life. Trust it. Trust your heart."

When Kale stepped away from him, her face crumpled with heartache. She looked sorrowfully toward Caine.

"Dad, why?" she asked with anguish in her voice. "Why from such wonderful dreams did you build so many horrors?"

"Kayla?" Caine stammered, and slowly he seemed to become another man.

"Why this, Daddy? Why like this?"

Everyone except Cyan stood in disbelief as father and daughter were reunited. Caine's memory of the life he lived before coming to Alpha Iridium slammed into him with so much force he staggered and stumbled before catching himself. The Darkness no longer able to hide it from him. Kale's friends couldn't believe what they were hearing and could only watch and wonder as Caine spoke to his daughter.

"Kayla," he repeated as he stepped back from her in fear and shame. "I wanted to give you the world. Those people weren't your parents. They didn't deserve you. I'm your father. I thought I could make you love me again. I thought I could make it up to you somehow but it all got out of hand. Then I lost my way. I thought I could make a wonderful world and that you might be proud of me. I thought..." Caine couldn't finish, past and present a confusing mess inside him, as he took another step back.

"Daddy," Kale said sadly and the sight of Randall Caine returned to a man who could be ashamed of his sins was enough to break her heart.

"Forgive me, Kayla. Please, forgive me," he began to weep as he stepped further away from her. Backing away from his shame.

She watched him, sorrowfully, knowing exactly where he would be in another moment, yet she let him go. She wished she could hug him and have him cradle her head in his lap and tell her everything would be okay. But those were fantasies for another life, for other people, not for her and Randall Caine, her father.

"I forgive you. I'll keep you in my heart as you were so many years ago. Before all this and lives torn in two." She smiled at him then, and it seemed a peace that no one but Kale had ever seen in him before, returned to his eyes and his face. "I forgive you, Daddy," she repeated as Randall Caine took one last step away from her and over the edge of the cliff.

For a single moment, Kale wondered whether she should have warned him. But she realized that at least in death, he could be forgiven and given the peace for which he had longed for and never found in life.


## ONE-HUNDRED-FIVE

Kale flinched and closed her eyes so she wouldn't have to see the spot where her father had just been. When she finally opened them more horrors would ask to be seen. She spotted Derin's lifeless body. That halo of blood and heartache spread out around him. Tears, like liquid moonbeams, traced pathways down her cheeks as a deep and painful realization dawned. Theirs would be a story mostly unwritten.

She walked over and kneeled at Derin's side, taking his head in her lap. Stroking his face gently Kale was carried back a few hours to the evening Cyan had visited her on Earth. Words then misunderstood became clear. She looked up into Cyan's eyes and waited for her answer.

"Do you understand the consequences of what you ask?" Cyan asked watching Kale with a mixture of sadness and hope.

Kale could only nod, as her voice betrayed her.

"I understand," Kale finally replied with a smile. "It's how it should be. I've had two, he hasn't even really had one yet."
She turned her attention back to Derin and the silver light that still surrounded her spread outward and enveloped his body. Everyone watched in wonder and amazement as the pool of blood began to shrink. Only Cyan wept. Filled with both gratitude and heartache. Fourteen long years she'd served Caine. Forced to do things she'd have trouble facing for the rest of her life. This, though voluntary, would be another of those.

"Derin," Kale leaned in close and whispered. The light surrounding them pulsed brightly and Derin's body shook as if an electric current had been passed through it. Then the silver light went out slowly and Derin suddenly sucked in a huge breath and opened his eyes.

Staring up at Kale, looking dazed, Derin began to smile, as if he was uncertain of where he was and thought that maybe he'd been the victim of a prank.

"I dreamed of you," he said quietly as a lazy smile spread across his face. "I dreamed of so many happy days that must be ahead of us. Where all is peaceful and we're together, and every day there is happiness."

"How nice," Kale said with a smile while tears, now clear, ran down her cheeks. "Like a fairytale. How very nice." She looked up and off into the distance fondly as if seeing the future Derin had just described. She closed her eyes for a long drawn out moment, wanting to hold onto it.

"Where was I?" he asked suddenly as he sat up and looked around him.

"Not too far from here," Kale said as she helped him to his feet. "Remember that, always, not too far from here."


ONE-HUNDRED-SIX

Falling to his death, Caine let all the pain, hatred, and fury go. The Darkness no longer whispered to him. All was quiet. He fell with relief and dared not look back over the life he despised. Instead he thought of Kayla, his beautiful and precious daughter, who'd saved him in both his lives. It was with thoughts of her forgiveness ringing through his mind and heart that Caine met the ground.

The moment he reached the end of his fall the ground shook and the dark sky was blasted apart by glorious light. The five watery rays of Sunshine Bay were lit up so that it seemed the sun had finally risen on the people of Berdune again and the Darkness had passed.

Not so far away in Empris, the slaves emerging from the mines and factories cheered and embraced the brave people who'd just risked their lives to free them. In their hearts, they all knew it was over and the light had won.

On the cliff at Sunshine Bay, the group cheered, overwhelmed with joy and relief. They all knew that the long battle was not only over, but won. They danced, they hugged, they rejoiced, they sang, they screamed with relief. They were free. It was over. The light had prevailed.

The J'Kahl who'd held them captive only minutes before fled into the woods in fear, defeated, and no one made any attempt to stop them.

The blazing, bright, dawn that Caine's destruction brought was dimming slowly but it was still the most radiant and glorious thing any of them had ever seen.

When she got her chance, Cyan took Kale in her arms and hugged her fiercely. "I can never repay you for what you've done and I don't know if I can ever forgive myself for letting you do it."

Kale stepped back and smiled at Cyan graciously. "This is what I want. I did what I was born to do. You already knew that in your heart. As for repaying me, keep him happy and make up for all the lost time."

"Kale," Cyan began but she was lost to tears immediately and simply wrapped her arms around Kale again and held her tight.

"Tears of joy?" Derin asked as he joined in their hug.

"Yeah, something like that," Cyan confirmed as she stepped away, leaving Kale and Derin hugging on their own.

"What did you do back there for me?" Derin whispered in her ear.

"It isn't important right now," Kale said stepping away from him but taking his hands in hers. "Derin, listen, we don't have much time and I just want you to know..."

"What? What is it, Kale?"

"Thank you for helping me to understand..."

"Kale, what's wrong? We won. It's over."

"I know. I just didn't think it would end like this." She said sadly and wished there was enough time to make him understand.

"Hey, this is just the beginning, right? We have all the time in the world."

"The beginning," Kale confirmed. "Remember that for me."

Again, they hugged, but Kale said nothing more. Around them, the bright light continued to shrink away into the night sky. Finally, it stopped shrinking when it hung overhead as the first moon Alpha Iridium had seen in fourteen long years. A million sparkling bodies danced within the heavens above them and they all looked upward to see the beauty and marvel at it as if they were seeing it for the first time ever. Kale wanted to weep with all that she was seeing and feeling, and all that was happening around her. So much joy, such wonderful triumph, and infinite love, that thread that weaves all lives together in the intricate fabric of eternity. *Yes*, she thought, *that's how it should be. Now I get it.*

Her head sagged a little and she let it rest on Derin's shoulder as she took a long look out over Sunshine Bay where she'd spent so many dawns with her father. She felt near to him again. 'What stories I have to tell you dad,' she thought as the cool breeze nestled her cheek and within it she felt a greeting.

She let Derin's warmth rock her calmly to sleep. *In another life, in some other dream, maybe...* she thought hopefully.

"I love you," she whispered, "I always will." But it was too quiet for him to hear.

"Kale, look," Derin said turning his face up to the sky. "Have you ever seen anything more wonderful?"

But Kale didn't reply and with a sudden flash of understanding Derin realized she was far too heavy in his arms. He tore his eyes from the beauty hovering above them all and pulled her back so he could see her face. The tears were still drying on her cheeks, so pale, and her eyes were turned upward to the heavens yet Derin knew right away she was no longer seeing the same world he was.

He hugged her fiercely again, unwilling to face the truth. The others began turning toward him, growing silent with the fear they all knew would be confirmed, drawn by the change her departure had created, though they didn't understand how.

Kale was gone.

Corin wrapped his arms around Medea and she clung to him like a child. Jaren stood beside them but sought no comfort from them just yet. He could only stand and watch as Derin held Kale tightly, unwilling to let her go, unable to believe she'd left them with such ease, unaware she hadn't traveled all that far from the people who'd truly loved her.

Cyan watched helplessly as her son held onto the one thing he would have to let go of. She was ashamed and sorry, and she knew it would be a long time before her son could forgive her. She turned the Prophecy over and over again in her mind and realized that even now she didn't completely understand it. A chosen one fulfilling three qualities or three chosen ones each possessing one, she wasn't sure and she realized that maybe those things were better left to lay in mystery much like the most wonderful and awful things in the universe usually are.

Kale never really had the chance to know who and what she truly was but the greatest among us rarely do.

With all that had happened, and all they'd seen, and all they would come to be told over the weeks that followed, her friends could never have imagined how rare Kale really was. If only they'd known while she was still alive, though in so many ways they had. And truly, with Kale, most was a mystery and the rest speculation.

As Derin looked up to the stars that were now shining brightly in the night sky, he was certain through the mist his tears created that they were weeping too.

ONE-HUNDRED-SEVEN

On Alpha Iridium, Randall Caine would be remembered in many ways. It is true the Darkness came at his heels but the people never knew that the Darkness always chose someone to look through and lead it. The Darkness is as blind as those who stumble through it.

On Earth, Randall Caine would be remembered for many things. But it had all started one night long ago when he found the key and lost it for a moment when his five-year-old daughter woke from a dream that had frightened her. That was the moment that everything began. The moment Kayla was no longer just Kayla but Kale as well. The moment Alpha Iridium was given the chance to prove it was more than just a dream.

Randall Caine had been well known on Earth within the scientific community for his research on sleep disorders and his specialization in dream psychology but the night he found the key his vision changed. Or rather a vision was given to him.

He came to publish his first book, Awake While Dreaming, which discussed the possibility of an alternate universe existing in the realm of sleep that he believed was the answer to saving humanity. The work earned him nothing but ridicule and shame and he disappeared without a trace not long after the work was published.

Because time had yet to begin for Alpha Iridium in relation to the rest of the Universe Caine found himself on that same day, in that same moment when his five-year old daughter had arrived. On Earth she was now fifteen but on Alpha Iridium she was still a child.

Randall Caine thought he found the answer to saving humanity but he'd truly found the answer to Alpha Iridium's salvation. The same salvation humanity had passed on many years ago. That truth had brought Froste, the Ocean Widow, to the shores of Earth to salvage five perfect beings and guide them to their new home, Alpha Iridium, and they'd brought with them Cyan.

Four years after he'd disappeared without a trace his daughter Kayla Caine did the same.

There were no survivors of the bus crash in Emery. Though strangely the body of Kayla Caine was never recovered. That wasn't the only mystery that surrounded the case. Randall Caine's body was found in the bus though no one could explain why or how. There was no record that he'd boarded the bus. Stranger still was when they autopsied the body it seemed he had aged well over fifteen years since his disappearance almost four years prior.

Many people thought it was a hoax or a publicity stunt and those who knew what kind of strange things were possible in the universe were no longer on Earth to chime in one way or another.

Randall Caine's work was being dissected in hopes of finding a clue as to where he'd been and why he'd returned. Even if they find the answers there is a good chance they won't believe them and maybe that's how things are meant to be. Earth had already met the Darkness and only the six Founders and a being called Froste knew what had come of that.

Every day, Max collected every article, story and speculation he could find about what had happened. Trying to ease his broken heart by finding some sense in it all. He walked the beach and whispered Kayla's name over and over again to the sea and salt breeze, but all he ever got in return was a whispering back that she'd never fully been there in the first place. The waves asked him over and over again, how can you hold onto something you never really had? So that he knew in his heart that he would heal, eventually.

## ONE-HUNDRED-EIGHT

Derin sat on the cliff at Sunshine Bay and watched the sun break over the mountains to the east. For the last three months he'd gone there every single morning to greet the dawn. That was where he met Kale, in the first golden light of morning. When the day had yet to begin and all was fresh and new and exciting. Just like Kale had been.

Much had changed since she'd left them. The people of Berdune were already building the better world they'd all dreamed of for so long.

The J'Kahl who were loyal to Caine either disappeared or were found dead, often by their own hand. Caine's castle was left in ruin, a monument to all that was lost yet a reminder that even rubble and ruins are a place to begin.

Cyan, Kedall, Milar, Arwyn, and Beran had headed north toward their home almost right after Caine's end. The people watched them go sadly but with promises they would be visited again soon. They journeyed north swiftly, filled with anticipation. The parents they'd been without for so long were awake and eagerly awaiting the reunion. Cyan returned to the love of her life and it made her ache to think her son had lost just that.

Drawn together by their loss Derin had become friends with Jaren, Medea, and Corin and they now worked together to build a better world. They talked about Kale often despite the pain it brought. They laughed about Kale's stubbornness and jokingly cursed her inability to let people help her even when she needed it.

Alex, Joah, and Arin had stayed with them as well, planning on making the trip north when Derin was ready. They'd all taken up residence in Medea's house and though it was crowded the house had never seen more laughter or joy.

Jet, Archer and James had also made their way in to the group of friends and were equally as active in rebuilding the community of Breadon Ridge. They'd paid their penance and now they worked for the sheer joy of making the better world they all knew they deserved.

Things were steadily improving and with everyone working together they would be a proud and thriving people once again.

"Today is the first official day of new time, Kale. It is our first day of the year 1 AD. After the Darkness," Derin paused and took a deep breath. "There's a huge celebration and everything. You'd really like it. Well maybe not." He chuckled a little to himself.

Always, when talking to Kale at Sunshine Bay, he expected a response yet none came.

"We miss you a lot. I miss you a lot." Derin felt moisture come to his eyes. "I just wanted you to know that you weren't alone in life Kale and you're not alone in death. A piece of me, of all of us, went with you when you...left." Derin wiped furiously at his eyes with the palms of his hands. "Just keep those pieces with you okay. I know you're strong enough to go without them but we're not. I'm not. Just keep a piece of me with you so I know you're okay."

Derin stood and wiped his eyes on the sleeve of his shirt.

"I came today to say goodbye. We're heading north tomorrow; Medea, Corin and Jaren are actually coming with us, I can't believe it. I guess they need a break from this place. I do, too." Derin laughed a little. "Going to meet my dad. I guess I'm kind of scared but he can't be worse than my last father, right?" He laughed a little more before choking up. "And I guess sooner or later I'll have to forgive my mother for letting you... well, you know."

"Anyway, I wanted to let you know I won't be around for awhile. But you know where to find me. You'll be with me while I'm gone."

In many ways, Kale would be with him always. Looking to the night sky and reading the stars Derin couldn't help but be reminded of Kale and how she'd returned them to him. He also looked to the moon. The glorious light that had come with Caine's death had faded to that single glowing orb. It always reminded him of her.

The people had named the new moon Kale and Derin felt that was appropriate. It made him feel like she returned every night to visit them and make sure they were all okay. He never had nightmares despite all he'd been through and he liked to think each night she watched over him and brought him pleasant dreams.

Derin turned and began to walk away. There were too many things to say and if Kale could truly hear him then she already knew what they were. Suddenly he stopped and looked back to the cliff and the newborn day beyond.

"And just so you know," Derin smiled deviously though sadness lined the corners of his mouth, "I know you loved me, Kale, so all of your fighting was for nothing 'cause I know. If you want me to believe otherwise you'd better come back and tell me yourself."

Derin looked to the heavens expecting something to happen. Expecting within himself to have Kale returned to him somehow. Certain that she'd come back just to disagree with him. He saw the last bright star in the morning sky glitter with enthusiasm and then wink out.

The ocean crashed upon the shore and the wind tossed his dark blue hair playfully. Walking back to the house Derin was overwhelmed once again by the irony in life. His new friends were once his sworn enemies. His true family he'd once thought of as a myth, a legend. And the truest love he'd ever known had lasted only a moment.

Sometimes the logic behind life eluded Derin and it made him ache, the irony that had been the affliction of Kale's life. You could have huge dreams yet never see them come true, just like Kale had never seen the better world she'd lived and died to create. Of course, it's not the dream that's important but the dreaming itself, and no one had dreamed greater wonders than Kale had, in either of her lives.

END

# ABOUT THE AUTHOR

NIKKI MARTIN is a writer and full time yoga teacher living on the east coast of Canada with her partner Paul and two playful kittens, Tris and Lu.

Her love of stories, both reading and creating them, started very young when she realized they could be both escape and salvation for a shy, sensitive and awkward kid who always felt a little bit out of place despite having friends and being very social. She drafted her first novel in grade nine and her first feature length screenplay not long after that, and has written many of both genres since. She hopes to share her work with readers over the coming years and to continue to share her passion for yoga while teaching and traveling.

She is an avid reader, a daydreamer, a movie lover, a sunset chaser, a stargazer, a love warrior, a tree hugger, a beach walker, a storyteller, and an ocean soul.

She was a contributor for *BreatheYourOMBalance: Writings about Yoga by Women* (Thorncraft, 2015). Her first novel, *A Momentary Darkness*, in the fictional series *Awake While Dreaming* will be available in 2018. Find Nikki on Instagram as @nikki_possibilities.

Nikki Martin

# BOOKS BY THORNCRAFT PUBLISHING

Nonfiction
*BreatheYourOMBalance: Yoga and Healing,* Volume Two, Introduced by Kelsy Timas, Founder and CEO of Guiding Wellness Institute, Inc. (March 2018). This second volume of nonfiction and poetry delves into the poignant journey of yoga as it heals, restores, and revitalizes life after life. Many of the contributors worked together in workshops and practices at Yoga Mat studio to infuse their work with not only the personal yoga journey, but the roots of the yoga community that connect us together as well.
ISBN-13: 978-0-9979687-2-9
Library of Congress Control Number: 2017959537

*BreatheYourOMBalance: Writings about Yoga by Women,* Volume One, Selected and introduced by S. Teague (October 2016). A collection of poetry, fiction, and nonfiction that focuses on breath and balance, this volume celebrates the life-changing practice of yoga. Thirty contributors share their experiences in this first collection.
ISBN-13: 978-0-9979687-0-5
Library of Congress Control Number: 2016953726

*Seasons of Balance: On Creativity & Mindfulness* by S. Teague and Shana Thornton (March 2016). Teague and Thornton co-write a book about creativity, meditations, affirmations, expressions of gratitude and mindfulness to help you through the seasons of life. Use this book as a creativity journal to inspire you and to prompt artistic creations.
ISBN-13: 978-0-9857947-9-8
Library of Congress Control Number: 2016931608

Fiction
*Talking Underwater* by Melissa Corliss DeLorenzo (August 2015). Authors have declared that this novel is a "literary gift" and that "book clubs will love this." Cattail, the adored beach near her coastal New England home, is Amy's place of refuge. When a mistake there ends tragically, almost destroying everything that Amy holds as sacred, she doesn't

know how she'll continue, nor mend the rift with her sister that results. *Talking Underwater* explores the balance between the elation of family summers at the ocean and the ways we navigate unbearable heartache to find new ways of being.
ISBN-13: 978-0-9857947-6-7
Library of Congress Control Number: 2015938787

*Poke Sallet Queen & the Family Medicine Wheel* by Shana Thornton (March 2015). When narrator Robin Ballard takes a writing course in college, she goes searching for her homeless father and wanders into the secret lives of her ancestors and relatives. Set in Nashville and the surrounding communities, this novel offers a glimpse into the superstitions and changes of a middle Tennessee family.
ISBN-13: 978-0-9857947-5-0
Library of Congress Control Number: 2015901106

*The Mosquito Hours* by Melissa Corliss DeLorenzo (April 2014). One turning-point summer places the grandmother, aunt, daughter, granddaughters, and great-grandchildren in the same home. An OnPoint Radio suggestion as Best Summer Reads 2014, *The Mosquito Hours* is a multi-generational story about how the women in a family attempt to keep secrets about their desires, spirituality, and motherhood.
ISBN-13: 978-0-9857947-2-9
Library of Congress Control Number: 2013957635

*Grace Among the Leavings* by Beverly Fisher (August 2013). Hailed by award-winning author Barry Kitterman as "a deeply moving story, one not given to easy resolution," this historical novella is a child's perspective of the Civil War. Playwrights Kari Catton and Dennis Darling adapted the book for the stage. Visit thorncraftpublishing.com for upcoming performances.
ISBN-13: 978-0-9857947-3-6
Library of Congress Control Number: 2013938285

*Multiple Exposure* by Shana Thornton (August 2012). The "war on terror" has captured the lives of the U.S. military and their families for over ten years, and Ellen Masters' husband has been repeatedly deployed. In the process, she shares her desires to connect with people and to discover her own strength by training for a marathon.

ISBN-13: 978-0-615-65508-6
Library of Congress Control Number: 2012941646

Forthcoming
*The Adventures to Pawnassus* by Shana Thornton and Brittany Brown (TBA 2018). A Children's book for the child explorer in all of us, journey with Luna & Salty on their Adventures to Pawnassus where they meet the literary dogs of their time and try to fulfill their dreams. After being abandoned, Luna finds a home close to Nashville, but her troubles are not over, and she needs the friendship of Salty, the Texas raccoon, to inspire a belief in the future.

For information about authors, books, upcoming reading events, new titles, and more, visit http://www.thorncraftpublishing.com

Like Thorncraft Publishing on Facebook. Find Thorncraft Publishing on Twitter as @ThorncraftBooks and on Instagram as @thorncraftpublishing